Quest for Meaning

Quest for Meaning

MODERN SHORT STORIES

Glenn O. Carey

DAVID McKAY CO., INC.
NEW YORK

QUEST FOR MEANING: MODERN SHORT STORIES

International Standard Book Number 0-679-30273-5
LIBRARY OF CONGRESS CATALOG CARD NUMBER: 74-27168
MANUFACTURED IN THE UNITED STATES OF AMERICA
Designed by Angela Foote

ACKNOWLEDGMENTS

"The Grave" by Katherine Anne Porter is reprinted from *The Leaning Tower and Other Stories*, copyright, 1944, 1972, by Katherine Anne Porter. Reprinted by permission of Harcourt Brace Jovanovich, Inc.

"The Drunkard" by Frank O'Connor. Copyright 1951 by Frank O'Connor. Reprinted from *The Stories of Frank O'Connor* by permission of Alfred A. Knopf. Inc. and A. D. Peters and Co. Originally appeared in *The New Yorker*.

"The Use of Force" by William Carlos Williams is reprinted from *The Farmers' Daughters*. Copyright 1938 by William Carlos Williams. Reprinted by permission of New Directions Publishing Corporation.

"Silent Snow, Secret Snow" copyright © 1922, 1923, 1924, 1925, 1927, 1928, 1929, 1930, 1931, 1932, 1933, 1934, 1935, 1941, 1950, 1952, 1953, 1955, 1956, 1957, 1958, 1959, 1960 by Conrad Aiken. From *The Collected Short Stories of Conrad Aiken* with permission of Thomas Y. Crowell Company, Inc.

"The Peasant Marey" is reprinted from *An Honest Thief and Other Stories* by Feodor Dostoevsky. Translated from the Russian by Constance Garnett. Published in the United States by Macmillan Publishing Co., Inc., and in Britain by William Heinemann Ltd., Publishers.

"The Basement Room" is reprinted from *21 Stories* by Graham Greene. Copyright 1947 by Graham Greene. Reprinted by permission of The Viking Press, Inc. Also published in the United Kingdom in *Collected Stories* by Graham Greene. Reprinted by permission of The Bodley Head & William Heinemann.

"Big Boy Leaves Home" from *Uncle Tom's Children* by Richard Wright. Copyright, 1936 by Richard Wright; renewed, 1964 by Ellen Wright. Reprinted by permission of Harper & Row, Publishers, Inc.

"Barn Burning" by William Faulkner. Copyright 1939 and renewed 1967 by Estelle Faulkner and Jill Faulkner Summers. Reprinted from *Collected Stories of William Faulkner*, by permission of Random House, Inc.

"Health Card" by Frank Yerby is reprinted by permission of William Morris Agency, Inc. Copyright © 1944 (renewed) by Frank Yerby.

"The Horse Dealer's Daughter" is reprinted from *The Complete Short Stories of D. H. Lawrence*, Vol. II. Copyright 1922 by Thomas B. Seltzer, Inc., renewed 1950 by Frieda Lawrence. Reprinted by permission of The Viking Press, Inc.

"The Chinese Dog" by Alberto Moravia. Reprinted by permission of the author, Valentino Bompiani & Co. and their agent, James Brown Associates, Inc. Copyright © 1955 by Valentino Bompiani & Co.

"Love" by Jesse Stuart is reprinted by permission of the author. Copyright by Jesse Stuart.

"A Tree · A Rock · A Cloud" by Carson McCullers copyright 1942 by Carson McCullers is reprinted from *The Ballad of the Sad Cafe: the Novels and Stories of Carson McCullers*, by permission of Houghton Mifflin Company.

"Crossing into Poland" by Isaac Babel. Reprinted by permission of S. G. Phillips, Inc. from *The Collected Stories of Isaac Babel* edited and translated by Walter Morison. Copyright © 1955 by S. G. Phillips, Inc.

"The Lagoon" by Joseph Conrad is reprinted from *Tales of Unrest* by Joseph Conrad. By permission of J. M. Dent & Sons Ltd. Publishers and the Trustees of the Joseph Conrad Estate.

"Everything That Rises Must Converge" is reprinted with the permission of Farrar, Straus and Giroux, Inc. from *Everything That Rises Must Converge* by Flannery O'Connor, copyright © 1961, 1965, by the Estate of Mary Flannery O'Connor.

"Only the Dead Know Brooklyn" (first published in *The New Yorker*, copyright 1935 F. R. Publishing Corporation; renewal copyright © 1963 Paul Gitlin) is reprinted by permission of Charles Scribner's Sons from *Death to Morning* by Thomas Wolfe.

"Stigmata" by Joyce Carol Oates. Reprinted from *Upon the Sweeping Flood* by Joyce Carol Oates by permission of the publisher, Vanguard Press, Inc. Copyright © 1966 by Joyce Carol Oates.

"The Other Side of the Hedge" by E. M. Forster is reprinted from *The Collected Tales of E. M. Forster*. Published 1947 by Alfred A. Knopf, Inc. Reprinted by permission of the publisher and The Society of Authors as the literary representative of the Estate of E. M. Forster.

"The Guest" by Albert Camus. Copyright © 1957, 1958 by Alfred A. Knopf, Inc. Reprinted from *Exile and the Kingdom*, by Albert Camus, trans. by Justin O'Brien, by permission of the publisher.

to
Margaret
Gretchen
Christopher
John
Jack

Introduction

The title of this international selection of short stories comes from an essay by Robert Penn Warren on Hemingway's *A Farewell to Arms*, about which Warren wrote, "For there is a story behind the love story. That story is the quest for meaning and certitude in a world which seems to offer nothing of the sort." The purpose of this collection and its thematic divisions is to offer readers a challenge and some direction as they enter upon their quest for the meaning and understanding of short fiction, and perhaps also to help them open some doors and gain some insights as they continue their search for self-understanding and meaning in their lives.

The stories in the collection deal with three significant areas of a person's growth: childhood and youth; involvement with love; and acceptance and avoidance of the forces of life. These three parts—"The Days of the Young," "The Faces of Love," and "The Dreams and the Realities"—along with the thematically oriented quotes on divider pages mark the only editorial intrusions in the book. Stories themselves have been chosen for their emphasis on a variety of writing styles and levels of meaning and encompass a range of American and European writing by older as well as more recent authors. Author biographies, a glossary of literary terms, and a selected bibliography have also been planned to assist the reader without invasive editorial explications.

A superior short story typically presents within its organic framework a truth of life that sheds meaningful light on mankind and the way men live and die. As Henry Miller wrote, "Art teaches nothing, except the significance of life." Good literature brings about this awareness by expanding a person's angle of vision and enlarging his or her perception of life. As involved readers eventually discover, the quest for meaning in the reading of short stories is an adventure of the mind and spirit. As Joseph Conrad wrote about his own fiction, "If I succeed, you shall find there according to your deserts: encouragement, consolation, fear, charm—all you demand—and, perhaps also that glimpse of truth for which you have forgotten to ask."

Contents

Part One
THE DAYS OF THE YOUNG

Katherine Anne Porter, The Grave *3*
Frank O'Connor, The Drunkard *10*
William Carlos Williams, The Use of Force *21*
Conrad Aiken, Silent Snow, Secret Snow *26*
Feodor Dostoevsky, The Peasant Marey *44*
Graham Greene, The Basement Room *50*
Richard Wright, Big Boy Leaves Home *75*
William Faulkner, Barn Burning *112*

Part Two
THE FACES OF LOVE

Frank Yerby, Health Card *133*
D. H. Lawrence, The Horse Dealer's Daughter *143*
Alberto Moravia, The Chinese Dog *160*
Jesse Stuart, Love *166*
Carson McCullers, A Tree · A Rock · A Cloud *170*
Anton Chekhov, The Lament *179*
Isaac Babel, Crossing into Poland *185*
Joseph Conrad, The Lagoon *188*

Part Three
THE DREAMS AND THE REALITIES

Flannery O'Connor, Everything That Rises Must Converge *205*
Thomas Wolfe, Only the Dead Know Brooklyn *221*
Joyce Carol Oates, Stigmata *227*
E. M. Forster, The Other Side of the Hedge *245*
Albert Camus, The Guest *251*
Stephen Crane, The Open Boat *265*

A SELECTED GLOSSARY OF LITERARY TERMS *291*
A SELECTED BIBLIOGRAPHY *303*

Quest for Meaning

The childhood shows the man
As morning shows the day.

MILTON, *Paradise Regained*

When we are young
We long to tread a way none trod before.

YEATS, "The Land of Heart's Desire"

We think our fathers fools, so wise we grow;
Our wiser sons, no doubt, will think us so.

POPE, *An Essay on Criticism*

Part One

THE DAYS OF THE YOUNG

The Grave

Katherine Anne Porter

KATHERINE ANNE PORTER *(1890–   ) was born in Indian Creek, Texas, grew up in Texas and Louisiana, and was educated in convent schools. She has traveled a great deal in Germany and Mexico, locales she has used in her fiction. Three collections of short stories—*Flowering Judas *(1930),* Pale Horse, Pale Rider *(1939), and* The Leaning Tower *(1944)—not only have given her an international reputation but have also established her as one of America's most creative short-story writers. Her first, and so far her only novel,* Ship of Fools, *was published in 1962.*

The grandfather, dead for more than thirty years, had been twice disturbed in his long repose by the constancy and possessiveness of his widow. She removed his bones first to Louisiana and then to Texas as if she had set out to find her own burial place, knowing well she would never return to the places she had left. In Texas she set up a small cemetery in a corner of her first farm, and as the family connection grew, and oddments of relations came over from Kentucky to settle, it contained at last about twenty graves. After the grandmother's death, part of her land was to be sold for the benefit of certain of her children, and the cemetery happened to lie in the part set aside for sale. It was necessary to take up the bodies and bury them again in the family plot in the big new public cemetery, where the grandmother had been buried. At last her husband was to lie beside her for eternity, as she had planned.

The family cemetery had been a pleasant small neglected garden of tangled rose bushes and ragged cedar trees and cypress, the simple flat stones rising out of uncropped sweet-smelling wild grass. The graves were lying open and empty one burning day when Miranda and her brother Paul, who often went together to hunt rabbits and doves, propped their twenty-two Winchester rifles carefully against the rail fence, climbed over and explored among the graves. She was nine years old and he was twelve.

They peered into the pits all shaped alike with such purposeful accuracy, and looking at each other with pleased adventurous eyes, they said in solemn tones: "These were graves!" trying by words to shape a special, suitable emotion in their minds, but they felt nothing except an agreeable thrill of wonder: they were seeing a new sight, doing something they had not done before. In them both there was also a small disappointment at the entire commonplaceness of the actual spectacle. Even if it had once contained a coffin for years upon years, when the coffin was gone a grave was just a hole in the ground. Miranda leaped into the pit that had held her grandfather's bones. Scratching around aimlessly and pleasurably as any young animal, she scooped up a lump of earth and weighed it in her palm. It had a pleasantly sweet, corrupt smell, being mixed with cedar needles and small leaves, and as the crumbs fell apart, she saw a silver dove no larger than a hazel nut, with spread wings and a neat fan-shaped tail. The breast had a deep round hollow in it. Turning it up to the fierce sunlight, she saw that the inside of the hollow was cut in little whorls. She scrambled out, over the pile of loose earth that had fallen back into one end of the grave, calling to Paul that she had found something, he must guess what. . . . His head appeared smiling over the rim of another grave. He waved a closed hand at her. "I've got something too!" They ran to compare treasures, making a game of it, so many guesses each, all wrong, and a final showdown with opened palms. Paul had found a thin wide gold ring carved with intricate flowers and leaves. Miranda was smitten at sight of the ring and wished to have it. Paul seemed more impressed by the dove. They made a trade, with some little bickering. After he had got the dove in his hand, Paul said, "Don't you know what this is? This is a screw head for a *coffin!* . . . I'll bet nobody else in the world has one like this!"

Miranda glanced at it without covetousness. She had the gold ring on her thumb; it fitted perfectly. "Maybe we ought to go now," she said, "maybe one of the niggers 'll see us and tell somebody." They knew the land had been sold, the cemetery was no longer theirs, and they felt like trespassers. They climbed back over the fence, slung their rifles loosely under their arms—they had been shooting at targets with various kinds of firearms since they were seven years old—and set out to look for the rabbits and doves or whatever small game might happen along. On these expeditions Miranda always followed at Paul's heels along the path, obeying instructions about handling her gun when going through fences; learning how to stand it up properly so it would not slip and fire unexpectedly; how to wait her time for a shot and not just bang away in the air without looking, spoiling shots for Paul, who really could hit things if given a chance. Now and then, in her excitement at seeing birds whizz up suddenly before her face, or a rabbit leap across her very toes, she lost her head, and almost without sighting she flung her rifle up and pulled the trigger. She hardly ever hit any sort of mark. She had no proper sense of hunting at all. Her brother would be often completely disgusted with her. "You don't care whether you get your bird or not," he said. "That's no way to hunt." Miranda could not understand his indignation. She had seen him smash his hat and yell with fury when he had missed his aim. "What I like about shooting," said Miranda, with exasperating inconsequence, "is pulling the trigger and hearing the noise."

"Then, by golly," said Paul, "whyn't you go back to the range and shoot at bulls-eyes?"

"I'd just as soon," said Miranda, "only like this, we walk around more."

"Well, you just stay behind and stop spoiling my shots," said Paul, who, when he made a kill, wanted to be certain he had made it. Miranda, who alone brought down a bird once in twenty rounds, always claimed as her own any game they got when they fired at the same moment. It was tiresome and unfair and her brother was sick of it.

"Now, the first dove we see, or the first rabbit, is mine," he told her. "And the next will be yours. Remember that and don't get smarty."

"What about snakes?" asked Miranda idly. "Can I have the first snake?"

Waving her thumb gently and watching her gold ring glitter, Miranda lost interest in shooting. She was wearing her summer roughing outfit: dark blue overalls, a light blue shirt, a hired-man's straw hat, and thick brown sandals. Her brother had the same outfit except his was a sober hickory-nut color. Ordinarily Miranda preferred her overalls to any other dress, though it was making rather a scandal in the countryside, for the year was 1903, and in the back country the law of female decorum had teeth in it. Her father had been criticized for letting his girls dress like boys and go careering around astride barebacked horses. Big sister Maria, the really independent and fearless one, in spite of her rather affected ways, rode at a dead run with only a rope knotted around her horse's nose. It was said the motherless family was running down, with the grandmother no longer there to hold it together. It was known that she had discriminated against her son Harry in her will, and that he was in straits about money. Some of his old neighbors reflected with vicious satisfaction that now he would probably not be so stiffnecked, nor have any more high-stepping horses either. Miranda knew this, though she could not say how. She had met along the road old women of the kind who smoked corn-cob pipes, who had treated her grandmother with most sincere respect. They slanted their gummy old eyes side-ways at the granddaughter and said, "Ain't you ashamed of yoself, Missy? It's aginst the Scriptures to dress like that. Whut yo Pappy thinkin about?" Miranda, with her powerful social sense, which was like a fine set of antennae radiating from every pore of her skin, would feel ashamed because she knew well it was rude and ill-bred to shock anybody, even bad-tempered old crones, though she had faith in her father's judgment and was perfectly comfortable in the clothes. Her father had said, "They're just what you need, and they'll save your dresses for school. . . ." This sounded quite simple and natural to her. She had been brought up in rigorous economy. Wastefulness was vulgar. It was also a sin. These were truths; she had heard them repeated many times and never once disputed.

Now the ring, shining with the serene purity of fine gold on her rather grubby thumb, turned her feelings against her overalls and sockless feet, toes sticking through the thick brown leather straps. She wanted to go back to the farmhouse, take a good cold bath, dust herself with plenty of Maria's violet talcum powder—provided Maria was not present to object, of course—put on the thinnest, most becoming dress she owned, with a big sash, and sit in a wicker chair under the trees. . . . These things were not all she wanted, of course; she had vague stirrings of desire for luxury and a grand way of living which could not take precise form in her imagination but were founded on family legend of past wealth and leisure. These immediate comforts were what she could have, and she wanted them at once. She lagged rather far behind Paul, and once she thought of just turning back without a word and going home. She stopped, thinking that Paul would never do that to her, and so she would have to tell him. When a rabbit leaped, she let Paul have it without dispute. He killed it with one shot.

When she came up with him, he was already kneeling, examining the wound, the rabbit trailing from his hands. "Right through the head," he said complacently, as if he had aimed for it. He took out his sharp, competent bowie knife and started to skin the body. He did it very cleanly and quickly. Uncle Jimbilly knew how to prepare the skins so that Miranda always had fur coats for her dolls, for though she never cared much for her dolls she liked seeing them in fur coats. The children knelt facing each other over the dead animal. Miranda watched admiringly while her brother stripped the skin away as if he were taking off a glove. The flayed flesh emerged dark scarlet, sleek, firm; Miranda with thumb and finger felt the long fine muscles with the silvery flat strips binding them to the joints. Brother lifted the oddly bloated belly. "Look," he said, in a low amazed voice. "It was going to have young ones."

Very carefully he slit the thin flesh from the center ribs to the flanks, and a scarlet bag appeared. He slit again and pulled the bag open, and there lay a bundle of tiny rabbits, each wrapped in a thin scarlet veil. The brother pulled these off and there they were, dark gray, their sleek wet down lying in minute even ripples, like a baby's head just washed, their unbelievably small delicate ears folded close, their little blind faces almost featureless.

Miranda said, "Oh, I want to *see*," under her breath. She looked and looked—excited but not frightened, for she was accustomed to the sight of animals killed in hunting—filled with pity and astonishment and a kind of shocked delight in the wonderful little creatures for their own sakes, they were so pretty. She touched one of them ever so carefully, "Ah, there's blood running over them," she said and began to tremble without knowing why. Yet she wanted most deeply to see and to know. Having seen, she felt at once as if she had known all along. The very memory of her former ignorance faded, she had always known just this. No one had ever told her anything outright, she had been rather unobservant of the animal life around her because she was so accustomed to animals. They seemed simply disorderly and unaccountably rude in their habits, but altogether natural and not very interesting. Her brother had spoken as if he had known about everything all along. He may have seen all this before. He had never said a word to her, but she knew now a part at least of what he knew. She understood a little of the secret, formless intuitions in her own mind and body, which had been clearing up, taking form, so gradually and so steadily she had not realized that she was learning what she had to know. Paul said cautiously, as if he were talking about something forbidden: "They were just about ready to be born." His voice dropped on the last word. "I know," said Miranda, "like kittens. I know, like babies." She was quietly and terribly agitated, standing again with her rifle under her arm, looking down at the bloody heap. "I don't want the skin," she said, "I won't have it." Paul buried the young rabbits again in their mother's body, wrapped the skin around her, carried her to a clump of sage bushes, and hid her away. He came out again at once and said to Miranda, with an eager friendliness, a confidential tone quite unusual in him, as if he were taking her into an important secret on equal terms: "Listen now. Now you listen to me, and don't ever forget. Don't you ever tell a living soul that you saw this. Don't tell a soul. Don't tell Dad because I'll get into trouble. He'll say I'm leading you into things you ought not to do. He's always saying that. So now don't you go and forget and blab out sometime the way you're always doing. . . . Now, that's a secret. Don't you tell."

Miranda never told, she did not even wish to tell anybody. She thought about the whole worrisome affair with confused unhappiness for a few days. Then it sank quietly into her mind and was heaped over by accumulated thousands of impressions, for nearly twenty years. One day she was picking her path among the puddles and crushed refuse of a market street in a strange city of a strange country, when without warning, plain and clear in its true colors as if she looked through a frame upon a scene that had not stirred nor changed since the moment it happened, the episode of that far-off day leaped from its burial place before her mind's eye. She was so reasonlessly horrified she halted suddenly staring, the scene before her eyes dimmed by the vision back of them. An Indian vendor had held up before her a tray of dyed sugar sweets, in the shapes of all kinds of small creatures: birds, baby chicks, baby rabbits, lambs, baby pigs. They were in gay colors and smelled of vanilla, maybe. . . . It was a very hot day and the smell in the market, with its piles of raw flesh and wilting flowers, was like the mingled sweetness and corruption she had smelled that other day in the empty cemetery at home: the day she had remembered always until now vaguely as the time she and her brother had found treasure in the opened graves. Instantly upon this thought the dreadful vision faded, and she saw clearly her brother, whose childhood face she had forgotten, standing again in the blazing sunshine, again twelve years old, a pleased sober smile in his eyes, turning the silver dove over and over in his hands.

The Drunkard

Frank O'Connor

FRANK O'CONNOR *(1903–1966) was born in Cork, Ireland, as Michael John O'Donovan. As a young man he joined the Irish Republican Army, was imprisoned for his IRA activities, and while incarcerated wrote stories. He worked in Cork and Dublin as a librarian, and during the 1930s was a director for the Abbey Theatre. In his later years, from 1952, he lived in New York. O'Connor's fictional output was prodigious—thirty books, most of them short-story collections. In 1961 his autobiography,* An Only Child, *was published; his book on the short story,* The Lonely Voice, *came out in 1963.*

It was a terrible blow to Father when Mr. Dooley on the terrace died. Mr. Dooley was a commercial traveller with two sons in the Dominicans and a car of his own, so socially he was miles ahead of us, but he had no false pride. Mr. Dooley was an intellectual, and, like all intellectuals the thing he loved best was conversation, and in his own limited way Father was a well-read man and could appreciate an intelligent talker. Mr. Dooley was remarkably intelligent. Between business acquaintances and clerical contacts, there was very little he didn't know about what went on in town, and evening after evening he crossed the road to our gate to explain to Father the news behind the news. He had a low, palavering voice and a knowing smile, and Father would listen in astonishment, giving him a conversational lead now and again, and then stump triumphantly in to Mother with his face aglow and ask: "Do you know what Mr. Dooley is after telling me?" Ever since, when somebody has given me some bit of information off the record I have found myself on the point of asking: "Was it Mr. Dooley told you that?"

Till I actually saw him laid out in his brown shroud with the rosary beads entwined between his waxy fingers I did not take the report of his death seriously. Even then I felt there must be a catch and that some summer evening Mr. Dooley must reappear at our gate to give us the lowdown on the next world. But Father was very upset, partly because Mr. Dooley was about one age with himself, a thing that always gives a distinctly personal turn to another man's demise; partly because now he would have no one to tell him what dirty work was behind the latest scene at the Corporation. You could count on your fingers the number of men in Blarney Lane who read the papers as Mr. Dooley did, and none of these would have overlooked the fact that Father was only a laboring man. Even Sullivan, the carpenter, a mere nobody, thought he was a cut above Father. It was certainly a solemn event.

"Half past two to the Curragh," Father said meditatively, putting down the paper.

"But you're not thinking of going to the funeral?" Mother asked in alarm.

" 'Twould be expected," Father said, scenting opposition. "I wouldn't give it to say to them."

"I think," said Mother with suppressed emotion, "it will be as much as anyone will expect if you go to the chapel with him."

("Going to the chapel," of course, was one thing, because the body was removed after work, but going to a funeral meant the loss of a half-day's pay.)

"The people hardly know us," she added.

"God between us and all harm," Father replied with dignity, "we'd be glad if it was our own turn."

To give Father his due, he was always ready to lose a half day for the sake of an old neighbor. It wasn't so much that he liked funerals as that he was a conscientious man who did as he would be done by; and nothing could have consoled him so much for the prospect of his own death as the assurance of a worthy funeral. And, to give Mother her due, it wasn't the half-day's pay she begrudged, badly as we could afford it.

Drink, you see, was Father's great weakness. He could keep

steady for months, even for years, at a stretch, and while he did he was as good as gold. He was first up in the morning and brought the mother a cup of tea in bed, stayed at home in the evenings and read the paper; saved money and bought himself a new blue serge suit and bowler hat. He laughed at the folly of men who, week in and week out, left their hard-earned money with the publicans; and sometimes, to pass an idle hour, he took pencil and paper and calculated precisely how much he saved each week through being a teetotaller. Being a natural optimist he sometimes continued this calculation through the whole span of his prospective existence and the total was breathtaking. He would die worth hundreds.

If I had only known it, this was a bad sign; a sign he was becoming stuffed up with spiritual pride and imagining himself better than his neighbors. Sooner or later, the spiritual pride grew till it called for some form of celebration. Then he took a drink—not whisky, of course; nothing like that—just a glass of some harmless drink like lager beer. That was the end of Father. By the time he had taken the first he already realized that he had made a fool of himself, took a second to forget it and a third to forget that he couldn't forget, and at last came home reeling drunk. From this on it was "The Drunkard's Progress," as in the moral prints. Next day he stayed in from work with a sick head while Mother went off to make his excuses at the works, and inside a fortnight he was poor and savage and despondent again. Once he began he drank steadily through everything down to the kitchen clock. Mother and I knew all the phases and dreaded all the dangers. Funerals were one.

"I have to go to Dunphy's to do a half-day's work," said Mother in distress. "Who's to look after Larry?"

"I'll look after Larry," Father said graciously. "The little walk will do him good."

There was no more to be said, though we all knew I didn't need anyone to look after me, and that I could quite well have stayed at home and looked after Sonny, but I was being attached to the party to act as a brake on Father. As a brake I had never achieved anything, but Mother still had great faith in me.

Next day, when I got home from school, Father was there before me and made a cup of tea for both of us. He was very good at tea, but too heavy in the hand for anything else; the way he cut bread was shocking. Afterwards, we went down the hill to the church, Father wearing his best blue serge and a bowler cocked to one side of his head with the least suggestion of the masher. To his great joy he discovered Peter Crowley among the mourners. Peter was another danger signal, as I knew well from certain experiences after Mass on Sunday morning: a mean man, as Mother said, who only went to funerals for the free drinks he could get at them. It turned out that he hadn't even known Mr. Dooley! But Father had a sort of contemptuous regard for him as one of the foolish people who wasted their good money in public houses when they could be saving it. Very little of his own money Peter Crowley wasted!

It was an excellent funeral from Father's point of view. He had it all well studied before we set off after the hearse in the afternoon sunlight.

"Five carriages!" he exclaimed. "Five carriages and sixteen covered cars! There's one alderman, two councillors and 'tis unknown how many priests. I didn't see a funeral like this from the road since Willie Mack, the publican, died."

"Ah, he was well liked," said Crowley in his husky voice.

"My goodness, don't I know that?" snapped Father. "Wasn't the man my best friend? Two nights before he died—only two nights—he was over telling me the goings-on about the housing contract. Them fellows in the Corporation are night and day robbers. But even I never imagined he was as well connected as that."

Father was stepping out like a boy, pleased with everything: the other mourners, and the fine houses along Sunday's Well. I knew the danger signals were there in full force: a sunny day, a fine funeral, and a distinguished company of clerics and public men were bringing out all the natural vanity and flightiness of Father's character. It was with something like genuine pleasure that he saw his old friend lowered into the grave; with the sense of having performed a duty and the pleasant awareness that however much he would miss poor Mr. Dooley in the long summer evenings, it was he and not poor Mr. Dooley who would do the missing.

"We'll be making tracks before they break up," he whispered to Crowley as the gravediggers tossed in the first shovelfuls of clay, and away he went, hopping like a goat from grassy hump to hump. The drivers, who were probably in the same state as himself, though without months of abstinence to put an edge on it, looked up hopefully.

"Are they nearly finished, Mick?" bawled one.

"All over now bar the last prayers," trumpeted Father in the tone of one who brings news of great rejoicing.

The carriages passed us in a lather of dust several hundred yards from the public house, and Father, whose feet gave him trouble in hot weather, quickened his pace, looking nervously over his shoulder for any sign of the main body of mourners crossing the hill. In a crowd like that a man might be kept waiting.

When we did reach the pub the carriages were drawn up outside, and solemn men in black ties were cautiously bringing out consolation to mysterious females whose hands reached out modestly from behind the drawn blinds of the coaches. Inside the pub there were only the drivers and a couple of shawly women. I felt if I was to act as a brake at all, this was the time, so I pulled Father by the coattails.

"Dadda, can't we go home now?" I asked.

"Two minutes now," he said, beaming affectionately. "Just a bottle of lemonade and we'll go home."

This was a bribe, and I knew it, but I was always a child of weak character. Father ordered lemonade and two pints. I was thirsty and swallowed my drink at once. But that wasn't Father's way. He had long months of abstinence behind him and an eternity of pleasure before. He took out his pipe, blew through it, filled it, and then lit it with loud pops, his eyes bulging above it. After that he deliberately turned his back on the pint, leaned one elbow on the counter in the attitude of a man who did not know there was a pint behind him, and deliberately brushed the tobacco from his palms. He had settled down for the evening. He was steadily working through all the important funerals he had ever attended. The carriages departed and the minor mourners drifted in till the pub was half full.

"Dadda," I said, pulling his coat again, "can't we go home now?"

"Ah, your mother won't be in for a long time yet," he said benevolently enough. "Run out in the road and play, can't you?"

It struck me as very cool, the way grown-ups assumed that you could play all by yourself on a strange road. I began to get bored as I had so often been bored before. I knew Father was quite capable of lingering there till nightfall. I knew I might have to bring him home, blind drunk, down Blarney Lane, with all the old women at their doors, saying: "Mick Delaney is on it again." I knew that my mother would be half crazy with anxiety; that next day Father wouldn't go out to work; and before the end of the week she would be running down to the pawn with the clock under her shawl. I could never get over the lonesomeness of the kitchen without a clock.

I was still thirsty. I found if I stood on tiptoe I could just reach Father's glass, and the idea occurred to me that it would be interesting to know what the contents were like. He had his back to it and wouldn't notice. I took down the glass and sipped cautiously. It was a terrible disappointment. I was astonished that he could even drink such stuff. It looked as if he had never tried lemonade.

I should have advised him about lemonade but he was holding forth himself in great style. I heard him say that bands were a great addition to a funeral. He put his arms in the position of someone holding a rifle in reverse and hummed a few bars of Chopin's Funeral March. Crowley nodded reverently. I took a longer drink and began to see that porter might have its advantages. I felt pleasantly elevated and philosophic. Father hummed a few bars of the Dead March in *Saul.* It was a nice pub and a very fine funeral, and I felt sure that poor Mr. Dooley in Heaven must be highly gratified. At the same time I thought they might have given him a band. As Father said, bands were a great addition.

But the wonderful thing about porter was the way it made you stand aside, or rather float aloft like a cherub rolling on a cloud, and watch yourself with your legs crossed, leaning against a bar counter, not worrying about trifles but thinking deep, serious, grown-up thoughts about life and death. Looking at yourself like that, you couldn't help thinking after a while how funny you looked, and suddenly you got embarrassed and wanted to giggle. But by the time I had finished the pint, that phase too had passed; I found it hard to put back the glass, the counter seemed to have grown so high. Melancholia was supervening again.

"Well," Father said reverently, reaching behind him for his drink, "God rest the poor man's soul, wherever he is!" He stopped, looked first at the glass, and then at the people round him. "Hello," he said in a fairly good-humored tone, as if he were just prepared to consider it a joke, even if it was in bad taste, "who was at this?"

There was silence for a moment while the publican and the old women looked first at Father and then at his glass.

"There was no one at it, my good man," one of the women said with an offended air. "Is it robbers you think we are?"

"Ah, there's no one here would do a thing like that, Mick," said the publican in a shocked tone.

"Well, someone did it," said Father, his smile beginning to wear off.

"If they did, they were them that were nearer it," said the woman darkly, giving me a dirty look; and at the same moment the truth began to dawn on Father. I suppose I must have looked a bit starry-eyed. He bent and shook me.

"Are you all right, Larry?" he asked in alarm.

Peter Crowley looked down at me and grinned.

"Could you beat that?" he exclaimed in a husky voice.

I could, and without difficulty. I started to get sick. Father jumped back in holy terror that I might spoil his good suit, and hastily opened the back door.

"Run! run! run!" he shouted.

I saw the sunlit wall outside with the ivy overhanging it, and ran. The intention was good but the performance was exaggerated, because I lurched right into the wall, hurting it badly, as it seemed to me. Being always very polite, I said "Pardon" before the second bout came on me. Father, still concerned for his suit, came up behind and cautiously held me while I got sick.

"That's a good boy!" he said encouragingly. "You'll be grand when you get that up."

Begor, I was not grand! Grand was the last thing I was. I gave one unmerciful wail out of me as he steered me back to the pub and put me sitting on the bench near the shawlies. They drew themselves up with an offended air, still sore at the suggestion that they had drunk his pint.

"God help us!" moaned one, looking pityingly at me, "isn't it the likes of them would be fathers?"

"Mick," said the publican in alarm, spraying sawdust on my tracks, "that child isn't supposed to be in here at all. You'd better take him home quick in case a bobby would see him."

"Merciful God!" whimpered Father, raising his eyes to heaven and clapping his hands silently as he only did when distraught, "what misfortune was on me? Or what will his mother say? . . . If women might stop at home and look after their children themselves!" he added in a snarl for the benefit of the shawlies. "Are them carriages all gone, Bill?"

"The carriages are finished long ago, Mick," replied the publican.

"I'll take him home," Father said despairingly. . . . "I'll never bring you out again," he threatened me. "Here," he added, giving me the clean handkerchief from his breast pocket, "put that over your eyes."

The blood on the handkerchief was the first indication I got that I was cut, and instantly my temple began to throb and I set up another howl.

"Whisht, whisht, whisht!" Father said testily, steering me out the door. "One'd think you were killed. That's nothing. We'll wash it when we get home."

"Steady now, old scout!" Crowley said, taking the other side of me. "You'll be all right in a minute."

I never met two men who knew less about the effects of drink. The first breath of fresh air and the warmth of the sun made me groggier than ever and I pitched and rolled between wind and tide till Father started to whimper again.

"God Almighty, and the whole road out! What misfortune was on me didn't stop at my work! Can't you walk straight?"

I couldn't. I saw plain enough that, coaxed by the sunlight, every woman old and young in Blarney Lane was leaning over her half-door or sitting on her doorstep. They all stopped gabbling to gape at the strange spectacle of two sober, middle-aged men bringing home a drunken small boy with a cut over his eye. Father, torn between the shamefast desire to get me home as quick as he could, and the neighborly need to explain that it wasn't his fault, finally halted outside Mrs. Roche's. There was a gang of old women outside a door at the opposite side of the road. I didn't like the look of them from the first. They seemed altogether too interested in me. I leaned against the wall of Mrs. Roche's cottage with my hands in my trousers pockets, thinking mournfully of poor Mr. Dooley in his cold grave on the Curragh, who would never walk down the road again, and, with great feeling, I began to sing a favorite song of Father's.

Though lost to Mononia and cold in the grave
He returns to Kincora no more.

"Wisha, the poor child!" Mrs. Roche said. "Haven't he a lovely voice, God bless him!"

That was what I thought myself, so I was the more surprised when Father said "Whisht!" and raised a threatening finger at me. He didn't seem to realize the appropriateness of the song, so I sang louder than ever.

"Whisht, I tell you!" he snapped, and then tried to work up a smile for Mrs. Roche's benefit. "We're nearly home now. I'll carry you the rest of the way."

But, drunk and all as I was, I knew better than to be carried home ignominiously like that.

"Now," I said severely, "can't you leave me alone? I can walk all right. 'Tis only my head. All I want is a rest."

"But you can rest at home in bed," he said viciously, trying to pick me up, and I knew by the flush on his face that he was very vexed.

"Ah, Jasus," I said crossly, "what do I want to go home for? Why the hell can't you leave me alone?"

For some reason the gang of old women at the other side of the road thought this very funny. They nearly split their sides over it. A gassy fury began to expand in me at the thought that a fellow couldn't have a drop taken without the whole neighborhood coming out to make game of him.

"Who are ye laughing at?" I shouted, clenching my fists at them. "I'll make ye laugh at the other side of yeer faces if ye don't let me pass."

They seemed to think this funnier still; I had never seen such ill-mannered people.

"Go away, ye bloody bitches!" I said.

"Whisht, whisht, whisht, I tell you!" snarled Father, abandoning all pretence of amusement and dragging me along behind him by the hand. I was maddened by the women's shrieks of laughter. I was maddened by Father's bullying. I tried to dig in my heels but he was too powerful for me, and I could only see the women by looking back over my shoulder.

"Take care or I'll come back and show ye!" I shouted. "I'll teach ye to let decent people pass. Fitter for ye to stop at home and wash yeer dirty faces."

" 'Twill be all over the road," whimpered Father. "Never again, never again, not if I lived to be a thousand!"

To this day I don't know whether he was forswearing me or the drink. By way of a song suitable to my heroic mood I bawled "The Boys of Wexford," as he dragged me in home. Crowley, knowing he was not safe, made off and Father undressed me and put me to bed. I couldn't sleep because of the whirling in my head. It was very unpleasant, and I got sick again. Father came in with a wet cloth and mopped up after me. I lay in a fever, listening to him chopping sticks to start a fire. After that I heard him lay the table.

Suddenly the front door banged open and Mother stormed in with Sonny in her arms, not her usual gentle, timid self, but a wild, raging woman. It was clear that she had heard it all from the neighbors.

"Mick Delaney," she cried hysterically, "what did you do to my son?"

"Whisht, woman, whisht, whisht!" he hissed, dancing from one foot to the other. "Do you want the whole road to hear?"

"Ah," she said with a horrifying laugh, "the road knows all about it by this time. The road knows the way you filled your unfortunate innocent child with drink to make sport for you and that other rotten, filthy brute."

"But I gave him no drink," he shouted, aghast at the horrifying interpretation the neighbors had chosen to give his misfortune. "He took it while my back was turned. What the hell do you think I am?"

"Ah," she replied bitterly, "everyone knows what you are now. God forgive you, wasting our hard-earned few ha'pence on drink, and bringing up your child to be a drunken corner-boy like yourself."

Then she swept into the bedroom and threw herself on her knees by the bed. She moaned when she saw the gash over my eye. In the kitchen Sonny set up a loud bawl on his own, and a moment later Father appeared in the bedroom door with his cap over his eyes, wearing an expression of the most intense self-pity.

"That's a nice way to talk to me after all I went through," he whined. "That's a nice accusation, that I was drinking. Not one drop of drink crossed my lips the whole day. How could it when he drank it all? I'm the one that ought to be pitied, with my day ruined on me, and I after being made a show for the whole road."

But next morning, when he got up and went out quietly to work with his dinner basket, Mother threw herself on me in the bed and kissed me. It seemed it was all my doing, and I was being given a holiday till my eye got better.

"My brave little man!" she said with her eyes shining. "It was God did it you were there. You were his guardian angel."

The Use of Force

William Carlos Williams

WILLIAM CARLOS WILLIAMS (1883–1963) was born in Rutherford, New Jersey, attended Horace Mann High School in New York City and a preparatory school in Switzerland, then studied medicine at the University of Pennsylvania, receiving his M.D. degree in 1906. Williams lived his life as both doctor and author, achieving writing success as poet, novelist, playwright, and short-story writer. He combined his medical experiences and sensitive understanding of people in such works as "The Use of Force." Williams' significant works are novels: White Mule *(1937),* The Build-Up *(1952); poetry collections:* Complete Collected Poems *(1938),* Selected Poems *(1949),* Collected Later Poems *(1950),* Paterson *(1951–1958),* Journey to Love *(1955); and short-story collections:* The Knife of the Times *(1932);* Life Along the Passaic River *(1938);* Make Light of It *(1950).*

They were new patients to me, all I had was the name, Olson. Please come down as soon as you can, my daughter is very sick.

When I arrived I was met by the mother, a big startled looking woman, very clean and apologetic who merely said, Is this the doctor? and let me in. In the back, she added. You must excuse us, doctor, we have her in the kitchen where it is warm. It is very damp here sometimes.

The child was fully dressed and sitting on her father's lap near the kitchen table. He tried to get up, but I motioned for him not to bother, took off my overcoat and started to look things over. I could see that they were all very nervous, eyeing me up and down distrustfully. As often, in such cases, they weren't telling me more than they had to, it was up to me to tell them; that's why they were spending three dollars on me.

The child was fairly eating me up with her cold, steady eyes, and no expression to her face whatever. She did not move and seemed, inwardly, quiet; an unusually attractive little thing, and as strong as a heifer in appearance. But her face was flushed, she was breathing rapidly, and I realized that she had a high fever. She had magnificent blonde hair, in profusion. One of those picture children often reproduced in advertising leaflets and the photogravure sections of the Sunday papers.

She's had a fever for three days, began the father, and we don't know what it comes from. My wife has given her things, you know, like people do, but it don't do no good. And there's been a lot of sickness around. So we tho't you'd better look her over and tell us what is the matter.

As doctors often do I took a trial shot at it as a point of departure. Has she had a sore throat?

Both parents answered me together, No . . . No, she says her throat don't hurt her.

Does your throat hurt you? added the mother to the child. But the little girl's expression didn't change nor did she move her eyes from my face.

Have you looked?

I tried to, said the mother, but I couldn't see.

As it happens we had been having a number of cases of diphtheria in the school to which this child went during that month and we were all, quite apparently, thinking of that, though no one had as yet spoken of the thing.

Well, I said, suppose we take a look at the throat first. I smiled in my best professional manner and asking for the child's first name I said, come on, Mathilda, open your mouth and let's take a look at your throat.

Nothing doing.

Aw, come on, I coaxed, just open your mouth wide and let me take a look. Look, I said opening both hands wide, I haven't anything in my hands. Just open up and let me see.

Such a nice man, put in the mother. Look how kind he is to you. Come on, do what he tells you to. He won't hurt you.

At that I ground my teeth in disgust. If only they wouldn't use the word "hurt" I might be able to get somewhere. But I did not allow myself to be hurried or disturbed but speaking quietly and slowly I approached the child again.

As I moved my chair a little nearer suddenly with one catlike movement both her hands clawed instinctively for my eyes and she almost reached them too. In fact she knocked my glasses flying and they fell, though unbroken, several feet away from me on the kitchen floor.

Both the mother and father almost turned themselves inside out in embarrassment and apology. You bad girl, said the mother, taking her and shaking her by one arm. Look what you've done. The nice man . . .

For heaven's sake, I broke in. Don't call me a nice man to her. I'm here to look at her throat on the chance that she might have diphtheria and possibly die of it. But that's nothing to her. Look here, I said to the child, we're going to look at your throat. You're old enough to understand what I'm saying. Will you open it now by yourself or shall we have to open it for you?

Not a move. Even her expression hadn't changed. Her breaths however were coming faster and faster. Then the battle began. I had to do it. I had to have a throat culture for her own protection. But first I told the parents that it was entirely up to them. I explained the danger but said that I would not insist on a throat examination so long as they would take the responsibility.

If you don't do what the doctor says you'll have to go to the hospital, the mother admonished her severely.

Oh yeah? I had to smile to myself. After all, I had already fallen in love with the savage brat, the parents were contemptible to me. In the ensuing struggle they grew more and more abject, crushed, exhausted while she surely rose to magnificent heights of insane fury of effort bred of her terror of me.

The father tried his best, and he was a big man but the fact that she was his daughter, his shame at her behavior and his dread of hurting her made him release her just at the critical times when I had almost achieved success, till I wanted to kill him. But his dread also that she might have diphtheria made him tell me to go on, go on though he himself was almost fainting, while the mother moved back and forth behind us raising and lowering her hands in an agony of apprehension.

Put her in front of you on your lap, I ordered, and hold both her wrists.

But as soon as he did the child let out a scream. Don't, you're hurting me. Let go of my hands. Let them go I tell you. Then she shrieked terrifyingly, hysterically. Stop it! Stop it! You're killing me!

Do you think she can stand it, doctor! said the mother.

You get out, said the husband to his wife. Do you want her to die of diphtheria?

Come on now, hold her, I said.

Then I grasped the child's head with my left hand and tried to get the wooden tongue depressor between her teeth. She fought, with clenched teeth, desperately! But now I also had grown furious—at the child. I tried to hold myself down but I couldn't. I know how to expose a throat for inspection. And I did my best. When finally I got the wooden spatula behind the last teeth and just the point of it into the mouth cavity, she opened up for an instant but before I could see anything she came down again and gripping the wooden blade between her molars she reduced it to splinters before I could get it out again.

Aren't you ashamed, the mother yelled at her. Aren't you ashamed to act like that in front of the doctor?

Get me a smooth-handled spoon of some sort, I told the mother. We're going through with this. The child's mouth was already bleeding. Her tongue was cut and she was screaming in wild hysterical shrieks. Perhaps I should have desisted and come back in an hour or more. No doubt it would have been better. But I have seen at least two children lying dead in bed of neglect in such cases, and feeling that I must get a diagnosis now or never I went at it again. But the worst of it was that I too had got beyond reason. I could have torn the child apart in my own fury and enjoyed it. It was a pleasure to attack her. My face was burning with it.

The damned little brat must be protected against her own idiocy, one says to one's self at such times. Others must be protected against her. It is a social necessity. And all these things are true. But a blind fury, a feeling of adult shame, bred of a longing for muscular release are the operatives. One goes on to the end.

In a final unreasoning assault I overpowered the child's neck and jaws. I forced the heavy silver spoon back of her teeth and down her throat till she gagged. And there it was—both tonsils covered with membrane. She had fought valiantly to keep me from knowing her secret. She had been hiding that sore throat for three days at least and lying to her parents in order to escape just such an outcome as this.

Now truly she was furious. She had been on the defensive before but now she attacked. Tried to get off her father's lap and fly at me while tears of defeat blinded her eyes.

Silent Snow, Secret Snow

Conrad Aiken

CONRAD AIKEN *(1889–1973) was born in Savannah, Georgia. In 1900, after the deaths of his mother and father, he was taken to New Bedford, Massachusetts. Aiken was educated at Concord's Middlesex School and Harvard University, where among his classmates were Walter Lippmann, Heywood Broun, Robert Benchley, and T. S. Eliot. Choosing a writing career at an early age, Aiken had his first book published in 1914, and by 1929 his* Selected Poems *had won the Pulitzer Prize. Some of his other books are* The Short Stories of Conrad Aiken *(1950),* Ushant: An Essay *(1952),* Collected Poems *(1953),* Mr. Arcularis: A Play *(1957),* A Reviewer's ABC *(1958), and* Collected Novels *(1964). Over his long and productive career Aiken has written more than forty volumes of poetry, criticism, and fiction. Some critics believe Aiken's work has been too long neglected and underrated, partially, it seems, because some of Aiken's contemporaries, including T. S. Eliot and Ezra Pound, achieved such literary prominence that they pushed Aiken and his work into the shadows.*

I

Just why it should have happened, or why it should have happened just when it did, he could not, of course, possibly have said; nor perhaps could it even have occurred to him to ask. The thing was above all a secret, something to be preciously concealed from Mother and Father; and to that very fact it owed an enormous part of its deliciousness. It was like a peculiarly beautiful trinket to be carried unmentioned in one's trouser pocket—a rare stamp, an old coin, a few tiny gold links found trodden out of shape on the path in the park, a pebble of carnelian, a sea shell distinguishable from all others by an unusual spot or stripe—and, as if it were anyone of these, he carried around with him everywhere a warm and persistent and increasingly beautiful sense of possession. Nor was it only a sense of possession—it was also a sense of protection. It was as if, in some delightful way, his secret gave him a fortress, a wall behind which he could retreat into heavenly seclusion. This was almost the first thing he had noticed about it—apart from the oddness of the thing itself—and it was this that now again, for the fiftieth time, occurred to him, as he sat in the little schoolroom. It was the half hour for geography. Miss Buell was revolving with one finger, slowly, a huge terrestrial globe which had been placed on her desk. The green and yellow continents passed and repassed, questions were asked and answered, and now the little girl in front of him, Deirdre, who had a funny little constellation of freckles on the back of her neck, exactly like the Big Dipper, was standing up and telling Miss Buell that the equator was the line that ran round the middle.

Miss Buell's face, which was old and grayish and kindly, with gray stiff curls beside the cheeks, and eyes that swam very brightly, like little minnows, behind thick glasses, wrinkled itself into a complication of amusements.

"Ah! I see. The earth is wearing a belt, or a sash. Or someone drew a line round it!"

"Oh, no—not that—I mean—"

In the general laughter, he did not share, or only a very little. He was thinking about the Arctic and Antarctic regions, which of course, on the globe, were white. Miss Buell was now telling them about the tropics, the jungles, the steamy heat of equatorial swamps, where the birds and butterflies, and even the snakes, were like living jewels. As he listened to these things, he was already, with a pleasant sense of half effort, putting his secret between himself and the words. Was it really an effort at all? For effort implied something voluntary, and perhaps even something one did not especially want; whereas this was distinctly pleasant, and came almost of its own accord. All he needed to do was to think of that morning, the first one, and then of all the others—

But it was all so absurdly simple! It had amounted to so little. It was nothing, just an idea—and just why it should have become so wonderful, so permanent, was a mystery—a very pleasant one, to be sure, but also, in an amusing way, foolish. However, without ceasing to listen to Miss Buell, who had now moved up to the north temperate zones, he deliberately invited his memory of the first morning. It was only a moment or two after he had waked up—or perhaps the moment itself. But was there, to be exact, an exact moment? Was one awake all at once? or was it gradual? Anyway, it was after he had stretched a lazy hand up towards the head rail, and yawned, and then relaxed again among his warm covers, all the more grateful on a December morning, that the thing had happened. Suddenly, for no reason, he had thought of the postman, he remembered the postman. Perhaps there was nothing so odd in that. After all, he heard the postman almost every morning in his life—his heavy boots could be heard clumping round the corner at the top of the little cobbled hill street, and then, progressively nearer, progressively louder, the double knock at each door, the crossings and recrossings of the street, till finally the clumsy steps came stumbling across to the very door, and the tremendous knock came which shook the house itself.

(Miss Buell was saying, "Vast wheat-growing areas in North America and Siberia."

Deirdre had for the moment placed her left hand across the back of her neck.)

But on this particular morning, the first morning, as he lay there with his eyes closed, he had for some reason *waited* for the postman. He wanted to hear him come round the corner. And that was precisely the joke—he never did. He never came. He never had come—*round the corner*—again. For when at last the steps *were* heard, they had already, he was quite sure, come a little down the hill, to the first house; and even so, the steps were curiously different—they were softer, they had a new secrecy about them, they were muffled and indistinct; and while the rhythm of them was the same, it now said a new thing—it said peace, it said remoteness, it said cold, it said sleep. And he had understood the situation at once—nothing could have seemed simpler—there had been snow in the night, such as all winter he had been longing for; and it was this which had rendered the postman's first footsteps inaudible, and the later ones faint. Of course! How lovely! And even now it must be snowing—it was going to be a snowy day—the long white ragged lines were drifting and sifting across the street, across the faces of the old houses, whispering and hushing, making little triangles of white in the corners between cobblestones, seething a little when the wind blew them over the ground to a drifted corner; and so it would be all day, getting deeper and deeper and silenter and silenter.

(Miss Buell was saying, "Land of perpetual snow.")

All this time, of course (while he lay in bed), he had kept his eyes closed, listening to the nearer progress of the postman, the muffled footsteps thumping and slipping on the snow-sheathed cobbles; and all the other sounds—the double knocks, a frosty far-off voice or two, a bell ringing thinly and softly as if under a sheet of ice—had the same slightly abstracted quality, as if removed by one degree from actuality—as if everything in the world had been insulated by snow. But when at last, pleased, he opened his eyes, and turned them towards the window, to see for himself this long-desired and now so clearly imagined miracle—what he saw instead was brilliant sunlight on a roof; and when, astonished, he jumped out of bed and stared down into the street, expecting to see the cobbles obliterated by the snow, he saw nothing but the bare bright cobbles themselves.

Queer, the effect this extraordinary surprise had had upon him—all the following morning he had kept with him a sense as of snow falling about him, a secret screen of new snow between himself and the world. If he had not dreamed such a thing—and how could he have dreamed it while awake?—how else could one explain it? In any case, the delusion had been so vivid as to affect his entire behavior. He could not now remember whether it was on the first or the second morning—or was it even the third?—that his mother had drawn attention to some oddness in his manner.

"But, my darling—" she had said at the breakfast table—"what has come over you? You don't seem to be listening. . . ."

And how often that very thing had happened since!

(Miss Buell was now asking if anyone knew the difference between the North Pole and the Magnetic Pole. Deirdre was holding up her flickering brown hand, and he could see the four white dimples that marked the knuckles.)

Perhaps it hadn't been either the second or third morning—or even the fourth or fifth. How could he be sure? How could he be sure just when the delicious *progress* had become clear? Just when it had really *begun?* The intervals weren't very precise. . . . All he now knew was that at some point or other—perhaps the second day, perhaps the sixth—he had noticed that the presence of the snow was a little more insistent, the sound of it clearer; and, conversely, the sound of the postman's footsteps more indistinct. Not only could he not hear the steps come round the corner, he could not even hear them at the first house. It was below the first house that he heard them; and then, a few days later, it was below the second house that he heard them; and a few days later again, below the third. Gradually, gradually, the snow was becoming heavier, the sound of its seething louder, the cobblestones more and more muffled. When he found, each morning, on going to the window, after the ritual of listening, that the roofs and cobbles were as bare as ever, it made no difference. This was, after all, only what he had expected. It was even what pleased him, what rewarded him: the thing was his own, belonged to no one else. No one else knew about it, not even his mother and father. There, outside, were the bare cobbles; and here, inside, was the snow. Snow growing heavier each day, muffling the world, hiding the ugly, and deadening increasingly—above all—the steps of the postman.

"But, my darling—" she had said at the luncheon table—"what has come over you? You don't seem to listen when people speak to you. That's the third time I've asked you to pass your plate. . . ."

How was one to explain this to Mother? or to Father? There was, of course, nothing to be done about it: nothing. All one could do was to laugh embarrassedly, pretend to be a little ashamed, apologize, and take a sudden and somewhat disingenuous interest in what was being done or said. The cat had stayed out all night. He had a curious swelling on his left cheek—perhaps somebody had kicked him, or a stone had struck him. Mrs. Kempton was or was not coming to tea. The house was going to be house cleaned, or "turned out," on Wednesday instead of Friday. A new lamp was provided for his evening work—perhaps it was eyestrain which accounted for this new and so peculiar vagueness of his—Mother was looking at him with amusement as she said this, but with something else as well. A new lamp? A new lamp. Yes Mother, No Mother, Yes Mother. School is going very well. The geometry is very easy. The history is very dull.

The geography is very interesting—particularly when it takes one to the North Pole. Why the North Pole? Oh, well, it would be fun to be an explorer. Another Peary or Scott or Shackleton. And then abruptly he found his interest in the talk at an end, stared at the pudding on his plate, listened, waited, and began once more—ah how heavenly, too, the first beginnings—to hear or feel—for could he actually hear it?—the silent snow, the secret snow.

(Miss Buell was telling them about the search for the Northwest Passage, about Hendrik Hudson, the *Half Moon*.)

This had been, indeed, the only distressing feature of the new experience: the fact that it so increasingly had brought him into a kind of mute misunderstanding, or even conflict, with his father and mother. It was as if he were trying to lead a double life. On the one hand he had to be Paul Hasleman, and keep up the appearance of being that person—dress, wash, and answer intelligently when spoken to; on the other, he had to explore this new world which had been opened to him. Nor could there be the slightest doubt—not the slightest—that the new world was the profounder and more wonderful of the two. It was irresistible. It was miraculous. Its beauty was simply beyond anything—beyond speech as beyond thought—utterly incommunicable. But how then, between the two worlds, of which he was thus constantly aware, was he to keep a balance? One must get up, one must go to breakfast, one must talk with Mother, go to school, do one's lessons—and, in all this, try not to appear too much of a fool. But if all the while one was also trying to extract the full deliciousness of another and quite separate existence, one which could not easily (if at all) be spoken of—how was one to manage? How was one to explain? Would it be safe to explain? Would it be absurd? Would it merely mean that he would get into some obscure kind of trouble?

These thoughts came and went, came and went, as softly and secretly as the snow; they were not precisely a disturbance, perhaps they were even a pleasure; he liked to have them; their presence was something almost palpable, something he could stroke with his hand, without closing his eyes, and without ceasing to see Miss Buell and the schoolroom and the globe and the freckles on Deirdre's neck; nevertheless he did in a sense cease to see, or to see the obvious external world, and substituted for this vision the vision of snow, the sound of snow, and the slow, almost soundless, approach of the postman. Yesterday, it had been only at the sixth house that the postman had become audible; the snow was much deeper now, it was falling more swiftly and heavily, the sound of its seething was more distinct, more soothing, more persistent. And this morning, it had been—as nearly as he could figure—just above the seventh house—perhaps only a step or two above: at most, he had heard two or three footsteps before the knock had sounded. . . . And with each such narrowing of the sphere, each nearer approach of the limit at which the postman was first audible, it was odd how sharply was increased the amount of illusion which had to be carried into the ordinary business of daily life. Each day, it was harder to get out of bed, to go to the window, to look out at the—as always—perfectly empty and snowless street. Each day it was more difficult to go through the perfunctory motions of greeting Mother and Father at breakfast, to reply to their questions, to put his books together and go to school. And at school, how extraordinarily hard to conduct with success simultaneously the public life and the life that was secret. There were times when he longed—positively ached—to tell everyone about it—to burst out with it—only to be checked almost at once by a far-off feeling as of some faint absurdity which was inherent in it—but *was* it absurd?—and more importantly by a sense of mysterious power in his very secrecy. Yes: it must be kept secret. That, more and more, became clear. At whatever cost to himself, whatever pain to others—

(Miss Buell looked straight at him, smiling, and said, "Perhaps we'll ask Paul. I'm sure Paul will come out of his daydream long enough to be able to tell us. Won't you, Paul." He rose slowly from his chair, resting one hand on the brightly varnished desk, and deliberately stared through the snow towards the blackboard. It was an effort, but it was amusing to make it. "Yes," he said slowly, "it was what we now call the Hudson River. This he thought to be the Northwest Passage. He was disappointed." He sat down again, and as he did so Deirdre half turned in her chair and gave him a shy smile, of approval and admiration.)

At whatever pain to others.

This part of it was very puzzling, very puzzling. Mother was very nice, and so was Father. Yes, that was all true enough. He wanted to be nice to them, to tell them everything—and yet, was it really wrong of him to want to have a secret place of his own?

At bedtime, the night before, Mother had said, "If this goes on, my lad, we'll have to see a doctor, we will! We can't have our boy—" But what was it she had said? "Live in another world"? "Live so far away"? The word "far" had been in it, he was sure, and then Mother had taken up a magazine again and laughed a little, but with an expression which wasn't mirthful. He had felt sorry for her. . . .

The bell rang for dismissal. The sound came to him through long curved parallels of falling snow. He saw Deirdre rise, and had himself risen almost as soon—but not quite as soon—as she.

II

On the walk homeward, which was timeless, it pleased him to see through the accompaniment, or counterpoint, of snow, the items of mere externality on his way. There were many kinds of bricks in the sidewalks, and laid in many kinds of pattern. The garden walls too were various, some of wooden palings, some of plaster, some of stone. Twigs of bushes leaned over the walls; the little hard green winter buds of lilac, on gray stems, sheathed and fat; other branches very thin and fine and black and desiccated. Dirty sparrows huddled in the bushes, as dull in color as dead fruit left in leafless trees. A single starling creaked on a weather vane. In the gutter, beside a drain, was a scrap of torn and dirty newspaper, caught in a little delta of filth: the word ECZEMA appeared in large capitals, and below it was a letter from Mrs. Amelia D. Cravath, 2100 Pine Street, Fort Worth, Texas, to the effect that after being a sufferer for years she had been cured by Caley's Ointment. In the little delta, beside the fan-shaped and deeply runneled continent of brown mud, were lost twigs, descended from their parent trees, dead matches, a rusty horse-chestnut burr, a small concentration of sparkling gravel on the lip of the sewer, a fragment of eggshell, a streak of yellow sawdust which had been wet and was now dry and congealed, a brown pebble, and a broken feather. Further on was a cement sidewalk, ruled into geometrical parallelograms, with a brass inlay at one end commemorating the contractors who had laid it, and, halfway across, an irregular and random series of dog tracks, immortalized in synthetic stone. He knew these well, and always stepped on them; to cover the little hollows with his own foot had always been a queer pleasure; today he did it once more, but perfunctorily and detachedly, all the while thinking of something else. That was a dog, a long time ago, who had made a mistake and walked on the cement while it was still wet. He had probably wagged his tail, but that hadn't been recorded. Now, Paul Hasleman, aged twelve, on his way home from school, crossed the same river, which in the meantime had frozen into rock. Homeward through the snow, the snow falling in bright sunshine. Homeward?

Then came the gateway with the two posts surmounted by egg-shaped stones which had been cunningly balanced on their ends, as if by Columbus, and mortared in the very act of balance: a source of perpetual wonder. On the brick wall just beyond, the letter *H* had been stenciled, presumably for some purpose. *H? H.*

The green hydrant, with a little green-painted chain attached to the brass screw cap.

The elm tree, with the great gray wound in the bark, kidney-shaped, into which he always put his hand—to feel the cold but living wood. The injury, he had been sure, was due to the gnawings of a tethered horse. But now it deserved only a passing palm, a merely tolerant eye. There were more important things. Miracles. Beyond the thoughts of trees, mere elms. Beyond the thoughts of sidewalks, mere stone, mere brick, mere cement. Beyond the thoughts even of his own shoes, which trod these sidewalks obediently, bearing a burden—far above—of elaborate mystery. He watched them. They were not very well polished; he had neglected them, for a very good reason: they were one of the many parts of the increasing difficulty of the daily return to daily life, the morning struggle. To get up, having at last opened one's eyes, to go to the window, and discover no snow, to wash, to dress, to descend the curving stairs to breakfast—

At whatever pain to others, nevertheless, one must persevere in severance, since the incommunicability of the experience demanded it. It was desirable of course to be kind to Mother and Father, especially as they seemed to be worried, but it was also desirable to be resolute. If they should decide—as appeared likely—to consult the doctor, Doctor Howells, and have Paul inspected, his heart listened to through a kind of dictaphone, his lungs, his stomach—well, that was all right. He would go through with it. He would give them answer for question, too—perhaps such answers as they hadn't expected? No. That would never do. For the secret world must, at all costs, be preserved.

The birdhouse in the apple tree was empty—it was the wrong time of year for wrens. The little round black door had lost its pleasure. The wrens were enjoying other houses, other nests, remoter trees. But this too was a notion which he only vaguely and grazingly entertained—as if, for the moment, he merely touched an edge of it; there was something further on, which was already assuming a sharper importance; something which already teased at the corners of his eyes, teasing also at the corner of his mind. It was funny to think that he so wanted this, so awaited it—and yet found himself enjoying this momentary dalliance with the birdhouse, as if for a quite deliberate postponement and enhancement of the approaching pleasure. He was aware of his delay, of his smiling and detached and now almost uncomprehending gaze at the little birdhouse; he knew what he was going to look at next: it was his own little cobbled hill street, his own house, the little river at the bottom of the hill, the grocer's shop with the cardboard man in the window—and now, thinking of all this, he turned his head, still smiling, and looking quickly right and left through the snow-laden sunlight.

And the mist of snow, as he had foreseen, was still on it—a ghost of snow falling in the bright sunlight, softly and steadily floating and turning and pausing, soundlessly meeting the snow that covered, as with a transparent mirage, the bare bright cobbles. He loved it—he stood still and loved it. Its beauty was paralyzing—beyond all words, all experience, all dream. No fairy story he had ever read could be compared with it—none had ever given him this extraordinary combination of ethereal loveliness with a something else, unnamable, which was just faintly and deliciously terrifying. What was this thing? As he thought of it, he looked upward toward his own bedroom window, which was open—and it was as if he looked straight into the room and saw himself lying half awake in his bed. There he was—at this very instant he was still perhaps actually there—more truly there than standing here at the edge of the cobbled hill street, with one hand lifted to shade his eyes against the snow-sun. Had he indeed ever left his room, in all this time? since that very first morning? Was the whole progress still being enacted there, was it still the same morning, and himself not yet wholly awake? And even now, had the postman not yet come round the corner? . . .

This idea amused him, and automatically, as he thought of it, he turned his head and looked toward the top of the hill. There was, of course, nothing there—nothing and no one. The street was empty and quiet. And all the more because of its emptiness it occurred to him to count the houses—a thing which, oddly enough, he hadn't before thought of doing. Of course, he had known there weren't many—many, that is, on his own side of the street, which were the ones that figured in the postman's progress—but nevertheless it came to him as something of a shock to find that there were precisely *six*, above his own house—his own house was the seventh.

Six!

Astonished, he looked at his own house—looked at the door, on which was the number thirteen—and then realized that the whole thing was exactly and logically and absurdly what he ought to have known. Just the same, the realization gave him abruptly, and even a little frighteningly, a sense of hurry. He was being hurried—he was being rushed. For—he knit his brows—he couldn't be mistaken—it was just above the *seventh* house, his *own* house, that the postman had first been audible this very morning. But in that case—in that case—did it mean that tomorrow he would hear nothing? The knock he had heard must have been the knock of their own door. Did it mean—and this was an idea which gave him a really extraordinary feeling of surprise—that he would never hear the postman again?—that tomorrow morning the postman would already have passed the house, in a snow by then so deep as to render his footsteps completely inaudible? That he would have made his approach down the snow-filled street so soundlessly, so secretly, that he, Paul Hasleman, there lying in bed, would not have waked in time, or, waking, would have heard nothing?

But how could that be? Unless even the knocker should be muffled in the snow—frozen tight, perhaps? . . . But in that case—

A vague feeling of disappointment came over him; a vague sadness, as if he felt himself deprived of something which he had long looked forward to, something much prized. After all this, all this beautiful progress, the slow delicious advance of the postman through the silent and secret snow, the knock creeping closer each day, and the footsteps nearer, the audible compass of the world thus daily narrowed, narrowed, narrowed, as the snow soothingly and beautifully encroached and deepened, after all this, was he to be defrauded of the one thing he had so wanted—to be able to count, as it were, the last two or three solemn footsteps, as they finally approached his own door? Was it all going to happen, at the end, so suddenly? or indeed, had it already happened? with no slow and subtle gradations of menace, in which he could luxuriate?

He gazed upward again, toward his own window which flashed in the sun: and this time almost with a feeling that it would be better if he *were* still in bed, in that room; for in that case this must still be the first morning, and there would be six more mornings to come—or, for that matter, seven or eight or nine—how could he be sure?—or even more.

III

After supper, the inquisition began. He stood before the doctor, under the lamp, and submitted silently to the usual thumpings and tappings.

"Now will you please say 'Ah'?"

"Ah!"

"Now again please, if you don't mind."

"Ah."

"Say it slowly, and hold it if you can—"

"Ah-h-h-h-h-h—"

"Good."

How silly all this was. As if it had anything to do with his throat! Or his heart or lungs!

Relaxing his mouth, of which the corners, after all this absurd stretching, felt uncomfortable, he avoided the doctor's eyes, and stared towards the fireplace, past his mother's feet (in gray slippers) which projected from the green chair, and his father's feet (in brown slippers) which stood neatly side by side on the hearth rug.

"Hm. There is certainly nothing wrong there. . . ."

He felt the doctor's eyes fixed upon him, and, as if merely to be polite, returned the look, but with a feeling of justifiable evasiveness.

"Now, young man, tell me—do you feel all right?"

"Yes, sir, quite all right."

"No headaches? no dizziness?"

"No, I don't think so."

"Let me see. Let's get a book, if you don't mind—yes, thank you, that will do splendidly—and now, Paul, if you'll just read it, holding it as you would normally hold it—"

He took the book and read:

"And another praise have I to tell for this the city our mother, the gift of a great god, a glory of the land most high; the might of horses, the might of young horses, the might of the sea. . . . For thou, son of Cronus, our lord Poseidon, hast throned herein this pride, since in these roads first thou didst show forth the curb that cures the rage of steeds. And the shapely oar, apt to men's hands, hath a wondrous speed on the brine, following the hundred-footed Nereids. . . . O land that art praised above all lands, now is it for thee to make those bright praises seen in deeds."

He stopped, tentatively, and lowered the heavy book.

"No—as I thought—there is certainly no superficial sign of eyestrain."

Silence thronged the room, and he was aware of the focused scrutiny of the three people who confronted him. . . .

"He could have his eyes examined—but I believe it is something else."

"What could it be?" This was his father's voice.

"It's only this curious absent-minded—" This was his mother's voice.

In the presence of the doctor, they both seemed irritatingly apologetic.

"I believe it is something else. Now, Paul—I would like very much to ask you a question or two. You will answer them, won't you—you know I'm an old, old friend of yours, eh? That's right! . . ."

His back was thumped twice by the doctor's fat fist—then the doctor was grinning at him with false amiability, while with one fingernail he was scratching the top button of his waistcoat. Beyond the doctor's shoulder was the fire, the fingers of flame making light prestidigitation against the sooty fireback, the soft sound of their random flutter the only sound.

"I would like to know—is there anything that worries you?"

The doctor was again smiling, his eyelids low against the little black pupils, in each of which was a tiny white bead of light. Why answer him? why answer him at all? "At whatever pain to others"—but it was all a nuisance, this necessity for resistance, this necessity for attention: it was as if one had been stood up on a brilliantly lighted stage, under a great round blaze of spotlight; as if one were merely a trained seal, or a performing dog, or a fish, dipped out of an aquarium and held up by the tail. It would serve them right if he were merely to bark or growl. And meanwhile, to miss these last few precious hours, these hours of which every minute was more beautiful than the last, more menacing—? He still looked, as if from a great distance, at the beads of light in the doctor's eyes, at the fixed false smile, and then, beyond, once more at his mother's slippers, his father's slippers, the soft flutter of the fire. Even here, even amongst these hostile presences, and in this arranged light, he could see the snow, he could hear it—it was in the corners of the room, where the shadow was deepest, under the sofa, behind the half-opened door which led to the dining room. It was gentler here, softer, its seethe the quietest of whispers, as if, in deference to a drawing room, it had quite deliberately put on its "manners"; it kept itself out of sight, obliterated itself, but distinctly with an air of saying, "Ah, but just wait! Wait till we are alone together! Then I will begin to tell you something new! Something white! something cold! something sleepy! something of cease, and peace, and the long bright curve of space! Tell them to go away. Banish them. Refuse to speak. Leave them, go upstairs to your room, turn out the light and get into bed—I will go with you, I will be waiting for you, I will tell you a better story than Little Kay of the Skates, or The Snow Ghost—I will surround your bed, I will close the windows, pile a deep drift against the door, so that none will ever again be able to enter. Speak to them! . . ." It seemed as if the little hissing voice came from a slow white spiral of falling flakes in the corner by the front window—but he could not be sure. He felt himself smiling, then, and said to the doctor, but without looking at him, looking beyond him still—

"Oh, no, I think not—"

"But are you sure, my boy?"

His father's voice came softly and coldly then—the familiar voice of silken warning. . . .

"You needn't answer at once, Paul—remember we're trying to help you—think it over and be quite sure, won't you?"

He felt himself smiling again, at the notion of being quite sure. What a joke! As if he weren't so sure that reassurance was no longer necessary, and all this cross-examination a ridiculous farce, a grotesque parody! What could they know about it? These gross intelligences, these humdrum minds so bound to the usual, the ordinary? Impossible to tell them about it! Why, even now, even now, with the proof so abundant, so formidable, so imminent, so appallingly present here in this very room, could they believe it?—could even his mother believe it? No—it was only too plain that if anything were said about it, the merest hint given, they would be incredulous—they would laugh—they would say, "Absurd!"—think things about him which weren't true. . . .

"Why no, I'm not worried—why should I be?"

He looked then straight at the doctor's low-lidded eyes, looked from one of them to the other, from one bead of light to the other, and gave a little laugh.

The doctor seemed to be disconcerted by this. He drew back in his chair, resting a fat white hand on either knee. The smile faded slowly from his face.

"Well, Paul!" he said, and paused gravely, "I'm afraid you don't take this quite seriously enough. I think you perhaps don't quite realize—don't quite realize—" He took a deep quick breath, and turned, as if helplessly, at a loss for words, to the others. But Mother and Father were both silent—no help was forthcoming.

"You must surely know, be aware, that you have not been quite yourself, of late? don't you know that? . . ."

It was amusing to watch the doctor's renewed attempt at a smile, a queer disorganized look, as of confidential embarrassment.

"I feel all right, sir," he said, and again gave the little laugh.

"And we're trying to help you." The doctor's tone sharpened.

"Yes, sir, I know. But why? I'm all right. I'm just *thinking,* that's all."

His mother made a quick movement forward, resting a hand on the back of the doctor's chair.

"Thinking?" she said. "But my dear, about what?"

This was a direct challenge—and would have to be directly met.

But before he met it, he looked again into the corner by the door, as if for reassurance. He smiled again at what he saw, at what he heard. The little spiral was still there, still softly whirling, like the ghost of a white kitten chasing the ghost of a white tail, and making as it did so the faintest of whispers. It was all right! If only he could remain firm, everything was going to be all right.

"Oh, about anything, about nothing—*you* know the way you do!"

"You mean—daydreaming?"

"Oh, no—thinking!"

"But thinking about *what?*"

"Anything."

He laughed a third time—but this time, happening to glance upward towards his mother's face, he was appalled at the effect his laughter seemed to have upon her. Her mouth had opened in an expression of horror. . . . This was too bad! Unfortunate! He had known it would cause pain, of course—but he hadn't expected it to be quite so bad as this. Perhaps—perhaps if he just gave them a tiny gleaming hint—?

"About the snow," he said.

"What on earth!" This was his father's voice. The brown slippers came a step nearer on the hearth rug.

"But, my dear, what do you mean!" This was his mother's voice.

The doctor merely stared.

"Just *snow,* that's all. I like to think about it."

"Tell us about it, my boy."

"But that's all it is. There's nothing to tell. *You* know what snow is?"

This he said almost angrily, for he felt that they were trying to corner him. He turned sideways so as no longer to face the doctor, and the better to see the inch of blackness between the window sill and the lowered curtains—the cold inch of beckoning and delicious night. At once he felt better, more assured.

"Mother—can I go to bed, now, please? I've got a headache."

"But I thought you said—"

"It's just come. It's all these questions—! Can I, Mother?"

"You can go as soon as the doctor has finished."

"Don't you think this thing ought to be gone into thoroughly, and *now?*" This was Father's voice. The brown slippers again came a step nearer, the voice was the well-known "punishment" voice, resonant and cruel.

"Oh, what's the use, Norman—"

Quite suddenly, everyone was silent. And without precisely facing them, nevertheless he was aware that all three of them were watching him with an extraordinary intensity—staring hard at him—as if he had done something monstrous, or was himself some kind of monster. He could hear the soft irregular flutter of the flames; the cluck-click-cluck-click of the clock; far and faint, two sudden spurts of laughter from the kitchen, as quickly cut off as begun; a murmur of water in the pipes; and then, the silence seemed to deepen, to spread out, to become world-long and world-wide, to become timeless and shapeless, and to center inevitably and rightly, with a slow and sleepy but enormous concentration of all power, on the beginning of a new sound. What this new sound was going to be, he knew perfectly well. It might begin with a hiss, but it would end with a roar—there was no time to lose—he must escape. It mustn't happen here—

Without another word, he turned and ran up the stairs.

IV

Not a moment too soon. The darkness was coming in long white waves. A prolonged sibilance filled the night—a great seamless seethe of wild influence went abruptly across it—a cold low humming shook the windows. He shut the door and flung off his clothes in the dark. The bare black floor was like a little raft tossed in waves of snow, almost overwhelmed, washed under whitely, up again, smothered in curled billows of feather. The snow was laughing: it spoke from all sides at once: it pressed closer to him as he ran and jumped exulting into his bed.

"Listen to us!" it said. "Listen! We have come to tell you the story we told you about. You remember? Lie down. Shut your eyes, now—you will no longer see much—in this white darkness who could see, or want to see? We will take the place of everything. . . . Listen—"

A beautiful varying dance of snow began at the front of the

room, came forward and then retreated, flattened out toward the floor, then rose fountainlike to the ceiling, swayed, recruited itself from a new stream of flakes which poured laughing in through the humming window, advanced again, lifted long white arms. It said peace, it said remoteness, it said cold—it said—

But then a gash of horrible light fell brutally across the room from the opening door—the snow drew back hissing—something alien had come into the room—something hostile. This thing rushed at him, clutched at him, shook him—and he was not merely horrified, he was filled with such a loathing as he had never known. What was this? this cruel disturbance? this act of anger and hate? It was as if he had to reach up a hand toward another world for any understanding of it—an effort of which he was only barely capable. But of that other world he still remembered just enough to know the exorcising words. They tore themselves from his other life suddenly—

"Mother! Mother! Go away! I hate you!"

And with that effort, everything was solved, everything became all right: the seamless hiss advanced once more, the long white wavering lines rose and fell like enormous whispering sea waves, the whisper becoming louder, the laughter more numerous.

"Listen!" it said. "We'll tell you the last, the most beautiful and secret story—shut your eyes—it is a very small story—a story that gets smaller and smaller—it comes inward instead of opening like a flower—it is a flower becoming a seed—a little cold seed—do you hear? we are leaning closer to you—"

The hiss was now becoming a roar—the whole world was a vast moving screen of snow—but even now it said peace, it said remoteness, it said cold, it said sleep.

The Peasant Marey

Feodor Dostoevsky

FEODOR DOSTOEVSKY *(1821–1881) was born in Moscow, attended the College of Military Engineering in Saint Petersburg, then served two years in the army. In 1843 he finished a novel,* Poor Folk, *which helped him to decide to be a writer. In 1849, because of his affiliation with revolutionaries he was charged with political crimes against the czar and was sent to Siberia for a period of five years at hard labor. Out of this Siberian experience came* The House of the Dead *(1861). Four years later came* Crime and Punishment *(1866). During a period of poverty and an addiction to gambling, he wrote* The Gambler *(1867),* The Idiot *(1869), and* The Possessed *(1871). The novels* The Brothers Karamazov *(1880) and* Crime and Punishment *have established him as one of the world's greatest novelists. Dostoevsky's genius is marked by his remarkable capacity to reveal the spiritual potential, as well as the amazing contradictions, found within all men.*

It was the second day in Easter week. The air was warm, the sky was blue, the sun was high, warm, bright, but my soul was very gloomy. I sauntered behind the prison barracks. I stared at the palings of the stout prison fence, counting them; but I had no inclination to count them, though it was my habit to do so. This was the second day of the "holidays" in the prison; the convicts were not taken out to work, there were numbers of men drunk, loud abuse and quarreling were springing up continually in every corner. There were hideous, disgusting songs, and card parties installed beside the platform beds. Several of the convicts who had been sentenced by their comrades, for special violence, to be beaten till they were half dead, were lying on the platform bed, covered with sheepskins till they should recover and come to themselves again; knives had already been drawn several times. For these two days of holiday all this had been torturing me till it made me ill. And indeed I could never endure without repulsion the noise and disorder of drunken people, and especially in this place. On these days even the prison officials did not look into the prison, made no searches, did not look for vodka, understanding that they must allow even these outcasts to enjoy themselves once a year, and that things would be even worse if they did not. At last a sudden fury flamed up in my heart. A political prisoner called M. met me; he looked at me gloomily, his eyes flashed and his lips quivered. "*Je hais ces brigands!*"* he hissed at me through his teeth, and walked on. I returned to the prison ward, though only a quarter of an hour before I had rushed out of it as though I were crazy, when six stalwart fellows had all together flung themselves upon the drunken Tatar Gazin to suppress him and had begun beating him; they beat him stupidly, a camel might have been killed by such blows, but they knew that this Hercules was not easy to kill, and so they beat him without uneasiness. Now on returning I noticed on the bed in the further corner of the room Gazin lying unconscious, almost without sign of life. He lay covered with a sheepskin, and everyone walked round him, without speaking; though they confidently hoped that he would come to himself next morning, yet if luck was against him, maybe from a beating like that, the man would die. I made my way to my own place opposite the window with the iron grating, and lay on my back with my hands behind my head and my eyes shut. I liked to lie like that; a sleeping man is not molested, and meanwhile one can dream and think. But I could not dream, my heart was beating uneasily, and M.'s words, "*Je hais ces brigands!*" were echoing in my ears. But why describe my impressions? I sometimes dream even now of those times at night, and I have no dreams more agonizing. Perhaps it will be noticed that even to this day I have scarcely once spoken in print of my life in prison. *The House of the Dead* I wrote fifteen years ago in the

* "I detest these ruffians!"

character of an imaginary person, a criminal who had killed his wife. I may add by the way that since then, very many persons have supposed, and even now maintain, that I was sent to penal servitude for the murder of my wife.

Gradually I sank into forgetfulness and by degrees was lost in memories. During the whole course of my four years in prison I was continually recalling all my past, and seemed to live over again the whole of my life in recollection. These memories rose up of themselves, it was not often that I summoned them of my own will. Each would begin from some point, some little thing, at times unnoticed, and then by degrees there would rise up a complete picture, some vivid and complete impression. I used to analyze these impressions, give new features to what had happened long ago, and best of all, I used to correct it, correct it continually, that was my great amusement. On this occasion, I suddenly for some reason remembered an unnoticed moment in my early childhood when I was only nine years old—a moment which I should have thought I had utterly forgotten; but at that time I was particularly fond of memories of my early childhood. I remembered the month of August in our country house: a dry bright day but rather cold and windy; summer was waning and soon we should have to go to Moscow to be bored all winter with French lessons, and I was so sorry to leave the country. I walked past the threshing floor and, going down the ravine, I went up to the dense thicket of bushes that covered the further side of the ravine as far as the copse. And I plunged right into the midst of the bushes, and heard a peasant plowing alone on the clearing about thirty paces away. I knew that he was plowing up the steep hill and the horse was moving with effort, and from time to time the peasant's call "Come up!" floated upwards to me. I knew almost all our peasants, but I did not know who it was plowing now, and, indeed, I did not care, I was absorbed in my own affairs. I was busy, too; I was breaking off switches from the nut trees to whip the frogs with. Nut sticks made such fine whips, but they do not last; while birch twigs are just the opposite. I was interested, too, in beetles and other insects; I used to collect them, some were very ornamental. I was very fond, too, of the nimble red and yellow lizards with black spots on them, but I was afraid of snakes. Snakes, however, were much more rare than lizards. There were not many mushrooms there. To get mushrooms one had to go to the birch wood, and I was about to set off there. And there was nothing in the world that I loved so much as the wood with its mushrooms and wild berries, with its beetles and its birds, its hedgehogs and squirrels, with its damp smell of dead leaves which I loved so much, and even as I write I smell the fragrance of our birch wood: these impressions will remain for my whole life. Suddenly in the midst of the profound stillness I heard a clear and distinct shout, "Wolf!" I shrieked and, beside myself with terror, calling out at the top of my voice, ran out into the clearing and straight to the peasant who was plowing.

It was our peasant Marey. I don't know if there is such a name, but everyone called him Marey—a thick-set, rather well-grown peasant of fifty, with a good many gray hairs in his dark brown, spreading beard. I knew him, but had scarcely ever happened to speak to him till then. He stopped his horse on hearing my cry, and when, breathless, I caught with one hand at his plow and with the other at his sleeve, he saw how frightened I was.

"There is a wolf!" I cried, panting.

He flung up his head, and could not help looking round for an instant, almost believing me.

"Where is the wolf?"

"A shout . . . someone shouted: 'wolf'. . . ," I faltered out.

"Nonsense, nonsense! A wolf! Why, it was your fancy! How could there be a wolf?" he muttered, reassuring me. But I was trembling all over, and still kept tight hold of his smock frock, and I must have been quite pale. He looked at me with an uneasy smile, evidently anxious and troubled over me.

"Why, you have had a fright, *aïe, aïe!*" He shook his head. "There, dear. . . . Come little one, *aïe!*"

He stretched out his hand, and all at once stroked my cheek.

"Come, come, there; Christ be with you! Cross yourself!"

But I did not cross myself. The corners of my mouth were twitching, and I think that struck him particularly. He put out his thick, black-nailed, earth-stained finger and softly touched my twitching lips.

"*Aïe,* there, there," he said to me with a slow, almost motherly smile. "Dear, dear, what is the matter? There; come, come!"

I grasped at last that there was no wolf, and that the shout that I had heard was my fancy. Yet that shout had been so clear and distinct, but such shouts (not only about wolves) I had imagined once or twice before, and I was aware of that. (These hallucinations passed away later as I grew older.)

"Well, I will go then," I said, looking at him timidly and inquiringly.

"Well, do, and I'll keep watch on you as you go. I won't let the wolf get you," he added, still smiling at me with the same motherly expression. "Well, Christ be with you! Come, run along then." And he made the sign of the cross over me and then over himself. I walked away, looking back almost at every tenth step. Marey stood still with his mare as I walked away, and looked after me and nodded to me every time I looked round. I must own I felt a little ashamed at having let him see me so frightened, but I was still very much afraid of the wolf as I walked away, until I reached the first barn halfway up the slope of the ravine; there my fright vanished completely, and all at once our yard dog Volchok flew to meet me. With Volchok I felt quite safe, and I turned round to Marey for the last time; I could not see his face distinctly, but I felt that he was still nodding and smiling affectionately at me. I waved to him; he waved back at me and started his little mare. "Come up!" I heard his call in the distance again, and the little mare pulled at the plow again.

All this I recalled all at once, I don't know why, but with extraordinary minuteness of detail. I suddenly roused myself and sat up on the sleeping platform, and, I remember, found myself still smiling quietly at my memories. I brooded over them for another minute.

When I got home that day I told no one of my "adventure" with Marey. And indeed it was hardly an adventure. And in fact I soon forgot Marey. When I met him now and then afterwards, I never even spoke to him about the wolf or anything else; and all at once now, twenty years afterwards in Siberia, I remembered this meeting with such distinctness to the smallest detail. So it must have lain hidden in my soul, though I knew nothing of it, and rose suddenly to my memory when it was wanted; I remembered the soft motherly smile of the poor serf, the way he signed me with the cross and shook his head. "There, there, you have had a fright, little one!" And I remembered particularly the thick earth-stained finger with which he softly and with timid tenderness touched my quivering lips. Of course anyone would have reassured a child, but something quite different seemed to have happened in that solitary meeting; and if I had been his own son, he could not have looked at me with eyes shining with greater love. And what made him like that? He was our serf and I was his little master, after all. No one would know that he had been kind to me and reward him for it. Was he, perhaps, very fond of little children? Some people are. It was a solitary meeting in the deserted fields, and only God, perhaps, may have seen from above with what deep and humane civilized feeling, and with what a delicate, almost feminine tenderness, the heart of a coarse, brutally ignorant Russian serf, who had as yet no expectation, no idea even of his freedom, may be filled. Was not this, perhaps, what Konstantin Aksakov meant when he spoke of the high degree of culture of our peasantry?

And when I got down off the bed and looked around me, I remember I suddenly felt that I could look at these unhappy creatures with quite different eyes, and that suddenly by some miracle all hatred and anger had vanished utterly from my heart. I walked about, looking into the faces that I met. That shaven peasant, branded on his face as a criminal, bawling his hoarse, drunken song, may be that very Marey; I cannot look into his heart.

I met M. again that evening. Poor fellow! he could have no memories of Russian peasants, and no other view of these people but: *"Je hais ces brigands!"* Yes, the Polish prisoners had more to bear than I.

Translated by Constance Garnett

The Basement Room

Graham Greene

GRAHAM GREENE *(1904–   ), educated at Balliol College, Oxford, began his career as a newspaperman and movie critic. His early books, mainly adventure stories, are* Orient Express *(1932),* It's a Battlefield *(1934),* This Gun for Hire *(1936), and several later pieces—what Greene calls "entertainments"—*The Third Man *(1950),* Our Man in Havana *(1958). Many of his novels have received critical praise for their psychological and religious probings into right and wrong, good and evil; among them are* Brighton Rock *(1938),* The Power and the Glory *(1940),* The Heart of the Matter *(1948),* The End of the Affair *(1951),* A Burnt-Out Case *(1961).*

I

When the front door had shut them out and the butler Baines had turned back into the dark heavy hall, Philip began to live. He stood in front of the nursery door, listening until he heard the engine of the taxi die out along the street. His parents were gone for a fortnight's holiday; he was "between nurses," one dismissed and the other not arrived; he was alone in the great Belgravia house with Baines and Mrs. Baines.

He could go anywhere, even through the green baize door to the pantry or down the stairs to the basement living-room. He felt a stranger in his home because he could go into any room and all the rooms were empty.

You could only guess who had once occupied them: the rack of pipes in the smoking-room beside the elephant tusks, the carved wood tobacco jar; in the bedroom the pink hangings and pale perfumes and the three-quarter finished jars of cream which Mrs. Baines had not yet cleared away; the high glaze on the never-opened piano in the drawing-room, the china clock, the silly little tables and the silver: but here Mrs. Baines was already busy, pulling down the curtains, covering the chairs in dustsheets.

"Be off out of here, Master Philip," and she looked at him with her hateful peevish eyes, while she moved round, getting everything in order, meticulous and loveless and doing her duty.

Philip Lane went downstairs and pushed at the baize door; he looked into the pantry, but Baines was not there, then he set foot for the first time on the stairs to the basement. Again he had the sense: this is life. All his seven nursery years vibrated with the strange, the new experience. His crowded busy brain was like a city which feels the earth tremble at a distant earthquake shock. He was apprehensive, but he was happier than he had ever been. Everything was more important than before.

Baines was reading a newspaper in his shirtsleeves. He said: "Come in, Phil, and make yourself at home. Wait a moment and I'll do the honors," and going to a white cleaned cupboard he brought out a bottle of ginger beer and half a Dundee cake. "Half-past eleven in the morning," Baines said. "It's opening time, my boy," and he cut the cake and poured out the ginger beer. He was more genial than Philip had ever known him, more at his ease, a man in his own home.

"Shall I call Mrs. Baines?" Philip asked, and he was glad when Baines said no. She was busy. She liked to be busy, so why interfere with her pleasure?

"A spot of drink at half-past eleven," Baines said, pouring himself out a glass of ginger beer, "gives an appetite for chop and does no man any harm."

"A chop?" Philip asked.

"Old Coasters," Baines said, "call all food chop."

"But it's not a chop?"

"Well, it might be, you know, cooked with palm oil. And then some paw-paw to follow."

Philip looked out of the basement window at the dry stone yard, the ash can and the legs going up and down beyond the railings.

"Was it hot there?"

"Ah, you never felt such heat. Not a nice heat, mind, like you get in the park on a day like this. Wet," Baines said "corruption." He cut himself a slice of cake. "Smelling of rot," Baines said, rolling his eyes round the small basement room, from clean cupboard to clean cupboard, the sense of bareness, of nowhere to hide a man's secrets. With an air of regret for something lost he took a long draught of ginger beer.

"Why did father live out there?"

"It was his job," Baines said, "same as this is mine now. And it was mine then too. It was a man's job. You wouldn't believe it now, but I've had forty niggers under me, doing what I told them to."

"Why did you leave?"

"I married Mrs. Baines."

Philip took the slice of Dundee cake in his hand and munched it round the room. He felt very old, independent and judicial; he was aware that Baines was talking to him as man to man. He never called him Master Philip as Mrs. Baines did, who was servile when she was not authoritative.

Baines had seen the world; he had seen beyond the railings, beyond the tired legs of typists, the Pimlico parade to and from Victoria. He sat there over his ginger pop with the resigned dignity of an exile; Baines didn't complain; he had chosen his fate; and if his fate was Mrs. Baines he had only himself to blame.

But today, because the house was almost empty and Mrs. Baines was upstairs and there was nothing to do, he allowed himself a little acidity.

"I'd go back tomorrow if I had the chance."

"Did you ever shoot a nigger?"

"I never had any call to shoot," Baines said. "Of course I carried a gun. But you didn't need to treat them bad. That just made them stupid. Why," Baines said, bowing his thin gray hair with embarrassment over the ginger pop, "I loved some of those damned niggers. I couldn't help loving them. There they'd be, laughing, holding hands; they liked to touch each other; it made them feel fine to know the other fellow was round.

"It didn't mean anything we could understand; two of them would go about all day without loosing hold, grown men; but it wasn't love; it didn't mean anything we could understand."

"Eating between meals," Mrs. Baines said. "What would your mother say, Master Philip?"

She came down the steep stairs to the basement, her hands full of pots of cream and salve, tubes of grease and paste. "You oughtn't to encourage him, Baines," she said, sitting down in a wicker armchair and screwing up her small ill-humored eyes at the Coty lipstick, Pond's cream, the Leichner rouge and Cyclax powder and Elizabeth Arden astringent.

She threw them one by one into the wastepaper basket. She saved only the cold cream. "Telling the boy stories," she said. "Go along to the nursery, Master Philip, while I get lunch."

Philip climbed the stairs to the baize door. He heard Mrs. Baines's voice like the voice in a nightmare when the small Price light has guttered in the saucer and the curtains move; it was sharp and shrill and full of malice, louder than people ought to speak, exposed.

"Sick to death of your ways, Baines, spoiling the boy. Time you did some work about the house," but he couldn't hear what Baines said in reply. He pushed open the baize door, came up like a small earth animal in his grey flannel shorts into a wash of sunlight on a parquet floor, the gleam of mirrors dusted and polished and beautified by Mrs. Baines.

Something broke downstairs, and Philip sadly mounted the stairs to the nursery. He pitied Baines; it occurred to him how happily they could live together in the empty house if Mrs. Baines were called away. He didn't want to play with his Meccano sets; he wouldn't take out his train or his soldiers; he sat at the table with his chin on his hands: this is life; and suddenly he felt responsible for Baines, as if he were the master of the house and Baines an aging servant who deserved to be cared for. There was not much one could do; he decided at least to be good.

He was not surprised when Mrs. Baines was agreeable at lunch; he was used to her changes. Now it was "another helping of meat, Master Philip," or "Master Philip, a little more of this nice pudding." It was a pudding he liked, Queen's pudding with a perfect meringue, but he wouldn't eat a second helping lest she might count that a victory. She was the kind of woman who thought that any injustice could be counterbalanced by something good to eat.

She was sour, but she liked making sweet things; one never had to complain of a lack of jam or plums; she ate well herself and added soft sugar to the meringue and the strawberry jam. The half light through the basement window set the motes moving above her pale hair like dust as she sifted the sugar, and Baines crouched over his plate saying nothing.

Again Philip felt responsibility. Baines had looked forward to this, and Baines was disappointed: everything was being spoilt. The sensation of disappointment was one which Philip could share; knowing nothing of love or jealousy or passion, he could understand better than anyone this grief, something hoped for not happening, something promised not fulfilled, something exciting turning dull. "Baines," he said, "will you take me for a walk this afternoon?"

"No," Mrs. Baines said, "no. That he won't. Not with all the silver to clean."

"There's a fortnight to do it in," Baines said.

"Work first, pleasure afterwards." Mrs. Baines helped herself to some more meringue.

Baines suddenly put down his spoon and fork and pushed his plate away. "Blast," he said.

"Temper," Mrs. Baines said softly, "temper. Don't you go breaking any more things, Baines, and I won't have you swearing in front of the boy. Master Philip, if you've finished you can get down." She skinned the rest of the meringue off the pudding.

"I want to go for a walk," Philip said.

"You'll go and have a rest."

"I will go for a walk."

"Master Philip," Mrs. Baines said. She got up from the table, leaving her meringue unfinished, and came towards him, thin, menacing, dusty in the basement room. "Master Philip, you do as you're told." She took him by the arm and squeezed it gently; she watched him with a joyless passionate glitter and above her head the feet of the typists trudged back to the Victoria offices after the lunch interval.

"Why shouldn't I go for a walk?" But he weakened; he was scared and ashamed of being scared. This was life; a strange passion he couldn't understand moving in the basement room. He saw a small pile of broken glass swept into a corner by the wastepaper basket. He looked to Baines for help and only intercepted hate; the sad hopeless hate of something behind bars.

"Why shouldn't I?" he repeated.

"Master Philip," Mrs. Baines said, "you've got to do as you're told. You mustn't think just because your father's away there's nobody here to—"

"You wouldn't dare," Philip cried, and was startled by Baines's low interjection, "There's nothing she wouldn't dare."

"I hate you," Philip said to Mrs. Baines. He pulled away from her and ran to the door, but she was there before him; she was old, but she was quick.

"Master Philip," she said, "you'll say you're sorry." She stood in front of the door quivering with excitement. "What would your father do if he heard you say that?"

She put a hand out to seize him, dry and white with constant soda, the nails cut to the quick, but he backed away and put the table between them, and suddenly to his surprise she smiled; she became again as servile as she had been arrogant. "Get along with you, Master Philip," she said with glee. "I see I'm going to have my hands full till your father and mother come back."

She left the door unguarded and when he passed her she slapped him playfully. "I've got too much to do today to trouble about you. I haven't covered half the chairs," and suddenly even the upper part of the house became unbearable to him as he thought of Mrs. Baines moving round shrouding the sofas, laying out the dustsheets.

So he wouldn't go upstairs to get his cap but walked straight out across the shining hall into the street, and again, as he looked this way and looked that way, it was life he was in the middle of.

II

It was the pink sugar cakes in the window on a paper doily, the ham, the slab of mauve sausage, the wasps driving like small torpedoes across the pane that caught Philip's attention. His feet were tired by pavements; he had been afraid to cross the road, had simply walked first in one direction, then in the other. He was nearly home now; the square was at the end of the street; this was a shabby outpost of Pimlico, and he smudged the pane with his nose, looking for sweets, and saw between the cakes and ham a different Baines.

He hardly recognized the bulbous eyes, the bald forehead. It was a happy, bold and buccaneering Baines, even though it was, when you looked closer, a desperate Baines.

Philip had never seen the girl. He remembered Baines had a niece and he thought that this might be her. She was thin and drawn, and she wore a white mackintosh; she meant nothing to Philip; she belonged to a world about which he knew nothing at all. He couldn't make up stories about her, as he could make them up about withered Sir Hubert Reed, the Permanent Secretary, about Mrs. Wince-Dudley, who came up once a year from Penstanley in Suffolk with a green umbrella and an enormous black handbag, as he could make them up about the upper servants in all the houses where he went to tea and games. She just didn't belong; he thought of mermaids and Undine; but she didn't belong there either, nor to the adventures of Emil, nor to the Bastables. She sat there looking at an iced pink cake in the detachment and mystery of the completely disinherited, looking at the half-used pots of powder which Baines had set out on the marble-topped table between them.

Baines was urging, hoping, entreating, commanding, and the girl looked at the tea and the china pots and cried. Baines passed his handkerchief across the table, but she wouldn't wipe her eyes; she screwed it in her palm and let the tears run down, wouldn't do anything, wouldn't speak, would only put up a silent despairing resistance to what she dreaded and wanted and refused to listen to at any price. The two brains battled over the teacups loving each other, and there came to Philip outside, beyond the ham and wasps and dusty Pimlico pane, a confused indication of the struggle.

He was inquisitive and he didn't understand and he wanted to know. He went and stood in the doorway to see better, he was less sheltered than he had ever been; other people's lives for the first time touched and pressed and molded. He would never escape that scene. In a week he had forgotten it, but it conditioned his career, the long austerity of his life; when he was dying he said, "Who is she?"

Baines had won; he was cocky and the girl was happy. She wiped her face, she opened a pot of powder, and their fingers touched across the table. It occurred to Philip that it would be amusing to imitate Mrs. Baines's voice and call "Baines" to him from the door.

It shrivelled them; you couldn't describe it in any other way; it made them smaller, they weren't happy any more and they weren't bold. Baines was the first to recover and trace the voice, but that didn't make things as they were. The sawdust was spilled out of the afternoon; nothing you did could mend it, and Philip was scared. "I didn't mean . . ." He wanted to say that he loved Baines, that he had only wanted to laugh at Mrs. Baines. But he had discovered that you couldn't laugh at Mrs. Baines. She wasn't Sir Hubert Reed, who used steel nibs and carried a pen-wiper in his pocket; she wasn't Mrs. Wince-Dudley; she was darkness when the night-light went out in a draught; she was the frozen blocks of earth he had seen one winter in a graveyard when someone said, "They need an electric drill"; she was the flowers gone bad and smelling in the little closet room at Penstanley. There was nothing to laugh about. You had to endure her when she was there and forget about her quickly when she was away, suppress the thought of her, ram it down deep.

Baines said, "It's only Phil," beckoned him in and gave him the pink iced cake the girl hadn't eaten, but the afternoon was broken, the cake was like dry bread in the throat. The girl left them at once; she even forgot to take the powder; like a small blunt icicle in her white mackintosh she stood in the doorway with her back to them, then melted into the afternoon.

"Who is she?" Philip asked. "Is she your niece?"

"Oh, yes," Baines said, "that's who she is; she's my niece," and poured the last drops of water on to the coarse black leaves in the teapot.

"May as well have another cup," Baines said.

"The cup that cheers," he said hopelessly, watching the bitter black fluid drain out of the spout.

"Have a glass of ginger pop, Phil?"

"I'm sorry. I'm sorry, Baines."

"It's not your fault, Phil. Why, I could believe it wasn't you at all, but her. She creeps in everywhere." He fished two leaves out of his cup and laid them on the back of his hand, a thin soft flake and a hard stalk. He beat them with his hand: "Today," and the stalk detached itself, "tomorrow, Wednesday, Thursday, Friday, Saturday, Sunday," but the flake wouldn't come, stayed where it was, drying under his blows, with a resistance you wouldn't believe it to possess. "The tough one wins," Baines said.

He got up and paid the bill and out they went into the street.

Baines said, "I don't ask you to say what isn't true. But you needn't mention to Mrs. Baines you met us here."

"Of course not," Philip said, and catching something of Sir Hubert Reed's manner, "I understand, Baines." But he didn't understand a thing; he was caught up in other people's darkness.

"It was stupid," Baines said. "So near home, but I hadn't time to think, you see. I'd got to see her."

"Of course, Baines."

"I haven't time to spare," Baines said. "I'm not young. I've got to see that she's all right."

"Of course you have, Baines."

"Mrs. Baines will get it out of you if she can."

"You can trust me, Baines," Philip said in a dry important Reed voice; and then, "Look out. She's at the window watching." And there indeed she was, looking up at them, between the lace curtains, from the basement room, speculating. "Need we go in, Baines?" Philip asked, cold lying heavy on his stomach like too much pudding; he clutched Baines's arm.

"Careful," Baines said softly, "careful."

"But need we go in, Baines? It's early. Take me for a walk in the park."

"Better not."

"But I'm frightened, Baines."

"You haven't any cause," Baines said. "Nothing's going to hurt you. You just run along upstairs to the nursery. I'll go down by the area and talk to Mrs. Baines." But even he stood hesitating at the top of the stone steps, pretending not to see her where she watched between the curtains. "In at the front door, Phil, and up the stairs."

Philip didn't linger in the hall; he ran, slithering on the parquet Mrs. Baines had polished, to the stairs. Through the drawing-room doorway on the first floor he saw the draped chairs; even the china clock on the mantel was covered like a canary's cage; as he passed it, it chimed the hour, muffled and secret under the duster. On the nursery table he found his supper laid out: a glass of milk and a piece of bread and butter, a sweet biscuit and a little cold Queen's pudding without the meringue. He had no appetite; he strained his ears for Mrs. Baines's coming, for the sound of voices, but the basement held its secrets; the green baize door shut off that world. He drank the milk and ate the biscuit, but he didn't touch the rest, and presently he could hear the soft precise footfalls of Mrs. Baines on the stairs: she was a good servant, she walked softly; she was a determined woman, she walked precisely.

But she wasn't angry when she came in; she was ingratiating as she opened the night nursery door—"Did you have a good walk, Master Philip?"—pulled down the blinds, laid out his pajamas, came back to clear his supper. "I'm glad Baines found you. Your mother wouldn't have liked your being out alone." She examined the tray. "Not much appetite, have you, Master Philip? Why don't you try a little of this nice pudding? I'll bring you up some more jam for it."

"No, no, thank you, Mrs. Baines," Philip said.

"You ought to eat more," Mrs. Baines said. She sniffed round the room like a dog. "You didn't take any pots out of the wastepaper basket in the kitchen, did you, Master Philip?"

"No," Philip said.

"Of course you wouldn't. I just wanted to make sure." She patted his shoulder and her fingers flashed to his lapel; she picked off a tiny crumb of pink sugar. "Oh, Master Philip," she said, "that's why you haven't any appetite. You've been buying sweet cakes. That's not what your pocket money's for."

"But I didn't," Philip said. "I didn't."

She tasted the sugar with the tip of her tongue.

"Don't tell lies to me, Master Philip. I won't stand for it any more than your father would."

"I didn't, I didn't," Philip said. "They gave it me. I mean Baines," but she had pounced on the word "they." She had got what she wanted; there was no doubt about that, even when you didn't know what it was she wanted. Philip was angry and miserable and disappointed because he hadn't kept Baines's secret. Baines oughtn't to have trusted him; grown-up people should keep their own secrets, and yet here was Mrs. Baines immediately entrusting him with another.

"Let me tickle your palm and see if you can keep a secret." But he put his hand behind him; he wouldn't be touched. "It's a secret between us, Master Philip, that I know all about them. I suppose she was having tea with him," she speculated.

"Why shouldn't she?" he said, the responsibility for Baines

weighing on his spirit, the idea that he had got to keep her secret when he hadn't kept Baines's making him miserable with the unfairness of life. "She was nice."

"She was nice, was she?" Mrs. Baines said in a bitter voice he wasn't used to.

"And she's his niece."

"So that's what he said," Mrs. Baines struck softly back at him like the clock under the duster. She tried to be jocular. "The old scoundrel. Don't you tell him I know, Master Philip." She stood very still between the table and the door, thinking very hard, planning something. "Promise you won't tell. I'll give you that Meccano set, Master Philip. . . ."

He turned his back on her; he wouldn't promise, but he wouldn't tell. He would have nothing to do with their secrets, the responsibilities they were determined to lay on him. He was only anxious to forget. He had received already a larger dose of life than he had bargained for, and he was scared. "A 2A Meccano set, Master Philip." He never opened his Meccano set again, never built anything, never created anything, died, the old dilettante, sixty years later, with nothing to show rather than preserve the memory of Mrs. Baines's malicious voice saying good night, her soft determined footfalls on the stairs to the basement, going down, going down.

III

The sun poured in between the curtains and Baines was beating a tattoo on the watercan. "Glory, glory," Baines said. He sat down on the end of the bed and said, "I beg to announce that Mrs. Baines has been called away. Her mother's dying. She won't be back till tomorrow."

"Why did you wake me up so early?" Philip said. He watched Baines with uneasiness; he wasn't going to be drawn in; he'd learnt his lesson. It wasn't right for a man of Baines's age to be so merry. It made a grown person human in the same way that you were human. For if a grown-up could behave so childishly, you were liable too to find yourself in their world. It was enough that it came at you in dreams: the witch at the corner, the man with a knife. So "It's very early," he complained, even though he loved Baines, even though he couldn't help being glad that Baines was happy. He was divided by the fear and the attraction of life.

"I want to make this a long day," Baines said. "This is the best time." He pulled the curtains back. "It's a bit misty. The cat's been out all night. There she is, sniffing round the area. They haven't taken in any milk at 59. Emma's shaking out the mats at 63." He said, "This was what I used to think about on the Coast: somebody shaking mats and the cat coming home. I can see it today," Baines said, "just as if I was still in Africa. Most days you don't notice what you've got. It's a good life if you don't weaken." He put a penny on the washstand. "When you've dressed, Phil, run and get a *Mail* from the barrow at the corner. I'll be cooking the sausages."

"Sausages?"

"Sausages," Baines said. "We're going to celebrate today. A fair bust." He celebrated at breakfast, reckless, cracking jokes, unaccountably merry and nervous. It was going to be a long, long day, he kept on coming back to that: for years he had waited for a long day, he had sweated in the damp Coast heat, changed shirts, gone down with fever, lain between the blankets and sweated, all in the hope of this long day, that cat sniffing round the area, a bit of mist, the mats beaten at 63. He propped the *Mail* in front of the coffee-pot and read pieces aloud. He said, "Cora Down's been married for the fourth time." He was amused, but it wasn't his idea of a long day. His long day was the Park, watching the riders in the Row, seeing Sir Arthur Stillwater pass beyond the rails ("He dined with us once in Bo; up from Freetown; he was governor there"), lunch at the Corner House for Philip's sake (he'd have preferred himself a glass of stout and some oysters at the York bar), the Zoo, the long bus ride home in the last summer light: the leaves in the Green Park were beginning to turn and the motors nuzzled out of Berkeley Street with the low sun gently glowing on their wind-screens. Baines envied no one, not Cora Down, or Sir Arthur Stillwater, or Lord Sandale, who came out on to the steps of the Army and Navy and then went back again because he hadn't got anything to do and might as well look at another paper. "I said don't let me see you touch that black again." Baines had led a man's life; everyone on top of the bus pricked their ears when he told Philip all about it.

"Would you have shot him?" Philip asked, and Baines put his head back and tilted his dark respectable man-servant's hat to a better angle as the bus swerved round the artillery memorial.

"I wouldn't have thought twice about it. I'd have shot to kill," he boasted, and the bowed figure went by, the steel helmet, the heavy cloak, the down-turned rifle and the folded hands.

"Have you got the revolver?"

"Of course I've got it," Baines said. "Don't I need it with all the burglaries there've been?" This was the Baines whom Philip loved: not Baines singing and carefree, but Baines responsible, Baines behind barriers, living his man's life.

All the buses streamed out from Victoria like a convoy of airplanes to bring Baines home with honor. "Forty blacks under me," and there waiting near the area steps was the proper conventional reward, love at lighting-up time.

"It's your niece," Philip said, recognizing the white mackintosh, but not the happy sleepy face. She frightened him like an unlucky number; he nearly told Baines what Mrs. Baines had said; but he didn't want to bother, he wanted to leave things alone.

"Why, so it is," Baines said. "I shouldn't wonder if she was going to have a bite of supper with us." But he said they'd play a game, pretend they didn't know her, slip down the area steps, "and here," Baines said, "we are," lay the table, put out the cold sausages, a bottle of beer, a bottle of ginger pop, a flagon of harvest burgundy. "Everyone his own drink," Baines said. "Run upstairs, Phil, and see if there's been a post."

Philip didn't like the empty house at dusk before the lights went on. He hurried. He wanted to be back with Baines. The hall lay there in quiet and shadow prepared to show him something he didn't want to see. Some letters rustled down, and someone knocked. "Open in the name of the Republic." The tumbrils rolled, the head bobbed in the bloody basket. Knock, knock, and the postman's footsteps going away. Philip gathered the letters. The slit in the door was like the grating in a jeweller's window. He remembered the policeman he had seen peer through. He had said to his nurse, "What's he doing?" and when she said, "He's seeing if everything's all right," his brain immediately filled with images of all that might be wrong. He ran to the baize door and the stairs. The girl was already there and Baines was kissing her. She leant breathless against the dresser.

"This is Emmy, Phil."

"There's a letter for you, Baines."

"Emmy," Baines said, "it's from her." But he wouldn't open it. "You bet she's coming back."

"We'll have supper, anyway," Emmy said. "She can't harm that."

"You don't know her," Baines said. "Nothing's safe. Damn it," he said, "I was a man once," and he opened the letter.

"Can I start?" Philip asked, but Baines didn't hear; he presented in his stillness and attention an example of the importance grown-up people attached to the written word: you had to write your thanks, not wait and speak them, as if letters couldn't lie. But Philip knew better than that, sprawling his thanks across a page to Aunt Alice who had given him a doll he was too old for. Letters could lie all right, but they made the lie permanent: they lay as evidence against you; they made you meaner than the spoken word.

"She's not coming back till tomorrow night," Baines said. He opened the bottles, he pulled up the chairs, he kissed Emmy again against the dresser.

"You oughtn't to," Emmy said, "with the boy here."

"He's got to learn," Baines said, "like the rest of us," and he helped Philip to three sausages. He only took one himself; he said he wasn't hungry; but when Emmy said she wasn't hungry either he stood over her and made her eat. He was timid and rough with her; he made her drink the harvest burgundy because he said she needed building up; he wouldn't take no for an answer, but when he touched her his hands were light and clumsy too, as if he were afraid to damage something delicate and didn't know how to handle anything so light.

"This is better than milk and biscuits, eh?"

"Yes," Philip said, but he was scared, scared for Baines as much as for himself. He couldn't help wondering at every bite, at every draught of the ginger pop, what Mrs. Baines would say if she ever learnt of this meal; he couldn't imagine it, there was a depth of bitterness and rage in Mrs. Baines you couldn't sound. He said, "She won't be coming back tonight?" but you could tell by the way they immediately understood him that she wasn't really away at all; she was there in the basement with them, driving them to longer drinks and louder talk, biding her time for the right cutting word. Baines wasn't really happy; he was only watching happiness from close to instead of from far away.

"No," he said, "she'll not be back till late tomorrow." He couldn't keep his eyes off happiness; he'd played around as much as other men, he kept on reverting to the Coast as if to excuse himself for his innocence; he wouldn't have been so innocent if he'd lived his life in London, so innocent when it came to tenderness. "If it was you, Emmy," he said, looking at the white dresser, the scrubbed chairs, "this'd be like a home." Already the room was not quite so harsh; there was a little dust in corners, the silver needed a final polish, the morning's paper lay untidily on a chair. "You'd better go to bed, Phil; it's been a long day."

They didn't leave him to find his own way up through the dark shrouded house; they went with him, turning on lights, touching each other's fingers on the switches; floor after floor they drove the night back; they spoke softly among the covered chairs; they watched him undress, they didn't make him wash or clean his teeth, they saw him into bed and lit his nightlight and left his door ajar. He could hear their voices on the stairs, friendly, like the guests he heard at dinner-parties when they moved down to the hall, saying good night. They belonged; wherever they were they made a home. He heard a door open and a clock strike, he heard their voices for a long while, so that he felt they were not far away and he was safe. The voices didn't dwindle, they simply went out, and he could be sure that they were still somewhere not far from him, silent together in one of the many empty rooms, growing sleepy together as he grew sleepy after the long day.

He just had time to sigh faintly with satisfaction, because this too perhaps had been life, before he slept and the inevitable terrors of sleep came round him: a man with a tricolor hat beat at the door on His Majesty's service, a bleeding head lay on the kitchen table in a basket, and the Siberian wolves crept closer. He was bound hand and foot and couldn't move; they leapt round him breathing heavily; he opened his eyes and Mrs. Baines was there, her gray untidy hair in threads over his face, her black hat askew. A loose hairpin fell on the pillow and one musty thread brushed his mouth. "Where are they?" she whispered. "Where are they?"

IV

Philip watched her in terror. Mrs. Baines was out of breath as if she had been searching all the empty rooms, looking under loose covers.

With her untidy gray hair and her black dress buttoned to her throat, her gloves of black cotton, she was so like the witches of his dreams that he didn't dare to speak. There was a stale smell in her breath.

"She's here," Mrs. Baines said; "you can't deny she's here." Her face was simultaneously marked with cruelty and misery; she wanted to "do things" to people, but she suffered all the time. It would have done her good to scream, but she daren't do that: it would warn them. She came ingratiatingly back to the bed where Philip lay rigid on his back and whispered, "I haven't forgotten the Meccano set. You shall have it tomorrow, Master Philip. We've got secrets together, haven't we? Just tell me where they are."

He couldn't speak. Fear held him as firmly as any nightmare. She said, "Tell Mrs. Baines, Master Philip. You love your Mrs. Baines, don't you?" That was too much; he couldn't speak, but he could move his mouth in terrified denial, wince away from her dusty image.

She whispered, coming closer to him, "Such deceit. I'll tell your father. I'll settle with you myself when I've found them. You'll smart; I'll see you smart." Then immediately she was still, listening. A board had creaked on the floor below, and a moment later, while she stooped listening above his bed, there came the whispers of two people who were happy and sleepy together after a long day. The nightlight stood beside the mirror and Mrs. Baines could see bitterly there her own reflection, misery and cruelty wavering in the glass, age and dust and nothing to hope for. She sobbed without tears, a dry, breathless sound; but her cruelty was a kind of pride which kept her going; it was her best quality, she would have been merely pitiable without it. She went out of the door on tiptoe, feeling her way across the landing, going so softly down the stairs that no one behind a shut door could hear her. Then there was complete silence again; Philip could move; he raised his knees; he sat up in bed; he wanted to die. It wasn't fair, the walls were down again between his world and theirs; but this time it was something worse than merriment that the grown people made him share; a passion moved in the house he recognized but could not understand.

It wasn't fair, but he owed Baines everything: the Zoo, the ginger pop, the bus ride home. Even the supper called on his loyalty. But he was frightened; he was touching something he touched in dreams: the bleeding head, the wolves, the knock, knock, knock. Life fell on him with savagery: you couldn't blame him if he never faced it again in sixty years. He got out of bed, carefully from habit put on his bedroom slippers, and tiptoed to the door: it wasn't quite dark on the landing below because the curtains had been taken down for the cleaners and the light from the street came in through the tall windows. Mrs. Baines had her hand on the glass doorknob; she was very carefully turning it; he screamed, "Baines, Baines."

Mrs. Baines turned and saw him cowering in his pajamas by the banisters; he was helpless, more helpless even than Baines, and cruelty grew at the sight of him and drove her up the stairs. The nightmare was on him again and he couldn't move; he hadn't any more courage left for ever; he'd spent it all, had been allowed no time to let it grow, no years of gradual hardening; he couldn't even scream.

But the first cry had brought Baines out of the best spare bedroom and he moved quicker than Mrs. Baines. She hadn't reached the top of the stairs before he'd caught her round the waist. She drove her black cotton gloves at his face and he bit her hand. He hadn't time to think, he fought her savagely like a stranger, but she fought back with knowledgeable hate. She was going to teach them all and it didn't really matter whom she began with; they had all deceived her; but the old image in the glass was by her side, telling her she must be dignified, she wasn't young enough to yield her dignity; she could beat his face, but she mustn't bite; she could push, but she mustn't kick.

Age and dust and nothing to hope for were her handicaps. She went over the banisters in a flurry of black clothes and fell into the hall; she lay before the front door like a sack of coals which should have gone down the area into the basement. Philip saw; Emmy saw; she sat down suddenly in the doorway of the best spare bedroom with her eyes open as if she were too tired to stand any longer. Baines went slowly down into the hall.

It wasn't hard for Philip to escape; they'd forgotten him

completely; he went down the back, the servants' stairs because Mrs. Baines was in the hall; he didn't understand what she was doing lying there; like the startling pictures in a book no one had read to him, the things he didn't understand terrified him. The whole house had been turned over to the grown-up world; he wasn't safe in the night nursery; their passions had flooded it. The only thing he could do was to get away, by the back stair, and up through the area, and never come back. You didn't think of the cold, of the need of food and sleep; for an hour it would seem quite possible to escape from people for ever.

He was wearing pajamas and bedroom slippers when he came up into the square, but there was no one to see him. It was that hour of the evening in a residential district when everyone is at the theater or at home. He climbed over the iron railings into the little garden: the plane-trees spread their large pale palms between him and the sky. It might have been an illimitable forest into which he had escaped. He crouched behind a trunk and the wolves retreated; it seemed to him between the little iron seat and the tree-trunk that no one would ever find him again. A kind of embittered happiness and self-pity made him cry; he was lost; there wouldn't be any more secrets to keep; he surrendered responsibility once and for all. Let grown-up people keep to their world and he would keep to his, safe in the small garden between the plane-trees. "In the lost childhood of Judas Christ was betrayed"; you could almost see the small unformed face hardening into the deep dilettante selfishness of age.

Presently the door of 48 opened and Baines looked this way and that; then he signalled with his hand and Emmy came; it was as if they were only just in time for a train, they hadn't a chance of saying goodby; she went quickly by, like a face at a window swept past the platform, pale and unhappy and not wanting to go. Baines went in again and shut the door; the light was lit in the basement, and a policeman walked round the square, looking into the areas. You could tell how many families were at home by the lights behind the first-floor curtains.

Philip explored the garden: it didn't take long: a twenty-yard square of bushes and plane-trees, two iron seats and a gravel path, a padlocked gate at either end, a scuffle of old leaves. But he couldn't stay: something stirred in the bushes and two illuminated eyes peered out at him like a Siberian wolf, and he thought how terrible it would be if Mrs. Baines found him there. He'd have no time to climb the railings; she'd seize him from behind.

He left the square at the unfashionable end and was immediately among the fish-and-chip shops, the little stationers selling Bagatelle, among the accommodation addresses and the dingy hotels with open doors. There were few people about because the pubs were open, but a blowzy woman carrying a parcel called out to him across the street and the commissionaire outside a cinema would have stopped him if he hadn't crossed the road. He went deeper: you could go farther and lose yourself more completely here than among the plane-trees. On the fringe of the square he was in danger of being stopped and taken back: it was obvious where he belonged: but as he went deeper he lost the marks of his origin. It was a warm night: any child in those free-living parts might be expected to play truant from bed. He found a kind of camaraderie even among grown-up people; he might have been a neighbor's child as he went quickly by, but they weren't going to tell on him, they'd been young once themselves. He picked up a protective coating of dust from the pavements, of smuts from the trains which passed along the backs in a spray of fire. Once he was caught in a knot of children running away from something or somebody, laughing as they ran; he was whirled with them round a turning and abandoned, with a sticky fruit-drop in his hand.

He couldn't have been more lost; but he hadn't the stamina to keep on. At first he feared that someone would stop him; after an hour he hoped that someone would. He couldn't find his way back, and in any case he was afraid of arriving home alone; he was afraid of Mrs. Baines, more afraid than he had ever been. Baines was his friend, but something had happened which gave Mrs. Baines all the power. He began to loiter on purpose to be noticed, but no one noticed him. Families were having a last breather on the doorsteps, the refuse bins had been put out and bits of cabbage stalks soiled his slippers. The air was full of voices, but he was cut off; these people were strangers and would always now be strangers; they were marked by Mrs. Baines and he shied away from them into a deep class-consciousness. He had been afraid of policemen, but now he wanted one to take him home; even Mrs. Baines could do nothing against a policeman. He sidled past a constable who was directing traffic, but he was too busy to pay him any attention. Philip sat down against a wall and cried.

It hadn't occurred to him that that was the easiest way, that all you had to do was to surrender, to show you were beaten and accept kindness. . . . It was lavished on him at once by two women and a pawnbroker. Another policeman appeared, a young man with a sharp incredulous face. He looked as if he noted everything he saw in pocketbooks and drew conclusions. A woman offered to see Philip home, but he didn't trust her: she wasn't a match for Mrs. Baines immobile in the hall. He wouldn't give his address; he said he was afraid to go home. He had his way; he got his protection. "I'll take him to the station," the policeman said, and holding him awkwardly by the hand (he wasn't married; he had his career to make) he led him round the corner, up the stone stairs into the little bare overheated room where Justice waited.

V

Justice waited behind a wooden counter on a high stool; it wore a heavy moustache; it was kindly and had six children ("three of them nippers like yourself"); it wasn't really interested in Philip, but it pretended to be, it wrote the address down and sent a constable to fetch a glass of milk. But the young constable was interested; he had a nose for things.

"Your home's on the telephone, I suppose," Justice said. "We'll ring them up and say you are safe. They'll fetch you very soon. What's your name, sonny?"

"Philip."

"Your other name."

"I haven't got another name." He didn't want to be fetched; he wanted to be taken home by someone who would impress even Mrs. Baines. The constable watched him, watched the way he drank the milk, watched him when he winced away from questions.

"What made you run away? Playing truant, eh?"

"I don't know."

"You oughtn't to do it, young fellow. Think how anxious your father and mother will be."

"They are away."

"Well, your nurse."

"I haven't got one."

"Who looks after you, then?" That question went home. Philip saw Mrs. Baines coming up the stairs at him, the heap of black cotton in the hall. He began to cry.

"Now, now, now," the sergeant said. He didn't know what to do; he wished his wife were with him; even a policewoman might have been useful.

"Don't you think it's funny," the constable said, "that there hasn't been an inquiry?"

"They think he's tucked up in bed."

"You are scared, aren't you?" the constable said. "What scared you?"

"I don't know."

"Somebody hurt you?"

"No."

"He's had bad dreams," the sergeant said. "Thought the house was on fire, I expect. I've brought up six of them. Rose is due back. She'll take him home."

"I want to go home with you," Philip said; he tried to smile at the constable, but the deceit was immature and unsuccessful.

"I'd better go," the constable said. "There may be something wrong."

"Nonsense," the sergeant said. "It's a woman's job. Tact is what you need. Here's Rose. Pull up your stockings, Rose. You're a disgrace to the Force. I've got a job of work for you." Rose shambled in: black cotton stockings drooping over her boots, a gawky Girl Guide manner, a hoarse hostile voice. "More tarts, I suppose."

"No, you've got to see this young man home." She looked at him owlishly.

"I won't go with her," Philip said. He began to cry again. "I don't like her."

"More of that womanly charm, Rose," the sergeant said. The telephone rang on his desk. He lifted the receiver. "What? What's that?" he said. "Number 48? You've got a doctor?" He put his hand over the telephone mouth. "No wonder this nipper wasn't reported," he said. "They've been too busy. An accident. Woman slipped on the stairs."

"Serious?" the constable asked. The sergeant mouthed at him; you didn't mention the word death before a child (didn't he know? he had six of them), you made noises in the throat, you grimaced, a complicated shorthand for a word of only five letters anyway.

"You'd better go, after all," he said, "and make a report. The doctor's there."

Rose shambled from the stove; pink apply-dapply cheeks, loose stockings. She stuck her hands behind her. Her large morgue-like mouth was full of blackened teeth. "You told me to take him and now just because something interesting . . . I don't expect justice from a man. . . ."

"Who's at the house?" the constable asked.

"The butler."

"You don't think," the constable said, "he saw . . ."

"Trust me," the sergeant said. "I've brought up six. I know 'em through and through. You can't teach me anything about children."

"He seemed scared about something."

"Dreams," the sergeant said.

"What name?"

"Baines."

"This Mr. Baines," the constable said to Philip, "you like him, eh? He's good to you?" They were trying to get something out of him; he was suspicious of the whole roomful of them; he said "yes" without conviction because he was afraid at any moment of more responsibilities, more secrets.

"And Mrs. Baines?"

"Yes."

They consulted together by the desk: Rose was hoarsely aggrieved; she was like a female impersonator, she bore her womanhood with an unnatural emphasis even while she scorned it in her creased stockings and her weather-exposed face. The charcoal shifted in the stove; the room was overheated in the mild late summer evening. A notice on the wall described a body found in the Thames, or rather the body's clothes: wool vest, wool pants, wool shirt with blue stripes, size ten boots, blue serge suit worn at the elbows, fifteen and a half celluloid collar. They couldn't find anything to say about the body, except its measurements, it was just an ordinary body.

"Come along," the constable said. He was interested, he was

glad to be going, but he couldn't help being embarrassed by his company, a small boy in pajamas. His nose smelt something, he didn't know what, but he smarted at the sight of the amusement they caused: the pubs had closed and the streets were full again of men making as long a day of it as they could. He hurried through the less frequented streets, chose the darker pavements, wouldn't loiter, and Philip wanted more and more to loiter, pulling at his hand, dragging with his feet. He dreaded the sight of Mrs. Baines waiting in the hall: he knew now that she was dead. The sergeant's mouthings had conveyed that; but she wasn't buried, she wasn't out of sight; he was going to see a dead person in the hall when the door opened.

The light was on in the basement, and to his relief the constable made for the area steps. Perhaps he wouldn't have to see Mrs. Baines at all. The constable knocked on the door because it was too dark to see the bell, and Baines answered. He stood there in the doorway of the neat bright basement room and you could see the sad complacent plausible sentence he had prepared wither at the sight of Philip; he hadn't expected Philip to return like that in the policeman's company. He had to begin thinking all over again; he wasn't a deceptive man; if it hadn't been for Emmy he would have been quite ready to let the truth lead him where it would.

"Mr. Baines?" the constable asked.

He nodded; he hadn't found the right words; he was daunted by the shrewd knowing face, the sudden appearance of Philip there.

"This little boy from here?"

"Yes," Baines said. Philip could tell that there was a message he was trying to convey, but he shut his mind to it. He loved Baines, but Baines had involved him in secrets, in fears he didn't understand. The glowing morning thought, "This is life," had become under Baines's tuition the repugnant memory, "That was life": the musty hair across the mouth, the breathless cruel tortured inquiry, "Where are they?" the heap of black cotton tipped into the hall. That was what happened when you loved: you got involved; and Philip extricated himself from life, from love, from Baines, with a merciless egotism.

There had been things between them, but he laid them low, as a retreating army cuts the wires, destroys the bridges. In the abandoned country you may leave much that is dear—a morning in the Park, an ice at a corner house, sausages for supper—but more is concerned in the retreat than temporary losses. There are old people who, as the tractors wheel away, implore to be taken, but you can't risk the rearguard for their sake: a whole prolonged retreat from life, from care, from human relationships is involved.

"The doctor's here," Baines said. He nodded at the door, moistened his mouth, kept his eyes on Philip, begging for something like a dog you can't understand. "There's nothing to be done. She slipped on these stone basement stairs. I was in here. I heard her fall." He wouldn't look at the notebook, at the constable's tiny spidery writing which got a terrible lot on one page.

"Did the boy see anything?"

"He can't have done. I thought he was in bed. Hadn't he better go up? It's a shocking thing. Oh," Baines said, losing control, "it's a shocking thing for a child."

"She's through there?" the constable asked.

"I haven't moved her an inch," Baines said.

"He'd better then—"

"Go up the area and through the hall," Baines said and again he begged dumbly like a dog: one more secret, keep this secret, do this for old Baines, he won't ask another.

"Come along," the constable said. "I'll see you up to bed. You're a gentleman; you must come in the proper way through the front door like the master should. Or will you go along with him, Mr. Baines, while I see the doctor?"

"Yes," Baines said, "I'll go." He came across the room to Philip, begging, begging, all the way with his soft old stupid expression: this is Baines, the old Coaster; what about a palm-oil chop, eh?; a man's life; forty niggers; never used a gun; I tell you I couldn't help loving them: it wasn't what we call love, nothing we could understand. The messages flickered out from the last posts at the border, imploring, beseeching, reminding: this is your old friend Baines; what about an eleven's; a glass of ginger pop won't do you any harm; sausages; a long day. But the wires were cut, the messages just faded out into the enormous vacancy of the neat scrubbed room in which there had never been a place where a man could hide his secrets.

"Come along, Phil, it's bedtime. We'll just go up the steps. . . ." Tap, tap, tap, at the telegraph; you may get through, you can't tell, somebody may mend the right wire. "And in at the front door."

"No," Philip said, "no. I won't go. You can't make me go. I'll fight. I won't see her."

The constable turned on them quickly. "What's that? Why won't you go?"

"She's in the hall," Philip said. "I know she's in the hall. And she's dead. I won't see her."

"You moved her then?" tne constable said to Baines. "All the way down here? You've been lying, eh? That means you had to tidy up. . . . Were you alone?"

"Emmy," Philip said, "Emmy." He wasn't going to keep any more secrets: he was going to finish once and for all with everything, with Baines and Mrs. Baines and the grown-up life beyond him; it wasn't his business and never, never again, he decided, would he share their confidences and companionship. "It was all Emmy's fault," he protested with a quaver which reminded Baines that after all he was only a child; it had been hopeless to expect help there; he was a child; he didn't understand what it all meant; he couldn't read this shorthand of terror; he'd had a long day and he was tired out. You could see him dropping asleep where he stood against the dresser, dropping back into the comfortable nursery peace. You couldn't blame him. When he woke in the morning, he'd hardly remember a thing.

"Out with it," the constable said, addressing Baines with professional ferocity, "who is she?" just as the old man sixty years later startled his secretary, his only watcher, asking, "Who is she? Who is she?" dropping lower and lower into death, passing on the way perhaps the image of Baines: Baines hopeless, Baines letting his head drop, Baines "coming clean."

Big Boy Leaves Home

Richard Wright

RICHARD WRIGHT *(1908–1960) was born in Natchez, Mississippi, grew up in Memphis, and at age nineteen moved to Chicago, experiencing early in life many of the problems a black person then encountered in a white-dominated society in both the North and the South. Not long after World War II, he settled in France, where he was held in high esteem by French writers.* Uncle Tom's Children *(1938), which contains stories such as "Big Boy Leaves Home," and the novel* Native Son *(1940) have solidly established Wright's reputation in American literature. Among his other books are* Black Boy *(1945), an autobiographical account of his early years, and novels—*The Outsider *(1953),* Savage Holiday *(1954), and* The Long Dream *(1958). Wright dramatically and effectively brought to American and world literature the struggles for social acceptance and self-realization of a black man in the first half of twentieth-century American life.*

I

Yo mama don wear no drawers . . .

Clearly, the voice rose out of the woods, and died away. Like an echo another voice caught it up:

Ah seena when she pulled em off . . .

Another, shrill, cracking, adolescent:

N she washed 'em in alcohol . . .

Then a quartet of voices, blending in harmony, floated high above the tree tops:

N she hung 'em out in the hall . . .

Laughing easily, four black boys came out of the woods into cleared pasture. They walked lollingly in bare feet, beating tangled vines and bushes with long sticks.

"Ah wished Ah knowed some mo lines t tha song."

"Me too."

"Yeah, when yuh gits t where she hangs em out in the hall yuh has t stop."

"Shucks, what goes wid *hall*"

"Call."
"Fall."
"Wall."
"Quall."

They threw themselves on the grass, laughing.

"Big Boy?"

"Huh?"

"Yuh know one thing?"

"Whut?"

"Yuh sho is crazy!"

"Crazy?"

"Yeah, yuh crazys a bed-bug!"

"Crazy bout whut?"

"Man, whoever hearda *quall?*"

"Yuh said yuh wanted something t go wid *hall*, didnt yuh?"

"Yeah, but whuts a *quall?*"

"Nigger, a *qualls* a *quall.*"

They laughed easily, catching and pulling long green blades of grass with their toes.

"Waal, ef a *qualls* a *quall*, whut IS a *quall?*"

"Oh, Ah know."

"Whut?"

"Tha ol song goes something like this:

Yo mama don wear no drawers,
Ah seena when she pulled em off,

N she washed em in alcohol,
N she hung em out in the hall,
N then she put em back on her QUALL!"

They laughed again. Their shoulders went flat to the earth, their knees propped up, and their faces square to the sun.

"Big Boy, yuhs CRAZY!"

"Don ax me nothin else."

"Nigger, yuhs CRAZY!"

They fell silent, smiling, drooping the lids of their eyes softly against the sunlight.

"Man, don the groun feel warm?"

"Jus lika bed."

"Jeeesus, Ah could stay here ferever."

"Me too."

"Ah kin feel tha ol sun goin all thu me."

"Feels like mah bones is warm."

In the distance a train whistled mournfully.

"There goes number fo!"

"Hittin on all six!"

"Highballin it down the line!"

"Boun fer up Noth, Lawd, boun fer up Noth!"

They began to chant, pounding bare heels in the grass.

Dis train boun fo Glory
Dis train, Oh Hallelujah
Dis train boun fo Glory
Dis train, Oh Hallelujah
Dis train boun fo Glory
Ef yuh ride no need fer fret er worry
Dis train, Oh Hallelujah
Dis train . . .

Dis train don carry no gambler
Dis train, Oh Hallelujah
Dis train don carry no gambler
Dis train, Oh Hallelujah
Dis train don carry no gambler
No fo day creeper er midnight rambler
Dis train, Oh Hallelujah
Dis train . . .

When the song ended they burst out laughing, thinking of a train bound for Glory.

"Gee, thas a good ol song!"

"Huuuuummmmmmmmman . . ."

"Whut?"

"Geeee whiiiiiiz . . ."

"Whut?"

"Somebody don let win! Das whut!"

Buck, Bobo and Lester jumped up. Big Boy stayed on the ground, feigning sleep.

"Jeeesus, tha sho stinks!"

"Big Boy!"

Big Boy feigned to snore.

"Big Boy!"

Big Boy stirred as though in sleep.

"Big Boy!"

"Hunh?"

"Yuh rotten inside!"

"Rotten?"

"Lawd, cant yuh smell it?"

"Smell whut?"

"Nigger, yuh mus gotta bad col!"

"*Smell whut?*"

"NIGGER, YUH BROKE WIN!"

Big Boy laughed and fell back on the grass, closing his eyes.

"The hen whut cackles is the hen whut laid the egg."

"We ain no hens."

"Yuh cackled, didnt yuh?"

The three moved off with noses turned up.

"C mon!"

"Where yuh-all goin?"

"T the creek fer a swim."

"Yeah, les swim."

"Naw buddy naw!" said Big Boy, slapping the air with a scornful palm.

"Aw, c mon! Don be a heel!"

"N git *lynched?* Hell naw!"

"He ain gonna see us."

"How yuh know?"

"Cause he ain."

"Yuh-all go on. Ahma stay right here," said Big Boy.

"Hell, let im stay! C mon, les go," said Buck.

The three walked off, swishing at grass and bushes with sticks. Big Boy looked lazily at their backs.

"Hey!"

Walking on, they glanced over their shoulders.

"Hey, niggers!"

"C mon!"

Big Boy grunted, picked up his stick, pulled to his feet, and stumbled off.

"Wait!"

"C mon!"

He ran, caught up with them, leaped upon their backs, bearing them to the ground.

"Quit, Big Boy!"

"Gawddam, nigger!"

"Git t hell offa me!"

Big Boy sprawled in the grass beside them, laughing and pounding his heels in the ground.

"Nigger, whut yuh think we is, hosses?"

"How come yuh awways hoppin on us?"

"Lissen, wes gonna double-team on yuh one of these days n beat yo ol ass good."

Big Boy smiled.

"Sho nough?"

"Yeah, don yuh like it?"

"We gonna beat yuh sos yuh cant walk!"

"N dare yuh t do nothin erbout it!"

Big Boy bared his teeth.

"C mon! Try it now!"

The three circled around him.

"Say, Buck, yuh grab his feets!"

"N yuh git his head, Lester!"

"N Bobo, yuh git berhin n grab his arms!"

Keeping more than arm's length, they circled round and round Big Boy.

"C mon!" said Big Boy, feinting at one and then the other.

Round and round they circled, but could not seem to get any closer. Big Boy stopped and braced his hands on his hips.

"Is all three of yuh-all scareda me?"

"Les git im some other time," said Bobo, grinning.

"Yeah, we kin ketch yuh when yuh ain thinkin," said Lester.

"We kin trick yuh," said Buck.

They laughed and walked together.

Big Boy belched.

"Ahm hongry," he said.

"Me too."

"Ah wished Ah hada big hot pota belly-busters!"

"Cooked wid some good ol salty ribs . . ."

"N some good ol egg cornbread . . ."

"N some buttermilk . . ."

"N some hot peach cobbler swimmin in juice . . ."

"Nigger, hush!"

They began to chant, emphasizing the rhythm by cutting at grass with sticks.

Bye n bye
Ah wanna piece of pie
Pies too sweet
Ah wanna piece of meat
Meats too red
Ah wanna piece of bread
Breads too brown
Ah wanna go t town
Towns too far
Ah wanna ketch a car
Cars too fas
Ah fall n break mah ass
Ahll understan it better bye n bye . . .

They climbed over a barbed-wire fence and entered a stretch of thick woods. Big Boy was whistling softly, his eyes half-closed.

"LES GIT IM!"

Buck, Lester, and Bobo whirled, grabbed Big Boy about the neck, arms, and legs, bearing him to the ground. He grunted and kicked wildly as he went back into weeds.

"Hol im tight!"

"Git his arms! Git his arms!"

"Set on his legs so he cant kick!"

Big Boy puffed heavily, trying to get loose.

"WE GOT YUH NOW, GAWDDAMMIT, WE GOT YUH NOW!"

"Thas a Gawddam lie!" said Big Boy. He kicked, twisted, and clutched for a hold on one and then the other.

"Say, yuh-all hep me hol his arms!" said Bobo.

"Aw, we got this bastard now!" said Lester.

"Thas a Gawddam lie!" said Big Boy again.

"Say, yuh-all hep me hol his arms!" called Bobo.

Big Boy managed to encircle the neck of Bobo with his left arm. He tightened his elbow scissors-like and hissed through his teeth:

"Yuh got me, ain yuh?"

"Hol im!"

"Les beat this bastard's ass!"

"Say, hep me hol his *arms!* Hes got aholda mah *neck!*" cried Bobo.

Big Boy squeezed Bobo's neck and twisted his head to the ground.

"Yuh got me, ain yuh?"

"Quit, Big Boy, yuh chokin me; yuh hurtin mah neck!" cried Bobo.

"Turn me loose!" said Big Boy.

"Ah ain got yuh! Its the others whut got yuh!" pleaded Bobo.

"Tell them others t git t hell offa me or Ahma break yo neck," said Big Boy.

"Ssssay, yyyuh-all gggit ooooffa Bbig Boy. Hhhes got me," gurgled Bobo.

"Cant yuh hol im?"

"Nnaw, hhes ggot mmah nneck . . ."

Big Boy squeezed tighter.

"N Ahma break it too less yuh tell em t git t hell offa me!"

"Ttturn mmmeee lllloose," panted Bobo, tears gushing.

"Cant yuh hol im, Bobo?" asked Buck.

"Nnaw, yuh-all tturn im lloose; hhhes got mah nnneck . . ."

"Grab his neck, Bobo . . ."

"Ah cant; yugurgur . . ."

To save Bobo, Lester and Buck got up and ran to a safe distance. Big Boy released Bobo, who staggered to his feet, slobbering and trying to stretch a crick out of his neck.

"Shucks, nigger, yuh almos broke mah neck," whimpered Bobo.

"Ahm gonna break yo ass nex time," said Big Boy.

"Ef Bobo coulda hel yuh we woulda had yuh," yelled Lester.

"Ah waznt gonna let im do that," said Big Boy.

They walked together again, swishing sticks.

"Yuh see," began Big Boy, "when a ganga guys jump on yuh, all yuh gotta do is just put the heat on one of them n make im tell the others t let up, see?"

"Gee, thas a good idee!"

"Yeah, thas a good idee!"

"But yuh almos broke mah neck, man," said Bobo.

"Ahma smart nigger," said Big Boy, thrusting out his chest.

II

They came to the swimming hole.

"Ah ain goin in," said Bobo.

"Done got scared?" asked Big Boy.

"Naw, Ah ain scared . . ."

"How come yuh ain goin in?"

"Yuh know ol man Harvey don erllow no niggers t swim in this hole."

"N jus las year he took a shot at Bob fer swimmin in here," said Lester.

"Shucks, ol man Harvey ain studyin bout us niggers," said Big Boy.

"Hes at home thinkin about his jelly-roll," said Buck.

They laughed.

"Buck, yo mins lowern a snakes belly," said Lester.

"Ol man Harveys too doggone ol t think erbout jelly-roll," said Big Boy.

"Hes dried up: all the saps done lef im," said Bobo.

"C mon, les go!" said Big Boy.

Bobo pointed.

"See tha sign over yonder?"

"Yeah."

"Whut it say?"

"NO TRESPASSIN," read Lester.

"Know whut tha mean?"

"Mean ain no dogs n niggers erllowed," said Buck.

"Waal, wes here now," said Big Boy. "Ef he ketched us even like this thered be trouble, so we just as waal go on in . . ."

"Ahm wid the nex one!"

"Ahl go ef anybody else goes!"

Big Boy looked carefully in all directions. Seeing nobody, he began jerking off his overalls.

"LAS ONE INS A OL DEAD DOG!"

"THAS YO MA!"

"THAS YO PA!"

"THAS BOTH YO MA N YO PA!"

They jerked off their clothes and threw them in a pile under a tree. Thirty seconds later they stood, black and naked, on the edge of the hole under a sloping embankment. Gingerly Big Boy touched the water with his foot.

"Man, this waters col," he said.

"Ahm gonna put mah cloes back on," said Bobo, withdrawing his foot.

Big Boy grabbed him about the waist.

"Like hell yuh is!"

"Git outta the way, nigger!" Bobo yelled.

"Throw im in!" said Lester.

"Duck im!"

Bobo crouched, spread his legs, and braced himself against Big Boy's body. Locked in each other's arms, they tussled on the edge of the hole, neither able to throw the other.

"C mon, les me n yuh push em in."

Laughing, Lester and Buck gave the two locked bodies a running push. Big Boy and Bobo splashed, sending up silver spray in the sunlight. When Big Boy's head came up he yelled:

"Yuh bastard!"

"That wuz yo ma yuh pushed!" said Bobo, shaking his head to clear the water from his eyes.

They did a surface dive, came up and struck out across the creek. The muddy water foamed. They swam back, waded into shallow water, breathing heavily and blinking eyes.

"C mon in!"

"Man, the waters fine!"

Lester and Buck hesitated.

"Les wet em," Big Boy whispered to Bobo.

Before Lester and Buck could back away, they were dripping wet from handsful of scooped water.

"Hey, quit!"

"Gawddam, nigger! Tha waters col!"

"C mon in!" called Big Boy.

"We jus as waal go on in now," said Buck.

"Look n see ef anybodys comin."

Kneeling, they squinted among the trees.

"Ain nobody."

"C mon, les go."

They waded in slowly, pausing each few steps to catch their breath. A desperate water battle began. Closing eyes and backing away, they shunted water into one another's faces with the flat palms of hands.

"Hey, cut it out!"

"Yeah, Ahm bout drownin!"

They came together in water up to their navels, blowing and blinking. Big Boy ducked, upsetting Bobo.

"Look out, nigger!"

"Don holler so loud!"

"Yeah, they kin hear yo ol big mouth a mile erway."

"This waters too col fer me."

"Thas cause it rained yistiddy."

They swam across and back again.

"Ah wish we hada bigger place t swim in."

"The white folks got plenty swimmin pools n we ain got none."

"Ah useta swim in the ol Missippi when we lived in Vicksburg."

Big Boy put his head under the water and blew his breath. A sound came like that of a hippopotamus.

"C mon, les be hippos."

Each went to a corner of the creek and put his mouth just below the surface and blew like a hippopotamus. Tiring, they came and sat under the embankment.

"Look like Ah gotta chill."

"Me too."

"Les stay here n dry off."

"Jeeesus, Ahm col!"

They kept still in the sun, suppressing shivers. After some of the water had dried off their bodies they began to talk through clattering teeth.

"Whut would yuh do ef ol man Harveyd come erlong right now?"

"Run like hell"

"Man, Ahd run so fas hed thinka black streaka lightnin shot pass im."

"But spose he hada gun?"

"Aw, nigger, shut up!"

They were silent. They ran their hands over wet, trembling legs, brushing water away. Then their eyes watched the sun sparkling on the restless creek.

Far away a train whistled.

"There goes number seven!"

"Headin fer up Noth!"

"Blazin it down the line!"

"Lawd, Ahm goin Noth some day."

"Me too, man."

"They say colored folks up Noth is got ekual rights."

They grew pensive. A black winged butterfly hovered at the water's edge. A bee droned. From somewhere came the sweet scent of honeysuckles. Dimly they could hear sparrows twittering in the woods. They rolled from side to side, letting sunshine dry their skins and warm their blood. They plucked blades of grass and chewed them.

"Oh!"

They looked up, their lips parting.

"Oh!"

A white woman, poised on the edge of the opposite embankment, stood directly in front of them, her hat in her hand and her hair lit by the sun.

"Its a woman!" whispered Big Boy in an underbreath. "A *white* woman!"

They stared, their hands instinctively covering their groins. Then they scrambled to their feet. The white woman backed slowly out of sight. They stood for a moment, looking at one another.

"Les git outta here!" Big Boy whispered.

"Wait till she goes erway."

"Les run, theyll ketch us here naked like this!"

"Mabbe theres a man wid her."

"C mon, les git our cloes," said Big Boy.

They waited a moment longer, listening.

"Whut t hell! Ahma git mah cloes," said Big Boy.

Grabbing at short tufts of grass, he climbed the embankment.

"Don run out there now!"

"C mon back, fool!"

Bobo hesitated. He looked at Big Boy, and then at Buck and Lester.

"Ahm goin wid Big Boy n git mah cloes," he said.

"Don run out there naked like tha, fool!" said Buck. "Yuh don know whos out there!"

Big Boy was climbing over the edge of the embankment.

"C mon," he whispered.

Bobo climbed after. Twenty-five feet away the woman stood. She had one hand over her mouth. Hanging by fingers, Buck and Lester peeped over the edge.

"C mon back; that womans scared," said Lester.

Big Boy stopped, puzzled. He looked at the woman. He looked at the bundle of clothes. Then he looked at Buck and Lester.

"C mon, les git our cloes!"

He made a step.

"Jim!" the woman screamed.

Big Boy stopped and looked around. His hands hung loosely at his sides. The woman, her eyes wide, her hand over her mouth, backed away to the tree where their clothes lay in a heap.

"Big Boy, come back n wait till shes gone!"

Bobo ran to Big Boy's side.

"Les go home! Theyll ketch us here," he urged.

Big Boy's throat felt tight.

"Lady, we wanna git our cloes," he said.

Buck and Lester climbed the embankment and stood indecisively. Big Boy ran toward the tree.

"Jim!" the woman screamed. "Jim! Jim!"

Black and naked, Big Boy stopped three feet from her.

"We wanna git our cloes," he said again, his words coming mechanically.

He made a motion.

"You go away! You go away! I tell you, you go away!"

Big Boy stopped again, afraid. Bobo ran and snatched the clothes. Buck and Lester tried to grab theirs out of his hands.

"You go away! You go away! You go away!" the woman screamed.

"Les go!" said Bobo, running toward the woods.

CRACK!

Lester grunted, stiffened, and pitched forward. His forehead struck a toe of the woman's shoes.

Bobo stopped, clutching the clothes. Buck whirled. Big Boy stared at Lester, his lips moving.

"Hes gotta gun; hes gotta gun!" yelled Buck, running wildly.

CRACK!

Buck stopped at the edge of the embankment, his head jerked backward, his body arched stiffly to one side; he toppled headlong, sending up a shower of bright spray to the sunlight. The creek bubbled.

Big Boy and Bobo backed away, their eyes fastened fearfully on a white man who was running toward them. He had a rifle and wore an army officer's uniform. He ran to the woman's side and grabbed her hand.

"You hurt, Bertha, you hurt?"

She stared at him and did not answer.

The man turned quickly. His face was red. He raised the rifle and pointed it at Bobo. Bobo ran back, holding the clothes in front of his chest.

"Don shoot me, Mistah, don shoot me . . ."

Big Boy lunged for the rifle, grabbing the barrel.

"You black sonofabitch!"

Big Boy clung desperately.

"Let go, you black bastard!"

The barrel pointed skyward.

CRACK!

The white man, taller and heavier, flung Big Boy to the ground. Bobo dropped the clothes, ran up, and jumped onto the white man's back.

"You black sonsofbitches!"

The white man released the rifle, jerked Bobo to the ground, and began to batter the naked boy with his fists. Then Big Boy swung, striking the man in the mouth with the barrel. His teeth caved in, and he fell, dazed. Bobo was on his feet.

"C mon, Big Boy, les go!"

Breathing hard, the white man got up and faced Big Boy. His lips were trembling, his neck and chin wet with blood. He spoke quietly.

"Give me that gun, boy!"

Big Boy leveled the rifle and backed away.

The white man advanced.

"Boy, I say give me that gun!"

Bobo had the clothes in his arms.

"Run, Big Boy, run!"

The man came at Big Boy.

"Ahll kill yuh; Ahll kill yuh!" said Big Boy.

His fingers fumbled for the trigger.

The man stopped, blinked, spat blood. His eyes were bewildered. His face whitened. Suddenly, he lunged for the rifle, his hands outstretched.

CRACK!

He fell forward on his face.

"Jim!"

Big Boy and Bobo turned in surprise to look at the woman.

"Jim!" she screamed again, and fell weakly at the foot of the tree.

Big Boy dropped the rifle, his eyes wide. He looked around. Bobo was crying and clutching the clothes.

"Big Boy, Big Boy . . ."

Big Boy looked at the rifle, started to pick it up, but didn't. He seemed at a loss. He looked at Lester, then at the white man; his eyes followed a thin stream of blood that seeped to the ground.

"Yuh don killed im," mumbled Bobo.

"Les go home!"

Naked, they turned and ran toward the woods. When they reached the barbed-wire fence they stopped.

"Les git our cloes on," said Big Boy.

They slipped quickly into overalls. Bobo held Lester's and Buck's clothes.

"Whut we gonna do wid these?"

Big Boy stared. His hands twitched.

"Leave em."

They climbed the fence and ran through the woods. Vines and leaves switched their faces. Once Bobo tripped and fell.

"C mon!" said Big Boy.

Bobo started crying, blood streaming from his scratches.

"Ahm scared!"

"C mon! Don cry! We wanna git home fo they ketches us!"

"Ahm scared!" said Bobo again, his eyes full of tears.

Big Boy grabbed his hand and dragged him along.

"C mon!"

III

They stopped when they got to the end of the woods. They could see the open road leading home, home to ma and pa. But they hung back, afraid. The thick shadows cast from the trees were friendly and sheltering. But the wide glare of sun stretching out over the fields was pitiless. They crouched behind an old log.

"We gotta git home," said Big Boy.

"Theys gonna lynch us," said Bobo, half questioningly.

Big Boy did not answer.

"Theys gonna lynch us," said Bobo again.

Big Boy shuddered.

"Hush!" he said. He did not want to think of it. He could not think of it; there was but one thought, and he clung to that one blindly. He had to get home, home to ma and pa.

Their heads jerked up. Their ears had caught the rhythmic jingle of a wagon. They fell to the ground and clung flat to the side of a log. Over the crest of the hill came the top of a hat. A white face. Then shoulders in a blue shirt. A wagon drawn by two horses pulled into full view.

Big Boy and Bobo held their breath, waiting. Their eyes followed the wagon till it was lost in dust around a bend of the road.

"We gotta git home," said Big Boy.

"Ahm scared," said Bobo.

"C mon! Les keep t the fields."

They ran till they came to the cornfields. Then they went slower, for last year's corn stubbles bruised their feet.

They came in sight of a brickyard.

"Wait a minute," gasped Big Boy.

They stopped.

"Ahm goin on t mah home n yuh better go on t yos."

Bobo's eyes grew round.

"Ahm scared!"

"Yuh better go on!"

"Lemme go wid yuh; theyll ketch me . . ."

"Ef yuh kin git home mabbe yo folks kin hep yuh t git erway."

Big Boy started off. Bobo grabbed him.

"Lemme go wid yuh!"

Big Boy shook free.

"Ef yuh stay here theys gonna lynch yuh!" he yelled, running.

After he had gone about twenty-five yards he turned and looked; Bobo was flying through the woods like the wind.

Big Boy slowed when he came to the railroad. He wondered if he ought to go through the streets or down the track. He decided on the tracks. He could dodge a train better than a mob.

He trotted along the ties, looking ahead and back. His cheek itched, and he felt it. His hand came away smeared with blood. He wiped it nervously on his overalls.

When he came to his back fence he heaved himself over. He landed among a flock of startled chickens. A bantam rooster tried to spur him. He slipped and fell in front of the kitchen steps, grunting heavily. The ground was slick with greasy dishwater.

Panting, he stumbled through the doorway.

"Lawd, Big Boy, whuts wrong wid yuh?"

His mother stood gaping in the middle of the floor. Big Boy flopped wordlessly onto a stool, almost toppling over. Pots simmered on the stove. The kitchen smelled of food cooking.

"Whuts the matter, Big Boy?"

Mutely, he looked at her. Then he burst into tears. She came and felt the scratches on his face.

"Whut happened t yuh, Big Boy? Somebody been botherin yuh?"

"They after me, Ma! They after me . . ."

"Who!"

"Ah . . . Ah . . . We . . ."

"Big Boy, whuts wrong wid yuh?"

"He killed Lester n Buck," he muttered simply.

"Killed!"

"Yessum."

"Lester n Buck!"

"Yessum, Ma!"

"How killed?"

"He shot em, Ma!"

"Lawd Gawd in Heaven, have mercy on us all! This is mo trouble, mo trouble," she moaned, wringing her hands.

"N Ah killed im, Ma . . ."

She stared, trying to understand.

"Whut happened, Big Boy?"

"We tried t git our cloes from the tree . . ."

"Whut tree?"

"We wuz swimmin, Ma. N the white woman . . ."

"*White* woman? . . ."

"Yessum. She wuz at the swimmin hole . . ."

"Lawd have mercy! Ah knowed yuh boys wuz gonna keep on till yuh got into somethin like this!"

She ran into the hall.

"Lucy!"

"Mam?"

"C mere!"

"Mam?"

"C mere, Ah say!"

"Wutcha wan, Ma? Ahm sewin."

"Chile, will yuh c mere like Ah ast yuh?"

Lucy came to the door holding an unfinished apron in her hands. When she saw Big Boy's face she looked wildly at her mother.

"Whuts the matter?"

"Wheres Pa?"

"Hes out front, Ah reckon."

"Git im, quick!"

"Whuts the matter, Ma?"

"Go git yo Pa, Ah say!"

Lucy ran out. The mother sank into a chair, holding a dish rag. Suddenly, she sat up.

"Big Boy, Ah thought yuh wuz at school?"

Big Boy looked at the floor.

"How come yuh didnt go t school?"

"We went t the woods."

She sighed.

"Ah done done all Ah kin fer yuh, Big Boy. Only Gawd kin hep yuh now."

"Ma, don let em git me; don let em git me . . ."

His father came into the doorway. He stared at Big Boy, then at his wife.

"Whuts Big Boy inter now?" he asked sternly.

"Saul, Big Boys done gone n got inter trouble wid the white folks."

The old man's mouth dropped, and he looked from one to the other.

"Saul, we gotta git im erway from here."

"Open yo mouth n talk! Whut yuh been doin?" The old man gripped Big Boy's shoulders and peered at the scratches on his face.

"Me n Lester n Buck n Bobo wuz out on ol man Harveys place swimmin . . ."

"Saul, its a *white* woman!"

Big Boy winced. The old man compressed his lips and stared at his wife. Lucy gaped at her brother as though she had never seen him before.

"Whut happened? Cant yuh-all talk?" the old man thundered with a certain helplessness in his voice.

"We wuz swimmin," Big Boy began, "n then a white woman comes up t the hole. We got up right erway t git our cloes sos we could git erway, n she started screamin. Our cloes wuz right by the tree where she wuz standin, n when we started t git em she jus screamed. We tol her we wanted our cloes . . . Yuh see, Pa, she wuz standin right *by* our cloes; n when we went t git em she jus screamed . . . Bobo got the cloes, n then he shot Lester . . ."

"*Who* shot Lester?"

"The white man."

"Whut white man?"

"Ah dunno, Pa. He wuz a soljer, n he had a rifle."

"A soljer?"

"Yessuh."

"A *soljer?*"

"Yessuh, Pa. A soljer."

The old man frowned.

"N then whut yuh-all do?"

"Waal, Buck said, 'He's gotta gun!' N we started runnin. N then he shot Buck, n he fell in the swimmin hole. We didnt see im no mo . . . He wuz close on us then. He looked at the white woman n then he started t shoot Bobo. Ah grabbed the gun, n we started fightin. Bobo jumped on his back. He started beatin Bobo. Then Ah hit im wid the gun. Then he started at me n Ah shot im. Then we run . . ."

"Who seen?"

"Nobody."

"Wheres Bobo?"

"He went home."

"Anybody run after yuh-all?"

"Nawsuh."

"Yuh see anybody?"

"Nawsuh. Nobody but a white man. But he didnt see us."

"How long fo yuh-all lef the swimmin hole?"

"Little while ergo."

The old man nervously brushed his hand across his eyes and walked to the door. His lips moved, but no words came.

"Saul, whut we gonna do?"

"Lucy," began the old man, "go t Brother Sanders n tell im Ah said c mere; n go t Brother Jenkins n tell im Ah said c mere; n go t Elder Peters n tell im Ah said c mere. N don say nothin t nobody but whut Ah tol yuh. N when yuh git thu come straight back. Now go!"

Lucy dropped her apron across the back of a chair and ran down the steps. The mother bent over, crying and praying. The old man walked slowly over to Big Boy.

"Big Boy?"

Big Boy swallowed.

"Ahm talkin t yuh!"

"Yessuh."

"How come yuh didnt go t school this mawnin?"

"We went t the woods."

"Didnt yo ma send yuh t school?"

"Yessuh."

"How come yuh didnt go?"

"We went t the woods."

"Don yuh know thas wrong?"

"Yessuh."

"How come yuh go?"

Big Boy looked at his fingers, knotted them, and squirmed in his seat.

"AHM TALKIN T YUH!"

His wife straightened up and said reprovingly:

"Saul!"

The old man desisted, yanking nervously at the shoulder straps of his overalls.

"How long wuz the woman there?"

"Not long."

"Wuz she young?"

"Yessuh. Lika gal."

"Did yuh-all say anythin t her?"

"Nawsuh. We jus said we wanted our cloes."

"N whut she say?"

"Nothin, Pa. She jus backed erway t the tree n screamed."

The old man stared, his lips trying to form a question.

"Big Boy, did yuh-all bother her?"

"Nawsuh, Pa. We didnt *touch* her."

"How long fo the white man come up?"

"Right erway."

"Whut he say?"

"Nothin. He jus cussed us."

Abruptly the old man left the kitchen.

"Ma, cant Ah go fo they ketches me?"

"Sauls doin whut he kin."

"Ma, Ma, Ah don wan em t ketch me . . ."

"Sauls doin whut he kin. Nobody but the good Lawd kin hep us now."

The old man came back with a shotgun and leaned it in a corner. Fascinatedly, Big Boy looked at it.

There was a knock at the front door.

"Liza, see whos there."

She went. They were silent, listening. They could hear her talking.

"Whos there?"

"Me."

"Who?"

"Me, Brother Sanders."

"C mon in. Sauls waitin fer yuh."

Sanders paused in the doorway, smiling.

"Yuh sent fer me, Brother Morrison?"

"Brother Sanders, wes in deep trouble here."

Sanders came all the way into the kitchen.

"Yeah?"

"Big Boy done gone n killed a white man."

Sanders stopped short, then came forward, his face thrust out, his mouth open. His lips moved several times before he could speak.

"A *white* man?"

"They gonna kill me; they gonna kill me!" Big Boy cried, running to the old man.

"Saul, cant we git im erway somewhere?"

"Here now, take it easy; take it easy," said Sanders, holding Big Boy's wrists.

"They gonna kill me; they gonna lynch me!"

Big Boy slipped to the floor. They lifted him to a stool. His mother held him closely, pressing his head to her bosom.

"Whut we gonna do?" asked Sanders.

"Ah done sent fer Brother Jenkins n Elder Peters."

Sanders leaned his shoulders against the wall. Then, as the full meaning of it all came to him, he exclaimed:

"Theys gonna git a mob! . . ." His voice broke off and his eyes fell on the shotgun.

Feet came pounding on the steps. They turned toward the door. Lucy ran in crying. Jenkins followed. The old man met him in the middle of the room, taking his hand.

"Wes in bad trouble here, Brother Jenkins. Big Boy's done gone n killed a white man. Yuh-alls gotta hep me . . ."

Jenkins looked hard at Big Boy.

"Elder Peters says hes comin," said Lucy.

"When all this happen?" asked Jenkins.

"Near bout a hour ergo, now," said the old man.

"Whut we gonna do?" asked Jenkins.

"Ah wanna wait till Elder Peters come," said the old man helplessly.

"But we gotta work fas ef we gonna do anythin," said Sanders. "Well git in trouble jus standin here like this."

Big Boy pulled away from his mother.

"Pa, lemme go now! Lemme go now!"

"Be still, Big Boy!"

"Where kin yuh go?"

"Ah could ketch a freight!"

"Thas *sho* death!" said Jenkins. "Theyll be watchin em all!"

"Kin yuh-all hep me wid some money?" the old man asked.

They shook their heads.

"Saul, whut kin we do? Big Boy cant stay here."

There was another knock at the door.

The old man backed stealthily to the shotgun.

"Lucy go!"

Lucy looked at him, hesitating.

"Ah better go," said Jenkins.

It was Elder Peters. He came in hurriedly.

"Good evenin, everybody!"

"How yuh, Elder?"

"Good evenin."

"How yuh today?"

Peters looked around the crowded kitchen.

"Whuts the matter?"

"Elder, wes in deep trouble," began the old man. "Big Boy n some mo boys . . ."

". . . Lester n Buck n Bobo . . ."

". . . wuz over on old man Harveys place swimmin . . ."

"N he don like us niggers *none*," said Peters emphatically. He widened his legs and put his thumbs in the armholes of his vest.

". . . n some white woman . . ."

"Yeah?" said Peters, coming closer.

". . . comes erlong n the boys tries t git their cloes where they done lef em under a tree. Waal, she started screamin n all, see?

Reckon she thought the boys wuz after her. Then a white man in a soljers suit shoots two of em . . ."

". . . Lester n Buck . . ."

"Huummm," said Peters. "Tha wuz old man Harveys son."

"Harveys son?"

"Yuh mean the one tha wuz in the Army?"

"Yuh mean Jim?"

"Yeh," said Peters. "The papers said he wuz here for a vacation from his regiment. N tha woman the boys saw wuz just erbout his wife . . ."

They stared at Peters. Now that they knew what white person had been killed, their fears became definite.

"N whut else happened?"

"Big Boy shot the man . . ."

"Harveys *son?*"

"He had t, Elder. He wuz gonna shoot im ef he didnt . . ."

"Lawd!" said Peters. He looked around and put his hat back on.

"How long ergo wuz this?"

"Mighty near an hour, now, Ah reckon."

"Do the white folks know yit?"

"Don know, Elder."

"Yuh-all better git this boy outta here right now," said Peters. "Cause ef yuh don theres gonna be a lynchin . . ."

"Where kin Ah go, Elder?" Big Boy ran up to him.

They crowded around Peters. He stood with his legs wide apart, looking up at the ceiling.

"Mabbe we kin hide im in the church till he kin git erway," said Jenkins.

Peters' lips flexed.

"Naw, Brother, thall never do! Theyll git im there sho. N anyhow, ef they ketch im there itll ruin us all. We gotta git the boy outta town . . ."

Sanders went up to the old man.

"Lissen," he said in a whisper. "Mah son, Will, the one whut drives for the Magnolia Express Company, is taking a truck o goods t Chicawgo in the mawnin. If we kin hide Big Boy somewhere till then, we kin put im on the truck . . ."

"Pa, please, lemme go wid Will when he goes in the mawnin," Big Boy begged.

The old man stared at Sanders.

"Yuh reckon thas safe?"

"Its the only thing yuh *kin* do," said Peters.

"But where we gonna hide im till then?"

"Whut time yo boy leavin out in the mawnin?"

"At six."

They were quiet, thinking. The water kettle on the stove sang.

"Pa, Ah knows where Will passes erlong wid the truck out on Bullards Road. Ah kin hide in one of them ol kilns . . ."

"Where?"

"In one of them kilns we built . . ."

"But theyll git yuh there," wailed the mother.

"But there ain no place else fer im t go."

"Theres some holes big ernough fer me t git in n stay till Will comes erlong," said Big Boy. "Please, Pa, lemme go fo they ketches me . . ."

"Let im go!"

"Please, Pa . . ."

The old man breathed heavily.

"Lucy, git his things!"

"Saul, theyll git im out there!" wailed the mother, grabbing Big Boy.

Peters pulled her way.

"Sister Morrison, ef yuh don let im go n git erway from here hes gonna be caught shos theres a Gawd in Heaven!"

Lucy came running with Big Boy's shoes and pulled them on his feet. The old man thrust a battered hat on his head. The mother went to the stove and dumped the skillet of corn pone into her apron. She wrapped it, and unbuttoning Big Boy's overalls, pushed it into his bosom.

"Heres somethin fer yuh t eat; n pray, Big Boy, cause thas all anybody kin do now . . ."

Big Boy pulled to the door, his mother clinging to him.

"Let im go, Sister Morrison!"

"Run fas, Big Boy!"

Big Boy raced across the yard, scattering the chickens. He paused at the fence and hollered back:

"Tell Bobo where Ahm hidin n tell im t c mon!"

IV

He made for the railroad, running straight toward the sunset. He held his left hand tightly over his heart, holding the hot pone of corn bread there. At times he stumbled over the ties, for his shoes were tight and hurt his feet. His throat burned from thirst; he had had no water since noon.

He veered off the track and trotted over the crest of a hill, following Bullard's Road. His feet slipped and slid in the dust. He kept his eyes straight ahead, fearing every clump of shrubbery, every tree. He wished it were night. If he could only get to the kilns without meeting anyone. Suddenly a thought came to him like a blow. He recalled hearing the old folks tell tales of blood-hounds, and fear made him run slower. None of them had thought of that. Spose blood-houns wuz put on his trail? Lawd! Spose a whole pack of em, foamin n howlin, tore im t pieces? He went limp and his feet dragged. Yeah, thas whut they wuz gonna send after im, blood-houns! N then thered be no way fer im to dodge! Why hadnt Pa let im take tha shotgun? He stopped. He oughta go back n git tha shotgun. And then when the mob came he would take some with him.

In the distance he heard the approach of a train. It jarred him back to a sharp sense of danger. He ran again, his big shoes sopping up and down in the dust. He was tired and his lungs were bursting from running. He wet his lips, wanting water. As he turned from the road across a plowed field he heard the train roaring at his heels. He ran faster, gripped in terror.

He was nearly there now. He could see the black clay on the sloping hillside. Once inside a kiln he would be safe. For a little while, at least. He thought of the shotgun again. If he only had something; someone to talk to . . . Thas right! Bobo! Bobod be wid im. Hed almost fergot Bobo. Bobod bringa gun; he knowed he would. N tergether they could kill the whole mob. Then in the mawning theyd git inter Will's truck n go far erway, t Chicawgo . . .

He slowed to a walk, looking back and ahead. A light wind skipped over the grass. A beetle lit on his cheek and he brushed it off. Behind the dark pines hung a red sun. Two bats flapped against that sun. He shivered, for he was growing cold; the sweat on his body was drying.

He stopped at the foot of the hill, trying to choose between two patches of black kilns high above him. He went to the left, for there lay the ones he, Bobo, Lester, and Buck had dug only last week. He looked around again; the landscape was bare. He climbed the embankment and stood before a row of black pits sinking four and five feet deep into the earth. He went to the largest and peered in. He stiffened when his ears caught the sound of a whir. He ran back a few steps and poised on his toes. Six foot of snake slid out of the pit and went into coil. Big Boy looked around wildly for a stick. He ran down the slope, peering into the grass. He stumbled over a tree limb. He picked it up and tested it by striking it against the ground.

Warily, he crept back up the slope, his stick poised. When about seven feet from the snake he stopped and waved the stick. The coil grew tighter, the whir sounded louder, and a flat head reared to strike. He went to the right, and the flat head followed him, the blue-black tongue darting forth; he went to the left, and the flat head followed him there too.

He stopped, teeth clenched. He had to kill this snake. Jus had t kill im! This wuz the safest pit on the hillside. He waved the stick again, looking at the snake before, thinking of a mob behind. The flat head reared higher. With stick over shoulder, he jumped in, swinging. The stick sang through the air, catching the snake on the side of the head, sweeping him out of coil. There was a brown writhing mass. Then Big Boy was upon him, pounding blows home, one on top of the other. He fought viciously, his eyes red, his teeth bared in a snarl. He beat till the snake lay still; then he stomped it with his heel, grinding its head into the dirt.

He stopped, limp, wet. The corners of his lips were white with spittle. He spat and shuddered.

Cautiously, he went to the hole and peered. He longed for a match. He imagined whole nests of them in there waiting. He put the stick into the hole and waved it around. Stooping, he peered again. It mus be awright. He looked over the hillside, his eyes coming back to the dead snake. Then he got to his knees and backed slowly into the hole.

When inside he felt there must be snakes all about him, ready to strike. It seemed he could see and feel them there, waiting tensely in coil. In the dark he imagined long white fangs ready to sink into his neck, his side, his legs. He wanted to come out, but kept still. Shucks, he told himself, ef there wuz any snakes in here they sho woulda done bit me by now. Some of his fear left, and he relaxed.

With elbows on ground and chin on palms, he settled. The clay was cold to his knees and thighs, but his bosom was kept warm by the hot pone of corn bread. His thirst returned and he longed for a drink. He was hungry, too. But he did not want to eat the corn pone. Naw, not now. Mabbe after erwhile, after Bobo came. Then theyd both eat the corn pone.

The view from his hole was fringed by the long tufts of grass. He could see all the way to Bullard's Road, and even beyond. The wind was blowing, and in the east the first touch of dusk was rising. Every now and then a bird floated past, a spot of wheeling black printed against the sky. Big Boy sighed, shifted his weight, and chewed at a blade of grass. A wasp droned. He heard number nine, far away and mournful.

The train made him remember how they had dug these kilns on long hot summer days, how they had made boilers out of big tin cans, filled them with water, fixed stoppers for steam, cemented them in holes with wet clay, and built fires under them. He recalled how they had danced and yelled when a stopper blew out of a boiler, letting out a big spout of steam and a shrill whistle. There were times when they had the whole hillside blazing and smoking. Yeah, yuh see, Big Boy wuz Casey Jones n wuz speedin it down the gleamin rails of the Southern Pacific. Bobo had number two on the Santa Fe. Buck wuz on the Illinoy Central. Lester the Nickel Plate. Lawd, how they shelved the wood in! The boiling water would almost jar the cans loose from the clay. More and more pine-knots and dry leaves would be piled under the cans. Flames would grow so tall they would have to shield their eyes. Sweat would pour off their faces. Then, suddenly, a peg would shoot high into the air, and

Pssseeeezzzzzzzzzzzzzzzzzzzz . . .

Big Boy sighed and stretched out his arm, quenching the flames and scattering the smoke. Why didnt Bobo c mon? He looked over the fields; there was nothing but dying sunlight. His mind drifted back to the kilns. He remembered the day when Buck, jealous of his winning, had tried to smash his kiln. Yeah, that ol sonofabitch! Naw, Lawd! He didnt go t say tha! Whut wuz he thinkin erbout? Cussin the dead! Yeah, po ol Buck wuz dead now. N Lester too. Yeah, it wuz awright fer Buck t smash his kiln. Sho. N he wished he hadn't socked ol Buck so hard tha day. He wuz sorry fer Buck now. N he sho wished he hadnt cussed po ol Bucks ma, neither. Tha wuz sinful! Mabbe Gawd would git im fer tha? But he didnt go t do it! Po Buck! Po Lester! Hed never treat anybody like tha ergin, never . . .

Dusk was slowly deepening. Somewhere, he could not tell exactly where, a cricket took up a fitful song. The air was growing soft and heavy. He looked over the fields, longing for Bobo . . .

He shifted his body to ease the cold damp of the ground, and thought back over the day. Yeah, hed been dam right erbout not wantin t go swimmin. N ef hed followed his right min hed neverve gone n got inter all this trouble. At first hed said naw. But shucks, somehow hed just went on wid the res. Yeah, he shoulda went on t school tha mawnin, like Ma told im t do. But, hell, who wouldnt git tireda school? T hell wid school! Tha wuz the big trouble, awways drivin a guy t school. He wouldnt be in all this trouble now ef it wuznt for that Gawddam school! Impatiently, he took the grass out of his mouth and threw it away, demolishing the little red school house . . .

Yeah, ef they had all kept still n quiet when that ol white woman showed-up, mabbe shedve went on off. But yuh never kin tell erbout these white folks. Mabbe she wouldntve went. Mabbe that white man woulda killed all of em! All *fo* of em! Yeah, yuh never kin tell erbout white folks. Then, ergin, mabbe tha white woman woulda went on off n laffed. Yeah, mabbe tha white man woulda said: *Yuh nigger bastards git t hell outta here! Yuh know Gawddam well yuh don berlong here!* N then they woulda grabbed their cloes n run like all hell . . . He blinked the white man away. Where wuz Bobo? Why didnt he hurry up n c mon?

He jerked another blade and chewed. Yeah, ef pa had only let im have tha shotgun? He could stan off a whole mob wid a shotgun. He looked at the ground as he turned a shotgun over in his hands. Then he leveled it at an advancing white man. *Boooom!* The man curled up. Another came. He reloaded quickly, and let him have what the other had got. He too curled up. Then another came. He got the same medicine. Then the whole mob swirled around him, and he blazed away, getting as many as he could. They closed in; but, by Gawd, he had done his part, hadnt he? N the newspapersd say: NIGGER KILLS DOZEN OF MOB BEFO LYNCHED! Er mabbe theyd say: TRAPPED NIGGER SLAYS TWENTY BEFO KILLED! He smiled a little. Tha wouldnt be so bad, would it? Blinking the newspaper away, he looked over the fields. Where wuz Bobo? Why didnt he hurry up n c mon?

He shifted, trying to get a crick out of his legs. Shucks, he wuz gittin tireda this. N it wuz almos dark now. Yeah, there wuz a little bittie star way over yonder in the eas. Mabbe that white man wuznt dead? Mabbe they wuznt even lookin for im? Mabbe he could go back home now? Naw, better wait erwhile. Thad be bes. But, Lawd, ef he only had some water! He could hardly swallow, his throat was so dry. Gawddam them white folks! Thas all they wuz good fer, t run a nigger down lika rabbit! Yeah, they git yuh in a corner n then they let yuh have it. A thousan of em! He shivered, for the cold of the clay was chilling his bones. Lawd, spose they foun im here in this hole? N wid nobody t hep im? . . . But ain no use in thinkin erbout tha; wait till trouble come fo yuh start fightin it. But ef tha mob came one by one hed wipe em all out. Clean up the whole bunch. He caught one by the neck and choked him long and hard, choked him till his tongue and eyes popped out. Then he jumped upon his chest and stomped him like he had stomped that snake. When he had finished with one, another came. He choked him too. Choked till he sank slowly to the ground, gasping . . .

"Hoalo!"

Big Boy snatched his fingers from the white man's neck and looked over the fields. He saw nobody. Had someone spied him? He was sure that somebody had hollered. His heart pounded. But, shucks, nobody couldnt see im here in this hole . . . But mabbe theyd seen im when he wuz comin n had laid low n wuz now closin in on im! Praps they wuz signalin fer the others? Yeah, they wuz creepin up on im! Mabbe he oughta git up n run . . . Oh! Mabbe tha wuz Bobo! Yeah, Bobo! He oughta clim out n see ef Bobo wuz lookin fer im . . . He stiffened.

"Hoalo!"

"Hoalo!"

"Wheres yuh?"

"Over here on Bullards Road!"

"C mon over!"

"Awright!"

He heard footsteps. Then voices came again, low and far away this time.

"Seen anybody?"

"Naw. Yuh?"

"Naw."

"Yuh reckon they got erway?"

"Ah dunno. Its hard t tell."

"Gawddam them sonofabitchin niggers!"

"We oughta kill ever black bastard in this country!"

"Waal, Jim got two of em, anyhow."

"But Bertha said there wuz *fo!*"

"Where in hell they hidin?"

"She said one of em wuz named Big Boy, or somethin like tha."

"We went t his shack lookin fer im."

"Yeah?"

"But we didnt fin im."

"These niggers stick tergether; they don never tell on each other."

"We looked all thu the shack n couldnt fin hide ner hair of im. Then we drove the ol woman n man out n set the shack on fire . . ."

"Jeesus! Ah wished Ah coulda been there!"

"Yuh shoulda heard the old nigger woman howl . . ."

"Hoalo!"

"C mon over!"

Big Boy eased to the edge and peeped. He saw a white man with a gun slung over his shoulder runnin down the slope. Wuz they gonna search the hill? Lawd, there wuz no way fer im t git erway now; he wuz caught! He shoulda knowed theyd git im here. N he didn't hava thing, notta thing t fight wid. Yeah, soon as the blood-houns came theyd fin im. Lawd, have mercy! They lynch im right here on the hill . . . Theyd git im n tie im t a stake n burn im erlive! Lawd! Nobody but the good Lawd could hep im now, nobody . . .

He heard more feet running. He nestled deeper. His chest ached. Nobody but the good Lawd could hep now. They wuz crowdin all round im n when they hada big crowd theyd close in on im. Then itd be over . . . The good Lawd would have t hep im, cause nobody could hep im now, nobody . . .

And then he went numb when he remembered Bobo. Spose Bobod come now? Hed be caught sho! Both of em would be caught! Theyd make Bobo tell where he wuz! Bobo oughta not try to come now. Somebody oughta tell im . . . But there wuz nobody; there wuz no way . . .

He eased slowly back to the opening. There was a large group of men. More were coming. Many had guns. Some had coils of rope slung over shoulders.

"Ah tell yuh they still here, somewhere . . ."

"But we looked all over!"

"What t hell! Wouldn't do t let em git erway!"

"Naw. Ef they git erway notta woman in this town would be safe."

"Say, whuts tha yuh got?"

"Er pillar."

"Fer whut?"

"Feathers, fool!"

"Chris! Thisll be hot ef we kin ketch them niggers!"

"Ol Anderson said he wuz gonna bringa barrela tar!"

"Ah got some gasoline in mah car ef yuh need it."

Big Boy had no feelings now. He was waiting. He did not wonder if they were coming after him. He just waited. He did not wonder about Bobo. He rested his cheek against the cold clay, waiting.

A dog barked. He stiffened. It barked again. He balled himself into a knot at the bottom of the hole, waiting. Then he heard the patter of dog feet.

"Look!"

"Whuts he got?"

"Its a snake!"

"Yeah, the dogs foun a snake!"

"Gee, its a big one!"

"Shucks, Ah wish he could fin one of them sonofabitchin niggers!"

The voices sank to low murmurs. Then he heard number twelve, its bell tolling and whistle crying as it slid along the rails. He flattened himself against the clay. Someone was singing:

"We'll hang ever nigger t a sour apple tree . . ."

When the song ended there was hard laughter. From the other side of the hill he heard the dog barking furiously. He listened. There was more than one dog now. There were many and they were barking their throats out.

"Hush, Ah hear them dogs!"

"When theys barkin like tha theys foun somethin!"

"Here they come over the hill!"

"WE GOT IM! WE GOT IM!"

There came a roar. Tha mus be Bobo; tha mus be Bobo . . . In spite of his fear, Big Boy looked. The road, and half of the hillside across the road, were covered with men. A few were at the top of the hill, stenciled against the sky. He could see dark forms moving up the slopes. They were yelling.

"By Gawd, we got im!"

"C mon!"

"Where is he?"

"Theyre bringin im over the hill!"

"Ah got a rope fer im!"

"Say, somebody go n git the others!"

"Where is he? Cant we see im, Mister?"

"They say Berthas comin, too."

"Jack! Jack! Don leave me! Ah wanna see im!"

"Theyre bringin im over the hill, sweetheart!"

"AH WANNA BE THE FIRS T PUT A ROPE ON THA BLACK BASTARDS NECK!"

"Les start the fire!"

"Heat the tar!"

"Ah got some chains t chain im."

"Bring im over this way!"

"Chris, Ah wished Ah hada drink . . ."

Big Boy saw men moving over the hill. Among them was a long dark spot. Tha mus be Bobo; tha mus be Bobo theys carryin . . . They'll git im here. He oughta git up n run. He clamped his teeth and ran his hand across his forehead, bringing it away wet. He tried to swallow, but could not; his throat was dry.

They had started the song again:

"We'll hang ever nigger t a sour apple tree . . ."

There were women singing now. Their voices made the song round and full. Song waves rolled over the top of pine trees. The sky sagged low, heavy with clouds. Wind was rising. Sometimes cricket cries cut surprisingly across the mob song. A dog had gone to the utmost top of the hill. At each lull of the song his howl floated full into the night.

Big Boy shrank when he saw the first tall flame light the hillside. Would they see im here? Then he remembered you could not see into the dark if you were standing in the light. As flames leaped higher he saw two men rolling a barrel up the slope.

"Say, gimme a han here, will yuh?"

"Awright, heave!"

"C mon! Straight up! Git t the other end!"

"Ah got the feathers here in this pillar!"

"BRING SOME MO WOOD!"

Big Boy could see the barrel surrounded by flames. The mob fell back, forming a dark circle. Theyd fin im here! He had a wild impulse to climb out and fly across the hills. But his legs would not move. He stared hard, trying to find Bobo. His eyes played over a long dark spot near the fire. Fanned by wind, flames leaped higher. He jumped. That dark spot had moved. Lawd, thas Bobo; thas Bobo . . .

He smelt the scent of tar, faint at first, then stronger. The wind brought it full into his face, then blew it away. His eyes burned and he rubbed them with his knuckles. He sneezed.

"LES GIT SOURVINEERS!"

He saw the mob close in around the fire. Their faces were hard and sharp in the light of the flames. More men and women were coming over the hill. The long dark spot was smudged out.

"Everybody git back!"

"Look! Hes gotta finger!"

"C MON! GIT THE GALS BACK FROM THE FIRE!"

"Hes got one of his ears, see?"

"Whuts the matter!"

"A woman fell out! Fainted, Ah reckon . . ."

The stench of tar permeated the hillside. The sky was black and the wind was blowing hard.

"HURRY UP N BURN THE NIGGER FO IT RAINS!"

Big Boy saw the mob fall back, leaving a small knot of men about the fire. Then, for the first time, he had a full glimpse of Bobo. A black body flashed in the light. Bobo was struggling, twisting; they were binding his arms and legs . . .

When he saw them tilt the barrel he stiffened. A scream quivered. He knew the tar was on Bobo. The mob fell back. He saw a tar-drenched body glistening and turning.

"THE BASTARDS GOT IT!"

There was a sudden quiet. Then he shrank violently as the wind carried, like a flurry of snow, a widening spiral of white feathers into the night. The flames leaped tall as the trees. The scream came again. Big Boy trembled and looked. The mob was running down the slopes, leaving the fire clear. Then he saw a writhing white mass cradled in yellow flame, and heard screams, one on top of the other, each shriller and shorter than the last. The mob was quiet now, standing still, looking up the slopes at the writhing white mass gradually growing black, growing black in a cradle of yellow flame.

"PO ON MO GAS!"

"Gimme a lif, will yuh!"

Two men were struggling, carrying between them a heavy can. They set it down, tilted it, leaving it so that the gas would trickle down to the hollowed earth around the fire.

Big Boy slid back into the hole, his face buried in clay. He had no feelings now, no fears. He was numb, empty, as though all blood had been drawn from him. Then his muscles flexed taut when he heard a faint patter. A tiny stream of cold water seeped to his knees, making him push back to a drier spot. He looked up; rain was beating in the grass.

"Its rainin!"

"C mon, les git t town!"

". . . don worry, when the fire git thu wid im hell be gone . . ."

"Wait, Charles! Don leave me; its slippery here . . ."

"Ahll take some of yuh ladies back in mah car . . ."

Big Boy heard the dogs barking again, this time closer. Running feet pounded past. Cold water chilled his ankles. He could hear raindrops steadily hissing.

Now a dog was barking at the mouth of the hole, barking furiously, sensing a presence there. He balled himself into a knot and clung to the bottom, his knees and shins buried in water. The bark came louder. He heard paws scraping and felt the hot scent of dog breath on his face. Green eyes glowed and drew nearer as the barking, muffled by the closeness of the hole, beat upon his eardrums. Backing till his shoulders pressed against the clay, he held his breath. He pushed out his hands, his fingers stiff. The dog yawped louder, advancing, his bark rising sharp and thin. Big Boy rose to his knees, his hands before him. Then he flattened out still more against the bottom, breathing lungsful of hot dog scent, breathing it slowly, hard, but evenly. The dog came closer, bringing hotter dog scent. Big Boy could go back no more. His knees were slipping and slopping in the water. He braced himself, ready. Then, he never exactly knew how—he never knew whether he had lunged or the dog had lunged—they were together, rolling in the water. The green eyes were beneath him, between his legs. Dognails bit into his arms. His knees slipped backward and he landed full on the dog; the dog's breath left in a heavy gasp. Instinctively, he fumbled for the throat as he felt the dog twisting between his knees. The dog snarled, long and low, as though gathering strength. Big Boy's hands traveled swiftly over the dog's back, groping for the throat. He felt dognails again and saw green eyes, but his fingers had found the throat. He choked, feeling his fingers sink; he choked, throwing back his head and stiffening his arms. He felt the dog's body heave, felt dognails digging into his loins. With strength flowing from fear, he closed his fingers, pushing his full weight on the dog's throat. The dog heaved again, and lay still . . . Big Boy heard the sound of his own breathing filling the hole, and heard shouts and footsteps above him going past.

For a long, long time he held the dog, held it long after the last footstep had died out, long after the rain had stopped.

V

Morning found him still on his knees in a puddle of rainwater, staring at the stiff body of a dog. As the air brightened he came to himself slowly. He held still for a long time, as though waking from a dream, as though trying to remember.

The chug of a truck came over the hill. He tried to crawl to the opening. His knees were stiff and a thousand needle-like pains shot from the bottom of his feet to the calves of his legs. Giddiness made his eyes blur. He pulled up and looked. Through brackish light he saw Will's truck standing some twenty-five yards away, the engine running. Will stood on the running board, looking over the slopes of the hill.

Big Boy scuffled out, falling weekly in the wet grass. He tried to call to Will, but his dry throat would make no sound. He tried again.

"Will!"

Will heard, answering:

"Big Boy, c mon!"

He tried to run, and fell. Will came, meeting him in the tall grass.

"C mon," Will said, catching his arm.

They struggled to the truck.

"Hurry up!" said Will, pushing him onto the running board.

Will pushed back a square trapdoor which swung above the back of the driver's seat. Big Boy pulled through, landing with a thud on the bottom. On hands and knees he looked around in the semi-darkness.

"Wheres Bobo?"

Big Boy stared.

"Wheres Bobo?"

"They got im."

"When?"

"Las night."

"The mob?"

Big Boy pointed in the direction of a charred sapling on the slope of the opposite hill. Will looked. The trapdoor fell. The engine purred, the gears whined, and the truck lurched forward over the muddy road, sending Big Boy on his side.

For a while he lay as he had fallen, on his side, too weak to move. As he felt the truck swing around a curve he straightened up and rested his back against a stack of wooden boxes. Slowly, he began to make out objects in the darkness. Through two long cracks fell thin blades of daylight. The floor was of smooth steel, and cold to his thighs. Splinters and bits of sawdust danced with the rumble of the truck. Each time they swung around a curve he was pulled over the floor; he grabbed at corners of boxes to steady himself. Once he heard the crow of a rooster. It made him think of home, of ma and pa. He thought he remembered hearing somewhere that the house had burned, but could not remember where . . . It all seemed unreal now.

He was tired. He dozed, swaying with the lurch. Then he jumped awake. The truck was running smoothly, on gravel. Far away he heard two short blasts from the Buckeye Lumber Mill. Unconsciously, the thought sang through his mind: Its six erclock . . .

The trapdoor swung in. Will spoke through a corner of his mouth.

"How yuh comin?"

"Awright."

"How they git Bobo?"

"He wuz comin over the hill."

"What they do?"

"They burnt im . . . Will, Ah wan some water; mah throats like fire . . ."

"Well git some when we pass a fillin station."

Big Boy leaned back and dozed. He jerked awake when the truck stopped. He heard Will git out. He wanted to peep through the trapdoor, but was afraid. For a moment, the wild fear he had known in the hole came back. Spose theyd search n fin im? He quieted when he heard Will's footstep on the running board. The trapdoor pushed in. Will's hat came through dripping.

"Take it quick!"

Big Boy grabbed, spilling water into his face. The truck lurched. He drank. Hard cold lumps of brick rolled into his hot stomach. A dull pain made him bend over. His intestines seemed to be drawing into a tight knot. After a bit it eased, and he sat up, breathing softly.

The truck swerved. He blinked his eyes. The blades of daylight had turned brightly golden. The sun had risen.

The truck sped over the asphalt miles, sped northward, jolting him, shaking out of his bosom the crumbs of corn bread, making them dance with the splinters and sawdust in the golden blades of sunshine.

He turned on his side and slept.

Barn Burning

William Faulkner

WILLIAM FAULKNER *(1897–1962) lived most of his life in Oxford, Mississippi, with some time spent in New Orleans, New York, Canada, Europe, and—in his later years—Virginia. Faulkner's short stories and novels have received critical acceptance throughout the world; in 1950 he was awarded the Nobel Prize. Among his most discussed novels are* The Sound and the Fury *(1929),* As I Lay Dying *(1930),* Light in August *(1932),* Absalom, Absalom! *(1936), and* The Hamlet *(1940); short-story collections are represented by* Go Down, Moses *(1942), which includes "The Bear,"* Dr. Martino and Other Stories *(1934),* These 13 *(1931), and* Collected Stories *(1950). Faulkner is considered to be among the best American writers of the twentieth century; a major creative contribution was his use of local Mississippi background, along with his unique style, to present so-called local color stories with universal application.*

The store in which the Justice of the Peace's court was sitting smelled of cheese. The boy, crouched on his nail keg at the back of the crowded room, knew he smelled cheese, and more: from where he sat he could see the ranked shelves close-packed with the solid, squat, dynamic shapes of tin cans whose labels his stomach read, not from the lettering which meant nothing to his mind but from the scarlet devils and the silver curve of fish—this, the cheese which he knew he smelled and the hermetic meat which his intestines believed he smelled coming in intermittent gusts momentary and brief between the other constant one, the smell and sense just a little of fear because mostly of despair and grief, the old fierce pull of blood. He could not see the table where the Justice sat and before which his father and his father's enemy (*our enemy* he thought in that despair; *ourn! mine and hisn both! He's my father!*) stood, but he could hear them, the two of them that is, because his father had said no word yet:

"But what proof have you, Mr. Harris?"

"I told you. The hog got into my corn. I caught it up and sent it back to him. He had no fence that would hold it. I told him so, warned him. The next time I put the hog in my pen. When he came to get it I gave him enough wire to patch up his pen. The next time I put the hog up and kept it. I rode down to his house and saw the wire I gave him still rolled on to the spool in his yard. I told him he could have the hog when he paid me a dollar pound fee. That evening a nigger came with the dollar and got the hog. He was a strange nigger. He said, 'He say to tell you wood and hay kin burn.' I said, 'What?' 'That whut he say to tell you,' the nigger said. 'Wood and hay kin burn.' That night my barn burned. I got the stock out but I lost the barn."

"Where is the nigger? Have you got him?"

"He was a strange nigger, I tell you. I don't know what became of him."

"But that's not proof. Don't you see that's not proof?"

"Get that boy up here. He knows." For a moment the boy thought too that the man meant his older brother until Harris said, "Not him. The little one. The boy," and, crouching, small for his age, small and wiry like his father, in patched and faded jeans even too small for him, with straight, uncombed, brown hair and eyes gray and wild as storm scud, he saw the men between himself and the table part and become a lane of grim faces, at the end of which he saw the Justice, a shabby, collarless, graying man in spectacles, beckoning him. He felt no floor under his bare feet; he seemed to walk beneath the palpable weight of the grim turning faces. His father, stiff in his black Sunday coat donned not for the trial but for the moving, did not even look at him. *He aims for me to lie,* he thought, again with that frantic grief and despair. *And I will have to do hit.*

"What's your name, boy?" the Justice said.

"Colonel Sartoris Snopes," the boy whispered.

"Hey?" the Justice said. "Talk louder. Colonel Sartoris? I reckon anybody named for Colonel Sartoris in this country can't help but tell the truth, can they?" The boy said nothing. *Enemy! Enemy!* he thought; for a moment he could not even see, could not see that the Justice's face was kindly nor discern that his voice was troubled when he spoke to the man named Harris: "Do you want me to question this boy?" But he could hear, and during those subsequent long seconds while there was absolutely no sound in the crowded little room save that of quiet and intent breathing it was as if he had swung outward at the end of a grape vine, over a ravine, and at the top of the swing had been caught in a prolonged instant of mesmerized gravity, weightless in time.

"No!" Harris said violently, explosively. "Damnation! Send him out of here!" Now time, the fluid world, rushed beneath him again, the voices coming to him again through the smell of cheese and sealed meat, the fear and despair and the old grief of blood:

"This case is closed. I can't find against you, Snopes, but I can give you advice. Leave this country and don't come back to it."

His father spoke for the first time, his voice cold and harsh, level, without emphasis: "I aim to. I don't figure to stay in a country among people who . . ." he said something unprintable and vile, addressed to no one.

"That'll do," the Justice said. "Take your wagon and get out of this country before dark. Case dismissed."

His father turned, and he followed the stiff black coat, the wiry figure walking a little stiffly from where a Confederate provost's man's musket ball had taken him in the heel on a stolen horse thirty years ago, followed the two backs now, since his older brother had appeared from somewhere in the crowd, no taller than the father but thicker, chewing tobacco steadily, between the two lines of grim-faced men and out of the store and across the worn gallery and down the sagging steps and among the dogs and half-grown boys in the mild May dust, where as he passed a voice hissed:

"Barn burner!"

Again he could not see, whirling; there was a face in a red haze, moonlike, bigger than the full moon, the owner of it half again his size, he leaping in the red haze toward the face, feeling no blow, feeling no shock when his head struck the earth, scrabbling up and leaping again, feeling no blow this time either and tasting no blood, scrabbling up to see the other boy in full flight and himself already leaping into pursuit as his father's hand jerked him back, the harsh, cold voice speaking above him: "Go get in the wagon."

It stood in a grove of locusts and mulberries across the road. His two hulking sisters in their Sunday dresses and his mother and her sister in calico and sunbonnets were already in it, sitting on and among the sorry residue of the dozen and more movings which even the boy could remember—the battered stove, the broken beds and chairs, the clock inlaid with mother-of-pearl, which would not run, stopped at some fourteen minutes past two o'clock of a dead and forgotten day and time, which had been his mother's dowry. She was crying, though when she saw him she drew her sleeve across her face and began to descend from the wagon. "Get back," the father said.

"He's hurt. I got to get some water and wash his . . ."

"Get back in the wagon," his father said. He got in too, over the tailgate. His father mounted to the seat where the older brother already sat and struck the gaunt mules two savage blows with the peeled willow, but without heat. It was not even sadistic; it was exactly that same quality which in later years would cause his descendants to over-run the engine before putting a motor car into motion, striking and reining back in the same movement. The wagon went on, the store with its quiet crowd of grimly watching men dropped behind; a curve in the road hid it. *Forever* he thought. *Maybe he's done satisfied now, now that he has . . .* stopping himself, not to say it aloud even to himself. His mother's hand touched his shoulder.

"Does hit hurt?" she said.

"Naw," he said. "Hit don't hurt. Lemme be."

"Can't you wipe some of the blood off before hit dries?"

"I'll wash to-night," he said. "Lemme be, I tell you."

The wagon went on. He did not know where they were going. None of them ever did or ever asked, because it was always somewhere, always a house of sorts waiting for them a day or two days or even three days away. Likely his father had already arranged to make a crop on another farm before he . . . Again he had to stop himself. He (the father) always did. There was something about his wolflike independence and even courage when the advantage was at least neutral which impressed strangers, as if they got from his latent ravening ferocity not so much a sense of dependability as a feeling that his ferocious conviction in the rightness of his own actions would be of advantage to all whose interest lay with his.

That night they camped, in a grove of oaks and beeches where a spring ran. The nights were still cool and they had a fire against it, of a rail lifted from a nearby fence and cut into lengths—a small fire, neat, niggard almost, a shrewd fire; such fires were his father's habit and custom always, even in freezing weather. Older, the boy might have remarked this and wondered why not a big one; why should not a man who had not only seen the waste and extravagance of war, but who had in his blood an inherent voracious prodigality with material not his own, have burned everything in sight? Then he might have gone a step farther and thought that that was the reason: that niggard blaze was the living fruit of nights passed during those four years in the woods hiding from all men, blue or gray, with his strings of horses (captured horses, he called them). And older still, he might have divined the true reason: that the element of fire spoke to some deep mainspring of his father's being, as the element of steel or of powder spoke to other men, as the one weapon for the preservation of integrity, else breath were not worth the breathing, and hence to be regarded with respect and used with discretion.

But he did not think this now and he had seen those same niggard blazes all his life. He merely ate his supper beside it and was already half asleep over his iron plate when his father called him, and once more he followed the stiff back, the stiff and ruthless limp, up the slope and on to the starlit road where, turning, he could see his father against the stars but without face or depth—a shape black, flat, and bloodless as though cut from tin in the iron folds of the frockcoat which had not been made for him, the voice harsh like tin and without heat like tin:

"You were fixing to tell them. You would have told him." He didn't answer. His father struck him with the flat of his hand on the side of the head, hard but without heat, exactly as he had struck the two mules at the store, exactly as he would strike either of them with any stick in order to kill a horse fly, his voice still without heat or anger: "You're getting to be a man. You got to learn. You got to learn to stick to your own blood or you ain't going to have any blood to stick to you. Do you think either of them, any man there this morning, would? Don't you know all they wanted was a chance to get at me because they knew I had them beat? Eh?" Later, twenty years later, he was to tell himself, "If I had said they wanted only truth, justice, he would have hit me again." But now he said nothing. He was not crying. He just stood there. "Answer me," his father said.

"Yes," he whispered. His father turned.

"Get on to bed. We'll be there to-morrow."

To-morrow they were there. In the early afternoon the wagon stopped before a paintless two-room house identical almost with the dozen others it had stopped before even in the boy's ten years, and again, as on the other dozen occasions, his mother and aunt got down and began to unload the wagon, although his two sisters and his father and brother had not moved.

"Likely hit ain't fitten for hawgs," one of the sisters said.

"Nevertheless, fit it will and you'll hog it and like it," his father said. "Get out of them chairs and help your Ma unload."

The two sisters got down, big, bovine, in a flutter of cheap ribbons; one of them drew from the jumbled wagon bed a battered lantern, the other a worn broom. His father handed the reins to the older son and began to climb stiffly over the wheel. "When they get unloaded, take the team to the barn and feed them." Then he said, and at first the boy thought he was still speaking to his brother: "Come with me."

"Me?" he said.

"Yes," his father said. "You."

"Abner," his mother said. His father paused and looked back—the harsh level stare beneath the shaggy, graying, irascible brows.

"I reckon I'll have a word with the man that aims to begin to-morrow owning me body and soul for the next eight months."

They went back up the road. A week ago—or before last night, that is—he would have asked where they were going, but not now. His father had struck him before last night but never before had he paused afterward to explain why; it was as if the blow and the following calm, outrageous voice still rang, repercussed, divulging nothing to him save the terrible handicap of being young, the light weight of his few years, just heavy enough to prevent his soaring free of the world as it seemed to be ordered but not heavy enough to keep him footed solid in it, to resist it and try to change the course of its events.

Presently he could see the grove of oaks and cedars and the other flowering trees and shrubs where the house would be, though not the house yet. They walked beside a fence massed with honeysuckle and Cherokee roses and came to a gate swinging open between two brick pillars, and now, beyond a sweep of drive, he saw the house for the first time and at that instant he forgot his father and the terror and despair both, and even when he remembered his father again (who had not stopped) the terror and despair did not return. Because, for all the twelve movings, they had sojourned until now in a poor country, a land of small farms and fields and houses, and he had never seen a house like this before. *Hit's big as a courthouse* he thought quietly, with a surge of peace and joy whose reason he could not have thought into words, being too young for that: *They are safe from him. People whose lives are a part of this peace and dignity are beyond his touch, he no more to them than a buzzing wasp: capable of stinging for a little moment but that's all; the spell of this peace and dignity rendering even the barns and stable and cribs which belong to it impervious to the puny flames he might contrive* . . . this, the peace and joy, ebbing for an instant as he looked again at the stiff black back, the stiff and implacable limp of the figure which was not dwarfed by the house, for the reason that it had never looked big anywhere and which now, against the serene columned backdrop, had more than ever that impervious quality of something cut ruthlessly from tin, depthless, as though, sidewise to the sun, it would cast no shadow. Watching him, the boy remarked the absolutely undeviating course which his father held and saw the stiff foot come squarely down in a pile of fresh droppings where a horse had stood in the drive and which his father could have avoided by a simple change of stride. But it ebbed only for a moment, though he could not have thought this into words either, walking on in the spell of the house, which he could even want but without envy, without sorrow, certainly never with that ravening and jealous rage which unknown to him walked in the ironlike black coat before him: *Maybe he will feel it too. Maybe it will even change him now from what maybe he couldn't help but be.*

They crossed the portico. Now he could hear his father's stiff foot as it came down on the boards with clocklike finality, a sound out of all proportion to the displacement of the body it bore and which was not dwarfed either by the white door before it, as though it had attained to a sort of vicious and ravening minimum not to be dwarfed by anything—the flat, wide, black hat, the formal coat of broadcloth which had once been black but which had now that friction-glazed greenish cast of the bodies of old house flies, the lifted sleeve which was too large, the lifted hand like a curled claw. The door opened so promptly that the boy knew the Negro must have been watching them all the time, an old man with neat grizzled hair, in a linen jacket, who stood barring the door with his body, saying, "Wipe yo foots, white man, fo you come in here. Major ain't home nohow."

"Get out of my way, nigger," his father said, without heat too, flinging the door back and the Negro also and entering, his hat still on his head. And now the boy saw the prints of the stiff foot on the doorjamb and saw them appear on the pale rug behind the machinelike deliberation of the foot which seemed to bear (or transmit) twice the weight which the body compassed. The Negro was shouting "Miss Lula! Miss Lula!" somewhere behind them, then the boy, deluged as though by a warm wave by a suave turn of carpeted stair and a pendant glitter of chandeliers and a mute gleam of gold frames, heard the swift feet and saw her too, a lady—perhaps he had never seen her like before either—in a gray, smooth gown with lace at the throat and an apron tied at the waist and the sleeves turned back, wiping cake or biscuit dough from her hands with a towel as she came up the hall, looking not at his father at all but at the tracks on the blond rug with an expression of incredulous amazement.

"I tried," the Negro cried. "I tole him to . . ."

"Will you please go away?" she said in a shaking voice. "Major de Spain is not at home. Will you please go away?"

His father had not spoken again. He did not speak again. He did not even look at her. He just stood stiff in the center of the rug, in his hat, the shaggy iron-gray brows twitching slightly above the pebble-colored eyes as he appeared to examine the house with brief deliberation. Then with the same deliberation he turned; the boy watched him pivot on the good leg and saw the stiff foot drag round the arc of the turning, leaving a final long and fading smear. His father never looked at it, he never once looked down at the rug. The Negro held the door. It closed behind them, upon the hysteric and indistinguishable woman-wail. His father stopped at the top of the steps and scraped his boot clean on the edge of it. At the gate he stopped again. He stood for a moment, planted stiffly on the stiff foot, looking back at the house. "Pretty and white, ain't it?" he said. "That's sweat. Nigger sweat. Maybe it ain't white enough yet to suit him. Maybe he wants to mix some white sweat with it."

Two hours later the boy was chopping wood behind the house within which his mother and aunt and the two sisters (the mother and aunt, not the two girls, he knew that; even at this distance and muffled by walls the flat loud voices of the two girls emanated an incorrigible idle inertia) were setting up the stove to prepare a meal, when he heard the hooves and saw the linen-clad man on a fine sorrel mare, whom he recognized even before he saw the rolled rug in front of the Negro youth following on a fat bay carriage horse—a suffused, angry face vanishing, still at full gallop, beyond the corner of the house where his father and brother were sitting in the two tilted chairs; and a moment later, almost before he could have put the axe down, he heard the hooves again and watched the sorrel mare go back out of the yard, already galloping again. Then his father began to shout one of the sisters' names, who presently emerged backward from the kitchen door dragging the rolled rug along the ground by one end while the other sister walked behind it.

"If you ain't going to tote, go on and set up the wash pot," the first said.

"You, Sarty!" the second shouted. "Set up the wash pot!" His father appeared at the door, framed against that shabbiness, as he had been against that other bland perfection, impervious to either, the mother's anxious face at his shoulder.

"Go on," the father said. "Pick it up." The two sisters stooped, broad, lethargic; stooping, they presented an incredible expanse of pale cloth and a flutter of tawdry ribbons.

"If I thought enough of a rug to have to git hit all the way from France I wouldn't keep hit where folks coming in would have to tromp on hit," the first said. They raised the rug.

"Abner," the mother said. "Let me do it."

"You go back and git dinner," his father said. "I'll tend to this."

From the woodpile through the rest of the afternoon the boy watched them, the rug spread flat in the dust beside the bubbling wash pot, the two sisters stooping over it with that profound and lethargic reluctance, while the father stood over them in turn, implacable and grim, driving them though never raising his voice again. He could smell the harsh homemade lye they were using; he saw his mother come to the door once and look toward them with an expression not anxious now but very like despair; he saw his father turn, and he fell to with the axe and saw from the corner of his eye his father raise from the ground a flattish fragment of field stone and examine it and return to the pot, and this time his mother actually spoke: "Abner. Abner. Please don't. Please, Abner."

Then he was done too. It was dusk; the whippoorwills had already begun. He could smell coffee from the room where they would presently eat the cold food remaining from the mid-afternoon meal, though when he entered the house he realized they were having coffee again probably because there was a fire on the hearth, before which the rug now lay spread over the backs of the two chairs. The tracks of his father's foot were gone. Where they had been were now long, water-cloudy scorifications resembling the sporadic course of a lilliputian mowing machine.

It still hung there while they ate the cold food and then went to bed, scattered without order or claim up and down the two rooms, his mother in one bed, where his father would later lie, the older brother in the other, himself, the aunt, and the two sisters on pallets on the floor. But his father was not in bed yet. The last thing the boy remembered was the depthless, harsh silhouette of the hat and coat bending over the rug and it seemed to him that he had not even closed his eyes when the silhouette was standing over him, the fire almost dead behind it, the stiff foot prodding him awake. "Catch up the mule," his father said.

When he returned with the mule his father was standing in the black door, the rolled rug over his shoulder. "Ain't you going to ride?" he said.

"No. Give me your foot."

He bent his knee into his father's hand, the wiry, surprising power flowed smoothly, rising, he rising with it, on to the mule's bare back (they had owned a saddle once; the boy could remember it though not when or where) and with the same effortlessness his father swung the rug up in front of him. Now in the starlight they retraced the afternoon's path, up the dusty road rife with honeysuckle, through the gate and up the black tunnel of the drive to the lightless house, where he sat on the mule and felt the rough warp of the rug drag across his thighs and vanish.

"Don't you want me to help?" he whispered. His father did not answer and now he heard again that stiff foot striking the hollow portico with that wooden and clocklike deliberation, that outrageous overstatement of the weight it carried. The rug, hunched, not flung (the boy could tell that even in the darkness) from his father's shoulder struck the angle of wall and floor with a sound unbelievably loud, thunderous, then the foot again, unhurried and enormous; a light came on in the house and the boy sat, tense, breathing steadily and quietly and just a little fast, though the foot itself did not increase its beat at all, descending the steps now; now the boy could see him.

"Don't you want to ride now?" he whispered. "We kin both ride now," the light within the house altering now, flaring up and sinking. *He's coming down the stairs now,* he thought. He had already ridden the mule up beside the horse block; presently his father was up behind him and he doubled the reins over and slashed the mule across the neck, but before the animal could begin to trot the hard, thin arm came round him, the hard, knotted hand jerking the mule back to a walk.

In the first red rays of the sun they were in the lot, putting plow gear on the mules. This time the sorrel mare was in the lot before he heard it at all, the rider collarless and even bare-headed, trembling, speaking in a shaking voice as the woman in the house had done, his father merely looking up once before stooping again to the hame he was buckling, so that the man on the mare spoke to his stooping back:

"You must realize you have ruined that rug. Wasn't there anybody here, any of your women . . ." he ceased, shaking, the boy watching him, the older brother leaning now in the stable door, chewing, blinking slowly and steadily at nothing apparently. "It cost a hundred dollars. But you never had a hundred dollars. You never will. So I'm going to charge you twenty bushels of corn against your crop. I'll add it in your contract and when you come to the commissary you can sign it. That won't keep Mrs. de Spain quiet but maybe it will teach you to wipe your feet off before you enter her house again."

Then he was gone. The boy looked at his father, who still had not spoken or even looked up again, who was now adjusting the logger-head in the hame.

"Pap," he said. His father looked at him—the inscrutable face, the shaggy brows beneath which the gray eyes glinted coldly. Suddenly the boy went toward him, fast, stopping as suddenly. "You done the best you could!" he cried. "If he wanted hit done different why didn't he wait and tell you how? He won't git no twenty bushels! He won't git none! We'll gether hit and hide hit! I kin watch . . ."

"Did you put the cutter back in that straight stock like I told you?"

"No, sir," he said.

"Then go do it."

That was Wednesday. During the rest of that week he worked steadily, at what was within his scope and some which was beyond it, with an industry that did not need to be driven nor even commanded twice; he had this from his mother, with the difference that some at least of what he did he liked to do, such as splitting wood with the half-size axe which his mother and aunt had earned, or saved money somehow, to present him with at Christmas. In company with the two older women (and on one afternoon, even one of the sisters), he built pens for the shoat and the cow which were a part of his father's contract with the landlord, and one afternoon, his father being absent, gone somewhere on one of the mules, he went to the field.

They were running a middle buster now, his brother holding the plow straight while he handled the reins, and walking beside the straining mule, the rich black soil shearing cool and damp against his bare ankles, he thought *Maybe this is the end of it. Maybe even that twenty bushels that seems hard to have to pay for just a rug will be a cheap price for him to stop forever and always from being what he used to be;* thinking, dreaming now, so that his brother had to speak sharply to him to mind the mule: *Maybe he even won't collect the twenty bushels. Maybe it will all add up and balance and vanish—corn, rug, fire; the terror and grief, the being pulled two ways like between two teams of horses—gone, done with for ever and ever.*

Then it was Saturday; he looked up from beneath the mule he was harnessing and saw his father in the black coat and hat. "Not that," his father said. "The wagon gear." And then, two hours later, sitting in the wagon bed behind his father and brother on the seat, the wagon accomplished a final curve, and he saw the weathered paintless store with its tattered tobacco- and patent-medicine posters and the tethered wagons and saddle animals below the gallery. He mounted the gnawed steps behind his father and brother, and there again was the lane of quiet, watching faces for the three of them to walk through. He saw the man in spectacles sitting at the plank table and he did not need to be told this was a Justice of the Peace; he sent one glare of fierce, exultant, partisan defiance at the man in collar and cravat now, whom he had seen but twice before in his life, and that on a galloping horse, who now wore on his face an expression not of rage but of amazed unbelief which the boy could not have known was at the incredible circumstance of being sued by one of his own tenants, and came and stood against his father and cried at the Justice: "He ain't done it! He ain't burnt . . ."

"Go back to the wagon," his father said.

"Burnt?" the Justice said. "Do I understand this rug was burned too?"

"Does anybody here claim it was?" his father said. "Go back to the wagon." But he did not, he merely retreated to the rear of the room, crowded as that other had been, but not to sit down this time, instead, to stand pressing among the motionless bodies, listening to the voices:

"And you claim twenty bushels of corn is too high for the damage you did to the rug?"

"He brought the rug to me and said he wanted the tracks washed out of it. I washed the tracks out and took the rug back to him."

"But you didn't carry the rug back to him in the same condition it was in before you made the tracks on it."

His father did not answer, and now for perhaps half a minute there was no sound at all save that of breathing, the faint, steady suspiration of complete and intent listening.

"You decline to answer that, Mr. Snopes?" Again his father did not answer. "I'm going to find against you, Mr. Snopes. I'm going to find that you were responsible for the injury to Major de Spain's rug and hold you liable for it. But twenty bushels of corn seems a little high for a man in your circumstances to have to pay. Major de Spain claims it cost a hundred dollars. October corn will be worth about fifty cents. I figure that if Major de Spain can stand a ninety-five dollar loss on something he paid cash for, you can stand a five-dollar loss you haven't earned yet. I hold you in damages to Major de Spain to the amount of ten bushels of corn over and above your contract with him, to be paid to him out of your crop at gathering time. Court adjourned."

It had taken no time hardly, the morning was but half begun. He thought they would return home and perhaps back to the field, since they were late, far behind all other farmers. But instead his father passed on behind the wagon, merely indicating with his hand for the older brother to follow with it, and crossed the road toward the blacksmith shop opposite, pressing on after his father, overtaking him, speaking, whispering up at the harsh, calm face beneath the weathered hat: "He won't git no ten bushels neither. He won't git one. We'll . . ." until his father glanced for an instant down at him, the face absolutely calm, the grizzled eyebrows tangled above the cold eyes, the voice almost pleasant, almost gentle:

"You think so? Well, we'll wait till October anyway."

The matter of the wagon—the setting of a spoke or two and the tightening of the tires—did not take long either, the business of the tires accomplished by driving the wagon into the spring branch behind the shop and letting it stand there, the mules nuzzling into the water from time to time, and the boy on the seat with the idle reins, looking up the slope and through the sooty tunnel of the shed where the slow hammer rang and where his father sat on an upended cypress bolt, easily, either talking or listening, still sitting there when the boy brought the dripping wagon up out of the branch and halted it before the door.

"Take them on to the shade and hitch," his father said. He did so and returned. His father and the smith and a third man squatting on his heels inside the door were talking, about crops and animals; the boy, squatting too in the ammoniac dust and hoof-parings and scales of rust, heard his father tell a long and unhurried story out of the time before the birth of the older brother even when he had been a professional horsetrader. And then his father came up beside him where he stood before a tattered last year's circus poster on the other side of the store, gazing rapt and quiet at the scarlet horses, the incredible poisings and convolutions of tulle and tights and the painted leers of comedians, and said, "It's time to eat."

But not at home. Squatting beside his brother against the front wall, he watched his father emerge from the store and produce from a paper sack a segment of cheese and divide it carefully and deliberately into three with his pocket knife and produce crackers from the same sack. They all three squatted on the gallery and ate, slowly, without talking; then in the store again, they drank from a tin dipper tepid water smelling of the cedar bucket and of living beech trees. And still they did not go home. It was a horse lot this time, a tall rail fence upon and along which men stood and sat and out of which one by one horses were led, to be walked and trotted and then cantered back and forth along the road while the slow swapping and buying went on and the sun began to slant westward, they—the three of them—watching and listening, the older brother with his muddy eyes and his steady, inevitable tobacco, the father commenting now and then on certain of the animals, to no one in particular.

It was after sundown when they reached home. They ate supper by lamplight, then, sitting on the doorstep, the boy watched the night fully accomplish, listening to the whippoorwills and the frogs, when he heard his mother's voice: "Abner! No! No! Oh, God. Oh, God. Abner!" and he rose, whirled, and saw the altered light through the door where a candle stub now burned in a bottleneck on the table and his father, still in the hat and coat, at once formal and burlesque as though dressed carefully for some shabby and ceremonial violence, emptying the reservoir of the lamp back into the five-gallon kerosene can from which it had been filled, while the mother tugged at his arm until he shifted the lamp to the other hand and flung her back, not savagely or viciously, just hard, into the wall, her hands flung out against the wall for balance, her mouth open and in her face the same quality of hopeless despair as had been in her voice. Then his father saw him standing in the door.

"Go to the barn and get that can of oil we were oiling the wagon with," he said. The boy did not move. Then he could speak.

"What . . ." he cried. "What are you . . ."

"Go get that oil," his father said. "Go."

Then he was moving, running, outside the house, toward the stable: this the old habit, the old blood which he had not been permitted to choose for himself, which had been bequeathed him willy nilly and which had run for so long (and who knew where, battening on what of outrage and savagery and lust) before it came to him. *I could keep on,* he thought. *I could run on and on and never look back, never need to see his face again. Only I can't. I can't,* the rusted can in his hand now, the liquid sploshing in it as he ran back to the house and into it, into the sound of his mother's weeping in the next room, and handed the can to his father.

"Ain't you going to even send a nigger?" he cried. "At least you sent a nigger before!"

This time his father didn't strike him. The hand came even faster than the blow had, the same hand which had set the can on the table with almost excruciating care flashing from the can toward him too quick for him to follow it, gripping him by the back of his shirt and on to tiptoe before he had seen it quit the can, the face stooping at him in breathless and frozen ferocity, the cold, dead voice speaking over him to the older brother who leaned against the table, chewing with that steady, curious, sidewise motion of cows.

"Empty the can into the big one and go on. I'll catch up with you."

"Better tie him up to the bedpost," the brother said.

"Do like I told you," the father said. Then the boy was moving, his bunched shirt and the hard, bony hand between his shoulder-blades, his toes just touching the floor, across the room and into the other one, past the sisters sitting with spread heavy thighs in the two chairs over the cold hearth, and to where his mother and aunt sat side by side on the bed, the aunt's arms about his mother's shoulders.

"Hold him," the father said. The aunt made a startled movement. "Not you," the father said. "Lennie. Take hold of him. I want to see you do it." His mother took him by the wrist. "You'll hold him better than that. If he gets loose don't you know what he is going to do? He will go up yonder." He jerked his head toward the road. "Maybe I'd better tie him."

"I'll hold him," his mother whispered.

"See you do then." Then his father was gone, the stiff foot heavy and measured upon the boards, ceasing at last.

Then he began to struggle. His mother caught him in both arms, he jerking and wrenching at them. He would be stronger in the end, he knew that. But he had no time to wait for it. "Lemme go!" he cried. "I don't want to have to hit you!"

"Let him go!" the aunt said. "If he don't go, before God, I am going up there myself!"

"Don't you see I can't?" his mother cried. "Sarty! Sarty! No! No! Help me, Lizzie!"

Then he was free. His aunt grasped at him but it was too late. He whirled, running, his mother stumbled forward onto her knees behind him, crying to the nearer sister: "Catch him, Net! Catch him!" But that was too late too, the sister (the sisters were twins, born at the same time, yet either of them now gave the impression of being, encompassing as much living meat and volume and weight as any other two of the family) not yet having begun to rise from the chair, her head, face, alone merely turned, presenting to him in the flying instant an astonishing expanse of young female features untroubled by any surprise even, wearing only an expression of bovine interest. Then he was out of the room, out of the house, in the mild dust of the starlit road and the heavy rifeness of honeysuckle, the pale ribbon unspooling with terrific slowness under his running feet, reaching the gate at last and turning in, running, his heart and lungs drumming, on up the drive toward the lighted house, the lighted door. He did not knock, he burst in, sobbing for breath, incapable for the moment of speech; he saw the astonished face of the Negro in the linen jacket without knowing when the Negro had appeared.

"De Spain!" he cried, panted. "Where's . . ." then he saw the white man too emerging from a white door down the hall. "Barn!" he cried. "Barn!"

"What?" the white man said. "Barn?"

"Yes!" the boy cried. "Barn!"

"Catch him!" the white man shouted.

But it was too late this time too. The Negro grasped his shirt, but the entire sleeve, rotten with washing, carried away, and he was out that door too and in the drive again, and had actually never ceased to run even while he was screaming into the white man's face.

Behind him the white man was shouting, "My horse! Fetch my horse!" and he thought for an instant of cutting across the park and climbing the fence into the road, but he did not know the park nor how high the vine-massed fence might be and he dared not risk it. So he ran on down the drive, blood and breath roaring; presently he was in the road again though he could not see it. He could not hear either: the galloping mare was almost upon him before he heard her, and even then he held his course, as if the very urgency of his wild grief and need must in a moment more find him wings, waiting until the ultimate instant to hurl himself aside and into the weed-choked roadside ditch as the horse thundered past and on, for an instant in furious silhouette against the stars, the tranquil early summer night sky which, even before the shape of the horse and rider vanished, stained abruptly and violently upward: a long, swirling roar incredible and soundless, blotting the stars, and he springing up and into the road again, running again, knowing it was too late yet still running even after he heard the shot and, an instant later, two shots, pausing now without knowing he had ceased to run, crying "Pap! Pap!", running again before he knew he had begun to run, stumbling, tripping over something and scrabbling up again without ceasing to run, looking backward over his shoulder at the glare as he got up, running on among the invisible trees, panting, sobbing, "Father! Father!"

At midnight he was sitting on the crest of a hill. He did not know it was midnight and he did not know how far he had come. But there was no glare behind him now and he sat now, his back toward what he had called home for four days anyhow, his face toward the dark woods which he would enter when breath was strong again, small, shaking steadily in the chill darkness, hugging himself into the remainder of his thin, rotten shirt, the grief and despair now no longer terror and fear but just grief and despair. *Father. My father,* he thought. "He was brave!" he cried suddenly, aloud but not loud, no more than a whisper: "He was! He was in the war! He was in Colonel Sartoris' cav'ry!" not knowing that his father had gone to that war a private in the fine old European sense, wearing no uniform, admitting the authority of and giving fidelity to no man or army or flag, going to war as Malbrouck himself did: for booty—it meant nothing and less than nothing to him if it were enemy booty or his own.

The slow constellations wheeled on. It would be dawn and then sun-up after a while and he would be hungry. But that would be to-morrow and now he was only cold, and walking would cure that. His breathing was easier now and he decided to get up and go on, and then he found that he had been asleep because he knew it was almost dawn, the night almost over. He could tell that from the whippoorwills. They were everywhere now among the dark trees below him, constant and inflectioned and ceaseless, so that, as the instant for giving over to the day birds drew nearer and nearer, there was no interval at all between them. He got up. He was a little stiff, but walking would cure that too as it would the cold, and soon there would be the sun. He went on down the hill, toward the dark woods within which the liquid silver voices of the birds called unceasing—the rapid and urgent beating of the urgent and quiring heart of the late spring night. He did not look back.

Doubt thou the stars are fire;
Doubt that the sun doth move;
Doubt truth to be a liar;
But never doubt I love.

SHAKESPEARE, *Hamlet*

They sin who tell us love can die;
With life all other passions flee,
All others are but vanity. . . .
Love is indestructible,
Its holy flame forever burneth.

SOUTHEY, *The Curse of Kehama*

Many loves of many a mood and many a kind
Fill the eye of man, and would the secret mind.

SWINBURNE, *Erechtheus*

Part Two

THE FACES OF LOVE

Health Card

Frank Yerby

FRANK YERBY *(1916–   ), born in Augusta, Georgia, now lives in Spain. Educated at Augusta's Haines Institute and Paine College (B.A.), Fiske University (M.A.), with further graduate work at the University of Chicago, Yerby in 1946 became quickly successful as an author of popular historical romances beginning with his novel* The Foxes of Harrow. *Today Yerby is among the best-known contemporary black novelists in America. Earlier, in 1944, Yerby won an O. Henry Memorial Award with his first-published short story, "Health Card," which appeared in* Harper's. *At that time he also had other stories published in magazines such as* Phylon. *After the publication of* The Foxes of Harrow, *while he was teaching in southern colleges, he began his lucrative career as a popular novelist, and to date has written over twenty commercially successful books.*

Johnny stood under one of the streetlights on the corner and tried to read the letter. The streetlights down in the Bottom were so dim that he couldn't make out half the words, but he didn't need to: he knew them all by heart anyway.

"Sugar," he read, "it took a long time but I done it. I got the money to come to see you. I waited and waited for them to give you a furlough, but it look like they don't mean to. Sugar, I can't wait no longer. I got to see you. I got to. Find a nice place for me to stay—where we can be happy together. You know what I mean. With all my love, Lily."

Johnny folded the letter up and put it back in his pocket. Then he walked swiftly down the street past all the juke joints with the music blaring out and the GI brogans pounding. He turned down a side street, scuffing up a cloud of dust as he did so. None of the streets down in Black Bottom was paved, and there were four inches of fine white powder over everything. When it rained the mud would come up over the tops of his army shoes, but it hadn't rained in nearly three months. There were no juke joints on this street, and the Negro shanties were neatly whitewashed. Johnny kept on walking until he came to the end of the street. On the corner stood the little whitewashed Baptist Church, and next to it was the neat, well-kept home of the pastor.

Johnny went up on the porch and hesitated. He thrust his hand in his pocket and the paper crinkled. He took his hand out and knocked on the door.

"Who's that?" a voice called.

"It's me," Johnny answered; "it's a sodjer."

The door opened a crack and a woman peered out. She was middle-aged and fat. Looking down, Johnny could see that her feet were bare.

"Whatcha want, sodjer?"

Johnny took off his cap.

"Please, ma'am, lemme come in. I kin explain it t' yuh better settin' down."

She studied his face for a minute in the darkness.

"Aw right," she said; "you kin come in, son."

Johnny entered the room stiffly and sat down on a cornshuck-bottomed chair.

"It's this way, ma'am," he said. "I got a wife up Nawth. I been tryin' an' tryin' t' git a furlough so I could go t' see huh. But they always put me off. So now she done worked an' saved enuff money t' come an' see me. I wants t' ax you t' rent me a room, ma'am. I doan' know nowheres t' ax."

"This ain't no hotel, son."

"I know it ain't. I cain't take Lily t' no hotel, not lak hotels in this heah town."

"Lily yo wife?"

"Yes'm. She my sho' nuff, honest t' Gawd wife. Married in th' Baptist Church in Deetroit."

The fat woman sat back, and her thick lips widened into a smile.

"She a good girl, ain't she? An' you doan' wanta take her t' one o' these heah ho'houses they calls hotels."

"That's it, ma'am."

"Sho' you kin bring huh heah, son. Be glad t' have huh. Reveren' be glad t' have huh too. What yo' name, son?"

"Johnny. Johnny Green. Ma'am—"

"Yas, son?"

"You understands that I wants t' come heah too?"

The fat woman rocked back in her chair and gurgled with laughter.

"Bless yo' heart, chile, I ain't always been a ole woman! And I ain't always been th' preacher's wife neither!"

"Thank you, ma'am. I gotta go now. Time fur me t' be gettin' back t' camp."

"When you bring Lily?"

"Be Monday night, ma'am. Pays you now if you wants it."

"Monday be aw right. Talk it over with th' Reveren', so he make it light fur yuh. Know sodjer boys ain't got much money."

"No, ma'am, sho' Lawd ain't. G'night, ma'am."

When he turned back into the main street of the Negro section the doors of the joints were all open and the soldiers were coming out. The girls were clinging onto their arms all the way to the bus stop. Johnny looked at the dresses that stopped halfway between the pelvis and the knee and hugged the backside so that every muscle showed when they walked. He saw the purple lipstick smeared across the wide full lips, and the short hair stiffened with smelly grease so that it covered their heads like a black lacquered cap. They went on down to the bus stop arm in arm, their knotty bare calves bunching with each step as they walked. Johnny thought about Lilly. He walked past them very fast without turning his head.

But just as he reached the bus stop he heard the whistles. When he turned around he saw the four MPs and the civilian policeman stopping the crowd. He turned around again and walked back until he was standing just behind the white men.

"Aw right," the MPs were saying, "you gals git your health cards out."

Some of the girls started digging in their handbags. Johnny could see them dragging out small yellow cardboard squares. But the others just stood there with blank expressions on their faces. The soldiers started muttering, a dark, deep-throated sound. The MPs started pushing their way through the crowd, looking at each girl's card as they passed. When they came to a girl who didn't have a card they called out to the civilian policemen:

"Aw right, mister, take A'nt Jemima for a little ride."

Then the city policemen would lead the girl away and put her in the Black Maria.

They kept this up until they had examined every girl except one. She hung back beside her soldier, and the first time the MPs didn't see her. When they came back through, one of them caught her by the arm.

"Lemme see your card, Mandy," he said.

The girl looked at him, her little eyes narrowing into slits in her black face.

"Tek yo' hands offen me, white man," she said.

The MP's face crimsoned, so that Johnny could see it, even in the darkness.

"Listen, black girl," he said, "I told you to lemme see your card."

"An' I tole you t' tek yo' han' offen me, white man!"

"Gawddammit, you little black bitch, you better do like I tell you!"

Johnny didn't see very clearly what happened after that. There was a sudden explosion of motion, and then the MP was trying to jerk his hand back, but he couldn't, for the little old black girl had it between her teeth and was biting it to the bone. He drew his other hand back and slapped her across the face so hard that it sounded like a pistol shot. She went over backwards and her tight skirt split, so that when she got up Johnny could see that she didn't have anything on under it. She came forward like a cat, her nails bared, straight for the MP's eyes. He slapped her down again, but the soldiers surged foward all at once. The MPs fell back and drew their guns and one of them blew a whistle.

Johnny, who was behind them, decided it was time for him to get out of there and he did; but not before he saw the squads of white MPs hurling around the corner and going to work on the Negroes with their clubs. He reached the bus stop and swung on board. The minute after he had pushed his way to the back behind all the white soldiers he heard the shots. The bus driver put the bus in gear and they roared off toward the camp.

It was after one o'clock when all the soldiers straggled in. Those of them who could still walk. Eight of them came in on the meat wagon, three with gunshot wounds. The colonel declared the town out of bounds for all Negro soldiers for a month.

"Dammit," Johnny said, "I gotta go meet Lily, I gotta. I cain't stay heah. I cain't!"

"Whatcha gonna do," Little Willie asked, "go AWOL?"

Johnny looked at him, his brow furrowed into a frown.

"Naw," he said, "I'm gonna go see th' colonel!"

"Whut! Man, you crazy! Colonel kick yo' black ass out fo' you gits yo' mouf open."

"I take a chanct on that."

He walked over to the little half mirror on the wall of the barracks. Carefully he readjusted his cap. He pulled his tie out of his shirt front and drew the knot tighter around his throat. Then he tucked the ends back in at just the right fraction of an inch between the correct pair of buttons. He bent down and dusted his shoes again, although they were already spotless.

"Man," Little Willie said, "you sho' is a fool!"

"Reckon I am," Johnny said; then he went out of the door and down the short wooden steps.

When he got to the road that divided the colored and white sections of the camp his steps faltered. He stood still a minute, drew in a deep breath, and marched very stiffly and erect across the road. The white soldiers gazed at him curiously, but none of them said anything. If a black soldier came over into their section it was because somebody sent him, so they let him alone.

In front of the colonel's headquarters he stopped. He knew what he had to say, but his breath was very short in his throat and he was going to have a hard time saying it.

"Whatcha want, soldier?" the sentry demanded.

"I wants t' see th' colonel."

"Who sent you?"

Johnny drew his breath in sharply.

"I ain't at liberty t' say," he declared, his breath coming out very fast behind the words.

"You ain't at liberty t' say," the sentry mimicked. "Well I'll be damned! If you ain't at liberty t' say, then I ain't at liberty t' let you see the colonel! Git tha hell outa here, nigger, before I pump some lead in you!"

Johnny didn't move.

The sentry started toward him, lifting his rifle butt, but another soldier, a sergeant, came around the corner of the building.

"Hold on there," he called. "What tha hell is th' trouble here?"

"This here nigger says he want t' see tha colonel an' when I ast him who sent him he says he ain't at liberty t' say!"

The sergeant turned to Johnny.

Johnny came to attention and saluted him. You aren't supposed to salute NCOs, but sometimes it helps.

"What you got t' say fur yourself, boy?" the sergeant said, not unkindly. Johnny's breath evened.

"I got uh message fur th' colonel, suh," he said; "I ain't s'posed t' give it t' nobody else but him. I ain't even s'posed t' tell who sont it, suh."

The sergeant peered at him sharply.

"You tellin' tha truth, boy?"

"Yassuh!"

"Aw right. Wait here a minute."

He went into HQ. After a couple of minutes he came back.

"Aw right, soldier, you kin go on in."

Johnny mounted the steps and went into the colonel's office. The colonel was a lean, white-haired soldier with a face tanned to the color of saddle leather. He was reading a letter through a pair of horn-rimmed glasses which had only one earhook left, so that he had to hold them up to his eyes with one hand. He put them down and looked up. Johnny saw that his eyes were pale blue, so pale that he felt as if he were looking into the eyes of an eagle or some other fierce bird of prey.

"Well?" he said, and Johnny stiffened into a salute. The colonel half smiled.

"At ease, soldier," he said. Then: "The sergeant tells me that you have a very important message for me."

Johnny gulped in the air.

"Beggin' th' sergeant's pardon, suh," he said, "but that ain't so."

"What!"

"Yassuh," Johnny rushed on, "nobody sent me. I come on m'

own hook. I had t' talk t' yuh, Colonel, suh! You kin sen' me t' th' guardhouse afterwards, but please, suh, lissen t' me fur jes' a minute!"

The colonel relaxed slowly. Something very like a smile was playing around the corners of his mouth. He looked at his watch.

"All right, soldier," he said. "You've got five minutes."

"Thank yuh, thank yuh, suh!"

"Speak your piece, soldier; you're wasting time!"

"It's about Lily, suh. She my wife. She done worked an' slaved fur nigh onto six months t' git the money t' come an' see me. An' now you give th' order that none of th' cullud boys kin go t' town. Beggin' yo' pahdon, suh, I wasn't in none of that trouble. I ain't neber been in no trouble. You kin ax my cap'n, if you wants to. All I wants is permission to go into town fur one week, an' I'll stay outa town fur two months if yuh wants me to."

The colonel picked up the phone.

"Ring Captain Walters for me," he said. Then: "What's your name, soldier?"

"It's Green, suh. Private Johnny Green."

"Captain Walters? This is Colonel Milton. Do you have anything in your files concerning Private Johnny Green? Oh yes, go ahead. Take all the time you need."

The colonel lit a long black cigar. Johnny waited. The clock on the wall spun its electric arms.

"What's that? Yes. Yes, yes, I see. Thank you, Captain."

He put down the phone and picked up a fountain pen. He wrote swiftly. Finally he straightened up and gave Johnny the slip of paper.

Johnny read it. It said: "Private Johnny Green is given express permission to go into town every evening of the week beginning August seventh and ending August fourteenth. He is further permitted to remain in town overnight every night during said week, so long as he returns to camp for reveille the following morning. By order of the commanding officer, Colonel H. H. Milton."

There was a hard knot at the base of Johnny's throat. He couldn't breathe. But he snapped to attention and saluted smartly.

"Thank yuh, suh," he said at last. Then: "Gawd bless you, suh!"

"Forget it, soldier. I was a young married man once myself. My compliments to Captain Walters."

Johnny saluted again and about-faced, then he marched out of the office and down the stairs. On the way back he saluted everybody—privates, NCOs, and civilian visitors, his white teeth gleaming in a huge smile.

"That's sure one happy darky," one of the white soldiers said.

Johnny stood in the station and watched the train running in. The yellow lights from the windows flickered on and off across his face as the alternating squares of light and darkness flashed past. Then it was slowing and Johnny was running beside it, trying to keep abreast of the Jim Crow coach. He could see her standing up, holding her bags. She came down the steps the first one and they stood there holding each other, Johnny's arms crushing all the breath out of her, holding her so hard against him that his brass buttons hurt through her thin dress. She opened her mouth to speak but he kissed her, bending her head backward on her neck until her little hat fell off. It lay there on the ground, unnoticed.

"Sugah," she said, "sugah. It was awful."

"I know," he said. "I know."

Then he took her bags and they started walking out of the station toward the Negro section of town.

"I missed yuh so much," Johnny said, "I thought I lose m' mind."

"Me too," she said. Then: "I brought th' marriage license with me like yuh tole me. I doan' wan th' preacher's wife t' think we bad."

"Enybody kin look at yuh an' see yuh uh angel!"

They went very quietly through all the dark streets and the white soldiers turned to look at Johnny and his girl.

Lak a queen, Johnny thought, lak a queen. He looked at the girl beside him, seeing the velvety nightshade skin, the glossy black lacquered curls, the sweet, wide hips and the long, clean legs striding beside him in the darkness. I am black, but comely, O ye daughters of Jerusalem!

They turned into the Bottom where the street lights were dim blobs on the pine poles and the dust rose up in little swirls around their feet. Johnny had his head half turned so that he didn't see the two MPs until he had almost bumped into them. He dropped one bag and caught Lily by the arm. Then he drew her aside quickly and the two men went by them without speaking.

They kept on walking, but every two steps Johnny would jerk his head around and look nervously back over his shoulder. The last time he looked the two MPs had stopped and were looking back at them. Johnny turned out the elbow of the arm next to Lily so that it hooked into hers a little and began to walk faster, pushing her along with him.

"What's yo' hurry, sugah?" she said. "I be heah a whole week!"

But Johnny was looking over his shoulder at the two MPs. They were coming toward them now, walking with long, slow strides, their reddish-white faces set. Johnny started to push Lily along faster, but she shook off his arm and stopped still.

"I do declare, Johnny Green! You th' beatines' man! Whut you walk me so fas' fur?"

Johnny opened his mouth to answer her, but the military police were just behind them now, and the sergeant reached out and laid his hand on her arm.

"C'mon, gal," he said, "lemme see it."

"Let you see whut? Whut he mean, Johnny?"

"Your card," the sergeant growled. "Lemme see your card."

"My card?" Lily said blankly. "Whut kinda card, mister?"

Johnny put the bags down. He was fighting for breath.

"Look heah, Sarge," he said; "this girl my wife!"

"Oh yeah? I said lemme see your card, sister!"

"I ain't got no card, mister. I dunno whut you talkin' about."

"Look, Sarge," the other MP said, "th' soldier's got bags. Maybe she's just come t' town."

"These your bags, gal?"

"Yessir."

"Aw right. You got twenty-four hours to git yourself a health card. If you don't have it by then we hafta run you in. Git goin' now."

"Listen," Johnny shouted; "this girl my wife! She ain't no ho'! I tell you she ain't—"

"What you say, nigger—" the MP sergeant growled. "Whatcha say?" He started toward Johnny.

Lily swung on Johnny's arm.

"C'mon, Johnny," she said; "they got guns. C'mon, Johnny, please! Please, Johnny!"

Slowly she drew him away.

"Aw, leave 'em be, Sarge," the MP corporal said; "maybe she is his wife."

The sergeant spat. The brown tobacco juice splashed in the dirt not an inch from Lily's foot. Then the two of them turned and started away.

Johnny stopped.

"Lemme go, Lily," he said, "lemme go!" He tore her arm loose from his and started back up the street. Lily leaped, her two arms fastening themselves around his neck. He fought silently but she clung to him, doubling her knees so that all her weight was hanging from his neck.

"No, Johnny! Oh Jesus no! You be kilt! Oh, Johnny, listen t' me, sugah! You's all I got!"

He put both hands up to break her grip but she swung her weight sidewise and the two of them went down in the dirt. The MPs turned the corner out of sight.

Johnny sat there in the dust staring at her. The dirt had ruined her dress. He sat there a long time looking at her until the hot tears rose up back of his eyelids faster than he could blink them away, so he put his face down in her lap and cried.

"I ain't no man!" he said. "I ain't no man!"

"Hush, sugah," she said. "You's a man aw right. You's my man!"

Gently she drew him to his feet. He picked up the bags and the two of them went down the dark street toward the preacher's house.

The Horse Dealer's Daughter

D. H. Lawrence

D. H. LAWRENCE *(1885–1930) was born into a coal-mining family in Nottinghamshire, England. For a time he taught school and then, in 1911, published his first novel,* The White Peacock. *Other novels soon followed:* Sons and Lovers *(1913),* The Rainbow *(1915),* Women in Love *(1920),* Lady Chatterley's Lover *(1928). His short-story collections include* The Prussian Officer *(1914),* England, My England *(1922),* The Captain's Doll*—English title* The Ladybird *(1923),* The Man Who Died *(1929). Lawrence became almost notorious for the sexual frankness in his stories; today, he is more justly evaluated for his creative sensitivity and for what some critics have called his mystical feeling for life.*

"Well, Mabel, and what are you going to do with yourself?" asked Joe, with foolish flippancy. He felt quite safe himself. Without listening for an answer, he turned aside, worked a grain of tobacco to the tip of his tongue, and spat it out. He did not care about anything, since he felt safe himself.

The three brothers and the sister sat round the desolate breakfast table, attempting some sort of desultory consultation. The morning's post had given the final tap to the family fortune, and all was over. The dreary dining room itself, with its heavy mahogany furniture, looked as if it were waiting to be done away with.

But the consultation amounted to nothing. There was a strange air of ineffectuality about the three men, as they sprawled at table, smoking, and reflecting vaguely on their own condition. The girl was alone, a rather short, sullen-looking young woman of twenty-seven. She did not share the same life as her brothers. She would have been good-looking, save for the impassive fixity of her face, "bulldog," as her brothers called it.

There was a confused tramping of horses' feet outside. The three men all sprawled round in their chairs to watch. Beyond the dark holly bushes that separated the strip of lawn from the highroad, they could see a cavalcade of shire horses swinging out of their own yard, being taken for exercise. This was the last time. These were the last horses that would go through their hands. The young men watched with critical, callous look. They were all frightened at the collapse of their lives, and the sense of disaster in which they were involved left them no inner freedom.

Yet they were three fine, well-set fellows enough. Joe, the eldest, was a man of thirty-three, broad and handsome in a hot, flushed way. His face was red, he twisted his black moustache over a thick finger, his eyes were shallow and restless. He had a sensual way of uncovering his teeth when he laughed, and his bearing was stupid. Now he watched the horses with a glazed look of helplessness in his eyes, a certain stupor of downfall.

The great draught horses swung past. They were tied head to tail, four of them, and they heaved along to where a lane branched off from the highroad, planting their great hoofs floutingly in the fine black mud, swinging their great rounded haunches sumptuously, and trotting a few sudden steps as they were led into the lane, round the corner. Every movement showed a massive, slumbrous strength, and a stupidity which held them in subjection. The groom at the head looked back, jerking the leading rope. And the cavalcade moved out of sight up the lane, the tail of the last horse, bobbed up tight and stiff, held out taut from the swinging great haunches as they rocked behind the hedges in a motion-like sleep.

Joe watched with glazed hopeless eyes. The horses were almost like his own body to him. He felt he was done for now. Luckily he was engaged to a woman as old as himself, and therefore her father, who was steward of a neighboring estate, would provide him with a job. He would marry and go into harness. His life was over, he would be a subject animal now.

He turned uneasily aside, the retreating steps of the horses echoing in his ears. Then, with foolish restlessness, he reached for the scraps of bacon rind from the plates, and making a faint whistling sound, flung them to the terrier that lay against the fender. He watched the dog swallow them, and waited till the creature looked into his eyes. Then a faint grin came on his face, and in a high, foolish voice he said:

"You won't get much more bacon, shall you, you little bitch?"

The dog faintly and dismally wagged its tail, then lowered its haunches, circled round, and lay down again.

There was another helpless silence at the table. Joe sprawled uneasily in his seat, not willing to go till the family conclave was dissolved. Fred Henry, the second brother, was erect, clean-limbed, alert. He had watched the passing of the horses with more sang-froid. If he was an animal, like Joe, he was an animal which controls, not one which is controlled. He was master of any horse, and he carried himself with a well-tempered air of mastery. But he was not master of the situations of life. He pushed his coarse brown moustache upwards, off his lip, and glanced irritably at his sister, who sat impassive and inscrutable.

"You'll go and stop with Lucy for a bit, shan't you?" he asked. The girl did not answer.

"I don't see what else you can do," persisted Fred Henry.

"Go as a skivvy," Joe interpolated laconically.

The girl did not move a muscle.

"If I was her, I should go in for training for a nurse," said Malcolm, the youngest of them all. He was the baby of the family, a young man of twenty-two, with a fresh, jaunty *museau.*

But Mabel did not take any notice of him. They had talked at her and round her for so many years, that she hardly heard them at all.

The marble clock on the mantelpiece softly chimed the half-hour, the dog rose uneasily from the hearthrug and looked at the party at the breakfast table. But still they sat on in ineffectual conclave.

"Oh, all right," said Joe suddenly, apropos of nothing. "I'll get a move on."

He pushed back his chair, straddled his knees with a downward jerk, to get them free, in horsey fashion, and went to the fire. Still he did not go out of the room; he was curious to know what the others would do or say. He began to charge his pipe, looking down at the dog and saying, in a high, affected voice:

"Going wi' me? Going wi' me are ter? Tha'rt goin' further than tha counts on just now, dost hear?"

The dog faintly wagged its tail, the man stuck out his jaw and covered his pipe with his hands, and puffed intently, losing himself in the tobacco, looking down all the while at the dog with an absent brown eye. The dog looked up at him in mournful distrust. Joe stood with his knees stuck out, in real horsey fashion.

"Have you had a letter from Lucy?" Fred Henry asked of his sister.

"Last week," came the neutral reply.

"And what does she say?"

There was no answer.

"Does she *ask* you to go and stop there?" persisted Fred Henry.

"She says I can if I like."

"Well, then, you'd better. Tell her you'll come on Monday."

This was received in silence.

"That's what you'll do then, is it?" said Fred Henry, in some exasperation.

But she made no answer. There was a silence of futility and irritation in the room. Malcolm grinned fatuously.

"You'll have to make up your mind between now and next Wednesday," said Joe loudly, "or else find yourself lodgings on the curbstone."

The face of the young woman darkened, but she sat on immutable.

"Here's Jack Fergusson!" exclaimed Malcolm, who was looking aimlessly out of the window.

"Where?" exclaimed Joe, loudly.

"Just gone past."

"Coming in?"

Malcolm craned his neck to see the gate.

"Yes," he said.

There was a silence. Mabel sat on like one condemned, at the head of the table. Then a whistle was heard from the kitchen. The dog got up and barked sharply. Joe opened the door and shouted:

"Come on."

After a moment a young man entered. He was muffled up in

overcoat and a purple woollen scarf, and his tweed cap, which he did not remove, was pulled down on his head. He was of medium height, his face was rather long and pale, his eyes looked tired.

"Hello, Jack! Well, Jack!" exclaimed Malcolm and Joe. Fred Henry merely said, "Jack."

"What's doing?" asked the newcomer, evidently addressing Fred Henry.

"Same. We've got to be out by Wednesday. Got a cold?"

"I have—got it bad, too."

"Why don't you stop in?"

"*Me* stop in? When I can't stand on my legs, perhaps I shall have a chance." The young man spoke huskily. He had a slight Scotch accent.

"It's a knock-out, isn't it," said Joe, boisterously, "if a doctor goes round croaking with a cold. Looks bad for the patients, doesn't it?"

The young doctor looked at him slowly.

"Anything the matter with *you*, then?" he asked sarcastically.

"Not as I know of. Damn your eyes, I hope not. Why?"

"I thought you were very concerned about the patients, wondered if you might be one yourself."

"Damn it, no, I've never been patient to no flaming doctor, and hope I never shall be," returned Joe.

At this point Mabel rose from the table, and they all seemed to become aware of her existence. She began putting the dishes together. The young doctor looked at her, but did not address her. He had not greeted her. She went out of the room with the tray, her face impassive and unchanged.

"When are you off then, all of you?" asked the doctor.

"I'm catching the eleven-forty," replied Malcolm. "Are you goin' down wi' th' trap, Joe?"

"Yes, I've told you I'm going down wi' th' trap, haven't I?"

"We'd better be getting her in then. So long, Jack, if I don't see you before I go," said Malcolm, shaking hands.

He went out, followed by Joe, who seemed to have his tail between his legs.

"Well, this is the devil's own," exclaimed the doctor, when he was left alone with Fred Henry. "Going before Wednesday, are you?"

"That's the orders," replied the other.

"Where, to Northampton?"

"That's it."

"The devil!" exclaimed Fergusson, with quiet chagrin.

And there was silence between the two.

"All settled up, are you?" asked Fergusson.

"About."

There was another pause.

"Well, I shall miss yer, Freddy, boy," said the young doctor.

"And I shall miss thee, Jack," returned the other.

"Miss you like hell," mused the doctor.

Fred Henry turned aside. There was nothing to say. Mabel came in again, to finish clearing the table.

"What are *you* going to do, then, Miss Pervin?" asked Fergusson. "Going to your sister's, are you?"

Mabel looked at him with her steady, dangerous eyes, that always made him uncomfortable, unsettling his superficial ease.

"No," she said.

"Well, what in the name of fortune *are* you going to do? Say what you mean to do," cried Fred Henry, with futile intensity.

But she only averted her head, and continued her work. She folded the white tablecloth, and put on the chenille cloth.

"The sulkiest bitch that ever trod!" muttered her brother.

But she finished her task with perfectly impassive face, the young doctor watching her interestedly all the while. Then she went out.

Fred Henry stared after her, clenching his lips, his blue eyes fixing in sharp antagonism, as he made a grimace of sour exasperation.

"You could bray her into bits, and that's all you'd get out of her," he said in a small, narrowed tone.

The doctor smiled faintly.

"What's she *going* to do, then?" he asked.

"Strike me if *I* know!" returned the other.

There was a pause. Then the doctor stirred.

"I'll be seeing you to-night, shall I?" he said to his friend.

"Ay—where's it to be? Are we going over to Jessdale?"

"I don't know. I've got such a cold on me. I'll come round to the Moon and Stars, anyway."

"Let Lizzie and May miss their night for once, eh?"

"That's it—if I feel as I do now."

"All's one—"

The two young men went through the passage and down to the back door together. The house was large, but it was servantless now, and desolate. At the back was a small bricked house yard, and beyond that a big square, gravelled fine and red, and having stables on two sides. Sloping, dank, winter-dark fields stretched away on the open sides.

But the stables were empty. Joseph Pervin, the father of the family, had been a man of no education, who had become a fairly large horse dealer. The stables had been full of horses, there was a great turmoil and come-and-go of horses and of dealers and grooms. Then the kitchen was full of servants. But of late things had declined. The old man had married a second time, to retrieve his fortunes. Now he was dead and everything was gone to the dogs, there was nothing but debt and threatening.

For months, Mabel had been servantless in the big house, keeping the home together in penury for her ineffectual brothers. She had kept house for ten years. But previously it was with unstinted means. Then, however brutal and coarse everything was, the sense of money had kept her proud, confident. The men might be foul-mouthed, the women in the kitchen might have bad reputations, her brothers might have illegitimate children. But so long as there was money, the girl felt herself established, and brutally proud, reserved.

No company came to the house, save dealers and coarse men. Mabel had no associates of her own sex, after her sister went away. But she did not mind. She went regularly to church, she attended to her father. And she lived in the memory of her mother, who had died when she was fourteen, and whom she had loved. She had loved her father, too, in a different way, depending upon him, and feeling secure in him, until at the age of fifty-four he married again. And then she had set hard against him. Now he had died and left them all hopelessly in debt.

She had suffered badly during the period of poverty. Nothing, however, could shake the curious sullen, animal pride that dominated each member of the family. Now, for Mabel, the end had come. Still she would not cast about her. She would follow her own way just the same. She would always hold the keys of her own situation. Mindless and persistent, she endured from day to day. Why should she think? Why should she answer anybody? It was enough that this was the end, and there was no way out. She need not pass any more darkly along the main street of the small town, avoiding every eye. She need not demean herself any more, going into the shops and buying the cheapest food. This was at an end. She thought of nobody, not even of herself. Mindless and persistent, she seemed in a sort of ecstasy to be coming nearer to her fulfilment, her own glorification, approaching her dead mother, who was glorified.

In the afternoon she took a little bag, with shears and sponge and a small scrubbing brush, and went out. It was a gray, wintry day, with saddened, dark green fields and an atmosphere blackened by the smoke of foundries not far off. She went quickly, darkly along the causeway, heeding nobody, through the town to the churchyard.

There she always felt secure, as if no one could see her, although as a matter of fact she was exposed to the stare of everyone who passed along under the churchyard wall. Nevertheless, once under the shadow of the great looming church, among the graves, she felt immune from the world, reserved within the thick churchyard wall as in another country.

Carefully she clipped the grass from the grave, and arranged the pinky white, small chrysanthemums in the tin cross. When this was done, she took an empty jar from a neighboring grave, brought water, and carefully, most scrupulously sponged the marble headstone and the coping stone.

It gave her sincere satisfaction to do this. She felt in immediate contact with the world of her mother. She took minute pains, went through the park in a state bordering on pure happiness, as if in performing this task she came into a subtle, intimate connection with her mother. For the life she followed here in the world was far less real than the world of death she inherited from her mother.

The doctor's house was just by the church. Fergusson, being a mere hired assistant, was slave to the countryside. As he hurried now to attend to the outpatients in the surgery, glancing across the graveyard with his quick eye, he saw the girl at her task at the grave. She seemed so intent and remote, it was like looking into another world. Some mystical element was touched in him. He slowed down as he walked, watching her as if spellbound.

She lifted her eyes, feeling him looking. Their eyes met. And each looked away again at once, each feeling, in some way, found out by the other. He lifted his cap and passed on down the road. There remained distinct in his consciousness, like a vision, the memory of her face, lifted from the tombstone in the churchyard, and looking at him with slow, large, portentous eyes. It *was* portentous, her face. It seemed to mesmerize him. There was a heavy power in her eyes which laid hold of his whole being, as if he had drunk some powerful drug. He had been feeling weak and done before. Now the life came back into him, he felt delivered from his own fretted, daily self.

He finished his duties at the surgery as quickly as might be, hastily filling up the bottle of the waiting people with cheap drugs. Then, in perpetual haste, he set off again to visit several cases in another part of his round, before teatime. At all times he preferred to walk if he could, but particularly when he was not well. He fancied the motion restored him.

The afternoon was falling. It was gray, deadened, and wintry, with a slow, moist, heavy coldness sinking in and deadening all the faculties. But why should he think or notice? He hastily climbed the hill and turned across the dark green fields, following the black cinder track. In the distance, across a shallow dip in the country, the small town was clustered like smoldering ash, a tower, a spire, a heap of low, raw, extinct houses. And on the nearest fringe of the town, sloping into the dip, was Oldmeadow, the Pervins' house. He could see the stables and the outbuildings distinctly, as they lay towards him on the slope. Well, he would not go there many more times! Another resource would be lost to him, another place gone: the only company he cared for in the alien, ugly little town he was losing. Nothing but work, drudgery, constant hastening from dwelling to dwelling among the colliers and the ironworkers. It wore him out, but at the same time he had a craving for it. It was a stimulant to him to be in the homes of the working people, moving as it were through the innermost body of their life. His nerves were excited and gratified. He could come so near, into the very lives of the rough, inarticulate, powerfully emotional men and women. He grumbled, he said he hated the hellish hole. But as a matter of fact it excited him, the contact with the rough, strongly-feeling people was a stimulant applied direct to his nerves.

Below Oldmeadow, in the green, shallow, soddened hollow of

fields, lay a square, deep pond. Roving across the landscape, the doctor's quick eye detected a figure in black passing through the gate of the field, down towards the pond. He looked again. It would be Mabel Pervin. His mind suddenly became alive and attentive.

Why was she going down there? He pulled up on the path on the slope above, and stood staring. He could just make sure of the small black figure moving in the hollow of the failing day. He seemed to see her in the midst of such obscurity, that he was like a clairvoyant, seeing rather with the mind's eye than with ordinary sight. Yet he could see her positively enough, whilst he kept his eye attentive. He felt, if he looked away from her, in the thick, ugly falling dusk, he would lose her altogether.

He followed her minutely as she moved, direct and intent, like something transmitted rather than stirring in voluntary activity, straight down the field towards the pond. There she stood on the bank for a moment. She never raised her head. Then she waded slowly into the water.

He stood motionless as the small black figure walked slowly and deliberately towards the centre of the pond, very slowly, gradually moving deeper into the motionless water, and still moving forward as the water got up to her breast. Then he could see her no more in the dusk of the dead afternoon.

"There!" he exclaimed. "Would you believe it?"

And he hastened straight down, running over the wet, soddened fields, pushing through the hedges, down into the depression of callous wintry obscurity. It took him several minutes to come to the pond. He stood on the bank, breathing heavily. He could see nothing. His eyes seemed to penetrate the dead water. Yes, perhaps that was the dark shadow of her black clothing beneath the surface of the water.

He slowly ventured into the pond. The bottom was deep, soft clay, he sank in, and the water clasped dead cold round his legs. As he stirred he could smell the cold, rotten clay that fouled up into the water. It was objectionable in his lungs. Still, repelled and yet not heeding, he moved deeper into the pond. The cold water rose over his thighs, over his loins, upon his abdomen. The lower part of his body was all sunk in the hideous cold element. And the bottom was so deeply soft and uncertain, he was afraid of pitching with his mouth underneath. He could not swim, and was afraid.

He crouched a little, spreading his hands under the water and moving them round, trying to feel for her. The dead cold pond swayed upon his chest. He moved again, a little deeper, and again, with his hands underneath, he felt all around under the water. And he touched her clothing. But it evaded his fingers. He made a desperate effort to grasp it.

And so doing he lost his balance and went under, horribly, suffocating in the foul earthy water, struggling madly for a few moments. At last, after what seemed an eternity, he got his footing, rose again into the air and looked around. He gasped, and knew he was in the world. Then he looked at the water. She had risen near him. He grasped her clothing, and drawing her nearer, turned to take his way to land again.

He went very slowly, carefully, absorbed in the slow progress. He rose higher, climbing out of the pond. The water was now only about his legs; he was thankful, full of relief to be out of the clutches of the pond. He lifted her and staggered on to the bank, out of the horror of wet, gray clay.

He laid her down on the bank. She was quite unconscious and running with water. He made the water come from her mouth, he worked to restore her. He did not have to work very long before he could feel the breathing begin again in her; she was breathing naturally. He worked a little longer. He could feel her live beneath his hands; she was coming back. He wiped her face, wrapped her in his overcoat, looked round into the dim, dark gray world, then lifted her and staggered down the bank and across the fields.

It seemed an unthinkably long way, and his burden so heavy he felt he would never get to the house. But at last he was in the stable yard, and then in the house yard. He opened the door and went into the house. In the kitchen he laid her down on the hearthrug, and called. The house was empty. But the fire was burning in the grate.

Then again he kneeled to attend to her. She was breathing regularly, her eyes were wide open and as if conscious, but there seemed something missing in her look. She was conscious in herself, but unconscious of her surroundings.

He ran upstairs, took blankets from a bed, and put them before the fire to warm. Then he removed her saturated, earthy-smelling clothing, rubbed her dry with a towel, and wrapped her naked in the blankets. Then he went into the dining room, to look for spirits.

There was a little whisky. He drank a gulp himself, and put some into her mouth.

The effect was instantaneous. She looked full into his face, as if she had been seeing him for some time, and yet had only just become conscious of him.

"Dr. Fergusson?" she said.

"What?" he answered.

He was divesting himself of his coat, intending to find some dry clothing upstairs. He could not bear the smell of the dead, clayey water, and he was mortally afraid for his own health.

"What did I do?" she asked.

"Walked into the pond," he replied. He had begun to shudder like one sick, and could hardly attend to her. Her eyes remained full on him, he seemed to be going dark in his mind, looking back at her helplessly. The shuddering became quieter in him, his life came back in him, dark and unknowing, but strong again.

"Was I out of my mind?" she asked, while her eyes were fixed on him all the time.

"Maybe, for the moment," he replied. He felt quiet, because his strength had come back. The strange fretful strain had left him.

"Am I out of my mind now?" she asked.

"Are you?" He reflected a moment. "No," he answered truthfully, "I don't see that you are." He turned his face aside. He was afraid now, because he felt dazed, and felt dimly that her power was stronger than his, in this issue. And she continued to look at him fixedly all the time. "Can you tell me where I shall find some dry things to put on?" he asked.

"Did you dive into the pond for me?" she asked.

"No," he answered. "I walked in. But I went in overhead as well."

There was silence for a moment. He hesitated. He very much wanted to go upstairs to get into dry clothing. But there was another desire in him. And she seemed to hold him. His will seemed to have gone to sleep, and left him, standing there slack before her. But he felt warm inside himself. He did not shudder at all, though his clothes were sodden on him.

"Why did you?" she asked.

"Because I didn't want you to do such a foolish thing," he said.

"It wasn't foolish," she said, still gazing at him as she lay on the floor, with a sofa cushion under her head. "It was the right thing to do. *I* knew best, then."

"I'll go and shift these wet things," he said. But still he had not the power to move out of her presence, until she sent him. It was as if she had the life of his body in her hands, and he could not extricate himself. Or perhaps he did not want to.

Suddenly she sat up. Then she became aware of her own immediate condition. She felt the blankets about her, she knew her own limbs. For a moment it seemed as if her reason were going. She looked round, with wild eye, as if seeking something. He stood still with fear. She saw her clothing lying scattered.

"Who undressed me?" she asked, her eyes resting full and inevitable on his face.

"I did," he replied, "to bring you round."

For some moments she sat and gazed at him awfully, her lips parted.

"Do you love me, then?" she asked.

He only stood and stared at her, fascinated. His soul seemed to melt.

She shuffled forward on her knees, and put her arms round him, round his legs, as he stood there, pressing her breasts against his knees and thighs, clutching him with strange, convulsive certainty, pressing his thighs against her, drawing him to her face, her throat, as she looked up at him with flaring, humble eyes of transfiguration, triumphant in first possession.

"You love me," she murmured, in strange transport, yearning and triumphant and confident. "You love me. I know you love me, I know."

And she was passionately kissing his knees, through the wet clothing, passionately and indiscriminately kissing his knees, his legs, as if unaware of everything.

He looked down at the tangled wet hair, the wild, bare, animal shoulders. He was amazed, bewildered, and afraid. He had never thought of loving her. He had never wanted to love her. When he rescued her and restored her, he was a doctor, and she was a patient. He had had no single personal thought of her. Nay, this introduction of the personal element was very distasteful to him, a violation of his professional honor. It was horrible to have her there embracing his knees. It was horrible. He revolted from it, violently. And yet—and yet—he had not the power to break away.

She looked at him again, with the same supplication of powerful love, and that same transcendent, frightening light of triumph. In view of the delicate flame which seemed to come from her face like a light, he was powerless. And yet he had never intended to love her. He had never intended. And something stubborn in him could not give way.

"You love me," she repeated, in a murmur of deep, rhapsodic assurance. "You love me."

Her hands were drawing him, drawing him down to her. He was afraid, even a little horrified. For he had, really, no intention of loving her. Yet her hands were drawing him towards her. He put out his hand quickly to steady himself, and grasped her bare shoulder. A flame seemed to burn the hand that grasped her soft shoulder. He had no intention of loving her: his whole will was against his yielding. It was horrible. And yet wonderful was the touch of her shoulders, beautiful the shining of her face. Was she perhaps mad? He had a horror of yielding to her. Yet something in him ached also.

He had been staring away at the door, away from her. But his hand remained on her shoulder. She had gone suddenly very still. He looked down at her. Her eyes were now wide with fear, with doubt, the light was dying from her face, a shadow of terrible grayness was returning. He could not bear the touch of her eyes' question upon him, and the look of death behind the question.

With an inward groan he gave way, and let his heart yield towards her. A sudden gentle smile came on his face. And her eyes, which never left his face, slowly, slowly filled with tears. He watched the strange water rise in her eyes, like some slow fountain coming up. And his heart seemed to burn and melt away in his breast.

He could not bear to look at her any more. He dropped on his knees and caught her head with his arms and pressed her face against his throat. She was very still. His heart, which seemed to have broken, was burning with a kind of agony in his breast. And he felt her slow, hot tears wetting his throat. But he could not move.

He felt the hot tears wet his neck and the hollows of his neck, and he remained motionless, suspended through one of man's eternities. Only now it had become indispensable to him to have her face pressed close to him; he could never let her go again. He could never let her head go away from the close clutch of his arm. He wanted to remain like that for ever, with his heart hurting him in a pain that was also life to him. Without knowing, he was looking down on her damp, soft brown hair.

Then, as it were suddenly, he smelt the horrid stagnant smell of that water. And at the same moment she drew away from him and looked at him. Her eyes were wistful and unfathomable. He was afraid of them, and he fell to kissing her, not knowing what he was doing. He wanted her eyes not to have that terrible, wistful, unfathomable look.

When she turned her face to him again, a faint delicate flush was glowing, and there was again dawning that terrible shining of joy in her eyes, which really terrified him, and yet which he now wanted to see, because he feared the look of doubt still more.

"You love me?" she said, rather faltering.

"Yes." The word cost him a painful effort. Not because it wasn't true. But because it was too newly true, the *saying* seemed to tear open again his newly torn heart. And he hardly wanted it to be true, even now.

She lifted her face to him, and he bent forward and kissed her on the mouth, gently, with the one kiss that is an eternal pledge. And as he kissed her his heart strained again in his breast. He never intended to love her. But now it was over. He had crossed over the gulf to her, and all that he had left behind had shrivelled and become void.

After the kiss, her eyes again slowly filled with tears. She sat still, away from him, with her face drooped aside, and her hands folded in her lap. The tears fell very slowly. There was complete silence. He too sat there motionless and silent on the hearthrug. The strange pain of his heart that was broken seemed to consume him. That he should love her? That this was love! That he should be ripped open in this way! Him, a doctor! How they would all jeer if they knew! It was agony to him to think they might know.

In the curious naked pain of the thought he looked again to her. She was sitting there drooped into a muse. He saw a tear fall, and his heart flared hot. He saw for the first time that one of her shoulders was quite uncovered, one arm bare, he could see one of her small breasts; dimly, because it had become almost dark in the room.

"Why are you crying?" he asked, in an altered voice.

She looked up at him, and behind her tears the consciousness of her situation for the first time brought a dark look of shame to her eyes.

"I'm not crying, really," she said, watching him half frightened.

He reached his hand, and softly closed it on her bare arm.

"I love you! I love you!" he said in a soft, low vibrating voice, unlike himself.

She shrank, and dropped her head. The soft, penetrating grip of his hand on her arm distressed her. She looked up at him.

"I want to go," she said. "I want to go and get you some dry things."

"Why?" he said. "I'm all right."

"But I want to go," she said. "And I want you to change your things."

He released her arm, and she wrapped herself in the blanket, looking at him rather frightened. And still she did not rise.

"Kiss me," she said wistfully.

He kissed her, but briefly, half in anger.

Then, after a second, she rose nervously, all mixed up in the blanket. He watched her in her confusion, as she tried to extricate herself and wrap herself up so that she could walk. He watched her relentlessly, as she knew. And as she went, the blanket trailing, and as he saw a glimpse of her feet and her white leg, he tried to remember her as she was when he had wrapped her in the blanket. But then he didn't want to remember, because she had been nothing to him then, and his nature revolted from remembering her as she was when she was nothing to him.

A tumbling, muffled noise from within the dark house startled him. Then he heard her voice:—"There are clothes." He rose and went to the foot of the stairs, and gathered up the garments she had thrown down. Then he came back to the fire to rub himself down and dress. He grinned at his own appearance when he had finished.

The fire was sinking, so he put on coal. The house was now quite dark, save for the light of a street-lamp that shone in faintly from beyond the holly trees. He lit the gas with matches he found on the mantelpiece. Then he emptied the pockets of his own clothes, and threw all his wet things in a heap into the scullery. After which he gathered up her sodden clothes, gently, and put them in a separate heap on the copper top in the scullery.

It was six o'clock on the clock. His own watch had stopped. He ought to go back to the surgery. He waited, and still she did not come down. So he went to the foot of the stairs and called:

"I shall have to go."

Almost immediately he heard her coming down. She had on her best dress of black voile, and her hair was tidy, but still damp. She looked at him—and in spite of herself, smiled.

"I don't like you in those clothes," she said.

"Do I look a sight?" he answered.

They were shy of one another.

"I'll make you some tea," she said.

"No, I must go."

"Must you?" And she looked at him again with the wide, strained, doubtful eyes. And again, from the pain of his breast, he knew how he loved her. He went and bent to kiss her, gently, passionately, with his heart's painful kiss.

"And my hair smells so horrible," she murmured in distraction. "And I'm so awful, I'm so awful! Oh, no, I'm too awful." And she broke into bitter, heartbroken sobbing. "You can't want to love me, I'm horrible."

"Don't be silly, don't be silly," he said, trying to comfort her, kissing her, holding her in his arms. "I want you, I want to marry you, we're going to be married, quickly, quickly—tomorrow if I can."

But she only sobbed terribly, and cried:

"I feel awful. I feel awful. I feel I'm horrible to you."

"No, I want you, I want you," was all he answered, blindly, with that terrible intonation which frightened her almost more than her horror lest he should *not* want her.

The Chinese Dog

Alberto Moravia

ALBERTO MORAVIA *(1907–) was born in Rome as Alberto Pincherle, the son of an architect. At age twenty-two, Moravia became famous for his first novel,* The Time of Indifference *(published in 1953 in the United States). A journalist, short-story writer, and novelist, Moravia soon became internationally known. During the Fascist regime in Italy, which Moravia opposed, his books were banned. His other major works (with English-translation dates) are* The Woman of Rome *(1949),* Two Adolescents: The Stories of Agostino and Luca *(1950),* Conjugal Love *(1951),* A Ghost at Noon *(1955),* Two Women *(1958),* The Empty Canvas *(1961). His collections of short stories include* Bitter Honeymoon *(1954),* Roman Tales *(1957),* The Wayward Wife *(1960),* More Roman Tales *(1963),* Fetish and Other Stories *(1965). "The Chinese Dog," which first appeared in* Esquire *in 1956, has not as yet been included in collections of Moravia's translated short stories published in America.*

That winter, in order to make a living, I finally had to resort to dog catching. Not on the payroll of the city, which then has the dogs exterminated, but on my own, in view of the tips I was given for each of the dogs stolen by me. I would go to one of the prosperous sections of town at the time of day when the maids take the dogs walking, and in my pocket I would have a cord with a slide knot tied into it. As soon as one of those maids came out, I would start following her, at a distance. Maidservants, as is known, have few chances to take their minds off things, and take advantage of these respites to meet with some woman friend or else with their male friends. The maid would let the dog run loose, and immediately he would trot on ahead, sniffing and stopping to lift his leg at each corner or tree. When I saw that the maid was deep in conversation, I would approach the dog, slip the cord over his head, and duck round the street corner. Then the next problem was getting to Tormarancio, where I lived. Partly by foot, and partly with the help of some taxi drivers who lived out that way, I would get as far as the Garbatella stop, and from there on one of those open trucks that did bus service I would finally get home. Home? Don't make me laugh. Let's put it this way: I would finally get to that corner of a room that, along with a narrow cot, I rented from Bonifazi, a worker friend of mine. That same room served as sleeping quarters for him, his wife and his three children; with the result that at night the floor was one whole spread of mattresses and if you wanted to get out, some one of them had to get up and make a roll of his mattress, to let you through. I would leave the dog with Bonifazi, who knew of this traffic, and the following day I would go back to that building from which I had seen the maid emerge. I would tell the superintendent how I had found such and such a dog. Immediately they would send for me, let me into an entrance hall that was all marble and mirrors, and almost throw their arms around me out of gratitude. The morning after, I would bring back the dog, pocket the tip, and start in all over again.

One day, with this system of the cord, I rounded up a strange dog, of a kind I had never seen before. He looked like a lion—large head, round and covered with fur, a smoothly shaved body, a stubby snout, and a tongue that was purplish black. He was a good animal, but not very lively; more on the sad side, and almost thoughtful. He followed me with his head hanging low, as though he knew what was in store for him.

That day it was raining. All I had on my back was a thin ragged jacket and an undershirt; my shoes were full of holes—in a word I got so drenched that on the truck my teeth started chattering, and when I moved my toes I could feel the water ooze through my socks and out through the shoe leather. Then in Tormarancio, which is in one of those low spots, the rain, as usual, had flooded the houses, and, instead of warmth, what I found was more water; and Bonifazi's wife shouting in despair, the children in tears, and Bonifazi himself trying to construct some sort of gangway across the flooded floor. I went straight to bed, without eating. That same night I broke out in a fever, and the following day I stayed in bed. The fever did not leave me for an entire week. I was in that corner, on that bed; with two clotheslines strung up over me and my belongings hanging on them. From the depths of my fever I stared out at the room, with all its mattresses stacked into the corners, with other lines and other clothes on them, crisscrossing in all directions. It was almost always dark, since the rain did not let up, and two out of the three windows had cardboard panes. Bonifazi's wife did the cooking in the next room, which meant that I was always alone, but I didn't mind, for when I feel bad I prefer not to talk. As for the dog, he was really good and, in order to keep the humidity from getting at him and making him ill, I had made a bed for him out of old rags and shavings which I kept under my cot. I kept giving money to Bonifazi's wife to buy food for him; not because I had the tip on my mind, but because I like animals and hate to make them suffer. On the seventh day I started raving, and I got the fixation that they wanted to take the dog away from me. I asked Bonifazi to have him put on my bed. Bonifazi did that, and I put my arms around the dog's body, pressed my face into that warm fur of his, and fell asleep hugging him. The dog didn't budge. During the night, perhaps owing to that fur of his, I sweated so much that I was soaked; then I felt as though I were released from a grip, and in the morning the fever had gone. All night long the dog had not moved.

For the next few days I took it easy, and meanwhile the sun had come out again, and I went walking in the neighborhood, pulling the dog behind me, on the cord. Just outside Tormarancio there are a number of shacks that make the Tormarancio ones look good by comparison. Do I have to describe them?—wooden crates and gas containers, topped off by sheets of corrugated roofing, surrounded by cane fences, and with doorways so low that you have to stoop to get in. In one of these shacks there was a Chinese, of the kind that sells ties in Rome. He had come there a few years before, and then had stayed, and he lived with a woman who was called Fesseria. She plied the usual trade; was thin, white, underfed; with a long face and a pair of heavy black eyebrows, and black eyes. Her hair was thick, black and as soft as silk, and when she put on some lipstick she even managed to be good-looking. The Chinese was pure Chinese; seen from the rear he might have been taken for one of those peasants from up north, squat and sturdy; but then he turned and you saw that he was Chinese. Well, with the dog I went walking in front of the Chinaman's shack, and without delay both of them came out—she with a pail full of water that almost landed, when she emptied it, on my legs; and he holding a pot, since he was always cooking. The Chinese came up to me and, speaking good Italian since he talks the way I do, said, "This breed of dog comes from my country . . . he is Chinese." And he explained that in China these dogs are as common as poodles here. He also said that, if I wanted, he was willing to take him, since the dog reminded him of his country, and that he would cherish him. But all he had to give in exchange was a couple of those raw-silk ties. I refused; what good were the ties when what I wanted was the cash reward? Fesseria, holding the pail, called out to me, "Luigi . . . so you won't give us the dog?" She was tantalizing, gay, jumping around from one puddle to the next on those long thin legs of hers. Even though I still felt pretty low, I couldn't help feeling attracted by her, so thin and white, with that pair of black eyebrows. However, I said nothing at all, and went back to Bonifazi's.

The next day I went into Rome, to the building where I had first seen the maid. But then things start going wrong. . . . "He belonged to an American family," the woman of the building told me, "and the family had to leave; yesterday. After all the fuss they made about the dog. . . . But anyway they had to leave, and they did."

So there I was; a fine specimen of a dog on my hands, and no idea what to do with him. At first I tried selling him, but that was no go. People took one look at my tattered clothes and said that the dog was stolen goods, as was true. On the other hand, I did not want to take him to the dog pound, since there they would have put him to death, poor thing, whereas I still remembered the night when he had cured me with the warmth of his fur, and had never moved. Meanwhile, however, he was costing me money, since he ate a great deal and was not small-sized.

One of those afternoons, I decided against going to the city. I left Tormarancio, which the sun had transformed from a swamp into a desert of dust, and climbed up to one of the nearby hills. By then it was springtime; without a cloud in the sky, with all that soft air and sunshine. Seen from up there even Tormarancio, with its long low houses and red roofs, seemed less of a prison camp than usual. The hill was covered with fresh tender green grass that was pleasing to see, and in places it looked as though there had been a snowfall, because of an outcropping of small daisies so thick that the grass was hidden by them. I roamed around from hill to hill, my hands in my pockets, whistling. The illness had done me good and I could feel my heart filling with a kind of vague hope, looking out towards the horizon full of sun, and watching large white butterflies as they headed right into it. The dog had become quite lively for a change, and raced ahead. At a certain point I went downhill and started following a brook that flowed between two high hills. Then I heard the dog bark, raised my eyes, and saw Fesseria, who was out walking too, alone, her hair loose on her shoulders, a blade of grass set between her teeth, her hands in the pockets of a striped smock of the kind worn by factory girls. She stopped and started playing with the dog, and then said, laughing, "Well, are you going to give us the dog?" Without pausing to think, I said, "I'll give him to you, on one condition."

To make a long story short, we made love; on the ground, between those two high hills, beside the brook. The dog, meanwhile, had started lapping up the water in the brook with his purple tongue; then settled back and sat there on the grass, eyeing us; to the point that it almost unnerved me. And I did what I did not only because that woman appealed to me, but also because I liked the idea of giving the dog away in return for some lovemaking; since by then I had grown fond of him and it seemed to me that that was the right price for him. In the end, we got up and Fesseria took the cord for the dog, saying, "He will be glad because it reminds him of his country." I stayed there, watching her go off with the dog, and I still had that feeling for her. Then I stretched out on the ground and slept for a couple of hours.

The next morning I went into the city and stayed there overnight, with a dachshund that I had picked up near Piazza Santiago del Cile. I slept in a city dormitory, and then went back to Tormarancio. That afternoon I went out walking again, with the dachshund, and happened to find myself in front of the shack of the Chinaman.

Fesseria was away, probably having gone to Rome. But he was

there, and he came out with a garbage can, which he emptied behind the shack. Why, I don't know, but I would have liked him to thank me for the dog, so I asked him where he was. He smiled and made a gesture which I didn't understand, and went back into the shack. The dachshund was poking around in the garbage. I went over and then I saw, in among the refuse, the paw of the dog, smeared with blood but with all its hair.

Later I was told that in their country the people eat dogs, everybody does, and there is no harm in it. But, at the time, the blood mounted to my head. I entered the shack; he had his back to me and was bent over the stove. He turned round, smiling, with a plate that contained a piece of dark-colored meat, in a sauce; and I realised that it was the meat of the dog and that he was inviting me to eat it. With my fist I sent the plate into his face, shouting, "Murderer! What have you done to the dog?" Immediately I realized that he did not understand why I was so mad. He ducked, ran out of the shack and headed towards Tormarancio. I scooped up a stone and hurled it at him; then I caught up with him and seized him by the neck. People rushed out and he kept hollering, "Grab him, he's crazy!" and I kept shaking him by the neck and shouting, "What did you do to the dog? Murderer! What did you do to the dog?" Finally they separated us, and got me on to the truck for Rome.

That same day I took the dachshund back to its owners and they gave me a tip. But I did not go back to Tormarancio. I had no belongings anyway, and had left nothing at Bonifazi's. I owed him one month's rent and thought that, after all, not all ills are one hundred per cent harmful. At the same time, that affair of the Chinese dog had given me a feeling of disgust for my livelihood, and I decided to change. I set myself up as a pedlar, pushing around a cart filled with almost everything—green olives, melon seeds, peeled chestnuts, peanuts, dried figs and walnuts. I twirled the wrapping paper into cones all day long, at the new bridge, at the entrance to the Aurelia tunnel, and more or less succeeded in keeping body and soul together. In that period I was always sad and life had little meaning for me, perhaps because of the dog. Only once I saw Fesseria, from a distance, but I did not speak to her. If she had told me that she too had eaten the dog, I think I would have killed her.

Love

Jesse Stuart

JESSE STUART *(1907–   ) was born in eastern Kentucky, where he has lived and worked almost all his life. Today he owns a farm of 723 acres at W-Hollow, near Greenup, on land where he was born. Proud of his heritage and strongly influenced by Kentucky's rich but demanding land and its resilient people, Stuart has frequently taken both this rural setting and these people—sometimes adding his life's experiences such as his years as a teacher and principal—and used them as themes for his poems, short stories, and novels. From 1934 to 1951, to illustrate his prodigious productivity, Stuart wrote 190 stories, many of them with deceptively simple themes that are deep in meaning and understanding. Today he is recognized as one of America's best-known regional writers. Among his many books are* Man with a Bull-Tongue Plow *(1934),* Taps for Private Tussie *(1943),* The Thread That Runs So True *(1949),* Kentucky Is My Land *(1952),* My Land Has a Voice *(1966), and* A Jesse Stuart Reader *(1963), stories and poems selected and introduced by Stuart.*

Yesterday when the bright sun blazed down on the wilted corn my father and I walked around the edge of the new ground to plan a fence. The cows kept coming through the chestnut oaks on the cliff and running over the young corn. They bit off the tips of the corn and trampled down the stubble.

My father walked in the cornbalk. Bob, our Collie, walked in front of my father. We heard a ground squirrel whistle down over the bluff among the dead treetops at the clearing's edge. "Whoop, take him, Bob," said my father. He lifted up a young stalk of corn, with wilted dried roots, where the ground squirrel had dug it up for the sweet grain of corn left on its tender roots. This has been a dry spring and the corn has kept well in the earth where the grain has sprouted. The ground squirrels love this corn. They dig up rows of it and eat the sweet grains. The young corn stalks are killed and we have to replant the corn.

I can see my father keep sicking Bob after the ground squirrel. He jumped over the corn rows. He started to run toward the ground squirrel. I, too, started running toward the clearing's edge where Bob was jumping and barking. The dust flew in tiny swirls behind our feet. There was a cloud of dust behind us.

"It's a big bull blacksnake," said my father. "Kill him, Bob! Kill him, Bob!"

Bob was jumping and snapping at the snake so as to make it strike and throw itself off guard. Bob had killed twenty-eight copperheads this spring. He knows how to kill a snake. He doesn't rush to do it. He takes his time and does the job well.

"Let's don't kill the snake," I said. "A blacksnake is a harmless snake. It kills poison snakes. It kills the copperhead. It catches more mice from the fields than a cat."

I could see the snake didn't want to fight the dog. The snake wanted to get away. Bob wouldn't let it. I wondered why it was crawling toward a heap of black loamy earth at the bench of the hill. I wondered why it had come from the chestnut oak sprouts and the matted greenbriars on the cliff. I looked as the snake lifted its pretty head in response to one of Bob's jumps. "It's not a bull blacksnake," I said. "It's a she-snake. Look at the white on her throat."

"A snake is an enemy to me," my father snapped. "I hate a snake. Kill it, Bob. Go in there and get that snake and quit playing with it!"

Bob obeyed my father. I hated to see him take this snake by the throat. She was so beautifully poised in the sunlight. Bob grabbed the white patch on her throat. He cracked her long body like an ox whip in the wind. He cracked it against the wind only. The blood spurted from her fine-curved throat. Something hit against my legs like pellets. Bob threw the snake down. I looked to see what had struck my legs. It was snake eggs. Bob had slung them from her body. She was going to the sand heap to lay her eggs, where the sun is the setting-hen that warms them and hatches them.

Bob grabbed her body there on the earth where the red blood was running down on the gray-piled loam. Her body was still writhing in pain. She acted like a greenweed held over a new-ground fire. Bob slung her viciously many times. He cracked her limp body against the wind. She was now limber as a shoestring in the wind. Bob threw her riddled body back on the sand. She quivered like a leaf in the lazy wind, then her riddled body lay perfectly still. The blood colored the loamy earth around the snake.

"Look at the eggs, won't you?" said my father. We counted thirty-seven eggs. I picked an egg up and held it in my hand. Only a minute ago there was life in it. It was an immature seed. It would not hatch. Mother sun could not incubate it on the warm earth. The egg I held in my hand was almost the size of a quail's egg. The shell on it was thin and tough and the egg appeared under the surface to be a watery egg.

"Well, Bob, I guess you see now why this snake couldn't fight," I said. "It is life. Weaker devour the stronger even among human beings. Dog kills snake. Snake kills birds. Birds kill the butterflies. Man conquers all. Man, too, kills for sport."

Bob was panting. He walked ahead of us back to the house. His tongue was out of his mouth. He was tired. He was hot under his shaggy coat of hair. His tongue nearly touched the dry dirt and white flecks of foam dripped from it. We walked toward the house. Neither my father nor I spoke. I still thought about the dead snake. The sun was going down over the chestnut ridge. A lark was singing. It was late for a lark to sing. The red evening clouds floated above the pine trees on our pasture hill. My father stood beside the path. His black hair was moved by the wind. His face was red in the blue wind of day. His eyes looked toward the sinking sun.

"And my father hates a snake," I thought.

I thought about the agony women know of giving birth. I thought about how they will fight to save their children. Then, I thought of the snake. I thought it was silly for me to think such thoughts.

This morning my father and I got up with the chickens. He says one has to get up with the chickens to do a day's work. We got the posthole digger, ax, spud, measuring pole and the mattock. We started for the clearing's edge. Bob didn't go along.

The dew was on the corn. My father walked behind with the posthole digger across his shoulder. I walked in front. The wind was blowing. It was a good morning wind to breathe and a wind that makes one feel like he can get under the edge of a hill and heave the whole hill upside down.

I walked out the corn row where we had come yesterday afternoon. I looked in front of me. I saw something. I saw it move. It was moving like a huge black rope winds around a windlass. "Steady," I says to my father. "Here is the bull blacksnake." He took one step up beside me and stood. His eyes grew wide apart.

"What do you know about this," he said.

"You have seen the bull blacksnake now," I said. "Take a good look at him! He is lying beside his dead mate. He has come to her. He, perhaps, was on her trail yesterday."

The male snake had trailed her to her doom. He had come in the night, under the roof of stars, as the moon shed rays of light on the quivering clouds of green. He had found his lover dead. He was coiled beside her, and she was dead.

The bull blacksnake lifted his head and followed us as we walked around the dead snake. He would have fought us to his death. He would have fought Bob to his death. "Take a stick," said my father, "and throw him over the hill so Bob won't find him. Did you ever see anything to beat that? I've heard they'd do that. But this is my first time to see it." I took a stick and threw him over the bank into the dewy sprouts on the cliff.

A Tree · A Rock · A Cloud

Carson McCullers

CARSON MC CULLERS *(1917–1967) was born in Georgia. During the Great Depression she went to New York City to study music, but instead turned to writing. Partially crippled by a series of strokes, she had chronic ill health for much of her life. Yet, in spite of her debilitating illnesses, her literary output is significant.* The Heart Is a Lonely Hunter *(1940), a novel, made her a literary success at age twenty-three. Other works are* Reflections in a Golden Eye *(1941),* The Member of the Wedding *(1946—a novel, 1949—a play);* The Ballad of the Sad Café *(1951),* Clock Without Hands *(1961), and, published after her death,* The Mortgaged Heart *(1971). Her writing, frequently including unusual characterizations, is piercing in its realistic portrayals of troubled people.*

It was raining that morning, and still very dark. When the boy reached the streetcar café he had almost finished his route and he went in for a cup of coffee. The place was an all-night café owned by a bitter and stingy man called Leo. After the raw, empty street the café seemed friendly and bright: along the counter there were a couple of soldiers, three spinners from the cotton mill, and in a corner a man who sat hunched over with his nose and half his face down in a beer mug. The boy wore a helmet such as aviators wear. When he went into the café he unbuckled the chin strap and raised the right flap up over his pink little ear; often as he drank his coffee someone would speak to him in a friendly way. But this morning Leo did not look into his face and none of the men were talking. He paid and was leaving the café when a voice called out to him:

"Son! Hey Son!"

He turned back and the man in the corner was crooking his finger and nodding to him. He had brought his face out of the beer mug and he seemed suddenly very happy. The man was long and pale, with a big nose and faded orange hair.

"Hey Son!"

The boy went toward him. He was an undersized boy of about twelve, with one shoulder drawn higher than the other because of the weight of the paper sack. His face was shallow, freckled, and his eyes were round child eyes.

"Yeah Mister?"

The man laid one hand on the paper boy's shoulders, then grasped the boy's chin and turned his face slowly from one side to the other. The boy shrank back uneasily.

"Say! What's the big idea?"

The boy's voice was shrill; inside the café it was suddenly very quiet.

The man said slowly: "I love you."

All along the counter the men laughed. The boy, who had scowled and sidled away, did not know what to do. He looked over the counter at Leo, and Leo watched him with a weary, brittle jeer. The boy tried to laugh also. But the man was serious and sad.

"I did not mean to tease you, Son," he said. "Sit down and have a beer with me. There is something I have to explain."

Cautiously, out of the corner of his eye, the paper boy questioned the men along the counter to see what he should do. But they had gone back to their beer or their breakfast and did not notice him. Leo put a cup of coffee on the counter and a little jug of cream.

"He is a minor," Leo said.

The paper boy slid himself up onto the stool. His ear beneath the upturned flap of the helmet was very small and red. The man was nodding at him soberly. "It is important," he said. Then he reached in his hip pocket and brought out something which he held up in the palm of his hand for the boy to see.

"Look very carefully," he said.

The boy stared, but there was nothing to look at very carefully. The man held in his big, grimy palm a photograph. It was the face of a woman, but blurred, so that only the hat and the dress she was wearing stood out clearly.

"See?" the man asked.

The boy nodded and the man placed another picture in his palm. The woman was standing on a beach in a bathing suit. The suit made her stomach very big, and that was the main thing you noticed.

"Got a good look?" He leaned over closer and finally asked "You ever seen her before?"

The boy sat motionless, staring slantwise at the man. "Not so I know of."

"Very well." The man blew on the photographs and put them back into his pocket. "That was my wife."

"Dead?" the boy asked.

Slowly the man shook his head. He pursed his lips as though about to whistle and answered in a long-drawn way: "Nuuu—" he said. "I will explain."

The beer on the counter before the man was in a large brown mug. He did not pick it up to drink. Instead he bent down and, putting his face over the rim, he rested there for a moment. Then with both hands he tilted the mug and sipped.

"Some night you'll go to sleep with your big nose in a mug and drown," said Leo. "Prominent transient drowns in beer. That would be a cute death."

The paper boy tried to signal to Leo. While the man was not looking he screwed up his face and worked his mouth to question soundlessly: "Drunk?" But Leo only raised his eyebrows and turned away to put some pink strips of bacon on the grill. The man pushed the mug away from him, straightened himself, and folded his loose crooked hands on the counter. His face was sad as he looked at the paper boy. He did not blink, but from time to time the lids closed down with delicate gravity over his pale green eyes. It was nearing dawn and the boy shifted the weight of the paper sack.

"I am talking about love," the man said. "With me it is a science."

The boy half slid down from the stool. But the man raised his forefinger, and there was something about him that held the boy and would not let him go away.

"Twelve years ago I married the woman in the photograph. She was my wife for one year, nine months, three days, and two nights. I loved her. Yes . . ." He tightened his blurred, rambling voice and said again: "I loved her. I thought also that she loved me. I was a railroad engineer. She had all home comforts and luxuries. It never crept into my brain that she was not satisfied. But do you know what happened?"

"Mgneeow!" said Leo.

The man did not take his eyes from the boy's face. "She left me. I came in one night and the house was empty and she was gone. She left me."

"With a fellow?" the boy asked.

Gently the man placed his palm down on the counter. "Why naturally, Son. A woman does not run off like that alone."

The café was quiet, the soft rain black and endless in the street outside. Leo pressed down the frying bacon with the prongs of his long fork. "So you have been chasing the floozie for eleven years. You frazzled old rascal!"

For the first time the man glanced at Leo. "Please don't be vulgar. Besides, I was not speaking to you." He turned back to the boy and said in a trusting and secretive undertone: "Let's not pay any attention to him. O.K.?"

The paper boy nodded doubtfully.

"It was like this," the man continued. "I am a person who feels many things. All my life one thing after another has impressed me. Moonlight. The leg of a pretty girl. One thing after another. But the point is that when I had enjoyed anything there was a peculiar sensation as though it was laying around loose in me. Nothing seemed to finish itself up or fit in with the other things. Women? I had my portion of them. The same. Afterwards laying around loose in me. I was a man who had never loved."

Very slowly he closed his eyelids, and the gesture was like a curtain drawn at the end of a scene in a play. When he spoke again his voice was excited and the words came fast—the lobes of his large, loose ears seemed to tremble.

"Then I met this woman. I was fifty-one years old and she always said she was thirty. I met her at a filling station and we were married within three days. And do you know what it was like? I just can't tell you. All I had ever felt was gathered together around this woman. Nothing lay around loose in me any more but was finished up by her."

The man stopped suddenly and stroked his long nose. His voice sank down to a steady and reproachful undertone: "I'm not explaining this right. What happened was this. There were these beautiful feelings and loose little pleasures inside me. And this woman was something like an assembly line for my soul. I run these little pieces of myself through her and I come out complete. Now do you follow me?"

"What was her name?" the boy asked.

"Oh," he said. "I called her Dodo. But that is immaterial."

"Did you try to make her come back?"

The man did not seem to hear. "Under the circumstances you can imagine how I felt when she left me."

Leo took the bacon from the grill and folded two strips of it between a bun. He had a gray face, with slitted eyes, and a pinched nose saddled by faint blue shadows. One of the mill workers signaled for more coffee and Leo poured it. He did not give refills on coffee free. The spinner ate breakfast there every morning, but the better Leo knew his customers the stingier he treated them. He nibbled his own bun as though he grudged it to himself.

"And you never got hold of her again?"

The boy did not know what to think of the man, and his child's face was uncertain with mingled curiosity and doubt. He was new on the paper route; it was still strange to him to be out in the town in the black, queer early morning.

"Yes," the man said. "I took a number of steps to get her back. I went around trying to locate her. I went to Tulsa where she had folks. And to Mobile. I went to every town she had ever mentioned to me, and I hunted down every man she had formerly been connected with. Tulsa, Atlanta, Chicago, Cheehaw, Memphis. . . . For the better part of two years I chased around the country trying to lay hold of her."

"But the pair of them had vanished from the face of the earth!" said Leo.

"Don't listen to him," the man said confidentially. "And also just forget those two years. They are not important. What matters is that around the third year a curious thing began to happen to me."

"What?" the boy asked.

The man leaned down and tilted his mug to take a sip of beer. But as he hovered over the mug his nostrils fluttered slightly; he sniffed the staleness of the beer and did not drink. "Love is a curious thing to begin with. At first I thought only of getting her back. It was a kind of mania. But then as time went on I tried to remember her. But do you know what happened?"

"No," the boy said.

"When I laid myself down on a bed and tried to think about her my mind became a blank. I couldn't see her. I would take out her pictures and look. No good. Nothing doing. A blank. Can you imagine it?"

"Say Mac!" Leo called down the counter. "Can you imagine this bozo's mind a blank!"

Slowly, as though fanning away flies, the man waved his hand. His green eyes were concentrated and fixed on the shallow little face of the paper boy.

"But a sudden piece of glass on a sidewalk. Or a nickel tune in a music box. A shadow on a wall at night. And I would remember. It might happen in a street and I would cry or bang my head against a lamppost. You follow me?"

"A piece of glass . . ." the boy said.

"Anything. I would walk around and I had no power of how and when to remember her. You think you can put up a kind of shield. But remembering don't come to a man face forward—it corners around sideways. I was at the mercy of everything I saw and heard. Suddenly instead of me combing the countryside to find her she begun to chase me around in my very soul. *She* chasing *me*, mind you! And in my soul."

The boy asked finally: "What part of the country were you in then?"

"Ooh," the man groaned. "I was a sick mortal. It was like smallpox. I confess, Son, that I boozed. I fornicated. I committed any sin that suddenly appealed to me. I am loath to confess it but I will do so. When I recall that period it is all curdled in my mind, it was so terrible."

The man leaned his head down and tapped his forehead on the counter. For a few seconds he stayed bowed over in this position, the back of his stringy neck covered with orange furze, his hands with their long warped fingers held palm to palm in an attitude of prayer.

Then the man straightened himself; he was smiling and suddenly his face was bright and tremulous and old.

"It was in the fifth year that it happened," he said. "And with it I started my science."

Leo's mouth jerked with a pale, quick grin. "Well none of we boys are getting any younger," he said. Then with sudden anger he balled up a dishcloth he was holding and threw it down hard on the floor. "You draggle-tailed old Romeo!"

"What happened?" the boy asked.

The old man's voice was high and clear: "Peace," he answered.

"Huh?"

"It is hard to explain scientifically, Son," he said. "I guess the logical explanation is that she and I had fleed around from each other for so long that finally we just got tangled up together and lay down and quit. Peace. A queer and beautiful blankness. It was spring in Portland and the rain came every afternoon. All evening I just stayed there on my bed in the dark. And that is how the science come to me."

The windows in the streetcar were pale blue with light. The two soldiers paid for their beers and opened the door—one of the soldiers combed his hair and wiped off his muddy puttees before they went outside. The three mill workers bent silently over their breakfasts. Leo's clock was ticking on the wall.

"It is this. And listen carefully. I meditated on love and reasoned it out. I realized what is wrong with us. Men fall in love for the first time. And what do they fall in love with?"

The boy's soft mouth was partly open and he did not answer.

"A woman," the old man said. "Without science, with nothing to go by, they undertake the most dangerous and sacred experience in God's earth. They fall in love with a woman. Is that correct, Son?"

"Yeah," the boy said faintly.

"They start at the wrong end of love. They begin at the climax. Can you wonder it is so miserable? Do you know how men should love?"

The old man reached over and grasped the boy by the collar of his leather jacket. He gave him a gentle little shake and his green eyes gazed down unblinking and grave.

"Son, do you know how love should be begun?"

The boy sat small and listening and still. Slowly he shook his head. The old man leaned closer and whispered:

"A tree. A rock. A cloud."

It was still raining outside in the street: a mild, gray, endless rain. The mill whistle blew for the six o'clock shift and the three spinners paid and went away. There was no one in the café but Leo, the old man, and the little paper boy.

"The weather was like this in Portland," he said. "At the time my science was begun. I meditated and I started very cautious. I would pick up something from the street and take it home with me. I bought a goldfish and I concentrated on the goldfish and I loved it. I graduated from one thing to another. Day by day I was getting this technique. On the road from Portland to San Diego—"

"Aw shut up!" screamed Leo suddenly. "Shut up! Shut up!"

The old man still held the collar of the boy's jacket; he was trembling and his face was earnest and bright and wild. "For six years now I have gone around by myself and built up my science. And now I am a master. Son. I can love anything. No longer do I have to think about it even. I see a street full of people and a beautiful light comes in me. I watch a bird in the sky. Or I meet a traveler on the road. Everything, Son. And anybody. All stranger and all loved! Do you realize what a science like mine can mean?"

The boy held himself stiffly, his hands curled tight around the counter edge. Finally he asked: "Did you ever really find that lady?"

"What? What say, Son?"

"I mean," the boy asked timidly. "Have you fallen in love with a woman again?"

The old man loosened his grasp on the boy's collar. He turned away and for the first time his green eyes had a vague and scattered look. He lifted the mug from the counter, drank down the yellow beer. His head was shaking slowly from side to side. Then finally he answered: "No, Son. You see that is the last step in my science. I go cautious. And I am not quite ready yet."

"Well!" said Leo. "Well well well!"

The old man stood in the open doorway. "Remember," he said. Framed there in the gray damp light of the early morning he looked shrunken and seedy and frail. But his smile was bright. "Remember I love you," he said with a last nod. And the door closed quietly behind him.

The boy did not speak for a long time. He pulled down the bangs on his forehead and slid his grimy little forefinger around the rim of his empty cup. Then without looking at Leo he finally asked:

"Was he drunk?"

"No," said Leo shortly.

The boy raised his clear voice higher. "Then was he a dope fiend?"

"No."

The boy looked up at Leo, and his flat little face was desperate, his voice urgent and shrill. "Was he crazy? Do you think he was a lunatic?" The paper boy's voice dropped suddenly with doubt. "Leo? Or not?"

But Leo would not answer him. Leo had run a night café for fourteen years, and he held himself to be a critic of craziness. There were the town characters and also the transients who roamed in from the night. He knew the manias of all of them. But he did not want to satisfy the questions of the waiting child. He tightened his pale face and was silent.

So the boy pulled down the right flap of his helmet and as he turned to leave he made the only comment that seemed safe to him, the only remark that could not be laughed down and despised:

"He sure has done a lot of traveling."

The Lament

Anton Chekhov

ANTON CHEKHOV *(1860–1904) was born in South Russia. He studied medicine at the University of Moscow, completed his studies, but did not practice except once during an epidemic. Chekhov gave most of his energies to writing, but because of his poor health—he had tuberculosis—he spent most of his last years at European health resorts. Chekhov wrote several novels, but his short stories and plays are outstanding. His short stories have been translated by Constance Garnett into thirteen volumes (1913–1922); his four best-known plays are* The Sea Gull *(1896),* Uncle Vanya *(1897),* The Three Sisters *(1901), and* The Cherry Orchard *(1904).*

It is twilight. A thick wet snow is twirling around the newly lighted street lamps, and lying in soft thin layers on roofs, on horses' backs, on people's shoulders and hats. The cabdriver Iona Potapov is quite white, and looks like a phantom; he is bent double as far as a human body can bend double; he is seated on his box; he never makes a move. If a whole snowdrift fell on him, it seems as if he would not find it necessary to shake it off. His little horse is also quite white, and remains motionless; its immobility, its angularity, and its straight wooden-looking legs, even close by, give it the appearance of a gingerbread horse worth a *kopek*. It is, no doubt, plunged in deep thought. If you were snatched from the plow, from your usual gray surroundings, and were thrown into this slough full of monstrous lights, unceasing noise, and hurrying people, you too would find it difficult not to think.

Iona and his little horse have not moved from their place for a long while. They left their yard before dinner, and up to now, not a fare. The evening mist is descending over the town, the white lights of the lamps replacing brighter rays, and the hubbub of the street getting louder. "Cabby for Viborg way!" suddenly hears Iona. "Cabby!"

Iona jumps, and through his snow-covered eyelashes sees an officer in a greatcoat, with his hood over his head.

"Viborg way!" the officer repeats. "Are you asleep, eh? Viborg way!"

With a nod of assent Iona picks up the reins, in consequence of which layers of snow slip off the horse's back and neck. The officer seats himself in the sleigh, the cabdriver smacks his lips to encourage his horse, stretches out his neck like a swan, sits up, and, more from habit than necessity, brandishes his whip. The little horse also stretches its neck, bends its wooden-looking legs, and makes a move undecidedly.

"What are you doing, werewolf!" is the exclamation Iona hears from the dark mass moving to and fro, as soon as they have started.

"Where the devil are you going? To the r-r-right!"

"You do not know how to drive. Keep to the right!" calls the officer angrily.

A coachman from a private carriage swears at him; a passerby, who has run across the road and rubbed his shoulder against the horse's nose, looks at him furiously as he sweeps the snow from his sleeve. Iona shifts about on his seat as if he were on needles, moves his elbows as if he were trying to keep his equilibrium, and gapes about like someone suffocating, who does not understand why and wherefore he is there.

"What scoundrels they all are!" jokes the officer; "one would think they had all entered into an agreement to jostle you or fall under your horse."

Iona looks around at the officer, and moves his lips. He evidently wants to say something, but the only sound that issues is a snuffle.

"What?" asks the officer.

Iona twists his mouth into a smile, and with an effort says hoarsely:

"My son, *barin,* died this week."

"Hm! What did he die of?"

Iona turns with his whole body toward his fare, and says:

"And who knows! They say high fever. He was three days in the hospital, and then died. . . . God's will be done."

"Turn around! The devil!" sounds from the darkness. "Have you popped off, old doggie, eh? Use your eyes!"

"Go on, go on," says the officer, "otherwise we shall not get there by tomorrow. Hurry up a bit!"

The cabdriver again stretches his neck, sits up, and, with a bad grace, brandishes his whip. Several times again he turns to look at his fare, but the latter has closed his eyes, and apparently is not disposed to listen. Having deposited the officer in the Viborg, he stops by the tavern, doubles himself up on his seat, and again remains motionless, while the snow once more begins to cover him and his horse. An hour, and another. . . . Then, along the footpath, with a squeak of galoshes, and quarreling, come three young men, two of them tall and lanky, the third one short and humpbacked.

"Cabby, to the Police Bridge!" in a cracked voice calls the humpback. "The three of us for two *griveniks!*"

Iona picks up his reins, and smacks his lips. Two *griveniks* is not a fair price, but he does not mind whether it is a *rouble* or five *kopeks*—to him it is all the same now, so long as they are fares. The young men, jostling each other and using bad language, approach the sleigh, and all three at once try to get onto the seat; then begins a discussion as to which two shall sit and who shall be the one to stand. After wrangling, abusing each other, and much petulance, it is at last decided that the humpback shall stand, as he is the smallest.

"Now then, hurry up!" says the humpback in a twanging voice, as he takes his place and breathes in Iona's neck. "Old furry! Here, mate, what a cap you have! There is not a worse one to be found in all Petersburg! . . ."

"He-he!—he-he!" giggles Iona. "Such a . . ."

"Now you, 'such a,' hurry up, are you going the whole way at this pace? Are you? . . . Do you want it in the neck?"

"My head feels like bursting," says one of the lanky ones. "Last night at the Donkmasovs, Vaska and I drank the whole of four bottles of cognac."

"I don't understand what you lie for," says the other lanky one angrily; "you lie like a brute."

"God strike me, it's the truth!"

"It's as much the truth as the louse coughs!"

"He, he," grins Iona, "what gay young gentlemen!"

"Pshaw, go to the devil!" says the humpback indignantly.

"Are you going to get on or not, you old pest? Is that the way to drive? Use the whip a bit! Go on, devil, go on, give it to him well!"

Iona feels at his back the little man wriggling, and the tremble in his voice. He listens to the insults hurled at him, sees the people, and little by little the feeling of loneliness leaves him. The humpback goes on swearing until he gets mixed up in some elaborate six-foot oath, or chokes with coughing. The lankies begin to talk about a certain Nadejda Petrovna. Iona looks round again, he murmurs:

"My son . . . died this week."

"We must all die," sighs the humpback, wiping his lips after an attack of coughing. "Now, hurry up, hurry up! Gentlemen, I really cannot go any farther like this! When will he get us there?"

"Well, just you stimulate him a little in the neck!"

"You old pest, do you hear, I'll bone your neck for you! If one treated the like of you with ceremony one would have to go on foot! Do you hear, old serpent Gorinytch! Or do you not care a spit?"

Iona hears rather than feels the blows they deal him.

"He, he," he laughs. "They are gay young gentlemen, God bless 'em!"

"Cabby, are you married?" asks a lanky one.

"I? He, he, gay young gentlemen! Now I have only a wife and the moist ground. . . . He, ho, ho . . . that is to say, the grave. My son has died, and I am alive. . . . A wonderful thing, death mistook the door . . . instead of coming to me, it went to my son. . . ."

Iona turns round to tell them how his son died, but at this moment the humpback, giving a little sigh, announces, "Thank God, we have at last reached our destination," and Iona watches them disappear through the dark entrance. Once more he is alone, and again surrounded by silence. . . . His grief, which has abated for a short while, returns and rends his heart with greater force. With an anxious and hurried look, he searches among the crowds passing on either side of the street to find whether there may be just one person who will listen to him. But the crowds hurry by without noticing him or his trouble. Yet it is such an immense, illimitable grief. Should his heart break and the grief pour out, it would flow over the whole earth, so it seems, and yet no one sees it. It has managed to conceal itself in such an insignificant shell that no one can see it even by day and with a light.

Iona sees a hall porter with some sacking, and decides to talk to him.

"Friend, what sort of time is it?" he asks.

"Past nine. What are you standing here for? Move on."

Iona moves on a few steps, doubles himself up, and abandons himself to his grief. He sees it is useless to turn to people for help. In less than five minutes he straightens himself, holds up his head as if he felt some sharp pain, and gives a tug at the reins; he can bear it no longer. "The stables," he thinks, and the little horse, as if it understood, starts off at a trot.

About an hour and a half later Iona is seated by a large dirty stove. Around the stove, on the floor, on the benches, people are snoring; the air is thick and suffocatingly hot. Iona looks at the sleepers, scratches himself, and regrets having returned so early.

"I have not even earned my fodder," he thinks. "That's what's my trouble. A man who knows his job, who has had enough to eat, and his horse too, can always sleep peacefully."

A young cabdriver in one of the corners half gets up, grunts sleepily, and stretches towards a bucket of water.

"Do you want a drink?" Iona asks him.

"Don't I want a drink!"

"That's so? Your good health! But listen, mate—you know, my son is dead. . . . Did you hear? This week, in the hospital. . . . It's a long story."

Iona looks to see what effect his words have, but sees none—the young man has hidden his face and is fast asleep again. The old man sighs, and scratches his head. Just as much as the young one wants to drink, the old man wants to talk. It will soon be a week since his son died, and he has not been able to speak about it properly to anyone. One must tell it slowly and carefully; how his son fell ill, how he suffered, what he said before he died, how he died. One must describe every detail of the funeral, and the journey to the hospital to fetch the dead son's clothes. His daughter Anissia has remained in the village—one must talk about her too. Is it nothing he has to tell? Surely the listener would gasp and sigh, and sympathize with him? It is better, too, to talk to women; although they are stupid, two words are enough to make them sob.

"I'll go and look after my horse," thinks Iona; "there's always time to sleep. No fear of that!"

He puts on his coat, and goes to the stables to his horse; he thinks of the corn, the hay, the weather. When he is alone, he dares not think of his son; he can speak about him to anyone, but to think of him, and picture him to himself, is unbearably painful.

"Are you tucking in?" Iona asks his horse, looking at its bright eyes; "go on, tuck in, though we've not earned our corn, we can eat hay. Yes! I am too old to drive—my son could have, not I. He was a first-rate cabdriver. If only he had lived!"

Iona is silent for a moment, then continues:

"That's how it is, my old horse. There's no more Kuzma Ionitch. He has left us to live, and he went off pop. Now let's say, you had a foal, you were the foal's mother, and suddenly, let's say, that foal went and left you to live after him. It would be sad, wouldn't it?"

The little horse munches, listens, and breathes over its master's hand. . . .

Iona's feelings are too much for him, and he tells the little horse the whole story.

Translated by Adeline Lister Kay

Crossing into Poland

Isaac Babel

ISAAC BABEL *(1894–1941) was born in Odessa, Russia, the son of a Jewish merchant. He studied Hebrew, the Bible, and the Talmud until he was sixteen. At age fifteen, after learning French from a teacher/friend, he began writing stories in French. In 1915, in Petrograd, he tried to get his stories (now being written in Russian) published but had no success. In 1916 Babel met Maxim Gorky who published Babel's stories in a magazine that Gorky edited. From 1914 to 1917 Babel was a volunteer soldier on the Rumanian front, and his experience is reflected in such stories as "Crossing into Poland." In 1923 Babel began his first collection of short stories,* Red Cavalry, *which appeared in 1926. Separate stories published in 1924 made him an overnight success. In1941, when Babel refused to write in sympathy with the Communist party line, he was arrested, tried by a military court, and shot. Two English translations of his stories are* Collected Stories *(1955) and* You Must Know Everything: Stories 1915–1937 *(1969). In 1964, his daughter Nathalie edited* Isaac Babel: The Lonely Years: 1925–1939, Unpublished Stories and Private Correspondence.

The Commander of the VI Division reported: Novgorod-Volynsk was taken at dawn today. The Staff had left Krapivno, and our baggage train was spread out in a noisy rearguard over the highroad from Brest to Warsaw built by Nicholas I upon the bones of peasants.

Fields flowered around us, crimson with poppies; a noontide

breeze played in the yellowing rye; on the horizon virginal buckwheat rose like the wall of a distant monastery. The Volyn's peaceful stream moved away from us in sinuous curves and was lost in the pearly haze of the birch groves; crawling between flowery slopes, it wound weary arms through a wilderness of hops. The orange sun rolled down the sky like a lopped-off head, and mild light glowed from the cloud gorges. The standards of the sunset flew above our heads. Into the cool of evening dripped the smell of yesterday's blood, of slaughtered horses. The blackened Zbruch roared, twisting itself into foamy knots at the falls. The bridges were down, and we waded across the river. On the waves rested a majestic moon. The horses were in to the cruppers, and the noisy torrent gurgled among hundreds of horses' legs. Somebody sank, loudly defaming the Mother of God. The river was dotted with the square black patches of the wagons, and was full of confused sounds, of whistling and singing, that rose above the gleaming hollows, the serpentine trails of the moon.

Far on in the night we reached Novgorod. In the house where I was billeted I found a pregnant woman and two red-haired, scraggy-necked Jews. A third, huddled to the wall with his head covered up, was already asleep. In the room I was given I discovered turned-out wardrobes, scraps of women's fur coats on the floor, human filth, fragments of the occult crockery the Jews use only once a year, at Eastertime.

"Clear this up," I said to the woman. "What a filthy way to live!"

The two Jews rose from their places and, hopping on their felt soles, cleared the mess from the floor. They skipped about noiselessly, monkey-fashion, like Japs in a circus act, their necks swelling and twisting. They put down for me a feather bed that had been disemboweled, and I lay down by the wall next to the third Jew, the one who was asleep. Faint-hearted poverty closed in over my couch.

Silence overcame all. Only the moon, clasping in her blue hands her round, bright, carefree face, wandered like a vagrant outside the window.

I kneaded my numbed legs and, lying on the ripped-open mattress, fell asleep. And in my sleep the Commander of the VI Division appeared to me; he was pursuing the Brigade Commander on a heavy stallion, fired at him twice between the eyes. The bullets pierced the Brigade Commander's head, and both his eyes dropped to the ground. "Why did you turn back the brigade?" shouted Savitsky, the Divisional Commander, to the wounded man—and here I woke up, for the pregnant woman was groping over my face with her fingers.

"Good sir," she said, "you're calling out in your sleep and you're tossing to and fro. I'll make you a bed in another corner, for you're pushing my father about."

She raised her thin legs and rounded belly from the floor and removed the blanket from the sleeper. Lying on his back was an old man, a dead old man. His throat had been torn out and his face cleft in two; in his beard blue blood was clotted like a lump of lead.

"Good sir," said the Jewess, shaking up the feather bed, "the Poles cut his throat, and he begging them: 'Kill me in the yard so that my daughter shan't see me die.' But they did as suited them. He passed away in this room, thinking of me. —And now I should wish to know," cried the woman with sudden and terrible violence, "I should wish to know where in the whole world you could find another father like my father?"

Translated by Walter Morison

The Lagoon

Joseph Conrad

JOSEPH CONRAD (1857–1924) was born Teodor Jósef Konrad Nalecz Korzeniowski in Russian Poland of Polish parents. Conrad's father was a Russian translator of Shakespeare. As a youth Conrad went to sea and worked on ships for twenty years, most of that time in the British merchant service where he concluded his career as master mariner in command of his own ship. His travels took him to many parts of the world, which gave him background, along with his sailing experiences, for his fiction. In 1894 Conrad settled in England, planning to become a writer. His novels include Almayer's Folly *(1895),* The Nigger of the "Narcissus" *(1897),* Lord Jim *(1900),* Typhoon *(1902),* Nostromo *(1904),* Chance *(1913), and* Victory *(1915). A master of style, Conrad explored the inner life of man, not only in many of his novels but also in short works such as "Youth" (1902), "Heart of Darkness" (1902), and "The Secret Sharer" (1912).*

The white man, leaning with both arms over the roof of the little house in the stern of the boat, said to the steersman—

"We will pass the night in Arsat's clearing. It is late."

The Malay only grunted, and went on looking fixedly at the river. The white man rested his chin on his crossed arms and gazed at the wake of the boat. At the end of the straight avenue of forests cut by the intense glitter of the river, the sun appeared unclouded and dazzling, poised low over the water that shone smoothly like a band of metal. The forests, somber and dull, stood motionless and silent on each side of the broad stream. At the foot of big, towering trees, trunkless nipa palms rose from the mud of the bank, in bunches of leaves enormous and heavy, that hung unstirring over the brown swirl of eddies. In the stillness of the air every tree, every leaf, every bough, every tendril of creeper and every petal of minute blossoms seemed to have been bewitched into an immobility perfect and final. Nothing moved on the river but the eight paddles that rose flashing regularly, dipped together with a single splash; while the steersman swept right and left with a periodic and sudden flourish of his blade describing a glinting semicircle above his head. The churned-up water frothed alongside with a confused murmur. And the white man's canoe, advancing upstream in the short-lived disturbance of its own making, seemed to enter the portals of a land from which the very memory of motion had forever departed.

The white man, turning his back upon the setting sun, looked along the empty and broad expanse of the sea-reach. For the last three miles of its course the wandering, hesitating river, as if enticed irresistibly by the freedom of an open horizon, flows straight into the sea, flows straight to the east—to the east that harbors both light and darkness. Astern of the boat the repeated call of some bird, a cry discordant and feeble, skipped along over the smooth water and lost itself, before it could reach the other shore, in the breathless silence of the world.

The steersman dug his paddle into the stream, and held hard with stiffened arms, his body thrown forward. The water gurgled aloud; and suddenly the long straight reach seemed to pivot on its center, the forest swung in a semicircle, and the slanting beams of sunset touched the broadside of the canoe with a fiery glow, throwing the slender and distorted shadows of its crew upon the streaked glitter of the river. The white man turned to look ahead. The course of the boat had been altered at right angles to the stream, and the carved dragon-head of its prow was pointing now at a gap in the fringing bushes of the bank. It glided through, brushing the overhanging twigs, and disappeared from the river like some slim and amphibious creature leaving the water for its lair in the forests.

The narrow creek was like a ditch: tortuous, fabulously deep; filled with gloom under the thin strip of pure and shining blue of the heaven. Immense trees soared up, invisible behind the festooned draperies of creepers. Here and there, near the glistening blackness of the water, a twisted root of some tall tree showed amongst the tracery of small ferns, black and dull, writhing and motionless, like an arrested snake. The short words of the paddlers reverberated loudly between the thick and somber walls of vegetation. Darkness oozed out from between the trees, through the tangled maze of the creepers, from behind the great fantastic and unstirring leaves; the darkness, mysterious and invincible; the darkness scented and poisonous of impenetrable forests.

The men poled in the shoaling water. The creek broadened, opening out into a wide sweep of a stagnant lagoon. The forests receded from the marshy bank, leaving a level strip of bright green, reedy grass to frame the reflected blueness of the sky. A fleecy pink cloud drifted high above, trailing the delicate coloring of its image under the floating leaves and the silvery blossoms of the lotus. A little house, perched on high piles, appeared black in the distance. Near it, two tall nibong palms, that seemed to have come out of the forests in the background, leaned slightly over the ragged roof, with a suggestion of sad tenderness and care in the droop of their leafy and soaring heads.

The steersman, pointing with his paddle, said, "Arsat is there. I see his canoe fast between the piles."

The polers ran along the sides of the boat glancing over their shoulders at the end of the day's journey. They would have preferred to spend the night somewhere else than on this lagoon of weird aspect and ghostly reputation. Moreover, they disliked Arsat, first as a stranger, and also because he who repairs a ruined house, and dwells in it, proclaims that he is not afraid to live amongst the spirits that haunt the places abandoned by mankind. Such a man can disturb the course of fate by glances or words; while his familiar ghosts are not easy to propitiate by casual wayfarers upon whom they long to wreak the malice of their human master. White men care not for such things, being unbelievers and in league with the Father of Evil, who leads them unharmed through the invisible dangers of this world. To the warnings of the righteous they oppose an offensive pretense of disbelief. What is there to be done?

So they thought, throwing their weight on the end of their long poles. The big canoe glided on swiftly, noiselessly, and smoothly, towards Arsat's clearing, till, in a great rattling of poles thrown down, and the loud murmurs of "Allah be praised!" it came with a gentle knock against the crooked piles below the house.

The boatmen with uplifted faces shouted discordantly, "Arsat! O Arsat!" Nobody came. The white man began to climb the rude ladder giving access to the bamboo platform before the house. The juragan of the boat said sulkily, "We will cook in the sampan, and sleep on the water."

"Pass my blankets and the basket," said the white man, curtly.

He knelt on the edge of the platform to receive the bundle. Then the boat shoved off, and the white man, standing up, confronted Arsat, who had come out through the low door of his hut. He was a man young, powerful, with broad chest and muscular arms. He had nothing on but his sarong. His head was bare. His big, soft eyes stared eagerly at the white man, but his voice and demeanor were composed as he asked, without any words of greeting—

"Have you medicine, Tuan?"

"No," said the visitor in a startled tone. "No. Why? Is there sickness in the house?"

"Enter and see," replied Arsat, in the same calm manner, and turning short round, passed again through the small doorway. The white man, dropping his bundles, followed.

In the dim light of the dwelling he made out on a couch of bamboos a woman stretched on her back under a broad sheet of red cotton cloth. She lay still, as if dead; but her big eyes, wide open, glittered in the gloom, staring upwards at the slender rafters, motionless and unseeing. She was in a high fever, and evidently unconscious. Her cheeks were sunk slightly, her lips were partly open, and on the young face there was the ominous and fixed expression—the absorbed, contemplating expression of the unconscious who are going to die. The two men stood looking down at her in silence.

"Has she been long ill?" asked the traveler.

"I have not slept for five nights," answered the Malay, in a deliberate tone. "At first she heard voices calling her from the water and struggled against me who held her. But since the sun of today rose she hears nothing—she hears not me. She sees nothing. She sees not me—me!"

He remained silent for a minute, then asked softly—

"Tuan, will she die?"

"I fear so," said the white man, sorrowfully. He had known Arsat years ago, in a far country in times of trouble and danger, when no friendship is to be despised. And since his Malay friend had come unexpectedly to dwell in the hut on the lagoon with a strange woman, he had slept many times there, in his journeys up and down the river. He liked the man who knew how to keep faith in council and how to fight without fear by the side of his white friend. He liked him—not so much perhaps as a man likes his favorite dog—but still he liked him well enough to help and ask no questions, to think sometimes vaguely and hazily in the midst of his own pursuits, about the lonely man and the long-haired woman with audacious face and triumphant eyes, who lived together hidden by the forests—alone and feared.

The white man came out of the hut in time to see the enormous conflagration of sunset put out by the swift and stealthy shadows that, rising like a black and impalpable vapor above the treetops, spread over the heaven, extinguishing the crimson glow of floating clouds and the red brilliance of departing daylight. In a few moments all the stars came out above the intense blackness of the earth and the great lagoon gleaming suddenly with reflected lights resembled an oval patch of night sky flung down into the hopeless and abysmal night of the wilderness. The white man had some supper out of the basket, then collecting a few sticks that lay about the platform, made up a small fire, not for warmth, but for the sake of the smoke, which would keep off the mosquitos. He wrapped himself in the blankets and sat with his back against the reed wall of the house, smoking thoughtfully.

Arsat came through the doorway with noiseless steps and squatted down by the fire. The white man moved his outstretched legs a little.

"She breathes," said Arsat in a low voice, anticipating the expected question. "She breathes and burns as if with a great fire. She speaks not; she hears not—and burns!"

He paused for a moment, then asked in a quiet, incurious tone—

"Tuan . . . will she die?"

The white man moved his shoulders uneasily and muttered in a hesitating manner—

"If such is her fate."

"No, Tuan," said Arsat, calmly. "If such is my fate. I hear, I see, I wait. I remember . . . Tuan, do you remember the old days? Do you remember my brother?"

"Yes," said the white man. The Malay rose suddenly and went in. The other, sitting still outside, could hear the voice in the hut. Arsat said: "Hear me! Speak!" His words were succeeded by a complete silence. "O Diamelen!" he cried, suddenly. After that cry there was a deep sigh. Arsat came out and sank down again in his old place.

They sat in silence before the fire. There was no sound within the house, there was no sound near them; but far away on the lagoon they could hear the voices of the boatmen ringing fitful and distinct on the calm water. The fire in the bows of the sampan shone faintly in the distance with a hazy red glow. Then it died out. The voices ceased. The land and the water slept invisible, unstirring and mute. It was as though there had been nothing left in the world but the glitter of stars streaming, ceaseless and vain, through the black stillness of the night.

The white man gazed straight before him into the darkness with wide-open eyes. The fear and fascination, the inspiration and the wonder of death—of death near, unavoidable, and unseen, soothed the unrest of his race and stirred the most indistinct, the most intimate of his thoughts. The ever-ready suspicion of evil, the gnawing suspicion that lurks in our hearts, flowed out into the stillness round him—into the stillness profound and dumb, and made it appear untrustworthy and infamous, like the placid and impenetrable mask of an unjustifiable violence. In that fleeting and powerful disturbance of his being the earth enfolded in the starlight peace became a shadowy country of inhuman strife, a battlefield of phantoms terrible and charming, august or ignoble, struggling ardently for the possession of our helpless hearts. An unquiet and mysterious country of inextinguishable desires and fears.

A plaintive murmur rose in the night; a murmur saddening and startling, as if the great solitudes of surrounding woods had tried to whisper into his ear the wisdom of their immense and lofty indifference. Sounds hesitating and vague floated in the air round him, shaped themselves slowly into words; and at last flowed on gently in a murmuring stream of soft and monotonous sentences. He stirred like a man waking up and changed his position slightly. Arsat, motionless and shadowy, sitting with bowed head under the stars, was speaking in a low and dreamy tone—

". . . for where can we lay down the heaviness of our trouble but in a friend's heart? A man must speak of war and of love. You, Tuan, know what war is, and you have seen me in time of danger seek death as other men seek life! A writing may be lost; a lie may be written; but what the eye has seen is truth and remains in the mind!"

"I remember," said the white man, quietly. Arsat went on with mournful composure—

"Therefore I shall speak to you of love. Speak in the night. Speak before both night and love are gone—and the eye of day looks upon my sorrow and my shame; upon my blackened face; upon my burnt-up heart."

A sigh, short and faint, marked an almost imperceptible pause, and then his words flowed on, without a stir, without a gesture.

"After the time of trouble and war was over and you went away from my country in the pursuit of your desires, which we, men of the islands, cannot understand, I and my brother became again, as we had been before, the sword bearers of the Ruler. You know we were men of family, belonging to a ruling race, and more fit than any to carry on our right shoulder the emblem of power. And in the time of prosperity Si Dendring showed us favor, as we, in time of sorrow, had showed to him the faithfulness of our courage. It was a time of peace. A time of deer hunts and cock fights; of idle talks and foolish squabbles between men whose bellies are full and weapons are rusty. But the sower watched the young rice shoots grow up without fear, and the traders came and went, departed lean and returned fat into the river of peace. They brought news, too. Brought lies and truth mixed together, so that no man knew when to rejoice and when to be sorry. We heard from them about you also. They had seen you here and had seen you there. And I was glad to hear, for I remembered the stirring times, and I always remembered you, Tuan, till the time came when my eyes could see nothing in the past, because they had looked upon the one who is dying there—in the house."

He stopped to exclaim in an intense whisper, "O Mara bahia! O Calamity!" then went on speaking a little louder.

"There's no worse enemy and no better friend than a brother, Tuan, for one brother knows another, and in perfect knowledge is strength for good or evil. I loved my brother, I went to him and told him that I could see nothing but one face, hear nothing but one voice. He told me: 'Open your heart so that she can see what is in it—and wait. Patience is wisdom. Inchi Midah may die or our Ruler may throw off his fear of a woman!' . . . I waited! . . . You remember the lady with the veiled face, Tuan, and the fear of our Ruler before her cunning and temper. And if she wanted her servant, what could I do? But I fed the hunger of my heart on short glances and stealthy words. I loitered on the path to the bath houses in the daytime, and when the sun had fallen behind the forest I crept along the jasmine hedges of the women's courtyard. Unseeing, we spoke to one another through the scent of flowers, through the veil of leaves, through the blades of long grass that stood still before our lips; so great was our prudence, so faint was the murmur of our great longing. The time passed swiftly . . . and there were whispers amongst women—and our enemies watched—my brother was gloomy, and I began to think of killing and of a fierce death. . . . We are of a people who take what they want—like you whites. There is a time when a man should forget loyalty and respect. Might and authority are given to rulers, but to all men is given love and strength and courage. My brother said, 'You shall take her from their midst. We are two who are like one.' And I answered, 'Let it be soon, for I find no warmth in sunlight that does not shine upon her.' Our time came when the Ruler and all the great people went to the mouth of the river to fish by torchlight. There were hundreds of boats, and on the white sand, between the water and the forests, dwellings of leaves were built for the households of the Rajahs. The smoke of cooking fires was like a blue mist in the evening, and many voices rang in it joyfully. While they were making the boats ready to beat up the fish, my brother came to me and said, 'Tonight!' I looked to my weapons, and when the time came our canoe took its place in the circle of boats carrying the torches. The lights blazed on the water, but behind the boats there was darkness. When the shouting began and the excitement made them like mad we dropped out. The water swallowed our fire, and we floated back to the shore that was dark with only here and there the glimmer of embers. We could hear the talk of slave girls amongst the sheds. Then we found a place deserted and silent. We waited there. She came. She came running along the shore, rapid and leaving no trace, like a leaf driven by the wind into the sea. My brother said gloomily, 'Go and take her; carry her into our boat.' I lifted her in my arms. She panted. Her heart was beating against my breast. I said, 'I take you from those people. You came to the cry of my heart, but my arms take you into my boat against the will of the great!' 'It is right,' said my brother. 'We are men who take what we want and can hold it against many. We should have taken her in daylight.' I said, 'Let us be off'; for since she was in my boat I began to think of our Ruler's many men. 'Yes. Let us be off,' said my brother. 'We are cast out and this boat is our country now—and the sea is our refuge.' He lingered with his foot on the shore, and I entreated him to hasten, for I remembered the strokes of her heart against my breast and thought that two men cannot withstand a hundred. We left, paddling downstream close to the bank; and as we passed by the creek where they were fishing, the great shouting had ceased, but the murmur of voices was loud like the humming of insects flying at noonday. The boats floated, clustered together, in the red light of torches, under a black roof of smoke; and men talked of their sport. Men that boasted, and praised, and jeered—men that would have been our friends in the morning, but on that night were already our enemies. We paddled swiftly past. We had no more friends in the country of our birth. She sat in the middle of the canoe with covered face; silent as she is now; unseeing as she is now—and I had no regret at what I was leaving because I could hear her breathing close to me—as I can hear her now."

He paused, listened with his ear turned to the doorway, then shook his head and went on:

"My brother wanted to shout the cry of challenge—one cry only—to let the people know we were freeborn robbers who trusted our arms and the great sea. And again I begged him in the name of our love to be silent. Could I not hear her breathing close to me? I knew the pursuit would come quick enough. My brother loved me. He dipped his paddle without a splash. He only said, 'There is a half a man in you now—the other half is in that woman. I can wait. When you are a whole man again, you will come back with me here to shout defiance. We are sons of the same mother.' I made no answer. All my strength and all my spirit were in my hands that held the paddle—for I longed to be with her in a safe place beyond the reach of men's anger and of women's spite. My love was so great, that I thought it could guide me to a country where death was unknown, if I could only escape from Inchi Midah's fury and from our Ruler's sword. We paddled with haste, breathing through our teeth. The blades bit deep into the smooth water. We passed out of the river; we flew in clear channels amongst the shallows. We skirted the black coast; skirted the sand beaches where the sea speaks in whispers to the land; and the gleam of white sand flashed back past our boat, so swiftly she ran upon the water. We spoke not. Only once I said, 'Sleep, Diamelen, for soon you may want all your strength.' I heard the sweetness of her voice, but I never turned my head. The sun rose and still we went on. Water fell from my face like rain from a cloud. We flew in the light and heat. I never looked back, but I knew that my brother's eyes, behind me, were looking steadily ahead, for the boat went as straight as a bushman's dart, when it leaves the end of the sumpitan. There was no better paddler, no better steersman than my brother. Many times, together, we had won races in that canoe. But we never had put out our strength as we did then—then, when for the last time we paddled together! There was no braver or stronger man in our country than my brother. I could not spare the strength to turn my head and look at him, but every moment I heard the hiss of his breath getting louder behind me. Still he did not speak. The sun was high. The heat clung to my back like a flame of fire. My ribs were ready to burst, but I could no longer get enough air into my chest. And then I felt I must cry out with my last breath, 'Let us rest!' . . . 'Good!' he answered; and his voice was firm. He was strong. He was brave. He knew not fear and no fatigue. . . . My brother!"

A murmur powerful and gentle, a murmur vast and faint; the murmur of trembling leaves, of stirring boughs, ran through the tangled depths of the forests, ran over the starry smoothness of the lagoon, and the water between the piles lapped the slimy timber once with a sudden splash. A breath of warm air touched the two men's faces and passed on with a mournful sound—a breath loud and short like an uneasy sigh of the dreaming earth.

Arsat went on in an even, low voice.

"We ran our canoe on the white beach of a little bay close to a long tongue of land that seemed to bar our road; a long wooden cape going far into the sea. My brother knew that place. Beyond the cape a river has its entrance, and through the jungle of that land there is a narrow path. We made a fire and cooked rice. Then we lay down to sleep on the soft sand in the shade of our canoe, while she watched.

No sooner had I closed my eyes than I heard her cry of alarm. We leaped up. The sun was halfway down the sky already, and coming in sight in the opening of the bay we saw a prau manned by many paddlers. We knew it at once; it was one of our Rajah's praus. They were watching the shore, and saw us. They beat the gong, and turned the head of the prau into the bay. I felt my heart become weak within my breast. Diamelen sat on the sand and covered her face. There was no escape by sea. My brother laughed. He had the gun you had given him, Tuan, before you went away, but there was only a handful of powder. He spoke to me quickly: 'Run with her along the path. I shall keep them back, for they have no firearms, and landing in the face of a man with a gun is certain death for some. Run with her. On the other side of that wood there is a fisherman's house—and a canoe. When I have fired all the shots I will follow. I am a great runner, and before they can come up we shall be gone. I will hold out as long as I can, for she is but a woman—that can neither run nor fight, but she has your heart in her weak hands.' He dropped behind the canoe. The prau was coming. She and I ran, and as we rushed along the path I heard shots. My brother fired—once—twice—and the booming of the gong ceased. There was silence behind us. That neck of land is narrow. Before I heard my brother fire the third shot I saw the shelving shore, and I saw the water again; the mouth of a broad river. We crossed a grassy glade. We ran down to the water. I saw a low hut above the black mud, and a small canoe hauled up. I heard another shot behind me. I thought, 'That is his last charge.' We rushed down to the canoe; a man came running from the hut, but I leaped on him, and we rolled together in the mud. Then I got up, and he lay still at my feet. I don't know whether I had killed him or not. I and Diamelen pushed the canoe afloat. I heard yells behind me, and I saw my brother run across the glade. Many men were bounding after him. I took her in my arms and threw her into the boat, then leaped in myself. When I looked back I saw that my brother had fallen. He fell and was up again, but the men were closing round him. He shouted, 'I am coming!' The men were close to him. I looked. Many men. Then I looked at her. Tuan, I pushed the canoe! I pushed it into deep water. She was kneeling forward looking at me, and I said, 'Take your paddle,' while I struck the water with mine. Tuan, I heard him cry. I heard him cry my name twice; and I heard voices shouting, 'Kill! Strike!' I never turned back. I heard him calling my name again with a great shriek, as when life is going out together with the voice—and I never turned my head. My own name! . . . My brother! Three times he called—but I was not afraid of life. Was she not there in that canoe? And could I not with her find a country where death is forgotten—where death is unknown!"

The white man sat up. Arsat rose and stood, an indistinct and silent figure above the dying embers of the fire. Over the lagoon a mist drifting and low had crept, erasing slowly the glittering images of the stars. And now a great expanse of white vapor covered the land: it flowed cold and gray in the darkness, eddied in noiseless whirls round the tree trunks and about the platform of the house, which seemed to float upon a restless and impalpable illusion of a sea. Only far away the tops of the trees stood outlined on the twinkle of heaven, like a somber and forbidding shore—a coast deceptive, pitiless and black.

Arsat's voice vibrated loudly in the profound peace.

"I had her there! I had her! To get her I would have faced all mankind. But I had her—and—"

His words went out ringing into the empty distances. He paused, and seemed to listen to them dying away very far—beyond help and beyond recall. Then he said quietly—

"Tuan, I loved my brother."

A breath of wind made him shiver. High above his head, high above the silent sea of mist the drooping leaves of the palms rattled together with a mournful and expiring sound. The white man stretched his legs. His chin rested on his chest, and he murmured sadly without lifting his head—

"We all love our brothers."

Arsat burst out with an intense whispering violence—

"What did I care who died? I wanted peace in my own heart."

He seemed to hear a stir in the house—listened—then stepped in noiselessly. The white man stood up. A breeze was coming in fitful puffs. The stars shone paler as if they had retreated into the frozen depths of immense space. After a chill gust of wind there were a few seconds of perfect calm and absolute silence. Then from behind the black and wavy line of the forest a column of golden light shot up into the heavens and spread over the semicircle of the eastern horizon. The sun had risen. The mist lifted, broke into drifting patches, vanished into thin flying wreaths; and the unveiled lagoon lay, polished and black, in the heavy shadows at the foot of the wall of trees. A white eagle rose over it with a slanting and ponderous flight, reached the clear sunshine and appeared dazzlingly brilliant for a moment, then soaring higher, became a dark and motionless speck before it vanished into the blue as if it had left the earth forever. The white man, standing gazing upwards before the doorway, heard in the hut a confused and broken murmur of distracted words ending with a loud groan. Suddenly Arsat stumbled out with outstretched hands, shivered, and stood still for some time with fixed eyes. Then he said—

"She burns no more."

Before his face the sun showed its edge above the treetops rising steadily. The breeze freshened; a great brilliance burst upon the lagoon, sparkled on the rippling water. The forests came out of the clear shadows of the morning, became distinct, as if they had rushed nearer—to stop short in a great stir of leaves, of nodding boughs, of swaying branches. In the merciless sunshine the whisper of unconscious life grew louder, speaking in an incomprehensible voice round the dumb darkness of that human sorrow. Arsat's eyes wandered slowly, then stared at the rising sun.

"I can see nothing," he said half aloud to himself.

"There is nothing," said the white man, moving to the edge of the platform and waving his hand to his boat. A shout came faintly over the lagoon and the sampan began to glide towards the abode of the friend of ghosts.

"If you want to come with me, I will wait all the morning," said the white man, looking away upon the water.

"No, Tuan," said Arsat, softly. "I shall not eat or sleep in this house, but I must first see my road. Now I can see nothing—see nothing! There is no light and no peace in the world; but there is death—death for many. We are sons of the same mother—and I left him in the midst of enemies; but I am going back now."

He drew a long breath and went on in a dreamy tone:

"In a little while I shall see clear enough to strike—to strike. But she has died, and . . . now . . . darkness."

He flung his arms wide open, let them fall along his body, then stood still with unmoved face and stony eyes, staring at the sun. The white man got down into his canoe. The polers ran smartly along the sides of the boat, looking over their shoulders at the beginning of a weary journey. High in the stern, his head muffled up in white rags, the juragan sat moody, letting his paddle trail in the water. The white man, leaning with both arms over the grass roof of the little cabin, looked back at the shining ripple of the boat's wake. Before the sampan passed out of the lagoon into the creek he lifted his eyes. Arsat had not moved. He stood lonely in the searching sunshine; and he looked beyond the great light of a cloudless day into the darkness of a world of illusions.

Life is a dream in the night, a fear among fears,
A naked runner lost in a storm of spears.

ARTHUR SYMONS,
"In the Wood of Finvara"

Is life, then, a dream and delusion, and where shall the
dreamer awake?
Is the world seen like shadows on water, and what if the
mirror break?

SIR ALFRED COMYN LYALL,
"Meditations of a Hindu Prince and Skeptic"

A young disciple asked of that saintly sage, Jiaffar:
"Master, what is life?"

In silence the master turned back the soiled sleeve of his sackcloth burnoose and showed the disciple a revolting sore that was eating into his arm.

And, at that time, the nightingales were trilling in full song, and all Seville was fragrant with the sweet odor of roses.

VSEVOLOD MICHAILOVICH GARSHIN,
"Life"

Part Three

THE DREAMS AND THE REALITIES

Everything That Rises Must Converge

Flannery O'Connor

FLANNERY O'CONNOR *(1925–1964) was born in Savannah, Georgia, and received her education at the Women's College of Georgia and the State University of Iowa. By age twenty-five she learned she had a serious disease that made her an invalid and finally took her life. Her short stories have given her a lasting memorial, and her books include* Wise Blood *(1952),* A Good Man Is Hard to Find *(1955),* The Violent Bear It Away *(1960), and* Everything That Rises Must Converge *(1965). Her fiction has received praise for its sharp and sometimes violent realism, and for its shocking penetration into life's mundaneness.*

Her doctor had told Julian's mother that she must lose twenty pounds on account of her blood pressure, so on Wednesday nights Julian had to take her downtown on the bus for a reducing class at the Y. The reducing class was designed for working girls over fifty and who weighed from 165 to 200 pounds. His mother was one of the slimmer ones, but she said ladies did not tell their age or weight. She would not ride the buses by herself at night since they had been integrated, and because the reducing class was one of her few pleasures, necessary for her health, and *free,* she said Julian could at least put himself out to take her, considering all she did for him. Julian did not like to consider all she did for him, but every Wednesday night he braced himself and took her.

She was almost ready to go, standing before the hall mirror, putting on her hat, while he, his hands behind him, appeared pinned to the door frame, waiting like Saint Sebastian for the arrows to begin piercing him. The hat was new and had cost her seven dollars and a half. She kept saying, "Maybe I shouldn't have paid that for it. No, I shouldn't have. I'll take it off and return it tomorrow. I shouldn't have bought it."

Julian raised his eyes to heaven. "Yes, you should have bought it," he said. "Put it on and let's go." It was a hideous hat. A purple velvet flap came down on one side of it and stood up on the other; the rest of it was green and looked like a cushion with the stuffing out. He decided it was less comical than jaunty and pathetic. Everything that gave her pleasure was small and depressed him.

She lifted the hat one more time and set it down slowly on top of her head. Two wings of gray hair protruded on either side of her florid face, but her eyes, sky-blue, were as innocent and untouched by experience as they must have been when she was ten. Were it not that she was a widow who had struggled fiercely to feed and clothe and put him through school and who was supporting him still, "until he got on his feet," she might have been a little girl that he had to take to town.

"It's all right, it's all right," he said. "Let's go." He opened the door himself and started down the walk to get her going. The sky was a dying violet and the houses stood out darkly against it, bulbous liver-colored monstrosities of a uniform ugliness though no two were alike. Since this had been a fashionable neighborhood forty years ago, his mother persisted in thinking they did well to have an apartment in it. Each house had a narrow collar of dirt around it in which sat, usually, a grubby child. Julian walked with his hands in his pockets, his head down and thrust forward and his eyes glazed with the determination to make himself completely numb during the time he would be sacrificed to her pleasure.

The door closed and he turned to find the dumpy figure, surmounted by the atrocious hat, coming toward him. "Well," she said, "you only live once and paying a little more for it, I at least won't meet myself coming and going."

"Some day I'll start making money," Julian said gloomily—he knew he never would—"and you can have one of those jokes whenever you take the fit." But first they would move. He visualized a place where the nearest neighbors would be three miles away on either side.

"I think you're doing fine," she said, drawing on her gloves. "You've only been out of school a year. Rome wasn't built in a day."

She was one of the few members of the Y reducing class who arrived in hat and gloves and who had a son who had been to college. "It takes time," she said, "and the world is in such a mess. This hat looked better on me than any of the others, though when she brought it out I said, 'Take that thing back. I wouldn't have it on my head,' and she said, 'Now wait till you see it on,' and when she put it on me, I said, 'We-ull,' and she said, 'If you ask me, that hat does something for you and you do something for the hat, and besides,' she said, 'with that hat, you won't meet yourself coming and going.' "

Julian thought he could have stood his lot better if she had been selfish, if she had been an old hag who drank and screamed at him. He walked along, saturated in depression, as if in the midst of his martyrdom he had lost his faith. Catching sight of his long, hopeless, irritated face, she stopped suddenly with a grief-stricken look, and pulled back on his arm. "Wait on me," she said. "I'm going back to the house and take this thing off and tomorrow I'm going to return it. I was out of my head. I can pay the gas bill with the seven-fifty."

He caught her arm in a vicious grip. "You are not going to take it back," he said. "I like it."

"Well," she said, "I don't think I ought . . ."

"Shut up and enjoy it," he muttered, more depressed than ever.

"With the world in the mess it's in," she said, "it's a wonder we can enjoy anything. I tell you, the bottom rail is on the top."

Julian sighed.

"Of course," she said, "if you know who you are, you can go anywhere." She said this every time he took her to the reducing class. "Most of them in it are not our kind of people," she said, "but I can be gracious to anybody. I know who I am."

"They don't give a damn for your graciousness," Julian said savagely. "Knowing who you are is good for one generation only. You haven't the foggiest idea where you stand now or who you are."

She stopped and allowed her eyes to flash at him. "I most certainly do know who I am," she said, "and if you don't know who you are, I'm ashamed of you."

"Oh hell," Julian said.

"Your great-grandfather was a former governor of this state," she said. "Your grandfather was a prosperous landowner. Your grandmother was a Godhigh."

"Will you look around you," he said tensely, "and see where you are now?" and he swept his arm jerkily out to indicate the neighborhood, which the growing darkness at least made less dingy.

"You remain what you are," she said. "Your great-grandfather had a plantation and two hundred slaves."

"There are no more slaves," he said irritably.

"They were better off when they were," she said. He groaned to see that she was off on that topic. She rolled onto it every few days like a train on an open track. He knew every stop, every junction, every swamp along the way, and knew the exact point at which her conclusion would roll majestically into the station: "It's ridiculous. It's simply not realistic. They should rise, yes, but on their own side of the fence."

"Let's skip it," Julian said.

"The ones I feel sorry for," she said, "are the ones that are half white. They're tragic."

"Will you skip it?"

"Suppose we were half white. We would certainly have mixed feelings."

"I have mixed feelings now," he groaned.

"Well let's talk about something pleasant," she said. "I remember going to Grandpa's when I was a little girl. Then the house had double stairways that went up to what was really the second floor—all the cooking was done on the first. I used to like to stay down in the kitchen on account of the way the walls smelled. I would sit with my nose pressed against the plaster and take deep breaths. Actually the place belonged to the Godhighs but your grandfather Chestny paid the mortgage and saved it for them. They were in reduced circumstances," she said, "but reduced or not, they never forgot who they were."

"Doubtless that decayed mansion reminded them," Julian muttered. He never spoke of it without contempt or thought of it without longing. He had seen it once when he was a child before it had been sold. The double stairways had rotted and been torn down. Negroes were living in it. But it remained in his mind as his mother had known it. It appeared in his dreams regularly. He would stand on the wide porch, listening to the rustle of oak leaves, then wander through the high-ceilinged hall into the parlor that opened onto it and gaze at the worn rugs and faded draperies. It occurred to him that it was he, not she, who could have appreciated it. He preferred its threadbare elegance to anything he could name and it was because of it that all the neighborhoods they had lived in had been a torment to him—whereas she had hardly known the difference. She called her insensitivity "being adjustable."

"And I remember the old darky who was my nurse, Caroline. There was no better person in the world. I've always had a great respect for my colored friends," she said. "I'd do anything in the world for them and they'd . . ."

"Will you for God's sake get off that subject?" Julian said. When he got on a bus by himself, he made it a point to sit down beside a Negro, in reparation as it were for his mother's sins.

"You're mighty touchy tonight," she said. "Do you feel all right?"

"Yes I feel all right," he said. "Now lay off."

She pursed her lips. "Well, you certainly are in a vile humor," she observed. "I just won't speak to you at all."

They had reached the bus stop. There was no bus in sight and Julian, his hands still jammed in his pockets and his head thrust forward, scowled down the empty street. The frustration of having to wait on the bus as well as ride on it began to creep up his neck like a hot hand. The presence of his mother was borne in upon him as she gave a pained sigh. He looked at her bleakly. She was holding herself very erect under the preposterous hat, wearing it like a banner of her imaginary dignity. There was in him an evil urge to break her spirit. He suddenly unloosened his tie and pulled it off and put it in his pocket.

She stiffened. "Why must you look like *that* when you take me to town?" she said. "Why must you deliberately embarrass me?"

"If you'll never learn where you are," he said, "you can at least learn where I am."

"You look like a—thug," she said.

"Then I must be one," he murmured.

"I'll just go home," she said. "I will not bother you. If you can't do a little thing like that for me . . ."

Rolling his eyes upward, he put his tie back on. "Restored to my class," he muttered. He thrust his face toward her and hissed, "True culture is in the mind, the *mind,*" he said, and tapped his head, "the mind."

"It's in the heart," she said, "and in how you do things and how you do things is because of who you *are.*"

"Nobody in the damn bus cares who you are."

"I care who I am," she said icily.

The lighted bus appeared on top of the next hill and as it approached, they moved out into the street to meet it. He put his hand under her elbow and hoisted her up on the creaking step. She entered with a little smile, as if she were going into a drawing room where everyone had been waiting for her. While he put in the tokens, she sat down on one of the broad front seats for three which faced the aisle. A thin woman with protruding teeth and long yellow hair was sitting on the end of it. His mother moved up beside her and left room for Julian beside herself. He sat down and looked at the floor across the aisle where a pair of thin feet in red and white canvas sandals were planted.

His mother immediately began a general conversation meant to attract anyone who felt like talking. "Can it get any hotter?" she said and removed from her purse a folding fan, black with a Japanese scene on it, which she began to flutter before her.

"I reckon it might could," the woman with the protruding teeth said, "but I know for a fact my apartment couldn't get no hotter."

"It must get the afternoon sun," his mother said. She sat forward and looked up and down the bus. It was half filled. Everybody was white. "I see we have the bus to ourselves," she said. Julian cringed.

"For a change," said the woman across the aisle, the owner of the red and white canvas sandals. "I come on one the other day and they were thick as fleas—up front and all through."

"The world is in a mess everywhere," his mother said. "I don't know how we've let it get in this fix."

"What gets my goat is all those boys from good families stealing automobile tires," the woman with the protruding teeth said. "I told my boy, I said you may not be rich but you been raised right and if I ever catch you in any such mess, they can send you on to the reformatory. Be exactly where you belong."

"Training tells," his mother said. "Is your boy in high school?"

"Ninth grade," the woman said.

"My son just finished college last year. He wants to write but he's selling typewriters until he gets started," his mother said.

The woman leaned forward and peered at Julian. He threw her such a malevolent look that she subsided against the seat. On the floor across the aisle there was an abandoned newspaper. He got up and got it and opened it out in front of him. His mother discreetly continued the conversation in a lower tone but the woman across the aisle said in a loud voice, "Well that's nice. Selling typewriters is close to writing. He can go right from one to the other."

"I tell him," his mother said, "that Rome wasn't built in a day."

Behind the newspaper Julian was withdrawing into the inner compartment of his mind where he spent most of his time. This was a kind of mental bubble in which he established himself when he could not bear to be a part of what was going on around him. From it he could see out and judge but in it he was safe from any kind of penetration from without. It was the only place where he felt free of the general idiocy of his fellows. His mother had never entered it but from it he could see her with absolute clarity.

The old lady was clever enough and he thought that if she had started from any of the right premises, more might have been expected of her. She lived according to the laws of her own fantasy world, outside of which he had never seen her set foot. The law of it was to sacrifice herself for him after she had first created the necessity to do so by making a mess of things. If he had permitted her sacrifices, it was only because her lack of foresight had made them necessary. All of her life had been a struggle to act like a Chestny without the Chestny goods, and to give him everything she thought a Chestny ought to have; but since, said she, it was fun to struggle, why complain? And when you had won, as she had won, what fun to look back on the hard times! He could not forgive her that she had enjoyed the struggle and that she thought *she* had won.

What she meant when she said she had won was that she had brought him up successfully and had sent him to college and that he had turned out so well—good-looking (her teeth had gone unfilled so that his could be straightened), intelligent (he realized he was too intelligent to be a success), and with a future ahead of him (there was of course no future ahead of him). She excused his gloominess on the grounds that he was still growing up and his radical ideas on his lack of practical experience. She said he didn't yet know a thing about "life," that he hadn't even entered the real world—when already he was as disenchanted with it as a man of fifty.

The further irony of all this was that in spite of her, he had turned out so well. In spite of going to only a third-rate college, he had, on his own initiative, come out with a first-rate education; in spite of growing up dominated by a small mind, he had ended up with a large one; in spite of all her foolish views, he was free of prejudice and unafraid to face facts. Most miraculous of all, instead of being blinded by love for her as she was for him, he had cut himself emotionally free of her and could see her with complete objectivity. He was not dominated by his mother.

The bus stopped with a sudden jerk and shook him from his meditation. A woman from the back lurched forward with little steps and barely escaped falling in his newspaper as she righted herself. She got off and a large Negro got on. Julian kept his paper lowered to watch. It gave him a certain satisfaction to see injustice in daily operation. It confirmed his view that with a few exceptions there was no one worth knowing within a radius of three hundred miles. The Negro was well dressed and carried a briefcase. He looked around and then sat down on the other end of the seat where the woman with the red and white canvas sandals was sitting. He immediately unfolded a newspaper and obscured himself behind it. Julian's mother's elbow at once prodded insistently into his ribs. "Now you see why I won't ride on these buses by myself," she whispered.

The woman with the red and white canvas sandals had risen at the same time the Negro sat down and had gone further back in the bus and taken the seat of the woman who had got off. His mother leaned forward and cast her an approving look.

Julian rose, crossed the aisle, and sat down in the place of the woman with the canvas sandals. From this position, he looked serenely across at his mother. Her face had turned an angry red. He stared at her, making his eyes the eyes of a stranger. He felt his tension suddenly lift as if he had openly declared war on her.

He would have liked to get in conversation with the Negro and to talk with him about art or politics or any subject that would be above the comprehension of those around him, but the man remained entrenched behind his paper. He was either ignoring the change of seating or had never noticed it. There was no way for Julian to convey his sympathy.

His mother kept her eyes fixed reproachfully on his face. The woman with the protruding teeth was looking at him avidly as if he were a type of monster new to her.

"Do you have a light?" he asked the Negro.

Without looking away from his paper, the man reached in his pocket and handed him a packet of matches.

"Thanks," Julian said. For a moment he held the matches foolishly. A NO SMOKING sign looked down upon him from over the door. This alone would not have deterred him; he had no cigarettes. He had quit smoking some months before because he could not afford it. "Sorry," he muttered and handed back the matches. The Negro lowered the paper and gave him an annoyed look. He took the matches and raised the paper again.

His mother continued to gaze at him but she did not take advantage of his momentary discomfort. Her eyes retained their battered look. Her face seemed to be unnaturally red, as if her blood pressure had risen. Julian allowed no glimmer of sympathy to show on his face. Having got the advantage, he wanted desperately to keep it and carry it through. He would have liked to teach her a lesson that would last her a while, but there seemed no way to continue the point. The Negro refused to come out from behind his paper.

Julian folded his arms and looked stolidly before him, facing her but as if he did not see her, as if he had ceased to recognize her existence. He visualized a scene in which, the bus having reached their stop, he would remain in his seat and when she said, "Aren't you going to get off?" he would look at her as at a stranger who had rashly addressed him. The corner they got off on was usually deserted, but it was well lighted and it would not hurt her to walk by herself the four blocks to the Y. He decided to wait until the time came and then decide whether or not he would let her get off by herself. He would have to be at the Y at ten to bring her back, but he could leave her wondering if he was going to show up. There was no reason for her to think she could always depend on him.

He retired again into the high-ceilinged room sparsely settled with large pieces of antique furniture. His soul expanded momentarily but then he became aware of his mother across from him and the vision shriveled. He studied her coldly. Her feet in little pumps dangled like a child's and did not quite reach the floor. She was training on him an exaggerated look of reproach. He felt completely detached from her. At that moment he could with pleasure have slapped her as he would have slapped a particularly obnoxious child in his charge.

He began to imagine various unlikely ways by which he could teach her a lesson. He might make friends with some distinguished Negro professor or lawyer and bring him home to spend the evening. He would be entirely justified but her blood pressure would rise to 300. He could not push her to the extent of making her have a stroke, and moreover, he had never been successful at making any Negro friends. He had tried to strike up an acquaintance on the bus with some of the better types, with ones that looked like professors or ministers or lawyers. One morning he had sat down next to a distinguished-looking dark brown man who had answered his questions with a sonorous solemnity but who had turned out to be an undertaker. Another day he had sat down beside a cigar-smoking Negro with a diamond ring on his finger, but after a few stilted pleasantries, the Negro had rung the buzzer and risen, slipping two lottery tickets into Julian's hand as he climbed over him to leave.

He imagined his mother lying desperately ill and his being able to secure only a Negro doctor for her. He toyed with that idea for a few minutes and then dropped it for a momentary vision of himself participating as a sympathizer in a sit-in demonstration. This was possible but he did not linger with it. Instead, he approached the ultimate horror. He brought home a beautiful suspiciously Negroid woman. Prepare yourself, he said. There is nothing you can do about it. This is the woman I've chosen. She's intelligent, dignified, even good, and she's suffered and she hasn't thought it *fun*. Now persecute us, go ahead and persecute us. Drive her out of here, but remember, you're driving me too. His eyes were narrowed and through the indignation he had generated, he saw his mother across the aisle, purple-faced, shrunken to the dwarflike proportions of her moral nature, sitting like a mummy beneath the ridiculous banner of her hat.

He was tilted out of his fantasy again as the bus stopped. The door opened with a sucking hiss and out of the dark a large, gaily dressed, sullen-looking colored woman got on with a little boy. The child, who might have been four, had on a short plaid suit and a

Tyrolean hat with a blue feather in it. Julian hoped that he would sit down beside him and that the woman would push in beside his mother. He could think of no better arrangement.

As she waited for her tokens, the woman was surveying the seating possibilities—he hoped with the idea of sitting where she was least wanted. There was something familiar-looking about her but Julian could not place what it was. She was a giant of a woman. Her face was set not only to meet opposition but to seek it out. The downward tilt of her large lower lip was like a warning sign: DON'T TAMPER WITH ME. Her bulging figure was encased in a green crepe dress and her feet overflowed in red shoes. She had on a hideous hat. A purple velvet flap came down on one side of it and stood up on the other; the rest of it was green and looked like a cushion with the stuffing out. She carried a mammoth red pocketbook that bulged throughout as if it were stuffed with rocks.

To Julian's disappointment, the little boy climbed up on the empty seat beside his mother. His mother lumped all children, black and white, into the common category, "cute," and she thought little Negroes were on the whole cuter than little white children. She smiled at the little boy as he climbed on the seat.

Meanwhile the woman was bearing down upon the empty seat beside Julian. To his annoyance, she squeezed herself into it. He saw his mother's face change as the woman settled herself next to him and he realized with satisfaction that this was more objectionable to her than it was to him. Her face seemed almost gray and there was a look of dull recognition in her eyes, as if suddenly she had sickened at some awful confrontation. Julian saw that it was because she and the woman had, in a sense, swapped sons. Though his mother would not realize the symbolic significance of this, she would feel it. His amusement showed plainly on his face.

The woman next to him muttered something unintelligible to herself. He was conscious of a kind of bristling next to him, muted growling like that of an angry cat. He could not see anything but the red pocketbook upright on the bulging green thighs. He visualized the woman as she had stood waiting for her tokens—the ponderous figure, rising from the red shoes upward over the solid hips, the mammoth bosom, the haughty face, to the green and purple hat.

His eyes widened.

The vision of the two hats, identical, broke upon him with the radiance of a brilliant sunrise. His face was suddenly lit with joy. He could not believe that Fate had thrust upon his mother such a lesson. He gave a loud chuckle so that she would look at him and see that he saw. She turned her eyes on him slowly. The blue in them seemed to have turned a bruised purple. For a moment he had an uncomfortable sense of her innocence, but it lasted only a second before principle rescued him. Justice entitled him to laugh. His grin hardened until it said to her as plainly as if he were saying aloud: Your punishment exactly fits your pettiness. This should teach you a permanent lesson.

Her eyes shifted to the woman. She seemed unable to bear looking at him and to find the woman preferable. He became conscious again of the bristling presence at his side. The woman was rumbling like a volcano about to become active. His mother's mouth began to twitch slightly at one corner. With a sinking heart, he saw incipient signs of recovery on her face and realized that this was going to strike her suddenly as funny and was going to be no lesson at all. She kept her eyes on the woman and an amused smile came over her face as if the woman were a monkey that had stolen her hat. The little Negro was looking up at her with large fascinated eyes. He had been trying to attract her attention for some time.

"Carver!" the woman said suddenly. "Come heah!"

When he saw that the spotlight was on him at last, Carver drew his feet up and turned himself toward Julian's mother and giggled.

"Carver!" the woman said. "You heah me? Come heah!"

Carver slid down from the seat but remained squatting with his back against the base of it, his head turned slyly around toward Julian's mother, who was smiling at him. The woman reached a hand across the aisle and snatched him to her. He righted himself and hung backwards on her knees, grinning at Julian's mother. "Isn't he cute?" Julian's mother said to the woman with the protruding teeth.

"I reckon he is," the woman said without conviction.

The Negress yanked him upright but he eased out of her grip and shot across the aisle and scrambled, giggling wildly, onto the seat beside his love.

"I think he likes me," Julian's mother said, and smiled at the woman. It was the smile she used when she was being particularly gracious to an inferior. Julian saw everything lost. The lesson had rolled off her like rain on a roof.

The woman stood up and yanked the little boy off the seat as if she were snatching him from contagion. Julian could feel the rage in her at having no weapon like his mother's smile. She gave the child a sharp slap across his leg. He howled once and then thrust his head into her stomach and kicked his feet against her shins. "Behave," she said vehemently.

The bus stopped and the Negro who had been reading the newspaper got off. The woman moved over and set the little boy down with a thump between herself and Julian. She held him firmly by the knee. In a moment he put his hands in front of his face and peeped at Julian's mother through his fingers.

"I see yoooooooo!" she said and put her hand in front of her face and peeped at him.

The woman slapped his hand down. "Quit yo' foolishness," she said, "before I knock the living Jesus out of you!"

Julian was thankful that the next stop was theirs. He reached up and pulled the cord. The woman reached up and pulled it at the same time. Oh my God, he thought. He had the terrible intuition that when they got off the bus together, his mother would open her purse and give the little boy a nickel. The gesture would be as natural to her as breathing. The bus stopped and the woman got up and lunged to the front, dragging the child, who wished to stay on, after her. Julian and his mother got up and followed. As they neared the door, Julian tried to relieve her of her pocketbook.

"No," she murmured, "I want to give the little boy a nickel."

"No!" Julian hissed. "No!"

She smiled down at the child and opened her bag. The bus door opened and the woman picked him up by the arm and descended with him, hanging at her hip. Once in the street she set him down and shook him.

Julian's mother had to close her purse while she got down the bus step but as soon as her feet were on the ground, she opened it again and began to rummage inside. "I can't find but a penny," she whispered, "but it looks like a new one."

"Don't do it!" Julian said fiercely between his teeth. There was a streetlight on the corner and she hurried to get under it so that she could better see into her pocketbook. The woman was heading off rapidly down the street with the child still hanging backward on her hand.

"Oh little boy!" Julian's mother called and took a few quick steps and caught up with them just beyond the lamppost. "Here's a bright new penny for you," and she held out the coin, which shone bronze in the dim light.

The huge woman turned and for a moment stood, her shoulders lifted and her face frozen with frustrated rage, and stared at Julian's mother. Then all at once she seemed to explode like a piece of machinery that had been given one ounce of pressure too much. Julian saw the black fist swing out with the red pocketbook. He shut his eyes and cringed as he heard the woman shout, "He don't take nobody's pennies!" When he opened his eyes, the woman was disappearing down the street with the little boy staring wide-eyed over her shoulder. Julian's mother was sitting on the sidewalk.

"I told you not to do that," Julian said angrily. "I told you not to do that!"

He stood over her for a minute, gritting his teeth. Her legs were stretched out in front of her and her hat was on her lap. He squatted down and looked her in the face. It was totally expressionless. "You got exactly what you deserved," he said. "Now get up."

He picked up her pocketbook and put what had fallen out back in it. He picked the hat up off her lap. The penny caught his eye on the sidewalk and he picked that up and let it drop before her eyes into the purse. Then he stood up and leaned over and held his hands out to pull her up. She remained immobile. He sighed. Rising above them on either side were black apartment buildings, marked with irregular rectangles of light. At the end of the block a man came out of a door and walked off in the opposite direction. "All right," he said, "suppose somebody happens by and wants to know why you're sitting on the sidewalk?"

She took the hand and, breathing hard, pulled heavily up on it and then stood for a moment, swaying slightly as if the spots of light in the darkness were circling around her. Her eyes, shadowed and confused, finally settled on his face. He did not try to conceal his irritation. "I hope this teaches you a lesson," he said. She leaned forward and her eyes raked his face. She seemed trying to determine his identity. Then, as if she found nothing familiar about him, she started off with a headlong movement in the wrong direction.

"Aren't you going on to the Y?" he asked.

"Home," she muttered.

"Well, are we walking?"

For answer she kept going. Julian followed along, his hands behind him. He saw no reason to let the lesson she had had go without backing it up with an explanation of its meaning. She might as well be made to understand what had happened to her. "Don't think that was just an uppity Negro woman," he said. "That was the whole colored race which will no longer take your condescending pennies. That was your black double. She can wear the same hat as you, and to be sure," he added gratuitously (because he thought it was funny), "it looked better on her than it did on you. What all this means," he said, "is that the old world is gone. The old manners are obsolete and your graciousness is not worth a damn." He thought bitterly of the house that had been lost for him. "You aren't who you think you are," he said.

She continued to plow ahead, paying no attention to him. Her hair had come undone on one side. She dropped her pocketbook and took no notice. He stooped and picked it up and handed it to her but she did not take it.

"You needn't act as if the world had come to an end," he said, "because it hasn't. From now on you've got to live in a new world and face a few realities for a change. Buck up," he said, "it won't kill you."

She was breathing fast.

"Let's wait on the bus," he said.

"Home," she said thickly.

"I hate to see you behave like this," he said. "Just like a child. I should be able to expect more of you." He decided to stop where he was and make her stop and wait for a bus. "I'm not going any farther," he said, stopping. "We're going on the bus."

She continued to go on as if she had not heard him. He took a few steps and caught her arm and stopped her. He looked into her face and caught his breath. He was looking into a face he had never seen before. "Tell Grandpa to come get me," she said.

He stared, stricken.

"Tell Caroline to come get me," she said.

Stunned, he let her go and she lurched forward again, walking as if one leg were shorter than the other. A tide of darkness seemed to be sweeping her from him. "Mother!" he cried. "Darling, sweetheart, wait!" Crumpling, she fell to the pavement. He dashed forward and fell at her side, crying, "Mamma, Mamma!" He turned her over. Her face was fiercely distorted. One eye, large and staring, moved slightly to the left as if it had become unmoored. The other remained fixed on him, raked his face again, found nothing and closed.

"Wait here, wait here!" he cried and jumped up and began to run for help toward a cluster of lights he saw in the distance ahead of him. "Help, help!" he shouted, but his voice was thin, scarcely a thread of sound. The lights drifted farther away the faster he ran and his feet moved numbly as if they carried him nowhere. The tide of darkness seemed to sweep him back to her, postponing from moment to moment his entry into the world of guilt and sorrow.

Only the Dead Know Brooklyn

Thomas Wolfe

THOMAS WOLFE *(1900–1938) was born in Asheville, North Carolina, and was educated at the University of North Carolina and at Harvard where his main interest was writing plays. By portraying his personal experience and depicting characters often based on his family, friends, and Asheville's townspeople, he channeled his materials into exceptionally long novels written in a prose style that some critics equate with poetry. His books include* Look Homeward, Angel *(1929),* Of Time and the River *(1935),* From Death to Morning *(1935),* The Story of a Novel *(1936). Among those published posthumously are* The Face of a Nation *(1939), which is made up of poetical passages from his writings,* The Web and the Rock *(1939),* You Can't Go Home Again *(1940), and* The Hills Beyond *(1941).*

Dere's no guy livin' dat knows Brooklyn t'roo an' t'roo, because it'd take a guy a lifetime just to find his way aroun' duh f—— town.

So like I say, I'm waitin' for my train t' come when I sees dis big guy standin' deh—dis is duh foist I eveh see of him. Well, he's lookin' wild, y'know, an' I can see dat he's had plenty, but still he's holdin' it; he talks good an' is walkin' straight enough. So den, dis big guy steps up to a little guy dat's standin' deh an' says, "How d'yuh get t' Eighteent' Avenoo an' Sixty-sevent' Street?" he says.

"Jesus! Yuh got me, chief," duh little guy says to him. "I ain't been heah long myself. Where is duh place?" he says. "Out in duh Flatbush sections somewhere?"

"Nah," duh big guy says. "It's out in Bensonhoist. But I was neveh deh befoeh. How d'yuh get deh?"

"Jesus," duh little guy says, scratchin' his head, y'know—yuh could see duh little guy didn't know his way about—"yuh got me, chief. I neveh hoid of it. Do any of youse guys know where it is?" he says to me.

"Sure," I says. "It's out in Bensonhoist. Yuh take duh Fourt' Avenoo express, get off at Fifty-nint' Street, change to a Sea Beach local deh, get off at Eighteent' Avenoo an' Sixty-toid, an' den walk down foeh blocks. Dat's all yuh got to do," I says.

"G'wan!" some wise guy dat I neveh seen befoeh pipes up. "Watcha talkin' about?" he says—oh, he was wise, y'know. "Duh guy is crazy! I tell yuh what yuh do," he says to duh big guy. "Yuh change to duh West End line at Toity-sixt'," he tells him. "Get off at Noo Utrecht and Sixteent' Avenoo," he says. "Walk two blocks oveh, foeh blocks up," he says, "an' you'll be right deh." Oh, a *wise* guy, y'know.

"Oh, yeah?" I says. "Who told *you* so much?" He got me sore because he was so wise about it. "How long you been livin' heah?" I says.

"All my life," he says. "I was bawn in Williamsboig," he says. "An' I can tell you t'ings about dis town you neveh hoid of," he says.

"Yeah?" I says.

"Yeah," he says.

"Well, den, you can tell me t'ings about dis town dat nobody else has eveh hoid of, either. Maybe you make it all up yoehself at night," I says, "befoeh you go to sleep—like cuttin' out papeh dolls, or somp'n."

"Oh, yeah?" he says. "You're pretty wise, ain't yuh?"

"Oh, I don't know," I says. "Duh boids ain't usin' my head for Lincoln's statue yet," I says. "But I'm wise enough to know a phony when I see one."

"Yeah?" he says. "A wise guy, huh? Well, you're so wise dat someone's goin' t'bust yuh one right on duh snoot some day," he says. "Dat's how wise *you* are."

Well, my train was comin', or I'da smacked him den and dere: but when I seen duh train was comin', all I said was, "All right, mug! I'm sorry I can't stay to take keh of you, but I'll be seein' yuh sometime, I hope, out in duh cemetery." So den I says to duh big guy, who'd been standin' deh all duh time, "You come wit me," I says. So when we get on to duh train I says to him, "Where yuh goin' out in Bensonhoist?" I says. "What number are yuh lookin' for?" I says. You know—I t'ought if he told me duh address I might be able to help him out.

"Oh," he says, "I'm not lookin' for no one. I don't know no one out deh."

"Then whatcha goin' out deh for?" I says.

"Oh," duh guy says, "I'm just goin' out to see duh place," he says. "I like duh sound of duh name—Bensonhoist, y'know—so I t'ought I'd go out an' have a look at it."

"Whatcha tryin' t'hand me?" I says. "Whatcha tryin' t'do—kid me?" *You* know I t'ought duh guy was bein' wise wit me.

"No," he says, "I'm tellin' yuh duh troot. I like to go out an' take a look at places wit nice names like dat. I like to go out an' look at all kinds of places," he says.

"How'd yuh know deh was such a place," I says, "if yuh neveh been deh befoeh?"

"Oh," he says, "I got a map."

"A *map?*" I says.

"Sure," he says, "I got a map dat tells me about all dese places. I take it wit me every time I come out heah," he says.

And Jesus! Wit dat, he pulls it out of his pocket, an' so help me, but he's *got* it—he's tellin' duh troot—a big map of duh whole f—— place with all duh different pahts mahked out. You know Canarsie an' East Noo Yawk an' Flatbush, Bensonhoist, Sout' Brooklyn, duh Heights, Bay Ridge, Greenpernt—duh whole goddam layout, he's got it right deh on duh map.

"You been to any of dose places?" I says.

"Sure," he says, "I been to most of 'em. I was down in Red Hook just last night," he says.

"Jesus! Red Hook!" I says. "Whatcha do down deh?"

"Oh," he says, "nuttin' much. I just walked aroun'. I went into a coupla places an' had a drink," he says, "but most of the time I just walked aroun'."

"Just walked aroun'?" I says.

"Sure," he says, "just lookin' at t'ings, y'know."

"Where'd yuh go?" I asts him.

"Oh," he says, "I don't know duh name of duh place, but I

could find it on my map," he says. "One time I was walkin' across some big fields where deh ain't no houses," he says, "but I could see ships oveh deh all lighted up. Dey was loadin'. So I walks across duh fields," he says, "to where duh ships are."

"Sure," I says, "I know where you was. You was down to duh Erie Basin."

"Yeah," he says, "I guess dat was it. Dey had some of dose big elevators an' cranes an' dey was loadin' ships, an' I could see some ships in dry dock all lighted up; so I walks across duh fields to where dey are," he says.

"Den what did yuh do?" I says.

"Oh," he says, "nuttin' much. I came on back across duh fields after a while an' went into a couple places an' had a drink."

"Didn't nuttin' happen while yuh was in dere?" I says.

"No," he says. "Nuttin' much. A coupla guys was drunk in one of duh places an' stahted a fight, but dey bounced 'em out," he says, "an' den one of duh guys stahted to come back again, but duh bartender gets his baseball bat out from under duh counteh; so duh guy goes on."

"Jesus!" I said. "Red Hook!"

"Sure," he says. "Dat's where it was, all right."

"Well, you keep outa deh," I says. "You stay away from deh."

"Why?" he says. "What's wrong wit it?"

"Oh," I says, "it's a good place to stay away from, dat's all. It's a good place to keep out of."

"Why?" he says. "Why is it?"

Jesus! Whatcha gonna do wit a guy as dumb as dat? I saw it wasn't no use to try to tell him nuttin'—he wouldn't know what I was talkin' about; so I just says to him, "Oh, nuttin'. Yuh might get lost down deh, dat's all."

"Lost?" he says. "No, I wouldn't get lost. I got a map," he says.

A map! Red Hook! Jesus!

So den duh guy begins to ast me all kinds of nutty questions: how big was Brooklyn, an' could I find my way aroun' in it, an' how long would it take a guy to know duh place.

"Listen!" I says. "You get dat idea outa yoeh head right now," I says. "You ain't neveh gonna get to know Brooklyn," I says. "Not in a hunderd yeahs. I been livin' heah all my life," I says, "an' I don't even know all deh is to know about it, so how do you expect to know duh town," I says, "when you don't even live heah?"

"Yes," he says, "but I got a map to help me find my way about."

"Map or no map," I says, "yuh ain't gonna get to know Brooklyn wit no map," I says.

"Can you swim?" he says, just like dat. Jesus! By dat time, y'know, I begun to see dat duh guy was some kind of nut. He'd had plenty to drink, of course, but he had dat crazy look in his eye I didn't like. "Can you swim?" he says.

"Sure," I says. "Can't you?"

"No," he says. "Not more'n a stroke or two. I neveh loined good."

"Well, it's easy," I says. "All yuh need is a little confidence. Duh way I loined, me older bruddeh pitched me off duh dock one day when I was eight yeahs old, cloes an' all. 'You'll swim,' he says. 'You'll swim all right—or drown.' An' believe me, I *swam!* When yuh know yuh got to, you'll do it. Duh only t'ing yuh need is confidence. An' once you've loined," I says, "you've got nuttin' else to worry about. You'll neveh forget it. It's somp'n dat stays wit yuh as long as yuh live."

"Can yuh swim good?" he says.

"Like a fish," I tells him. "I'm a regulah fish in duh wateh," I says. "I loined to swim right off duh docks with all duh oddeh kids," I says.

"What would you do if yuh saw a man drownin'?" duh guy says.

"Do? Why, I'd jump in an' pull him out," I says. "Dat's what I'd do."

"Did yuh eveh see a man drown?" he says.

"Sure," I says. "I see two guys—bot' times at Coney Island. Dey got out too far, an' neider one could swim. Dey drowned befoeh anyone could get to 'em."

"What becomes of people after dey've drowned out heah?" he says.

"Drowned out where?" I says.

"Out heah in Brooklyn."

"I don't know whatcha mean," I says. "Neveh hoid of no one drownin' heah in Brooklyn, unless you mean a swimmin' pool. Yuh can't drown in Brooklyn," I says. "Yuh gotta drown somewhere else—in duh ocean, where dere's wateh."

"Drownin'," duh guy says, lookin' at his map. "Drownin'." Jesus! I could see by den he was some kind of nut; he had dat crazy expression in his eyes when he looked at you, an' I didn't know what he might do. So we was comin' to a station, an' it wasn't my stop, but I got off anyway, an' waited for duh next train.

"Well, so long, chief," I says. "Take it easy, now."

"Drownin'," duh guy says, lookin' at his map. "Drownin'."

Jesus! I've t'ought about dat guy a t'ousand times since den an' wondered what eveh happened to 'm goin' out to look at Bensonhoist because he liked duh name! Walkin' roun' t'roo Red Hook by himself at night an' lookin' at his map! How many people did I see get drowned out heah in Brooklyn! How long would it take a guy wit a good map to know all deh was to know about Brooklyn!

Jesus! What a nut *he* was! I wondeh what eveh happened to 'im, anyway! I wondeh if someone knocked him on duh head or if he's still wanderin' aroun' in duh subway in duh middle of duh night wit his little map! Duh poor guy! Say, I've got to laugh, at dat, when I t'ink about him! Maybe he's found out by now dat he'll neveh live long enough to know duh whole of Brooklyn. It'd take a guy a lifetime to know Brooklyn t'roo an' t'roo. An' even den, yuh wouldn't know it all.

Stigmata

Joyce Carol Oates

JOYCE CAROL OATES *(1938–   ) grew up in the area around Lockport, New York, was graduated in 1960 from Syracuse University, and later received her master's degree in English from the University of Wisconsin. She has won many awards and recognitions for her fiction, including the National Book Award in 1970 for her novel,* Them. *Her short stories have been frequently cited for their excellence. In 1967 she was chosen as first-prize winner in the O. Henry Prize Awards. Her novels include* With Shuddering Fall *(1964),* A Garden of Earthly Delights *(1967),* Expensive People *(1968),* Wonderland *(1971). Her collections of short stories are widely known, such as* Upon the Sweeping Flood *(1966),* The Wheel of Love *(1970),* Marriages and Infidelities *(1972). For the past ten years her stories have been praised principally for their capacity to probe into areas of life that most of us cannot or do not want to see, let alone acknowledge.*

Though his father had been at St. Jerome's Home for the Aged for five or six years now, Walt Turner had never seen the home before—he had seen his father, of course, at various Christmases, at various houses of brothers and sisters, and the old man had journeyed down out of these saintly hills one fall to attend a Sunday High Mass sung by his second oldest son, newly ordained a priest—but Walt had never visited him at the home and had never imagined visiting him, since he did not like his father particularly. He had guessed that a visit to the home, with those faint mountains and hills peering in the old man's window, and that blue sky that was so fraudulently pure it offended one's credulity, would be, as his sister Clara reported sadly, "A visit to him in Heaven—all he does is smile."

Walt had driven alone up to the home, in spite of his distrust of this second-hand car, refusing a ride with his brothers— who drove carefully and looked at the scenery and talked about their jobs and their children and their father—and as he approached the nursing home the impact of its high, rigid, ascetic opulence struck him so that he felt the car slowing, as if weakened by the vision. St. Jerome's, as its worthy brochure had shown, was built on a hill: a kind of drumlin, perhaps, at any rate a freakish hill which lifted high above the level of the immediate area. It was jarring: a photograph or a vision made real. Oh, there were frills of nature attendant upon it, fir trees and slimly elegant shrubs; there were foothills and real mountains behind it, suggesting its location in nature; but the building itself, a heavy rectangular structure that surrendered nothing to art, that, constructed of some deliberate anonymous colorless rock, looked centuries old and simultaneously unrelated to time, showed by the very bluntness of its reality the illusion that nature conspired—there were meek dying trees beneath that green, and hills fated to erode beneath those slivers of leftover snow, and mountains so vague they might be erased by hand. And had not nature's great contribution to history, the wooden cross, become transformed into brilliant silver, gleaming over there above the chapel? It was human creation that would survive all worldly accidents.

Walt turned up the long gravel drive. The big building waited coyly atop its hill: the drive leaned this way, now that way, as if teasing. As it rose slowly Walt began to seek the parking lot behind the home; there were a large number of cars parked there, and he noticed in his rear-view mirror that a station wagon was just turning in from the road. He drove faster. On the bumper of the station wagon was a sticker with orange fluorescent letters—a politician's name? But it was months too early for that. Walt drove faster and heard with satisfaction gravel being picked up and churned around his wheels. He supposed the driver behind him had taken in, carefully, this car and was wondering about it—St. Jerome's, though planned as near-charity, was aristocratic, after all, and bluntly expensive. And who else would there be to wonder at him? There would be reporters and doctors and one or two psychiatrists and a university professor from downstate, not to mention his two frail sweet sisters whose letters he did not answer and his two successful brothers whose offer of money he refused (the third brother was now in Rome, regretted violently that he could not come). Walt parked along the edge of the driveway; his heart was pounding. The station wagon passed him, headed for the parking lot, and he found himself staring at the orange sticker: OBSERVE EASTER.

Walt was met inside by a young nun in a brown outfit, who smiled like his father smiled. He introduced himself with an absurd yet faintly proud sense of being important; he had noticed, sitting about the foyer on cheap modern chairs, men who must certainly be reporters. Other people drifted by, dumpy women in furs, young women holding back straining children, visitors to lesser patients, who looked about wonderingly. Was it possible a miracle might occur, and in this building? Walt's blood throbbed foolishly as he ascended the stairs.

But it was for nothing: his father was not in his room. A nurse explained politely, another young woman in a brown outfit, hardly more than a girl. No, not out in the sun porch either, this was his time of devotion; she spoke in short snatched enthusiastic phrases. "But your family is inside waiting. Won't you wait with them?" She was obviously shy and pleased and embarrassed.

As Walt knocked he heard his brother Art's voice, a solemn murmur that must be dragging down the corners of his mouth. The door opened—a dazzling flash of white like a glimpse of another world, beautifully white walls—his sister standing there chic in a dark tweed suit with black fur about its collar. "Walt, dear," she cried. She embraced him and he held his breath against the odor of cologne, though he liked Clara immensely: had she not always taken his side, the side of the youngest, the weakest, the nastiest? "It's so good to see you again," she said in her family-gathering voice. The others were on their feet and crowding in; welcomes were general. There was Carolyn and her husband, Carolyn now getting old—nearly forty—but smiling bravely, defying all wrinkles, trusting to a new complex sort of make-up: but Carolyn was a fine woman, a fine mother, wasn't that true? Walt accepted her embrace and saw over her shoulder the embarrassed expressions of his brothers. Then as he was released to them their expressions clicked into proper looks of solemn, cautious welcome, the professional greeting between older brothers. "Walt," Art said, shaking hands and cuffing his shoulder; Ronald did the same. "If only Tom had been able to come!" Clara said. In the awkward group they jostled about for a while, lighting cigarettes, helping Walt off with his coat; Carolyn and her husband exchanged domestic murmurs, nothing important, the sort of thing expected between husband and wife; Art—who was putting on weight, a round, well-fed, red-faced stranger—went back to his position by the window, where the fine glare burned around his head and blurred his features. "Here, sit down. I suppose you've driven all the way?" Clara said, leading him somewhere. "We're staying in town, at the hotel. *The* hotel. There's only one but it's rather nice—big and white, with a veranda. It was built in 1850." Walt made his way through the odor of cologne and cigar smoke and sat down. "So where is he?" he said. "Holding a press conference or something?"

He saw that look of pain shoot in several directions, ricochet off one face and hit another, become absorbed finally in Clara's shrill chatty voice. "He's at his devotions now," she said. "All the old people spend quite a bit of time at their devotions, especially during Holy Week. But Father more than anyone—you understand." Walt showed no understanding but lit a cigarette and everyone watched him drop the match into a dirty ashtray.

The room was smaller than he had expected: the brochure had hinted at larger rooms. This room, despite the esteem of its inmate, was hardly more than a cell—with a large window, it was true, viewing the parking lot; its walls were starkly white, a white so relentlessly clean and featureless that it turned Walt's eyes continually away from it and to the security of flesh—the familiar unfamiliar faces of his family. Their mother had died years ago and so there was only a brother missing, Tom, who was tall, angular, bony-faced, with a gift of venomous wit—Tom in Italy now humbling himself in a study of marriage law, Tom who had wanted to teach college: Walt missed him. How much easier these people were without him lurking in the background to ridicule and love them—how much straighter they stood! "If only Tom had been able to get permission!" Clara said, looking at Walt.

"The discipline is too strong," Carolyn's husband suggested without enthusiasm. Walt could not remember if he was Catholic—

maybe a convert. Didn't they have five children? Everyone murmured over this perhaps agreeing, perhaps disagreeing. "A bulwark against anarchy," Ronald said. He wore a gray vest that bulged gently about his abdomen. "But it is too strong!" Clara said. "What are you talking about, anarchy? His own father is a saint and the Church won't let him come! What are you talking about?" Clara's nose seemed to grow sharper; a dull red flush overtook her cheeks. "For God's sake don't start on that, that saint business," Art said. He looked at Walt. "We've been instructed about that. They've made it clear. Nobody's a saint when he's living, and there's no evidence—no final—" "But in your heart what do you feel?" Clara cried triumphantly.

An excited, embarrassed silence fell upon them. Walt's fingers were cold. "Oh, for Christ's sake," he said. "So you believe in this." They were too fond of him, or too dignified, to answer; Ronald, twelve years Walt's senior, blinked benignly at him as if at a child. It was odd that Walt's remark should hang in the air so clearly, as if it were cherished by them, examined by them, distinguishing him from them and their successful lives. . . . Walt, his face burning with anger and shame, felt catapulted back in time, sitting again at that big dinner table in the old parlor, with a napkin on his lap. Food being passed elegantly, in white dishes; his sisters' young faces, hair recently washed; his brothers in suits and ties; his mother with her heavy pearls; his father, there at the head of the table with his back reflected in the glass of the mahogany china cabinet: his father! While they murmured happily with the full fierce impersonal glare of their father's love falling upon them without distinction, like the sun's rays on the blind earth, Walt had grovelled backwards like a crab, staring down at his food and his dirt-edged fingernails, thinking that he was not related to them, could recognize nothing of himself in them, why did they pretend love for him? His mind shifted backward steadily, away from the candlelight, he retreated inside his bowed head from that half-smile on his father's lean attractive face. His father smiled that smile to all of them, Art who was so good in math, and Walt who had been caught stealing comic books in the drug store!

"It isn't the reporters I mind," Carolyn was saying. "I thought I would. It's the psychiatrist, the one from Chicago. Did you meet him? He's staying at the hotel." "He seemed cordial," Art said. "But they don't believe—any of them!" Carolyn said. "And," said Art carefully, "it's better that way—they'll be forced to believe. Why do you think they allow them here, to examine Father? They've been analyzing him for a week. —The bishop has finally come around, Walt, did you hear that?" Walt shrugged his shoulders. He had crossed his legs and noted now, with indifferent curiosity, that the cuffs of his trousers were dirty. "There's going to be a procession of the faithful on Friday, if everything is well," said Art. "If he starts to bleed on time," Walt said.

"Walt, how is Linda?" Carolyn said. She wore a hat with a seagreen feather twisting about it; it seemed to tense with the anticipation of putting Walt down.

"Fine, last time I saw her."

They looked at him sadly. "She was a sweet girl, but maybe a little too young. Immature," Clara offered.

"Not was but is. *Is* a sweet girl." Now that they watched him so closely he gloried, despite himself, in their attention. "And it hadn't anything much to do with her. Don't blame her."

"I wasn't blaming her," Clara said sharply.

"Well, don't. I know you all do." He leered at them, grinning. That would pierce their benevolent hearts. Or had they learned from their father that august generous indifference, that godly calm that stifles all anger, all love? He believed he could see something of their father in each of them, even in Clara, a girl forced into a woman, with bracelets and rings and clouds of perfume, to whose pretty smile so many young men had been drawn, eager at first, later perplexed, bored, retreating to firmer women. Especially in Art, the oldest, who leaned back against the window sill sucking at a cigar with the same look of tender concern their father had directed toward his own cigars, or his food, or Clara's recitations, at family reunions, of sprightly verse from "Alice in Wonderland." "I used to think it would be strange to be a father," Walt said. "But it isn't anything, is it? That's the hell of it. It meant something to Linda, having the baby—but not to me. That's the way it is, isn't it?"

They looked at him blankly; this was too personal. With a frown Art stretched his arm so he could consult his watch: "Twenty past five. He stays in the chapel from one until five-thirty. On his knees, a man that age. Do you know he's been fasting all this year? Since last Easter, Walt." Walt shivered, not at this sinister information, but at his own name; what kin was he to such insanity? "He insisted that communion every morning would be enough for him to live on, but they wouldn't allow it—there was quite a controversy, all the way up to the chancery office. It was thought to be too extreme—I think I agree—"

"He's such an old man now, Walt, wait till you see him! He's lost so much weight," Clara said.

"But if *he* feels communion would be enough they should let him fast," Carolyn pointed out. The sisters did not look at each other but toward each other, obliquely; their glances crossed in mid-air. "He knows more than they do. I *don't* care if they are the church, this is something special, obviously. It's a direct revelation from God."

"It isn't going through channels, that's sure," Ronald said.

"But if he were to die—!" Clara whispered.

"He's got to die," said Walt. "Then he's got to be resurrected, Sunday morning. Isn't that how it goes, and isn't he under contract to a television network for it?"

"Look, why the hell did you come?" Art said. Their father's look slid off his face and he stared over at Walt. "Just what are you doing here?"

Walt glanced away—at the unfinished bureau, the crucifix above it. His hands became loose and self-conscious. "I don't know."

"I know you've been under a strain, Walt, with the divorce and all," Art said slowly. "I don't want any quarrels. Not here. There's too much at stake. It's just that you don't seem to realize what this is—what's really happening and how important it is."

"Walt, the whole world is waiting," Clara said.

The horror of this remark calmed Walt. It was true that he believed in nothing, benevolence neither divine nor human; he expected nothing but age, perhaps cancer, perhaps a failing heart, since nature runs only one way; he expected no more abortive gestures of love; he was too ironical to care, really, about the college degrees he had never been able to use. He had begun to drink too much, as if fulfilling a role; it was true that his mind had no refuge: thoughts before sleep could center on nothing, neither the future nor the past nor the distant past, that sunless perplexing area of his childhood. On his mother? But she was dead too long, it was not a person he remembered but an image, an American formula. And yet, he wanted to assure them, there was something in him to which they could address themselves—if they wanted— They could speak with him singly, honestly, they could reveal the truth about their secret lives and he would listen—greedily, gratefully— He was not hard, his heart was not dead, he was waiting and vulnerable. He muttered, "Sorry."

Carolyn was speaking, slowly and elaborately, about the political machinations in the diocese, when the door was opened rather roughly, given these still surroundings—and a heavy white-faced nun stared in at them. "Could you please wait downstairs? Could you— You must leave, something has happened to your father—" The woman cried out; Walt got to his feet. Another nun appeared, an older woman. "Yes, your father has collapsed in the chapel but he is being attended. He is being attended. The doctors are going to bring him back up here and so we would like the room empty—you'll be able to visit him soon— No, it's nothing critical, he has regained consciousness. You understand he will have the best of medical care."

The women breathed audibly, trembling, the brothers moved tentatively toward the door: all stared at the nuns. "We weren't prepared for this," the older nun said suddenly, "since it—it began last year on Friday— And today is only Thursday— We weren't prepared—your father was not prepared, exactly, but he seems well—he is conscious, perfectly conscious— Pray for him. Pray for him," she said in excitement. "He is praying for us. God has visited this blessing upon him for us, for all of us, your father prays for all the world—"

Her fierce controlled hysteria followed Walt out into the hall. Ahead of him his sisters and brothers walked along in frightened obedience, like children; staring at their stiff backs, Walt was sickened with fear—was it possible that this miracle was going to happen? A miracle advertised in cheap Catholic pamphlets, a miracle insisted upon by factions within the Church—hinted at in his own newspaper, a sophisticated large-circulation daily? He saw the figures of old men in doorways, watching them as they passed, envious old men in bathrobes and slippers whose sunken mouths showed their despair over being no more than ordinary, dying old men.

They checked Walt into the hotel and had dinner there that evening with Father Mann—an old priest with a heavy, drooping head and an apologetic smile—and a writer introduced as a "special friend of the Church," a well-fed young man who did not take notes but listened to their conversation as if he were recording it. "Your father has concentrated his life upon Christ and the passion of Christ," the priest told them gently. They were at dinner, eating perfunctorily; an odor of baked fish rose about the table. "It was for this reason that he wanted to come to St. Jerome's. We know the unhappiness this caused—you felt that a man's children should take care of him in his old age. All this is true, true," he said, nodding, as Walt remembered the shrill quarrels that had shot back and forth from child to child, nervous refutations of earlier remarks, or accusations, insistences upon love, duty. No one had really wanted him since all were afraid of him, and yet all—except Walt—had wanted him desperately and viciously, afraid to surrender him to anyone else. "All this is true ordinarily, but you have always known that your father is no ordinary man. The miracle of his faith, the physical miracle, is but a symptom—you understand. A sign, a manifestation of inner faith. Here at St. Jerome's he was able to withdraw as far as possible from the world; he could contemplate Christ and the bitter crucifixion of Christ without having to return, except incidentally, to the world. . . ."

"He never recognized the world," Walt said.

"Never recognized it?" The reporter leaned forward.

"Never recognized it, yes, a good expression," Father Mann said. "Perhaps he spoke of his faith to you? Yes, he is a saintly man, a holy man—by contrast with us who are secular," he added carefully. "It's believed, you may have heard, that the manifestation of Our Saviour's wounds came to him earlier than last year. As long as three years ago. . . . One of the nurses has told us she remembered your father falling sometime during Holy Week, and suffering headaches, but of course nothing was suspected, nothing supernatural. And last year the wounds appeared unmistakably, on both hands, his feet, in his side. They bled slightly for about three hours on Good Friday, but your father did not seem to regain consciousness until Sunday morning. He came back to us as if from a great distance, and the wounds faded. . . . A miracle." The old man looked moved by his own words; his jaw had begun to tremble finely. A small piece of fish, newly cut from the rest, lay cooling on his plate. "Except for the miracle of the Mass there's never been anything like it, in my life—

Never so clear a sign of God's love, so obvious a blessing. The sharing of Christ's suffering by a human being, an ordinary man—this will be acclaimed as a miracle, this will be a lever for conversion and strengthening of faith all over the world."

"But why today? Why has it happened today?" Clara interrupted.

"God's time is not necessarily our time," the priest said coldly.

There was a long, intricate quarrel over the check, but Walt, who excused himself to head for the bar, did not notice who won. In the half-deserted lounge he sat at a small table in the rear, grateful for the dark. His eyes had begun to sting. He drank slowly, while the yawning bartender read through a newspaper, turning the pages noisily in the red glow from a neon sign. A little after ten Clara joined him. She had changed from the suit to a dark wool dress; gold jewelry tinkled about her wrist. "I'm going to try to make it with them for six o'clock services," she said, "but I couldn't sleep just now, I don't want to take more pills. . . ." She chattered on with the nervous coquettish energy that Walt had always pitied, knowing it must end slumped before a dressing-table mirror, nose a little shiny, powder smeared subtly by perspiration, lips heavy. She skipped from topic to topic, person to person, circling but steadily nearing the center of their worlds, the accident that bound them there together, at a small cheap-surfaced table in this dreary lounge— "I'm afraid that this will injure him," she said seriously. Her innocence alarmed Walt. "You mean you don't think he's suffering?" Walt asked. "Suffering? Suffering?" Clara murmured, looking in her purse for something. In the dull red light she looked suddenly young; she allowed him the calculated impact of her simplicity. "Why, yes, he's suffering . . . some. . . . That's part of it, I've done some reading and I was talking to the Mother Superior, she. . . . But how does he suffer?"

Her fingers paused inside her purse. Walt could see a tangle of objects, silver and gold, leather, the neat oval gleams of Clara's enameled nails. "Like Christ," said Walt with a grin. But Clara had begun to retreat. She took out a compact, opened it and looked at herself, dutifully, licking her lips; then she snapped it shut and replaced it. Her expression had the look of assurance that comes from having just been checked in a mirror. "But I hope it doesn't injure him so that he's different, so that he doesn't know us anymore," she said. "I've been up to see him, Walt, more than anyone, once a month, and he's so remote—always so remote—I could hardly talk to him. Oh, he wasn't impolite; you know Father, he's incapable of hurting anyone. . . . But he was so distracted that I felt later he wouldn't remember I had come. Or he wouldn't remember who had come." "Then why do you come to see him?" said Walt. "Because I love him," Clara said. "But why do you love him?" said Walt. "Because I love him," Clara said sharply. "He's our father."

They sat in silence for a while. Walt noticed a waitress with silver-blond hair uplifted and ballooning over the top of her head. She teetered skillfully on high heels. "I can't bear to think of anything happening to him," Clara went on, apologetically. "Anything to change him. What if he forgets? I can't sleep sometimes, or I wake up at night, thinking—what if he forgets me? Because I've always waited for him—I've always thought he might— Well, he might tell me something," she said, confused, "he might talk about home, when we were children, or he might ask me how I am, what my life is now— How could I have ever given everything over to some other man, some stranger, when— I thought he might tell me something, some secret about myself." They stared in embarrassment at each other. The kinship between them was so strong that Walt, to control his sudden nervousness, had to light a cigarette. "Do you understand?" Clara said. "Do you understand?"

Around three that morning, unable to sleep, Walt thought of calling his wife—his ex-wife—and had picked up the receiver, was dreamily awaiting the outside line, when he saw his reflection in the bureau mirror like a policeman popped up to accuse him: it was always a surprise to see that he was no longer really young, that last year between twenty-nine and thirty must have exhausted his youth. He had black hair, cut close against his head so that it looked like a cap, giving him an appearance of innocence—jocularity. His eyes, which were drooping like his brother Tom's, belied any innocence; they took in most things, including themselves, without enthusiasm. Yet he had a gift for irony, and if he prized it rather too much—if he sought in himself an academic salvation through it—it was because there was nothing else for him, really nothing. He had never believed in himself, any more than he had believed in the world: alien shapes, lines, colors, conversations, toothed smiles that convey whole dialogues, patterns of living, even passion—all had drifted by his sight with the watery instability of distractions in dreams, mere trifles to divert the mind from its true object. But what was this object? He had never been able to discover it, as his father so easily had; and perhaps it was only after struggle, relinquishing a part of their heritage, that his brothers had blinked away the glorious threat of this ideal and had surrendered to the complex material charms of the world. For these charms were complex and frightening; it was no coward who succumbed to them. Walt could appreciate the courage it took to sink oneself in the world, in its ponderous ways, yet he could not make the leap—any more than he could make the leap to the pleasant ghostly universe his father inhabited, gentlemanly man! He saw his fright in the mirror before he felt it: the telephone was speaking to him. "No, sorry, I've changed my mind." He put the receiver back. And he felt, then, half-smiling at the telephone, that he had, indeed, escaped—a clever escape—and that his father if he had known, would have been pleased.

Walt woke after eight, feeling drugged, and drove alone up to St. Jerome's. The air was cold, there was no hint of spring; slivers of ice lay in the ditches. There were already cars in the parking lot, and about the damp front steps groups of people stood, families, breathing in the cold air. A young man with an acne-ravaged face and a maroon scarf approached Walt. "You are a member of the Turner family?" he said. "No," said Walt. Evidently they were waiting for the doors to be opened. He looked around at the mild faces, country people like domesticated animals, calmed by impending excitement. Some, older women, were saying rosaries to themselves. Walt heard the man with the scarf and another man, who wore a hat, talking behind him. "Supposed to be an inside story," one said. "Born without eyes, the skin just growing over. Radiation poisoning. It's going to break in a week." "Is this the same one, the one in California?" the other said.

The meek crowd moved along up the wide stone steps, watching their feet., Inside the building was gleaming with cleanliness: the floor shone, windows shone in the brittle light, the nuns' shoes, when they peeked out from beneath the heavy brown skirts, were polished a shiny black. Walt met his sister Carolyn upstairs. She took his arm. "They've put Father in another room, in the sun porch," she whispered. Her face was pale and not very pretty; she had sacrificed lipstick for Good Friday. "He knows us, Walt. He knows us." Her whisper became throaty with triumph; Walt felt her shiver. "The tourists are here," Walt said brutally. "They're downstairs." "The audience of the faithful," Carolyn said, as if reading a sign on the wall. Walt looked up: there was a sign there, but it said NO SMOKING.

When he entered the antiseptic-smelling room—which was crowded quietly in the background—Walt understood that he had been preparing for this meeting for months. Carolyn urged him on as his heart thudded, and, yes, there was his father—no stranger after all, but his father, their father, familiar man!—that face leapt to Walt with the serenity of habit, the face of Walt's dreams, daydreams, and nothing in him protested as he approached the bed and sank to his knees on the tiled floor. . . . Was he supposed to pray? He supposed it was proper to pray a little, to mutter harmlessly, and to cross oneself; he crossed himself with care. He peered up at his father, who did not seem to notice him. There the old man lay, real as life! Weight gone out of his chest; his cheeks sunken (as if the stubborn rotted old teeth had finally been pulled); his face was pale, mottled slightly, mild, peaceful, charmed with itself or with this blessing, his eyes fastened upon something in the air, his throat quivering as if sustaining an inaudible dialogue. White, frail hair, that of a professional old man; and arms poking out of bony shoulders, narrow as rods, hands turned upward to catch the precise gleam of bright spring air from the great windows on the side wall—palms covered with blood! Beneath them, on a paper-thin bluish plastic sheet that protected the bedclothes, little beads of blood.

Walt felt a queer, half-pleasant paralysis. His legs were dead, his eyes fastened themselves greedily upon that shining blood and—to be recalled later with shame—he drew in a breath, slowly, sniffing to catch the odor of blood, legitimate blood. He smelled only antiseptic. "But the feet," he wanted to cry, "and the bleeding side—where are they? If I don't see them I won't believe!" But he simply got to his feet, allowed Carolyn to lead him away. He thought he was smiling, grinning, but the family—the nuns—the strange men—looked at him tenderly, with understanding.

The phenomenon continued throughout the day, the old man in a trance, and several hundred frightened visitors were allowed, singly, in the room to drop to their knees, pray, stare, and leave; but the bleeding did not abate, neither that evening nor the next day, and the audience of the faithful continued. There was an alarming swell on Saturday afternoon. Walt waited out these hours at the hotel, in the lounge, reading newspapers about the miracle at St. Jerome's, which the Church, though refusing comment, was viewing "with benevolent interest." There were side articles about other miracles, most of them in Italy, one in southern France. Opinions of doctors, who were baffled, opinions of other authorities, one of them—Walt read with anger—who attributed the bleeding to psychosomatic blisters! Walt did not see his brothers and sisters, they were at the home, near the old man, so he began to mutter to himself as he drank. Sometimes his mind, jolted naked by the insanity of this experience, called for flight, escape: if he did not escape soon he would be doomed. He forgot to eat and the inertia of half-pleasant nausea overtook him. On Saturday afternoon he was sick off and on for hours, waiting patiently on the edge of the bathtub, then he drank a little more until dinner. He came upon Ronald in the hotel lobby: Ronald looked aged, his hair had fallen loose about his forehead. But he smiled and gripped Walt's shoulders passionately. "He knows us!" he said. "The way he looks when we kneel by him—when you knelt too, did you see it? He recognizes us!"

Walt woke the next morning, oddly relaxed. Then he remembered that it was Sunday; all was over. Resurrection. He felt drained, pleased, his stomach ached with hunger. Perhaps his father would die before next Easter. Perhaps he would die. He ordered breakfast from room service, showered, shaved, hung out the door looking for someone familiar—saw no one—saw, out the window, people dressed for Easter Sunday, resplendent in the sunshine. On an impulse he opened the window, grunting. There was a sound of remote bells.

He ate ravenously—eggs fried in butter, bacon, toast with jelly of two sorts, grape and apple. Cups of hot coffee, sweetened with cream. He watched the food lovingly as he ate, later he brushed his teeth and watched himself in the mirror with approval, then he dressed himself with a sense of pleasure and freedom: some catharsis had taken place after all, the miracle had touched him. He sped out of town to St. Jerome's, which jutted out of the earth in a glory.

The foyer was radiant with lilies. Walt passed through the aisle which they bounded, frail white proud things that had blossomed out of the nursing home air itself. He exchanged greetings with young nuns, with strangers, men and women decked in fine warm clothes, little girls in patent leather shoes. It occurred to him, ascending the stairs for the last time, that he had not yet thought about his father—facing him now would be more difficult than facing him on Friday, when he was transfigured, another person. What did one say to such a being? But the Sunday air buoyed him, cheered him. Doors were opened upon domestic scenes—families sitting around beds, around old men in wheelchairs. Radios played, television sets were on. By one doorway a pile of breakfast dishes, plate smeared with hardened egg, were set carelessly on the floor—such was the vagabond holiday mood of Easter! But the door to his father's old room was closed, locked, and Walt wandered on, puzzled, down the corridor to the sun porch . . . which was blocked off by bureaus and bedframes dragged down from the attic, surely, and seeing this Walt's blood seemed to slow.

There were his brothers standing by a railing, looking down over a stairway, smoking. And Carolyn on a leather couch, legs crossed and stockings straining with muscle—legs nearly as girlish as ever. Ronald came up to Walt gravely. "Well, have you heard? It isn't over." "Isn't over?" Walt said. He saw immediately, in his mind's eye, a calendar; perhaps there was a confusion of dates. "The bleeding hasn't stopped," Ronald said, looking significantly at Walt. Walt wanted to say, "God's time is not necessarily man's time," but Ronald was so frightened—so *disappointed*—that Walt only stared abruptly down at his feet, as if something had dragged his gaze that way. "No one knows what's wrong," Ronald said. "Clara's in there with him, they can't get her to leave. It's been hell, Walt, you don't know—we think Clara might be—might need— You're so goddamed lucky, aren't you, off in your corner when things get tough!" Ronald's sickish face was puffy and distorted, like that of a bulldog. "Leave us to worry about it like you've always done!"

Walt pulled away and approached Ronald from another side, as if executing a dance step; this seemed to work. "What have they done about it? Do the newsmen know?" he whispered. "It's been kept a secret," Ronald said. "They expect it to stop soon. Today. For God's sake why hasn't it stopped? It's only supposed to bleed a few hours on Friday." "Is he in pain?" said Walt. But Ronald shrugged his shoulders. "Money couldn't get him any better care. I've got to get started back, my wife called, she's worried as hell," he said, "and if Art wants a ride, and Carolyn and. . . . The responsibility of it. . . . Could you take Clara home? It's sure to stop today, it started earlier and maybe that's why it kept on longer." "How's Clara?" said Walt. "Oh, God, Clara. . . . You remember the time she ripped some evening dress with her heel, putting it on? The same thing. . . ." "Does he talk?" said Walt. "Yes, he talks," Ronald said abruptly. "Art," he said, holding out his arm, "what time do you have?"

Walt stared at the closed door. He felt dizzy, isolated. Everything spun away from him, even time: here he was back on Friday again, forced to enter that door, approach that bed, kneel, cross himself, sniff at the blood. . . . He argued gently with a nun who came at him out of nowhere, was admitted, saw with shock Clara's disorderly figure jerking to its feet as he entered the room. There was his father in bed, the same position! Nothing had changed except that the room was empty now of people, filled sweetly with lilies. Clara, on the other side of the bed, stared resentfully across at Walt. The old man was covered now with a brown blanket—lovingly darned at one corner, by a solitary, smiling old nun—his hands still out, though bandaged thickly, face propped up against the pillows. There was a small metal crucifix propped up against a fold in the blanket. The old man squinted at Walt as he approached. The room was silent, only from afar could they hear the pleasant muffled sounds of televisions, conversations, children's cries. At the bedside Walt saw the old man's lips move. Walt stared, transfixed, he awaited his name . . . the old man said something but Walt's ears were deafened by blood, he had to stoop like a little old man himself and say, "I didn't hear." The old man's throat quivered and the lips moved again. "I hurt," he said. Walt, still bent, stared at nothing—at the pillow. "I hurt," his father said again.

Walt stared. Again he felt the sensation of being alone, of being lost, as if ordinary time and the ordinary people it involved had been sucked violently away from him; even Clara, ravaged by despair, looked on without involvement or comprehension. It was at that moment, judging finally that old, handsome, dying face, that Walt understood what had happened to his father. Safe in his old age, before that safe in his tranquillity, he had refined himself out of life—he had had, so easily, six children, he had given them nothing, not his own identity, not identities of their own, he had not distinguished one from the other, he had moved as a ghost among the mild, ghostly illusions of this world, as a young man and, now, an old man; he had never been a man; and he was being educated now in the pain of being human. "Why, this is a punishment," Walt said at once, almost laughing at the surprise of his discovery. "This isn't a blessing, who told you that? This is a punishment. A punishment." He looked up: Clara stared with hatred at him. And his father, was that not a sly look, sly and knowing behind the wincing pain? "You're being punished!" Walt cried.

There were others around him, nurses, and a man he had not seen before; they propelled him around. "A punishment! Or a penance—your word for it!" he shouted into the face of one of the nuns. "*He* knows! Ask *him!*" he said, jerking around to point with his jaw back at the old man. At the opened door they scuffled. Walt looked around again at the bed. Tears burned his eyes. "Punishment that you deserve! Goddam selfish old bastard, now you're getting it! God's on the right track! Got your number—never loved us, did you? Took all our love from us and—" They had pushed him out the door but he continued, laughing, seeing the faces of his brothers rush toward him— "Took it and kept taking it, a goddam sewer! a drain! down a toilet, anything we gave you! Now you're getting it good! —He is, he's getting it good," Walt was crying at his brothers. "He's laying in there and told me how he changed his mind and doesn't want the miracle any more, he told me it with his eyes. He says he hates God, hates Christ, says Christ had it easier than he does, if there ever was a real Christ—which he doubts! Told me it with his eyes!" He felt a sharp pain through his sleeve—a needle? He spun around and grabbed something—the doctor's jacket—and with rage born out of revenge for his father, for the joke played upon him, began to tear violently. Tears spilled out over his face, onto his own threshing hands.

Walt was not allowed in St. Jerome's again, so he waited down at the hotel, in his room, lying on his rumpled bed. He found out that Ronald and Art had gone—that was Monday afternoon. No change in his father. He tried to get in touch with Carolyn but there was never anyone in her room, his notes were never answered. . . . On Wednesday he paid part of his hotel bill, aware that the management was suspicious of him; he paid with a check which was worthless, but they would not know that immediately; he was elated with his own cunning. But as if to give him away his hands trembled as he made out the check. Upstairs he waited the hours away, lying on his bed. He forgot to drink. His eyes grew sore as if weakening from disuse. On Thursday he understood the peculiar inertia, the heavy calm that had dulled his brain for so long, when he was told of his father's death.

A professional-looking stranger who had knocked gently, whose eyes, in spite of the message of gravity to be given, could not help but wander about the smelling, cluttered room. If there were toast crusts on the floor there, those eyes would seek them out! The stranger spoke gently to Walt. "He managed to get out of the room during the night and found his way down to the visitors' restroom, the men's room, the room by the stairs— Strips of sheet he tore from his bedclothes—did harm to himself— If you'd like to get dressed and come with me— He was found in the morning—" Walt lay on the bed, his legs outstretched. Though he had heard only part of the man's speech he could see his father's skinny body dangling in the air as clearly as if the old man had hanged himself in the hotel closet, pushing the hangers to one side. Walt felt neither surprise nor relief. "Did the bleeding stop, then?" he said. "Your father was out of his mind with the pain, he wasn't responsible for what he did," the man said. "My father was responsible for what he did," Walt said with dignity.

The man waited for him outside. Time went slowly, it took time to dress. He ran his razor, dry over his jaw, lost interest, turned around in the white cramped bathroom as if looking for something—forgot what it was— The white walls blurred and dazzled his vision; a roaring began in his ears. What legacy had his father left him? His father had recognized him! He had known him, had talked to him—he had left him a legacy of death, spiteful death, but a work of art! Walt turned his palms up close to his face and stared at them. No blood. Nothing. No marks, no scars, no hints of anything, not even blisters.

Clean as a life never quite lived. There were wrinkles there, and hints of soft, blue veins beneath, far beneath, pinkish-gray skin that looked, upon examination, more like wood than flesh—the same hands he remembered looking at, idly, one day, as a child, as if those innocent palms might tell him something about the life to come.

The Other Side of the Hedge

E. M. Forster

E. M. FORSTER *(1879–1970), educated at King's College, Cambridge, was an English essayist, critic, and author of fiction, both novels and short stories. He twice traveled to India, and out of these experiences came the background and inspiration for his outstanding novel,* A Passage to India *(1924). Other novels include* Where Angels Fear to Tread *(1905),* The Longest Journey *(1907),* A Room with a View *(1908),* Howards End *(1910), and, published posthumously,* Maurice *(1971). His short-story collections are* The Celestial Omnibus and Other Stories *(1911),* The Eternal Moment and Other Stories *(1928), and* Collected Short Stories *(1948).* Abinger Harvest *(1936) is a mixture of articles, essays, reviews, poems;* Aspects of the Novel *(1927) is a superior consideration of fiction and the writing techniques involved.*

My pedometer told me that I was twenty-five; and, though it is a shocking thing to stop walking, I was so tired that I sat down on a milestone to rest. People outstripped me, jeering as they did so, but I was too apathetic to feel resentful, and even when Miss Eliza Dimbleby, the great educationist, swept past, exhorting me to persevere, I only smiled and raised my hat.

At first I thought I was going to be like my brother, whom I had had to leave by the roadside a year or two round the corner. He had wasted his breath on singing, and his strength on helping others. But I had travelled more wisely, and now it was only the monotony of the highway that oppressed me—dust under foot and brown crackling hedges on either side, ever since I could remember.

And I had already dropped several things—indeed, the road behind was strewn with the things we all had dropped; and the white dust was settling down on them, so that already they looked no better than stones. My muscles were so weary that I could not even bear the weight of those things I still carried. I slid off the milestone into the road, and lay there prostrate, with my face to the great parched hedge, praying that I might give up.

A little puff of air revived me. It seemed to come from the hedge; and, when I opened my eyes, there was a glint of light through the tangle of boughs and dead leaves. The hedge could not be as thick as usual. In my weak, morbid state, I longed to force my way in, and see what was on the other side. No one was in sight, or I should not have dared to try. For we of the road do not admit in conversation that there is another side at all.

I yielded to the temptation, saying to myself that I would come back in a minute. The thorns scratched my face, and I had to use my arms as a shield, depending on my feet alone to push me forward. Halfway through I would have gone back, for in the passage all the things I was carrying were scraped off me, and my clothes were torn. But I was so wedged that return was impossible, and I had to wriggle blindly forward, expecting every moment that my strength would fail me, and that I should perish in the undergrowth.

Suddenly cold water closed round my head, and I seemed sinking down for ever. I had fallen out of the hedge into a deep pool. I rose to the surface at last, crying for help, and I heard someone on the opposite bank laugh and say: "Another!" And then I was twitched out and laid panting on the dry ground.

Even when the water was out of my eyes, I was still dazed, for I had never been in so large a space, nor seen such grass and sunshine. The blue sky was no longer a strip, and beneath it the earth had risen gradually into hills—clean, bare buttresses, with beech trees in their folds, and meadows and clear pools at their feet. But the hills were not high, and there was in the landscape a sense of human occupation—so that one might have called it a park, or garden, if the words did not imply a certain triviality and constraint.

As soon as I got my breath, I turned to my rescuer and said:

"Where does this place lead to?"

"Nowhere, thank the Lord!" said he, and laughed. He was a man of fifty or sixty—just the kind of age we mistrust on the road—but there was no anxiety in his manner, and his voice was that of a boy of eighteen.

"But it must lead somewhere!" I cried, too much surprised at his answer to thank him for saving my life.

"He wants to know where it leads!" he shouted to some men on the hill side, and they laughed back, and waved their caps.

I noticed then that the pool into which I had fallen was really a moat which bent round to the left and to the right, and that the hedge followed it continually. The hedge was green on this side—its roots showed through the clear water, and fish swam about in them—and it was wreathed over with dog roses and Traveller's Joy. But it was a barrier, and in a moment I lost all pleasure in the grass, the sky, the trees, the happy men and women, and realized that the place was but a prison, for all its beauty and extent.

We moved away from the boundary, and then followed a path almost parallel to it, across the meadows. I found it difficult walking, for I was always trying to outdistance my companion, and there was no advantage in doing this if the place led nowhere. I had never kept step with anyone since I left my brother.

I amused him by stopping suddenly and saying disconsolately, "This is perfectly terrible. One cannot advance: one cannot progress. Now we of the road—"

"Yes. I know."

"I was going to say, we advance continually."

"I know."

"We are always learning, expanding, developing. Why, even in my short life I have seen a great deal of advance—the Transvaal War, the Fiscal Question, Christian Science, Radium. Here for example—"

I took out my pedometer, but it still marked twenty-five, not a degree more.

"Oh, it's stopped! I meant to show you. It should have registered all the time I was walking with you. But it makes me only twenty-five."

"Many things don't work in here," he said. "One day a man brought in a Lee-Metford, and that wouldn't work."

"The laws of science are universal in their application. It must be the water in the moat that has injured the machinery. In normal conditions everything works. Science and the spirit of emulation—those are the forces that have made us what we are."

I had to break off and acknowledge the pleasant greetings of people whom we passed. Some of them were singing, some talking, some engaged in gardening, hay-making, or other rudimentary industries. They all seemed happy; and I might have been happy too, if I could have forgotten that the place led nowhere.

I was startled by a young man who came sprinting across our path, took a little fence in fine style, and went tearing over a ploughed field till he plunged into a lake, across which he began to swim. Here was true energy, and I exclaimed: "A cross-country race! Where are the others?"

"There are no others," my companion replied; and, later on, when we passed some long grass from which came the voice of a girl singing exquisitely to herself, he said again: "There are no others." I was bewildered at the waste in production, and murmured to myself, "What does it all mean?"

He said: "It means nothing but itself"—and he repeated the words slowly, as if I were a child.

"I understand," I said quietly, "but I do not agree. Every achievement is worthless unless it is a link in the chain of development. And I must not trespass on your kindness any longer. I must get back somehow to the road, and have my pedometer mended."

"First, you must see the gates," he replied, "for we have gates, though we never use them."

I yielded politely, and before long we reached the moat again, at a point where it was spanned by a bridge. Over the bridge was a big gate, as white as ivory, which was fitted into a gap in the boundary hedge. The gate opened outwards, and I exclaimed in amazement, for from it ran a road—just such a road as I had left—dusty under foot, with brown crackling hedges on either side as far as the eye could reach.

"That's my road!" I cried.

He shut the gate and said: "But not your part of the road. It is through this gate that humanity went out countless ages ago, when it was first seized with the desire to walk."

I denied this, observing that the part of the road I myself had left was not more than two miles off. But with the obstinacy of his years he repeated: "It is the same road. This is the beginning, and though it seems to run straight away from us, it doubles so often, that it is never far from our boundary and sometimes touches it." He stooped down by the moat, and traced on its moist margin an absurd figure like a maze. As we walked back through the meadows, I tried to convince him of his mistake.

"The road sometimes doubles, to be sure, but that is part of our discipline. Who can doubt that its general tendency is onward? To what goal we know not—it may be to some mountain where we shall touch the sky, it may be over precipices into the sea. But that it goes forward—who can doubt that? It is the thought of that that makes us strive to excel, each in his own way, and gives us an impetus which is lacking with you. Now that man who passed us—it's true that he ran well, and jumped well, and swam well; but we have men who can run better, and men who can jump better, and who can swim better. Specialization has produced results which would surprise you. Similarly, that girl—"

Here I interrupted myself to exclaim: "Good gracious me! I could have sworn it was Miss Eliza Dimbleby over there, with her feet in the fountain!"

He believed that it was.

"Impossible! I left her on the road, and she is due to lecture this evening at Tunbridge Wells. Why, her train leaves Cannon Street in—of course my watch has stopped like everything else. She is the last person to be here."

"People always are astonished at meeting each other. All kinds come through the hedge, and come at all times—when they are drawing ahead in the race, when they are lagging behind, when they are left for dead. I often stand near the boundary listening to the sounds of the road—you know what they are—and wonder if anyone will turn aside. It is my great happiness to help someone out of the moat, as I helped you. For our country fills up slowly, though it was meant for all mankind."

"Mankind have other aims," I said gently, for I thought him well-meaning; "and I must join them." I bade him good evening, for the sun was declining, and I wished to be on the road by nightfall. To my alarm, he caught hold of me, crying: "You are not to go yet!" I tried to shake him off, for we had no interests in common, and his civility was becoming irksome to me. But for all my struggles the tiresome old man would not let go; and, as wrestling is not my specialty, I was obliged to follow him.

It was true that I could have never found alone the place where I came in, and I hoped that, when I had seen the other sights about which he was worrying, he would take me back to it. But I was determined not to sleep in the country, for I mistrusted it, and the people too, for all their friendliness. Hungry though I was, I would not join them in their evening meals of milk and fruit, and, when they gave me flowers, I flung them away as soon as I could do so unobserved. Already they were lying down for the night like cattle—some out on the bare hillside, others in groups under the beeches. In the light of an orange sunset I hurried on with my unwelcome guide, dead tired, faint for want of food, but murmuring indomitably: "Give me life, with its struggles and victories, with its failures and hatreds, with its deep moral meaning and its unknown goal!"

At last we came to a place where the encircling moat was spanned by another bridge, and where another gate interrupted the line of the boundary hedge. It was different from the first gate; for it was half transparent like horn, and opened inwards. But through it, in the waning light, I saw again just such a road as I had left—monotonous, dusty, with brown crackling hedges on either side, as far as the eye could reach.

I was strangely disquieted at the sight, which seemed to deprive me of all self-control. A man was passing us, returning for the night to the hills, with a scythe over his shoulder and a can of some liquid in his hand. I forgot the destiny of our race. I forgot the road that lay before my eyes, and I sprang at him, wrenched the can out of his hand, and began to drink.

It was nothing stronger than beer, but in my exhausted state it overcame me in a moment. As in a dream, I saw the old man shut the gate, and heard him say: "This is where your road ends, and through this gate humanity—all that is left of it—will come in to us."

Though my senses were sinking into oblivion, they seemed to expand ere they reached it. They perceived the magic song of nightingales, and the odor of invisible hay, and stars piercing the fading sky. The man whose beer I had stolen lowered me down gently to sleep off its effects, and, as he did so, I saw that he was my brother.

The Guest

Albert Camus

ALBERT CAMUS *(1913–1960) was born in Algeria, the son of a farm laborer. During his lifetime he was a teacher, actor, journalist, playwright, novelist. He fought as a French underground resistance leader during World War II; he and Jean-Paul Sartre also edited the underground paper* Combat. *Camus' first novel,* The Stranger *(1942), and his long essay* The Myth of Sisyphus *(1942) made him well known as an existentialist writer. His later works include* The Plague *(1947) and* The Fall *(1956), and another philosophical prose work,* The Rebel *(1951). He was awarded the Nobel Prize for Literature in 1957. A few years later he was killed in an automobile accident, leaving a void in modern literature that many believe still has not been filled. Camus said he wrote to increase the sum of responsibility in all men and women; some critics call him the conscience of the twentieth century.*

The schoolmaster was watching the two men climb toward him. One was on horseback, the other on foot. They had not yet tackled the abrupt rise leading to the schoolhouse built on the hillside. They were toiling onward, making slow progress in the snow, among the stones, on the vast expanse of the high, deserted plateau. From time to time the horse stumbled. Without hearing anything yet, he could see the breath issuing from the horse's nostrils. One of the men, at least, knew the region. They were following the trail although it had disappeared days ago under a layer of dirty white snow. The schoolmaster calculated that it would take them half an hour to get onto the hill. It was cold; he went back into the school to get a sweater.

He crossed the empty, frigid classroom. On the blackboard the four rivers of France, drawn with four different colored chalks, had been flowing toward their estuaries for the past three days. Snow had suddenly fallen in mid-October after eight months of drought without the transition of rain, and the twenty pupils, more or less, who lived in the villages scattered over the plateau had stopped coming. With fair weather they would return. Daru now heated only the single room that was his lodging, adjoining the classroom and giving also onto the plateau to the east. Like the class windows, his window looked to the south too. On that side the school was a few kilometers from the point where the plateau began to slope toward the south. In clear weather could be seen the purple mass of the mountain range where the gap opened onto the desert.

Somewhat warmed, Daru returned to the window from which he had first seen the two men. They were no longer visible. Hence they must have tackled the rise. The sky was not so dark, for the snow had stopped falling during the night. The morning had opened with a dirty light which had scarcely become brighter as the ceiling of clouds lifted. At two in the afternoon it seemed as if the day were merely beginning. But still this was better than those three days when the thick snow was falling amidst unbroken darkness with little gusts of wind that rattled the double door of the classroom. Then Daru had spent long hours in his room, leaving it only to go to the shed and feed the chickens or get some coal. Fortunately the delivery truck from Tadjid, the nearest village to the north, had brought his supplies two days before the blizzard. It would return in forty-eight hours.

Besides, he had enough to resist a siege, for the little room was cluttered with bags of wheat that the administration left as a stock to distribute to those of his pupils whose families had suffered from the drought. Actually they had all been victims because they were all poor. Every day Daru would distribute a ration to the children. They had missed it, he knew, during these bad days. Possibly one of the fathers or big brothers would come this afternoon and he could supply them with grain. It was just a matter of carrying them over to the next harvest. Now shiploads of wheat were arriving from France and the worst was over. But it would be hard to forget that poverty, that army of ragged ghosts wandering in the sunlight, the plateaus burned to a cinder month after month, the earth shriveled up little by little, literally scorched, every stone bursting into dust under one's foot. The sheep had died then by thousands and even a few men, here and there, sometimes without anyone's knowing.

In contrast with such poverty, he who lived almost like a monk in his remote schoolhouse, nonetheless satisfied with the little he had and with the rough life, had felt like a lord with his whitewashed walls, his narrow couch, his unpainted shelves, his well, and his weekly provision of water and food. And suddenly this snow, without warning, without the foretaste of rain. This is the way the region was, cruel to live in, even without men—who didn't help matters either. But Daru had been born here. Everywhere else, he felt exiled.

He stepped out onto the terrace in front of the schoolhouse. The two men were now halfway up the slope. He recognized the horseman as Balducci, the old gendarme he had known for a long time. Balducci was holding on the end of a rope an Arab who was walking behind him with hands bound and head lowered. The gendarme waved a greeting to which Daru did not reply, lost as he was in contemplation of the Arab dressed in a faded blue jellaba, his feet in sandals but covered with socks of heavy raw wool, his head surmounted by a narrow, short *chèche*. They were approaching. Balducci was holding back his horse in order not to hurt the Arab, and the group was advancing slowly.

Within earshot, Balducci shouted: "One hour to do the three kilometers from El Ameur!" Daru did not answer. Short and square in his thick sweater, he watched them climb. Not once had the Arab raised his head. "Hello," said Daru when they got up onto the terrace. "Come in and warm up." Balducci painfully got down from his horse without letting go of the rope. From under his bristling mustache he smiled at the schoolmaster. His little dark eyes, deep-set under a tanned forehead, and his mouth surrounded with wrinkles made him look attentive and studious. Daru took the bridle, led the horse to the shed, and came back to the two men, who were now waiting for him in the school. He led them into his room. "I am going to heat up the classroom," he said. "We'll be more comfortable there." When he entered the room again, Balducci was on the couch. He had undone the rope tying him to the Arab, who had squatted near the stove. His hands still bound, the *chèche* pushed back on his head, he was looking toward the window. At first Daru noticed only his huge lips, fat, smooth, almost Negroid; yet his nose was straight, his eyes were dark and full of fever. The *chèche* revealed an obstinate forehead and, under the weathered skin now rather discolored by the cold, the whole face had a restless and rebellious look that struck Daru when the Arab, turning his face toward him, looked him straight in the eyes. "Go into the other room," said the schoolmaster, "and I'll make you some mint tea." "Thanks," Balducci said. "What a chore! How I long for retirement." And addressing his prisoner in Arabic: "Come on, you." The Arab got up and, slowly, holding his bound wrists in front of him, went into the classroom.

With the tea, Daru brought a chair. But Balducci was already enthroned on the nearest pupil's desk and the Arab had squatted against the teacher's platform facing the stove, which stood between the desk and the window. When he held out the glass of tea to the prisoner, Daru hesitated at the sight of his bound hands. "He might perhaps be untied." "Sure," said Balducci. "That was for the trip." He started to get to his feet. But Daru, setting the glass on the floor, had knelt beside the Arab. Without saying anything, the Arab watched him with his feverish eyes. Once his hands were free, he rubbed his swollen wrists against each other, took the glass of tea, and sucked up the burning liquid in swift little sips.

"Good," said Daru. "And where are you headed?"

Balducci withdrew his mustache from the tea. "Here, son."

"Odd pupils! And you're spending the night?"

"No. I'm going back to El Ameur. And you will deliver this fellow to Tinguit. He is expected at police headquarters."

Balducci was looking at Daru with a friendly little smile.

"What's this story?" asked the schoolmaster. "Are you pulling my leg?"

"No, son. Those are the orders."

"The orders? I'm not . . ." Daru hesitated, not wanting to hurt the old Corsican. "I mean, that's not my job."

"What! What's the meaning of that? In wartime people do all kinds of jobs."

"Then I'll wait for the declaration of war!"

Balducci nodded.

"O.K. But the orders exist and they concern you too. Things are brewing, it appears. There is talk of a forthcoming revolt. We are mobilized, in a way."

Daru still had his obstinate look.

"Listen, son," Balducci said. "I like you and you must understand. There's only a dozen of us at El Ameur to patrol throughout the whole territory of a small department and I must get back in a hurry. I was told to hand this guy over to you and return without delay. He couldn't be kept there. His village was beginning to stir; they wanted to take him back. You must take him to Tinguit tomorrow before the day is over. Twenty kilometers shouldn't faze a husky fellow like you. After that, all will be over. You'll come back to your pupils and your comfortable life."

Behind the wall the horse could be heard snorting and pawing the earth. Daru was looking out the window. Decidedly, the weather was clearing and the light was increasing over the snowy plateau. When all the snow was melted, the sun would take over again and once more would burn the fields of stone. For days, still, the unchanging sky would shed its dry light on the solitary expanse where nothing had any connection with man.

"After all," he said, turning around toward Balducci, "what did he do?" And, before the gendarme had opened his mouth, he asked: "Does he speak French?"

"No, not a word. We had been looking for him for a month, but they were hiding him. He killed his cousin."

"Is he against us?"

"I don't think so. But you can never be sure."

"Why did he kill?"

"A family squabble, I think. One owed the other grain, it seems. It's not at all clear. In short, he killed his cousin with a billhook. You know, like a sheep, *kreezk!*"

Balducci made the gesture of drawing a blade across his throat and the Arab, his attention attracted, watched him with a sort of anxiety. Daru felt a sudden wrath against the man, against all men with their rotten spite, their tireless hates, their blood lust.

But the kettle was singing on the stove. He served Balducci more tea, hesitated, then served the Arab again, who, a second time, drank avidly. His raised arms made the jellaba fall open and the schoolmaster saw his thin, muscular chest.

"Thanks, kid," Balducci said. "And now, I'm off."

He got up and went toward the Arab, taking a small rope from his pocket.

"What are you doing?" Daru asked dryly.

Balducci, disconcerted, showed him the rope.

"Don't bother."

The old gendarme hesitated. "It's up to you. Of course, you are armed?"

"I have my shotgun."

"Where?"

"In the trunk."

"You ought to have it near your bed."

"Why? I have nothing to fear."

"You're crazy, son. If there's an uprising, no one is safe, we're all in the same boat."

"I'll defend myself. I'll have time to see them coming."

Balducci began to laugh, then suddenly the mustache covered the white teeth. "You'll have time? O.K. That's just what I was saying. You have always been a little cracked. That's why I like you, my son was like that."

At the same time he took out his revolver and put in on the desk.

"Keep it; I don't need two weapons from here to El Ameur."

The revolver shone against the black paint of the table. When the gendarme turned toward him, the schoolmaster caught the smell of leather and horseflesh.

"Listen, Balducci," Daru said suddenly, "every bit of this disgusts me, and first of all your fellow here. But I won't hand him over. Fight, yes, if I have to. But not that."

The old gendarme stood in front of him and looked at him severely.

"You're being a fool," he said slowly. "I don't like it either. You don't get used to putting a rope on a man even after years of it, and you're even ashamed—yes, ashamed. But you can't let them have their way."

"I won't hand him over," Daru said again.

"It's an order, son, and I repeat it."

"That's right. Repeat to them what I've said to you: I won't hand him over."

Balducci made a visible effort to reflect. He looked at the Arab and at Daru. At last he decided.

"No, I won't tell them anything. If you want to drop us, go ahead; I'll not denounce you. I have an order to deliver the prisoner and I'm doing so. And now you'll just sign this paper for me."

"There's no need. I'll not deny that you left him with me."

"Don't be mean with me. I know you'll tell the truth. You're from hereabouts and you are a man. But you must sign, that's the rule."

Daru opened his drawer, took out a little square bottle of purple ink, the red wooden penholder with the "sergeant-major" pen he used for making models of penmanship, and signed. The gendarme carefully folded the paper and put it into his wallet. Then he moved toward the door.

"I'll see you off," Daru said.

"No," said Balducci. "There's no use being polite. You insulted me."

He looked at the Arab, motionless in the same spot, sniffed peevishly, and turned away toward the door. "Good-by, son," he said. The door shut behind him. Balducci appeared outside the window and then disappeared. His footsteps were muffled by the snow. The horse stirred on the other side of the wall and several chickens fluttered in fright. A moment later Balducci reappeared outside the window leading the horse by the bridle. He walked toward the little rise without turning around and disappeared from sight with the horse following him. A big stone could be heard bouncing down. Daru walked back toward the prisoner, who, without stirring, never took his eyes off him. "Wait," the schoolmaster said in Arabic and went toward the bedroom. As he was going through the door, he had a second thought, went to the desk, took the revolver, and stuck it in his pocket. Then, without looking back, he went into his room.

For some time he lay on his couch watching the sky gradually close over, listening to the silence. It was this silence that had seemed painful to him during the first days here, after the war. He had requested a post in the little town at the base of the foothills separating the upper plateaus from the desert. There, rocky walls, green and black to the north, pink and lavender to the south, marked the frontier of eternal summer. He had been named to a post farther north, on the plateau itself. In the beginning, the solitude and the silence had been hard for him on these wastelands peopled only by stones. Occasionally, furrows suggested cultivation, but they had been dug to uncover a certain kind of stone good for building. The only plowing here was to harvest rocks. Elsewhere a thin layer of soil accumulated in the hollows would be scraped out to enrich paltry village gardens. This is the way it was: bare rock covered three quarters of the region. Towns sprang up, flourished, then disappeared; men came by, loved one another or fought bitterly, then died. No one in this desert, neither he nor his guest, mattered. And yet, outside this desert neither of them, Daru knew, could have really lived.

When he got up, no noise came from the classroom. He was amazed at the unmixed joy he derived from the mere thought that the Arab might have fled and that he would be alone with no decision to make. But the prisoner was there. He had merely stretched out between the stove and the desk. With eyes open, he was staring at the ceiling. In that position, his thick lips were particularly noticeable, giving him a pouting look. "Come," said Daru. The Arab got up and followed him. In the bedroom, the schoolmaster pointed to a chair near the table under the window. The Arab sat down without taking his eyes off Daru.

"Are you hungry?"

"Yes," the prisoner said.

Daru set the table for two. He took flour and oil, shaped a cake in a frying pan, and lighted the little stove that functioned on bottled gas. While the cake was cooking, he went out to the shed to get cheese, eggs, dates, and condensed milk. When the cake was done he set it on the window sill to cool, heated some condensed milk diluted with water, and beat up the eggs into an omelette. In one of his motions he knocked against the revolver stuck in his right pocket. He set the bowl down, went into the classroom, and put the revolver in his desk drawer. When he came back to the room, night was falling. He put on the light and served the Arab. "Eat," he said. The Arab took a piece of the cake, lifted it eagerly to his mouth, and stopped short.

"And you?" he asked.

"After you. I'll eat too."

The thick lips opened slightly. The Arab hesitated, then bit into the cake determinedly.

The meal over, the Arab looked at the schoolmaster. "Are you the judge?"

"No, I'm simply keeping you until tomorrow."

"Why do you eat with me?"

"I'm hungry."

The Arab fell silent. Daru got up and went out. He brought back a folding bed from the shed, set it up between the table and the stove, perpendicular to his own bed. From a large suitcase which, upright in a corner, served as a shelf for papers, he took two blankets and arranged them on the camp bed. Then he stopped, felt useless, and sat down on his bed. There was nothing more to do or to get ready. He had to look at this man. He looked at him, therefore, trying to imagine his face bursting with rage. He couldn't do so. He could see nothing but the dark yet shining eyes and the animal mouth.

"Why did you kill him?" he asked in a voice whose hostile tone surprised him.

The Arab looked away. "He ran away. I ran after him."

He raised his eyes to Daru again and they were full of a sort of woeful interrogation. "Now what will they do to me?"

"Are you afraid?"

He stiffened, turning his eyes away.

"Are you sorry?"

The Arab stared at him openmouthed. Obviously he did not understand. Daru's annoyance was growing. At the same time he felt awkward and self-conscious with his big body wedged between the two beds.

"Lie down there," he said impatiently. "That's your bed."

The Arab didn't move. He called to Daru:

"Tell me!"

The schoolmaster looked at him.

"Is the gendarme coming back tomorrow?"

"I don't know."

"Are you coming with us?"

"I don't know. Why?"

The prisoner got up and stretched out on top of the blankets, his feet toward the window. The light from the electric bulb shone straight into his eyes and he closed them at once.

"Why?" Daru repeated, standing beside the bed.

The Arab opened his eyes under the blinding light and looked at him, trying not to blink.

"Come with us," he said.

In the middle of the night, Daru was still not asleep. He had gone to bed after undressing completely; he generally slept naked. But when he suddenly realized that he had nothing on, he hesitated. He felt vulnerable and the temptation came to him to put his clothes back on. Then he shrugged his shoulders; after all, he wasn't a child and, if need be, he could break his adversary in two. From his bed he could observe him, lying on his back, still motionless with his eyes closed under the harsh light. When Daru turned out the light, the darkness seemed to coagulate all of a sudden. Little by little, the night came back to life in the window where the starless sky was stirring gently. The schoolmaster soon made out the body lying at his feet. The Arab still did not move, but his eyes seemed open. A faint wind was prowling around the schoolhouse. Perhaps it would drive away the clouds and the sun would reappear.

During the night the wind increased. The hens fluttered a little and then were silent. The Arab turned over on his side with his back to Daru, who thought he heard him moan. Then he listened for his guest's breathing, become heavier and more regular. He listened to that breath so close to him and mused without being able to go to sleep. In this room where he had been sleeping alone for a year, this presence bothered him. But it bothered him also by imposing on him a sort of brotherhood he knew well but refused to accept in the present circumstances. Men who share the same rooms, soldiers or prisoners, develop a strange alliance as if, having cast off their armor with their clothing, they fraternized every evening, over and above their differences, in the ancient community of dream and fatigue. But Daru shook himself; he didn't like such musings, and it was essential to sleep.

A little later, however, when the Arab stirred slightly, the schoolmaster was still not asleep. When the prisoner made a second move, he stiffened, on the alert. The Arab was lifting himself slowly on his arms with almost the motion of a sleepwalker. Seated upright in bed, he waited motionless without turning his head toward Daru, as if he were listening attentively. Daru did not stir; it had just occurred to him that the revolver was still in the drawer of his desk. It was better to act at once. Yet he continued to observe the prisoner, who, with the same slithery motion, put his feet on the ground, waited again, then began to stand up slowly. Daru was about to call out to him when the Arab began to walk, in a quite natural but extraordinary silent way. He was heading toward the door at the end of the room that opened into the shed. He lifted the latch with precaution and went out, pushing the door behind him but without shutting it. Daru had not stirred. "He is running away," he merely thought. "Good riddance!" Yet he listened attentively. The hens were not fluttering; the guest must be on the plateau. A faint sound of water reached him, and he didn't know what it was until the Arab again stood framed in the doorway, closed the door carefully, and came back to bed without a sound. Then Daru turned his back on him and fell asleep. Still later he seemed, from the depths of his sleep, to hear furtive steps around the schoolhouse. "I'm dreaming! I'm dreaming!" he repeated to himself. And he went on sleeping.

When he awoke, the sky was clear; the loose window let in a cold, pure air. The Arab was asleep, hunched up under the blankets now, his mouth open, utterly relaxed. But when Daru shook him, he started dreadfully, staring at Daru with wild eyes as if he had never seen him and such a frightened expression that the schoolmaster stepped back. "Don't be afraid. It's me. You must eat." The Arab nodded his head and said yes. Calm had returned to his face, but his expression was vacant and listless.

The coffee was ready. They drank it seated together on the folding bed as they munched their pieces of the cake. Then Daru led the Arab under the shed and showed him the faucet where he washed. He went back into the room, folded the blankets and the bed, made his own bed and put the room in order. Then he went through the classroom and out onto the terrace. The sun was already rising in the blue sky; a soft, bright light was bathing the deserted plateau. On the ridge the snow was melting in spots. The stones were about to reappear. Crouched on the edge of the plateau, the schoolmaster looked at the deserted expanse. He thought of Balducci. He had hurt him, for he had sent him off in a way as if he didn't want to be associated with him. He could still hear the gendarme's farewell and, without knowing why, he felt strangely empty and vulnerable. At that moment, from the other side of the schoolhouse, the prisoner coughed. Daru listened to him almost despite himself and then, furious, threw a pebble that whistled through the air before sinking into the snow. That man's stupid crime revolted him, but to hand him over was contrary to honor. Merely thinking of it made him smart with humiliation. And he cursed at one and the same time his own people who had sent him this Arab and the Arab too who had dared to kill and not managed to get away. Daru got up, walked in a circle on the terrace, waited motionless, and then went back into the schoolhouse.

The Arab, leaning over the cement floor of the shed, was washing his teeth with two fingers. Daru looked at him and said: "Come." He went back into the room ahead of the prisoner. He slipped a hunting jacket on over his sweater and put on walking shoes. Standing, he waited until the Arab had put on his *chèche* and sandals. They went into the classroom and the schoolmaster pointed to the exit, saying: "Go ahead." The fellow didn't budge. "I'm coming," said Daru. The Arab went out. Daru went back into the room and made a package of pieces of rusk, dates, and sugar. In the classroom, before going out, he hesitated a second in front of his desk, then crossed the threshold and locked the door. "That's the way," he said. He started toward the east, followed by the prisoner. But, a short distance from the schoolhouse, he thought he heard a slight sound behind them. He retraced his steps and examined the surroundings of the house; there was no one there. The Arab watched him without seeming to understand. "Come on," said Daru.

They walked for an hour and rested beside a sharp peak of limestone. The snow was melting faster and faster and the sun was drinking up the puddles at once, rapidly cleaning the plateau, which gradually dried and vibrated like the air itself. When they resumed walking, the ground rang under their feet. From time to time a bird rent the space in front of them with a joyful cry. Daru breathed in deeply the fresh morning light. He felt a sort of rapture before the vast familiar expanse, now almost entirely yellow under its dome of blue sky. They walked an hour more, descending toward the south. They reached a level height made up of crumbly rocks. From there on, the plateau sloped down, eastward toward a low plain where there were a few spindly trees and, to the south, toward outcroppings of rock that gave the landscape a chaotic look.

Daru surveyed the two directions. There was nothing but the

sky on the horizon. Not a man could be seen. He turned toward the Arab, who was looking at him blankly. Daru held out the package to him. "Take it," he said. "There are dates, bread, and sugar. You can hold out for two days. Here are a thousand francs too." The Arab took the package and the money but kept his full hands at chest level as if he didn't know what to do with what was being given him. "Now look," the schoolmaster said as he pointed in the direction of the east, "there's the way to Tinguit. You have a two-hour walk. At Tinguit you'll find the administration and the police. They are expecting you." The Arab looked toward the east, still holding the package and the money against his chest. Daru took his elbow and turned him rather roughly toward the south. At the foot of the height on which they stood could be seen a faint path. "That's the trail across the plateau. In a day's walk from here you'll find pasturelands and the first nomads. They'll take you in and shelter you according to their law." The Arab had now turned toward Daru and a sort of panic was visible in his expression. "Listen," he said. Daru shook his head: "No, be quiet. Now I'm leaving you." He turned his back on him, took two long steps in the direction of the school, looked hesitantly at the motionless Arab, and started off again. For a few minutes he heard nothing but his own step resounding on the cold ground and did not turn his head. A moment later, however, he turned around. The Arab was still there on the edge of the hill, his arms hanging now, and he was looking at the schoolmaster. Daru felt something rise in his throat. But he swore with impatience, waved vaguely, and started off again. He had already gone some distance when he again stopped and looked. There was no longer anyone on the hill.

Daru hesitated. The sun was now rather high in the sky and was beginning to beat down on his head. The schoolmaster retraced his steps, at first somewhat uncertainly, then with decision. When he reached the little hill, he was bathed in sweat. He climbed it as fast as he could and stopped, out of breath, at the top. The rock fields to the south stood out sharply against the blue sky, but on the plain to the east a steamy heat was already rising. And in that slight haze, Daru, with heavy heart, made out the Arab walking slowly on the road to prison.

A little later, standing before the window of the classroom, the schoolmaster was watching the clear light bathing the whole surface of the plateau, but he hardly saw it. Behind him on the blackboard, among the winding French rivers, sprawled the clumsily chalked-up words he had just read: "You handed over our brother. You will pay for this." Daru looked at the sky, the plateau, and, beyond, the invisible lands stretching all the way to the sea. In this vast landscape he had loved so much, he was alone.

Translated by Justin O'Brien

The Open Boat

Stephen Crane

A Tale intended to be after the fact.
Being the Experience of Four Men
from the Sunk Steamer "Commodore"

STEPHEN CRANE *(1871–1900) had a brief but creatively full life. Born in Newark, New Jersey, by age sixteen Crane was working as a journalist, and then went to Lafayette College and Syracuse University.* Maggie: A Girl of the Streets, *an excellent naturalistic novel, came out in 1892, privately printed and not generally recognized. But in 1895, when* The Red Badge of Courage *was published, Crane became well known. After the success of this novel, Crane accepted assignments as a newspaper correspondent, including coverage of the Spanish-American War. During his involvement in this war, Crane was shipwrecked, an incident he creatively converted into the story "The Open Boat." Known for his fidelity to a realistic depiction of life, Crane is also praised for his carefully honed writing style.*

I

None of them knew the color of the sky. Their eyes glanced level, and were fastened upon the waves that swept toward them. These waves were of the hue of slate, save for the tops, which were of foaming white, and all of the men knew the colors of the sea. The horizon narrowed and widened, and dipped and rose, and at all times its edge was jagged with waves that seemed thrust up in points like rocks.

Many a man ought to have a bathtub larger than the boat which here rode upon the sea. These waves were most wrongfully and barbarously abrupt and tall, and each froth-top was a problem in small boat navigation.

The cook squatted in the bottom and looked with both eyes at the six inches of gunwale which separated him from the ocean. His sleeves were rolled over his fat forearms, and the two flaps of his unbuttoned vest dangled as he bent to bail out the boat. Often he said: "Gawd! That was a narrow clip." As he remarked it he invariably gazed eastward over the broken sea.

The oiler, steering with one of the two oars in the boat, sometimes raised himself suddenly to keep clear of water that swirled in over the stern. It was a thin little oar and it seemed often ready to snap.

The correspondent, pulling at the other oar, watched the waves and wondered why he was there.

The injured captain, lying in the bow, was at this time buried in that profound dejection and indifference which comes, temporarily at least, to even the bravest and most enduring when, willy nilly, the firm fails, the army loses, the ship goes down. The mind of the master of a vessel is rooted deep in the timbers of her, though he command for a day or a decade, and this captain had on him the stern impression of a scene in the grays of dawn of seven turned faces, and later a stump of a topmast with a white ball on it that slashed to and fro at the waves, went low and lower, and down. Thereafter there was something strange in his voice. Although steady, it was deep with mourning, and of a quality beyond oration or tears.

"Keep 'er a little more south, Billie," said he.

"A little more south, sir," said the oiler in the stern.

A seat in this boat was not unlike a seat upon a bucking broncho, and, by the same token, a broncho is not much smaller. The craft pranced and reared, and plunged like an animal. As each wave came, and she rose for it, she seemed like a horse making at a fence outrageously high. The manner of her scramble over these walls of water is a mystic thing, and, moreover, at the top of them were ordinarily these problems in white water, the foam racing down from the summit of each wave, requiring a new leap, and a leap from the air. Then, after scornfully bumping a crest, she would slide, and race, and splash down a long incline, and arrive bobbing and nodding in front of the next menace.

A singular disadvantage of the sea lies in the fact that after successfully surmounting one wave you discover that there is another behind it just as important and just as nervously anxious to do something effective in the way of swamping boats. In a ten-foot dinghy one can get an idea of the resources of the sea in the line of waves that is not probable to the average experience which is never at sea in a dinghy. As each slaty wall of water approached, it shut all else from the view of the men in the boat, and it was not difficult to imagine that this particular wave was the final outburst of the ocean, the last effort of the grim water. There was a terrible grace in the move of the waves, and they came in silence, save for the snarling of the crests.

In the wan light, the faces of the men must have been gray. Their eyes must have glinted in strange ways as they gazed steadily astern. Viewed from a balcony, the whole thing would doubtless have been weirdly picturesque. But the men in the boat had no time to see it, and if they had had leisure there were other things to occupy their minds. The sun swung steadily up the sky, and they knew it was broad day because the color of the sea changed from slate to emerald green, streaked with amber lights, and the foam was like tumbling snow. The process of the breaking day was unknown to them. They were aware only of this effect upon the color of the waves that rolled toward them.

In disjointed sentences the cook and the correspondent argued as to the difference between a lifesaving station and a house of refuge. The cook had said: "There's a house of refuge just north of the Mosquito Inlet Light, and as soon as they see us, they'll come off in their boat and pick us up."

"As soon as who sees us?" said the correspondent.

"The crew," said the cook.

"Houses of refuge don't have crews," said the correspondent. "As I understand them, they are only places where clothes and grub are stored for the benefit of shipwrecked people. They don't carry crews."

"Oh yes, they do," said the cook.

"No, they don't," said the correspondent.

"Well, we're not there yet, anyhow," said the oiler, in the stern.

"Well," said the cook, "perhaps it's not a house of refuge that I'm thinking of as being near Mosquito Inlet Light. Perhaps it's a lifesaving station."

"We're not there yet," said the oiler, in the stern.

II

As the boat bounced from the top of each wave, the wind tore through the hair of the hatless men, and as the craft plopped her stern down again the spray slashed past them. The crest of each of these waves was a hill, from the top of which the men surveyed, for a moment, a broad tumultuous expanse, shining and wind driven. It was probably splendid. It was probably glorious, this play of the free sea, wild with lights of emerald and white and amber.

"Bully good thing it's an on-shore wind," said the cook. "If not, where would we be? Wouldn't have a show."

"That's right," said the correspondent.

The busy oiler nodded his assent.

Then the captain, in the bow, chuckled in a way that expressed humor, contempt, tragedy, all in one. "Do you think we've got much of a show now, boys?" said he.

Whereupon the three were silent, save for a trifle of hemming and hawing. To express any particular optimism at this time they felt to be childish and stupid, but they all doubtless possessed this sense of the situation in their mind. A young man thinks doggedly at such times. On the other hand, the ethics of their condition was decidedly against any open suggestion of hopelessness. So they were silent.

"Oh, well," said the captain, soothing his children, "we'll get ashore all right."

But there was that in his tone which made them think, so the oiler quoth: "Yes! If this wind holds!"

The cook was bailing: "Yes! If we don't catch hell in the surf."

Canton flannel gulls flew near and far. Sometimes they sat down on the sea, near patches of brown seaweed that rolled over the waves with a movement like carpets on a line in a gale. The birds sat comfortably in groups, and they were envied by some in the dinghy, for the wrath of the sea was no more to them than it was to a covey of prairie chickens a thousand miles inland. Often they came very close and stared at the men with black beadlike eyes. At these times they were uncanny and sinister in their unblinking scrutiny, and the men hooted angrily at them, telling them to be gone. One came, and evidently decided to alight on the top of the captain's head. The bird flew parallel to the boat and did not circle, but made short sidelong jumps in the air in chicken fashion. His black eyes were wistfully fixed upon the captain's head. "Ugly brute," said the oiler to the bird. "You look as if you were made with a jackknife." The cook and the correspondent swore darkly at the creature. The captain naturally wished to knock it away with the end of the heavy painter; but he did not dare to do it, because anything resembling an emphatic gesture would have capsized this freighted boat, and so with his open hand, the captain gently and carefully waved the gull away. After it had been discouraged from the pursuit the captain breathed easier on account of his hair, and others breathed easier because the bird struck their minds at this time as being somehow gruesome and ominous.

In the meantime the oiler and the correspondent rowed. And also they rowed.

They sat together in the same seat, and each rowed an oar. Then the oiler took both oars; then the correspondent took both oars; then the oiler; then the correspondent. They rowed and they rowed. The very ticklish part of the business was when the time came for the reclining one in the stern to take his turn at the oars. By the very last star of truth, it is easier to steal eggs from under a hen than it was to change seats in the dinghy. First the man in the stern slid his hand along the thwart and moved with care, as if he were of Sèvres. Then the man in the rowing seat slid his hand along the other thwart. It was all done with the most extraordinary care. As the two sidled past each other, the whole party kept watchful eyes on the coming wave, and the captain cried: "Look out now! Steady there!"

The brown mats of seaweed that appeared from time to time were like islands, bits of earth. They were travelling, apparently, neither one way nor the other. They were, to all intents, stationary. They informed the men in the boat that it was making progress slowly toward the land.

The captain, rearing cautiously in the bow, after the dinghy soared on a great swell, said that he had seen the lighthouse at

Mosquito Inlet. Presently the cook remarked that he had seen it. The correspondent was at the oars then, and for some reason he too wished to look at the lighthouse, but his back was toward the far shore and the waves were important, and for some time he could not seize an opportunity to turn his head. But at last there came a wave more gentle than the others, and when at the crest of it he swiftly scoured the western horizon.

"See it?" said the captain.

"No," said the correspondent slowly. "I didn't see anything."

"Look again," said the captain. He pointed. "It's exactly in that direction."

At the top of another wave, the correspondent did as he was bid, and this time his eyes chanced on a small still thing on the edge of the swaying horizon. It was precisely like the point of a pin. It took an anxious eye to find a lighthouse so tiny.

"Think we'll make it, captain?"

"If this wind holds and the boat don't swamp, we can't do much else," said the captain.

The little boat, lifted by each towering sea, and splashed viciously by the crests, made progress that in the absence of seaweed was not apparent to those in her. She seemed just a wee thing wallowing, miraculously top up, at the mercy of five oceans. Occasionally, a great spread of water, like white flames, swarmed into her.

"Bail her, cook," said the captain serenely.

"All right, captain," said the cheerful cook.

III

It would be difficult to describe the subtle brotherhood of men that was here established on the seas. No one said that it was so. No one mentioned it. But it dwelt in the boat, and each man felt it warm him. They were a captain, an oiler, a cook, and a correspondent, and they were friends, friends in a more curiously ironbound degree than may be common. The hurt captain, lying against the water jar in the bow, spoke always in a low voice and calmly, but he could never command a more ready and swiftly obedient crew than the motley three of the dinghy. It was more than a mere recognition of what was best for the common safety. There was surely in it a quality that was personal and heartfelt. And after this devotion to the commander of the boat there was this comradeship that the correspondent, for instance, who had been taught to be cynical of men, knew even at the time was the best experience of his life. But no one said that it was so. No one mentioned it.

"I wish we had a sail," remarked the captain. "We might try my overcoat on the end of an oar and give you two boys a chance to rest." So the cook and the correspondent held the mast and spread wide the overcoat. The oiler steered, and the little boat made good way with her new rig. Sometimes the oiler had to scull sharply to keep a sea from breaking into the boat, but otherwise sailing was a success.

Meanwhile the lighthouse had been growing slowly larger. It had now almost assumed color, and appeared like a little gray shadow on the sky. The man at the oars could not be prevented from turning his head rather often to try for a glimpse of this little gray shadow.

At last, from the top of each wave the men in the tossing boat could see land. Even as the lighthouse was an upright shadow on the sky, this land seemed but a long black shadow on the sea. It certainly was thinner than paper. "We must be about opposite New Smyrna," said the cook, who had coasted this shore often in schooners. "Captain, by the way, I believe they abandoned that lifesaving station there about a year ago."

"Did they?" said the captain.

The wind slowly died away. The cook and the correspondent were not now obliged to slave in order to hold high the oar. But the waves continued their old impetuous swooping at the dinghy, and the little craft, no longer under way, struggled woundily over them. The oiler or the correspondent took the oars again.

Shipwrecks are apropos of nothing. If men could only train for them and have them occur when the men had reached pink condition, there would be less drowning at sea. Of the four in the dinghy none had slept any time worth mentioning for two days and two nights previous to embarking in the dinghy, and in the excitement of clambering about the deck of a foundering ship they had also forgotten to eat heartily.

For these reasons, and for others, neither the oiler nor the correspondent was fond of rowing at this time. The correspondent wondered ingenuously how in the name of all that was sane could there be people who thought it amusing to row a boat. It was not an amusement; it was a diabolical punishment, and even a genius of mental aberrations could never conclude that it was anything but a horror to the muscles and a crime against the back. He mentioned to the boat in general how the amusement of rowing struck him, and the weary-faced oiler smiled in full sympathy. Previously to the foundering, by the way, the oiler had worked double watch in the engine room of the ship.

"Take her easy, now, boys," said the captain. "Don't spend yourselves. If we have to run a surf you'll need all your strength, because we'll sure have to swim for it. Take your time."

Slowly the land arose from the sea. From a black line it became a line of black and a line of white, trees and sand. Finally, the captain said that he could make out a house on the shore. "That's the house of refuge, sure," said the cook. "They'll see us before long, and come out after us."

The distant lighthouse reared high. "The keeper ought to be able to make us out now, if he's looking through a glass," said the captain. "He'll notify the lifesaving people."

"None of those other boats could have got ashore to give word of the wreck," said the oiler, in a low voice. "Else the lifeboat would be out hunting us."

Slowly and beautifully the land loomed out of the sea. The wind came again. It had veered from the northeast to the southeast. Finally, a new sound struck the ears of the men in the boat. It was the low thunder of the surf on the shore. "We'll never be able to make the lighthouse now," said the captain. "Swing her head a little more north, Billie."

"A little more north, sir," said the oiler.

Whereupon the little boat turned her nose once more down the wind, and all but the oarsman watched the shore grow. Under the influence of this expansion doubt and direful apprehension was leaving the minds of the men. The management of the boat was still most absorbing, but it could not prevent a quiet cheerfulness. In an hour, perhaps, they would be ashore.

Their backbones had become thoroughly used to balancing in the boat, and they now rode this wild colt of a dinghy like circus men. The correspondent thought that he had been drenched to the skin, but happening to feel in the top pocket of his coat, he found therein eight cigars. Four of them were soaked with seawater; four were perfectly scatheless. After a search, somebody produced three dry matches, and thereupon the four waifs rode impudently in their little boat, and with an assurance of an impending rescue shining in their eyes, puffed at the big cigars and judged well and ill of all men. Everybody took a drink of water.

IV

"Cook," remarked the captain, "There don't seem to be any signs of life about your house of refuge."

"No," replied the cook. "Funny they don't see us!"

A broad stretch of lowly coast lay before the eyes of the men. It was of low dunes topped with dark vegetation. The roar of the surf was plain, and sometimes they could see the white lip of a wave as it spun up the beach. A tiny house was blocked out black upon the sky. Southward, the slim lighthouse lifted its little gray length.

Tide, wind, and waves were swinging the dinghy northward. "Funny they don't see us," said the men.

The surf's roar was here dulled, but its tone was, nevertheless, thunderous and mighty. As the boat swam over the great rollers, the men sat listening to this roar. "We'll swamp sure," said everybody.

It is fair to say here that there was not a lifesaving station within twenty miles in either direction, but the men did not know this fact, and in consequence they made dark and opprobrious remarks concerning the eyesight of the nation's livesavers. Four scowling men sat in the dinghy and surpassed records in the invention of epithets.

"Funny they don't see us."

The lightheartedness of a former time had completely faded. To their sharpened minds it was easy to conjure pictures of all kinds of incompetency and blindness and, indeed, cowardice. There was the shore of the populous land, and it was bitter and bitter to them that from it came no sign.

"Well," said the captain, ultimately, "I suppose we'll have to make a try for ourselves. If we stay out here too long, we'll none of us have strength left to swim after the boat swamps."

And so the oiler, who was at the oars, turned the boat straight for the shore. There was a sudden tightening of muscles. There was some thinking.

"If we don't all get ashore—" said the captain. "If we don't all get ashore, I suppose you fellows know where to send news of my finish?"

They then briefly exchanged some addresses and admonitions. As for the reflections of the men, there was a great deal of rage in them. Perchance they might be formulated thus: "If I am going to be drowned—if I am going to be drowned—if I am going to be drowned, why, in the name of the seven mad gods who rule the sea, was I allowed to come thus far and contemplate sand and trees? Was I brought here merely to have my nose dragged away as I was about to nibble the sacred cheese of life? It is preposterous. If this old ninny-woman, Fate, cannot do better than this, she should be deprived of the management of men's fortunes. She is an old hen who knows not her intention. If she has decided to drown me, why did she not do it in the beginning and save me all this trouble? The whole affair is absurd. . . . But no, she cannot mean to drown me. She dare not drown me. She cannot drown me. Not after all this work." Afterward the man might have had an impulse to shake his fist at the clouds: "Just you drown me, and then hear what I call you!"

The billows that came at this time were more formidable. They seemed always just about to break and roll over the little boat in a turmoil of foam. There was a preparatory and long growl in the speech of them. No mind unused to the sea would have concluded that the dinghy could ascend these sheer heights in time. The shore was still afar. The oiler was a wily surfman. "Boys," he said swiftly, "she won't live three minutes more, and we're too far out to swim. Shall I take her to sea again, captain?"

"Yes! Go ahead!" said the captain.

This oiler, by a series of quick miracles, and fast and steady oarsmanship, turned the boat in the middle of the surf and took her safely to sea again.

There was a considerable silence as the boat bumped over the furrowed sea to deeper water. Then somebody in gloom spoke. "Well, anyhow, they must have seen us from the shore by now."

The gulls went in slanting flight up the wind toward the gray desolate east. A squall, marked by dingy clouds, and clouds brick-red, like smoke from a burning building, appeared from the southeast.

"What do you think of those lifesaving people? Ain't they peaches?"

"Funny they haven't seen us."

"Maybe they think we're out here for sport! Maybe they think we're fishin'. Maybe they think we're damned fools."

It was a long afternoon. A changed tide tried to force them southward, but wind and wave said northward. Far ahead, where coastline, sea and sky formed their mighty angle, there were little dots which seemed to indicate a city on the shore.

"St. Augustine?"

The captain shook his head. "Too near Mosquito Inlet."

And the oiler rowed, and then the correspondent rowed. Then the oiler rowed. It was a weary business. The human back can become the seat of more aches and pains than are registered in books for the composite anatomy of a regiment. It is a limited area, but it can become the theater of innumerable muscular conflicts, tangles, wrenches, knots, and other comforts.

"Did you ever like to row, Billie?" asked the correspondent.

"No," said the oiler. "Hang it."

When one exchanged the rowing seat for a place in the bottom of the boat, he suffered a bodily depression that caused him to be careless of everything save an obligation to wiggle one finger. There was cold seawater swashing to and fro in the boat, and he lay in it. His head, pillowed on a thwart, was within an inch of the swirl of a wave crest, and sometimes a particularly obstreperous sea came inboard and drenched him once more. But these matters did not annoy him. It is almost certain that if the boat had capsized he would have tumbled comfortably out upon the ocean as if he felt sure that it was a great soft mattress.

"Look! There's a man on the shore!"

"Where?"

"There! See 'im? See 'im?"

"Yes, sure! He's walking along."

"Now he's stopped. Look! He's facing us!"

"He's waving at us!"

"So he is! By thunder!"

"Ah, now we're all right! Now we're all right! There'll be a boat out here for us in half an hour."

"He's going on. He's running. He's going up to that house there."

The remote beach seemed lower than the sea, and it required a searching glance to discern the little black figure. The captain saw a floating stick and they rowed to it. A bath towel was by some weird chance in the boat, and, tying this on the stick, the captain waved it. The oarsman did not dare turn his head, so he was obliged to ask questions.

"What's he doing now?"

"He's standing still again. He's looking, I think. . . . There he goes again. Toward the house. . . . Now he's stopped again."

"Is he waving at us?"

"No, not now! he was, though."

"Look! There comes another man!"

"He's running."

"Look at him go, would you."

"Why, he's on a bicycle. Now he's met the other man. They're both waving at us. Look!"

"There comes something up the beach."

"What the devil is that thing?"

"Why, it looks like a boat."

"Why, certainly it's a boat."

"No, it's on wheels."

"Yes, so it is. Well, that must be the lifeboat. They drag them along shore on a wagon.

"That's the lifeboat, sure."

"No, by—, it's—it's an omnibus."

"I tell you it's a lifeboat."

"It is not! It's an omnibus. I can see it plain. See? One of these big hotel omnibuses."

"By thunder, you're right. It's an omnibus, sure as fate. What do you suppose they are doing with an omnibus? Maybe they are going around collecting the lifecrew, hey?"

"That's it, likely. Look! There's a fellow waving a little black flag. He's standing on the steps of the omnibus. There comes those other two fellows. Now they're all talking together. Look at the fellow with the flag. Maybe he ain't waving it."

"That ain't a flag, is it? That's his coat. Why, certainly, that's his coat."

"So it is. It's his coat. He's taken it off and is waving it around his head. But would you look at him swing it."

"Oh, say, there isn't any lifesaving station there. That's just a winter resort hotel omnibus that has brought over some of the boarders to see us drown."

"What's that idiot with the coat mean? What's he signalling, anyhow?"

"It looks as if he were trying to tell us to go north. There must be a lifesaving station up there."

"No! He thinks we're fishing. Just giving us a merry hand. See? Ah, there, Willie."

"Well, I wish I could make something out of those signals. What do you suppose he means?"

"He don't mean anything. He's just playing."

"Well, if he'd just signal us to try the surf again, or to go to sea and wait, or go north, or go south, or go to hell—there would be some reason in it. But look at him. He just stands there and keeps his coat revolving like a wheel. The ass!"

"There come more people."

"Now there's quite a mob. Look! Isn't that a boat?"

"Where? Oh, I see where you mean. No, that's no boat."

"That fellow is still waving his coat."

"He must think we like to see him do that. Why don't he quit it? It don't mean anything."

"I don't know. I think he is trying to make us go north. It must be that there's a lifesaving station there somewhere."

"Say, he ain't tired yet. Look at 'im wave."

"Wonder how long he can keep that up. He's been revolving his coat ever since he caught sight of us. He's an idiot. Why aren't they getting men to bring a boat out? A fishing boat—one of those big yawls—could come out here all right. Why don't he do something?"

"Oh, it's all right, now."

"They'll have a boat out here for us in less than no time, now that they've seen us."

A faint yellow tone came into the sky over the low land. The shadows on the sea slowly deepened. The wind bore coldness with it, and the men began to shiver.

"Holy smoke!" said one, allowing his voice to express his impious mood, "if we keep on monkeying out here! If we've got to flounder out here all night!"

"Oh, we'll never have to stay here all night! Don't you worry. They've seen us now, and it won't be long before they'll come chasing out after us."

The shore grew dusky. The man waving a coat blended gradually into this gloom, and it swallowed in the same manner the omnibus and the group of people. The spray, when it dashed uproariously over the side, made the voyagers shrink, and swear like men who were being branded.

"I'd like to catch the chump who waved that coat. I feel like soaking him one, just for luck."

"Why? What did he do?"

"Oh, nothing, but then he seemed so damned cheerful."

In the meantime the oiler rowed, and then the correspondent rowed, and then the oiler rowed. Gray-faced and bowed forward, they mechanically, turn by turn, plied the leaden oars. The form of the lighthouse had vanished from the southern horizon, but finally a pale star appeared, just lifting from the sea. The streaked saffron in the west passed before the all-merging darkness, and the sea to the east was black. The land had vanished, and was expressed only by the low and drear thunder of the surf.

"If I am going to be drowned—if I am going to be drowned—if I am going to be drowned, why, in the name of the seven mad gods who rule the sea, was I allowed to come thus far and contemplate sand and trees? Was I brought here merely to have my nose dragged away as I was about to nibble the sacred cheese of life?"

The patient captain, drooped over the water jar, was sometimes obliged to speak to the oarsman.

"Keep her head up! Keep her head up!"

" 'Keep her head up,' sir." The voices were weary and low.

This was surely a quiet evening. All save the oarsman lay heavily and listlessly in the boat's bottom. As for him, his eyes were just capable of noting the tall black waves that swept forward in a most sinister silence, save for an occasional subdued growl of a crest.

The cook's head was on a thwart, and he looked without interest at the water under his nose. He was deep in other scenes. Finally he spoke. "Billie," he murmured, dreamfully, "what kind of pie do you like best?"

V

"Pie," said the oiler and the correspondent, agitatedly. "Don't talk about those things, blast you!"

"Well," said the cook, "I was just thinking about ham sandwiches, and—"

A night on the sea in an open boat is a long night. As darkness settled finally, the shine of the light, lifting from the sea in the south, changed to full gold. On the northern horizon a new light appeared, a small bluish gleam on the edge of the waters. These two lights were the furniture of the world. Otherwise there was nothing but waves.

Two men huddled in the stern, and distances were so magnificent in the dinghy that the rower was enabled to keep his feet partly warmed by thrusting them under his companions. Their legs indeed extended far under the rowing seat until they touched the feet of the captain forward. Sometimes, despite the efforts of the tired oarsman, a wave came piling into the boat, an icy wave of the night, and the chilling water soaked them anew. They would twist their bodies for a moment and groan, and sleep the dead sleep once more, while the water in the boat gurgled about them as the craft rocked.

The plan of the oiler and the correspondent was for one to row until he lost the ability, and then arouse the other from his seawater couch in the bottom of the boat.

The oiler plied the oars until his head drooped forward, and the overpowering sleep blinded him. And he rowed yet afterward. Then he touched a man in the bottom of the boat, and called his name. "Will you spell me for a little while?" he said, meekly.

"Sure, Billie," said the correspondent, awakening and dragging himself to a sitting position. They exchanged places carefully, and the oiler, cuddling down in the seawater at the cook's side, seemed to go to sleep instantly.

The particular violence of the sea had ceased. The waves came without snarling. The obligation of the man at the oars was to keep the boat headed so that the tilt of the rollers would not capsize her, and to preserve her from filling when the crests rushed past. The black waves were silent and hard to be seen in the darkness. Often one was almost upon the boat before the oarsman was aware.

In a low voice the correspondent addressed the captain. He was not sure that the captain was awake, although this iron man seemed to be always awake. "Captain, shall I keep her making for that light north, sir?"

The same steady voice answered him. "Yes. Keep it about two points off the port bow."

The cook had tied a life belt around himself in order to get even the warmth which this clumsy cork contrivance could donate, and he seemed almost stove-like when a rower, whose teeth invariably chattered wildly as soon as he ceased his labor, dropped down to sleep.

The correspondent, as he rowed, looked down at the two men sleeping underfoot. The cook's arm was around the oiler's shoulders, and, with their fragmentary clothing and haggard faces, they were the babes of the sea, a grotesque rendering of the old babes in the wood.

Later he must have grown stupid at his work, for suddenly there was a growling of water, and a crest came with a roar and a swash into the boat, and it was a wonder that it did not set the cook afloat in his life belt. The cook continued to sleep, but the oiler sat up, blinking his eyes and shaking with the new cold.

"Oh, I'm awful sorry, Billie," said the correspondent, contritely.

"That's all right, old boy," said the oiler, and lay down again and was asleep.

Presently it seemed that even the captain dozed, and the correspondent thought that he was the one man afloat on all the oceans. The wind had a voice as it came over the waves, and it was sadder than the end.

There was a long, loud swishing astern of the boat, and a gleaming trail of phosphorescence, like blue flame, was furrowed on the black waters. It might have been made by a monstrous knife.

Then there came a stillness, while the correspondent breathed with the open mouth and looked at the sea.

Suddenly there was another swish and another long flash of bluish light, and this time it was alongside the boat, and might almost have been reached with an oar. The correspondent saw an enormous fin speed like a shadow through the water, hurling the crystalline spray and leaving the long glowing trail.

The correspondent looked over his shoulder at the captain. His face was hidden, and he seemed to be asleep. He looked at the babes of the sea. They certainly were asleep. So, being bereft of sympathy, he leaned a little way to one side and swore softly into the sea.

But the thing did not then leave the vicinity of the boat. Ahead or astern, on one side or the other, at intervals long or short, fled the long sparkling streak, and there was to be heard the whiroo of the dark fin. The speed and power of the thing was greatly to be admired. It cut the water like a gigantic and keen projectile.

The presence of this biding thing did not affect the man with the same horror that it would if he had been a picnicker. He simply looked at the sea dully and swore in an undertone.

Nevertheless, it is true that he did not wish to be alone with the thing. He wished one of his companions to awaken by chance and keep him company with it. But the captain hung motionless over the water jar, and the oiler and the cook in the bottom of the boat were plunged in slumber.

VI

"If I am going to be drowned—if I am going to be drowned—if I am going to be drowned, why, in the name of the seven mad gods who rule the sea, was I allowed to come thus far and contemplate sand and trees?"

During this dismal night, it may be remarked that a man would conclude that it was really the intention of the seven mad gods to drown him, despite the abominable injustice of it. For it was certainly an abominable injustice to drown a man who had worked so hard, so hard. The man felt it would be a crime most unnatural. Other people had drowned at sea since galleys swarmed with painted sails, but still—

When it occurs to a man that nature does not regard him as important, and that she feels she would not maim the universe by disposing of him, he at first wishes to throw bricks at the temple, and he hates deeply the fact that there are no bricks and no temples. Any visible expression of nature would surely be pelleted with his jeers.

Then, if there be no tangible thing to hoot he feels, perhaps, the desire to confront a personification and indulge in pleas, bowed to one knee, and with hands supplicant, saying: "Yes, but I love myself."

A high cold star on a winter's night is the word he feels that she says to him. Thereafter he knows the pathos of his situation.

The men in the dinghy had not discussed these matters, but each had, no doubt, reflected upon them in silence and according to his mind. There was seldom any expression upon their faces save the general one of complete weariness. Speech was devoted to the business of the boat.

To chime the notes of his emotion, a verse mysteriously entered the correspondent's head. He had even forgotten that he had forgotten this verse, but it suddenly was in his mind.

> A soldier of the Legion lay dying in Algiers,
> There was lack of woman's nursing, there was dearth of woman's
>   tears;
> But a comrade stood beside him, and he took that comrade's hand,
> And he said: "I shall never see my own, my native land."

In his childhood, the correspondent had been made acquainted with the fact that a soldier of the Legion lay dying in Algiers, but he had never regarded the fact as important. Myriads of his school fellows had informed him of the soldier's plight, but the dinning had naturally ended by making him perfectly indifferent. He had never considered it his affair that a soldier of the Legion lay dying in Algiers, nor had it appeared to him as a matter for sorrow. It was less to him than the breaking of a pencil's point.

Now, however, it quaintly came to him as a human, living thing. It was no longer merely a picture of a few throes in the breast of a poet, meanwhile drinking tea and warming his feet at the grate; it was an actuality—stern, mournful, and fine.

The correspondent plainly saw the soldier. He lay on the sand with his feet out straight and still. While his pale left hand was upon his chest in an attempt to thwart the going of his life, the blood came between his fingers. In the far Algerian distance, a city of low square forms was set against a sky that was faint with the last sunset hues.

The correspondent, plying the oars and dreaming of the slow and slower movements of the lips of the soldier, was moved by a profound and perfectly impersonal comprehension. He was sorry for the soldier of the Legion who lay dying in Algiers.

The thing which had followed the boat and waited had evidently grown bored at the delay. There was no longer to be heard the slash of the cutwater, and there was no longer the flame of the long trail. The light in the north still glimmered, but it was apparently no nearer to the boat. Sometimes the boom of the surf rang in the correspondent's ears, and he turned the craft seaward then and rowed harder. Southward, someone had evidently built a watch fire on the beach. It was too low and too far to be seen, but it made a shimmering, roseate reflection upon the bluff back of it, and this could be discerned from the boat. The wind came stronger, and sometimes a wave suddenly raged out like a mountain cat, and there was to be seen the sheen and sparkle of a broken crest.

The captain, in the bow, moved on his water jar and sat erect. "Pretty long night," he observed to the correspondent. He looked at the shore. "Those lifesaving people take their time."

"Did you see that shark playing around?"

"Yes, I saw him. He was a big fellow, all right."

"Wish I had known you were awake."

Later the correspondent spoke into the bottom of the boat.

"Billie!" There was a slow and gradual disentanglement. "Billie, will you spell me?"

"Sure," said the oiler.

As soon as the correspondent touched the cold comfortable seawater in the bottom of the boat, and had huddled close to the cook's life belt he was deep in sleep, despite the fact that his teeth played all the popular airs. This sleep was so good to him that it was but a moment before he heard a voice call his name in a tone that demonstrated the last stages of exhaustion. "Will you spell me?"

"Sure, Billie."

The light in the north had mysteriously vanished, but the correspondent took his course from the wide-awake captain.

Later in the night they took the boat farther out to sea, and the captain directed the cook to take one oar at the stern and keep the boat facing the seas. He was to call out if he should hear the thunder of the surf. This plan enabled the oiler and the correspondent to get respite together. "We'll give those boys a chance to get into shape again," said the captain. They curled down and, after a few preliminary chatterings and trembles, slept once more the dead sleep. Neither knew they had bequeathed to the cook the company of another shark, or perhaps the same shark.

As the boat caroused on the waves, spray occasionally bumped over the side and gave them a fresh soaking, but this had no power to break their repose. The ominous slash of the wind and the water affected them as it would have affected mummies.

"Boys," said the cook, with the notes of every reluctance in his voice, "she's drifted in pretty close. I guess one of you had better take her to sea again." The correspondent, aroused, heard the crash of the toppled crests.

As he was rowing, the captain gave him some whisky and water, and this steadied the chills out of him. "If I ever get ashore and anybody shows me even a photograph of an oar—"

At last there was a short conversation.

"Billie . . . Billie, will you spell me?"

"Sure," said the oiler.

VII

When the correspondent again opened his eyes, the sea and the sky were each of the gray hue of the dawning. Later, carmine and gold was painted upon the waters. The morning appeared finally, in its splendor, with a sky of pure blue, and the sunlight flamed on the tips of the waves.

On the distant dunes were set many little black cottages, and a tall white windmill reared above them. No man, nor dog, nor bicycle appeared on the beach. The cottages might have formed a deserted village.

The voyagers scanned the shore. A conference was held in the boat. "Well," said the captain, "if no help is coming, we might better try a run through the surf right away. If we stay out here much longer we will be too weak to do anything for ourselves at all." The others silently acquiesced in this reasoning. The boat was headed for the beach. The correspondent wondered if none ever ascended the tall windtower, and if then they never looked seaward. This tower was a giant, standing with its back to the plight of the ants. It represented in a degree, to the correspondent, the serenity of nature amid the struggles of the individual—nature in the wind, and nature in the vision of men. She did not seem cruel to him then, nor beneficent, nor treacherous, nor wise. But she was indifferent, flatly indifferent. It is, perhaps, plausible that a man in this situation, impressed with the unconcern of the universe, should see the innumerable flaws of his life, and have them taste wickedly in his mind and wish for another chance. A distinction between right and wrong seems absurdly clear to him, then, in this new ignorance of the grave edge, and he understands that if he were given another opportunity he would mend his conduct and his words, and be better and brighter during an introduction or at a tea.

"Now, boys," said the captain, "she is going to swamp sure. All we can do is to work her in as far as possible, and then when she swamps, pile out and scramble for the beach. Keep cool now, and don't jump until she swamps sure."

The oiler took the oars. Over his shoulders he scanned the surf. "Captain," he said, "I think I'd better bring her about, and keep her head-on to the seas and back her in."

"All right, Billie," said the captain. "Back her in." The oiler swung the boat then and, seated in the stern, the cook and the correspondent were obliged to look over their shoulders to contemplate the lonely and indifferent shore.

The monstrous inshore rollers heaved the boat high until the men were again enabled to see the white sheets of water scudding up the slanted beach. "We won't get in very close," said the captain. Each time a man could wrest his attention from the rollers, he turned his glance toward the shore, and in the expression of the eyes during this contemplation there was a singular quality. The correspondent, observing the others, knew that they were not afraid, but the full meaning of their glances was shrouded.

As for himself, he was too tired to grapple fundamentally with the fact. He tried to coerce his mind into thinking of it, but the mind was dominated at this time by the muscles, and the muscles said they did not care. It merely occurred to him that if he should drown it would be a shame.

There were no hurried words, no pallor, no plain agitation. The men simply looked at the shore. "Now, remember to get well clear of the boat when you jump," said the captain.

Seaward the crest of a roller suddenly fell with a thunderous crash, and the long white comber came roaring down upon the boat.

"Steady now," said the captain. The men were silent. They turned their eyes from the shore to the comber and waited. The boat slid up the incline, leaped at the furious top, bounced over it, and swung down the long back of the waves. Some water had been shipped and the cook bailed it out.

But the next crest crashed also. The tumbling, boiling flood of white water caught the boat and whirled it almost perpendicular. Water swarmed in from all sides. The correspondent had his hands on the gunwale at this time, and when the water entered at that place he swiftly withdrew his fingers, as if he objected to wetting them.

The little boat, drunken with this weight of water, reeled and snuggled deeper into the sea.

"Bail her out, cook! Bail her out," said the captain.

"All right, captain," said the cook.

"Now, boys, the next one will do for us, sure," said the oiler. "Mind to jump clear of the boat."

The third wave moved forward, huge, furious, implacable. It fairly swallowed the dinghy, and almost simultaneously the men tumbled into the sea. A piece of life belt had lain in the bottom of the boat, and as the correspondent went overboard he held this to his chest with his left hand.

The January water was icy, and he reflected immediately that it was colder than he had expected to find it off the coast of Florida. This appeared to his dazed mind as a fact important enough to be noted at the time. The coldness of the water was sad; it was tragic. This fact was somehow so mixed and confused with his opinion of his own situation that it seemed almost a proper reason for tears. The water was cold.

When he came to the surface he was conscious of little but the noisy water. Afterward he saw his companions in the sea. The oiler was ahead in the race. He was swimming strongly and rapidly. Off to the correspondent's left, the cook's great white and corked back bulged out of the water, and in the rear the captain was hanging with his one good hand to the keel of the overturned dinghy.

There is a certain immovable quality to a shore, and the correspondent wondered at it amid the confusion of the sea.

It seemed also very attractive, but the correspondent knew that it was a long journey, and he paddled leisurely. The piece of life preserver lay under him, and sometimes he whirled down the incline of a wave as if he were on a hand sled.

But finally he arrived at a place in the sea where travel was beset with difficulty. He did not pause swimming to inquire what manner of current had caught him, but there his progress ceased. The shore was set before him like a bit of scenery on a stage, and he looked at it and understood with his eyes each detail of it.

As the cook passed, much farther to the left, the captain was calling to him, "Turn over on your back, cook! Turn over on your back and use the oar."

"All right, sir." The cook turned on his back, and, paddling with an oar, went ahead as if he were a canoe.

Presently the boat also passed to the left of the correspondent with the captain clinging with one hand to the keel. He would have appeared like a man raising himself to look over a board fence, if it were not for the extraordinary gymnastics of the boat. The correspondent marvelled that the captain could still hold to it.

They passed on, nearer to shore—the oiler, the cook, the captain—and following them went the water jar, bouncing gaily over the seas.

The correspondent remained in the grip of this strange new enemy—a current. The shore, with its white slope of sand and its green bluff, topped with little silent cottages, was spread like a picture before him. It was very near to him then, but he was impressed as one who in a gallery looks at a scene from Brittany or Algiers.

He thought: "I am going to drown? Can it be possible? Can it be possible? Can it be possible?" Perhaps an individual must consider his own death to be the final phenomenon of nature.

But later a wave perhaps whirled him out of this small deadly current, for he found suddenly that he could again make progress toward the shore. Later still, he was aware that the captain, clinging with one hand to the keel of the dinghy, had his face turned away from the shore and toward him, and was calling his name. "Come to the boat! Come to the boat!"

In his struggle to reach the captain and the boat, he reflected that when one gets properly wearied, drowning must really be a comfortable arrangement, a cessation of hostilities accompanied by a large degree of relief, and he was glad of it, for the main thing in his mind for some moments had been horror of the temporary agony. He did not wish to be hurt.

Presently he saw a man running along the shore. He was undressing with most remarkable speed. Coat, trousers, shirt, everything flew magically off him.

"Come to the boat," called the captain.

"All right, captain." As the correspondent paddled, he saw the captain let himself down to bottom and leave the boat. Then the correspondent performed his one little marvel of the voyage. A large wave caught him and flung him with ease and supreme speed completely over the boat and far beyond it. It struck him even then as an event in gymnastics, and a true miracle of the sea. An overturned boat in the surf is not a plaything to a swimming man.

The correspondent arrived in water that reached only to his waist, but his condition did not enable him to stand for more than a moment. Each wave knocked him into a heap, and the undertow pulled at him.

Then he saw the man who had been running and undressing, and undressing and running, come bounding into the water. He dragged ashore the cook, and then waded toward the captain, but the captain waved him away, and sent him to the correspondent. He was naked, naked as a tree in winter, but a halo was about his head, and he shone like a saint. He gave a strong pull, and a long drag, and a bully heave at the correspondent's hand. The correspondent, schooled in the minor formulae, said: "Thanks, old man." But suddenly the man cried: "What's that?" He pointed a swift finger. The correspondent said: "Go."

In the shallows, face downward, lay the oiler. His forehead touched sand that was periodically, between each wave, clear of the sea.

The correspondent did not know all that transpired afterward. When he achieved safe ground he fell, striking the sand with each particular part of his body. It was as if he had dropped from a roof, but the thud was grateful to him.

It seems that instantly the beach was populated with men, with blankets, clothes, and flasks, and women with coffeepots and all the remedies sacred to their minds. The welcome of the land to the men from the sea was warm and generous, but a still and dripping shape was carried slowly up the beach, and the land's welcome for it could only be the different and sinister hospitality of the grave.

When it came night, the white waves paced to and fro in the moonlight, and the wind brought the sound of the great sea's voice to the men on shore, and they felt that they could then be interpreters.

A Selected Glossary of Literary Terms

Although these terms are not all-inclusive, their variety and scope are sufficient for much more than adequate coverage of terms useful for the interpretation and understanding of short stories. Used in conjunction with this book's bibliography, this glossary will be of strong assistance to the reader/student, and also very helpful in discussions of these short stories.

ACTION: A series of occurrences, events, or incidents that constitute the subject of a fiction or drama. The sum-total of the action can be called the *plot*. *See* PLOT.

ALLEGORY (from Greek—to imply something else): A form of writing where characters, ideas, or a series of events represent moral or spiritual truths beyond the significance of the objects or story itself. *See* FABLE, PARABLE, and SYMBOL.

AMBIGUITY: A story with ambiguity has two or more possible meanings or *interpretations*, making *explication* of the story highly important. *See* EXPLICATION, INTERPRETATION and MULTIPLE MEANINGS.

ANTAGONIST: The second most important character in fiction or drama, and who is in direct opposition and/or conflict with the *protagonist*. If the cause of the *protagonist* is heroic or noble, the antagonist is sometimes called the *villain*, especially in a melodramatic work. *See* CONFLICT, MELODRAMA, PROTAGONIST, and VILLAIN.

ANTICLIMAX: An incident or series of incidents whose action is disappointing or less serious than that of the major narrative event, often arranged deliberately for comic effect; the opposite of *climax*. *See* BATHOS and CLIMAX.

ANTI-HERO: A main character who does not possess the qualities commonly associated with heroism. *See* CHARACTER, HERO, and PROTAGONIST.

APPRENTICESHIP STORY: A story, usually a novel, that stresses the development in a character's philosophy and understanding of life, and his/her relationship with the world, with the character learning these aspects in youth and early adulthood. *See* BILDUNGSROMAN.

ATMOSPHERE: The *tone* or *mood* created by the author's arrangement of effects, such as a brooding or mysterious atmosphere, which brings about an emotional response by the reader. The *setting* complements the atmosphere. *See* MOOD, SETTING, and TONE.

AVANT-GARDE (from French—the vanguard or the troops that march for security in front of an army): The avant-garde in literature applies to those new writers and their writings that are ahead of their times and that are frequently not in harmony with established contemporary literary styles and traditions.

BACKGROUND: In literature background is used in a general sense as synonymous with *setting;* or background can be used to refer, for example, to the philosophical and/or religious background of a story. *See* SETTING.

BATHOS: The opposite of *pathos.* Action of a sentimental, insincere, or markedly less serious nature than the major events of a narrative, giving rise to a sense of that which is ridiculous rather than sublime. *See* ANTICLIMAX and PATHOS.

BILDUNGSROMAN (from German—a novel of development): A story that deals with the growth of a youth or a young person developing an awareness of himself/herself and the world, sometimes called an *erziehungsroman* (education novel) and/or *apprenticeship story. See* APPRENTICESHIP STORY and ERZIEHUNGSROMAN.

BLACK HUMOR: Humor that is mainly contemporary in its use, in which the morbid and the absurd are used for comic purposes in situations that are grotesque, sometimes involving death and suffering.

BLACK LITERATURE: A contemporary term used for literature that has been written by black writers.

BURLESQUE: An attitude, style of writing, or type of comedy in fiction/drama identified by the treatment of a serious issue in a ridiculous way, or a trivial issue in an exaggerated, mock-serious way. *See* FARCE and SATIRE.

CATASTROPHE: The conclusion of a story or play, especially a *tragedy,* and the final stage in the *falling action. See* FALLING ACTION, DENOUEMENT, and TRAGEDY.

CATHARSIS (from Greek—a cleansing or purgation, to make pure): One of the dictionary definitions is purification or purgation of the emotions by art, usually through pity and fear. The psychological interpretation of catharsis is that the readers/viewers identify themselves through *empathy* with a character in fiction or drama, and the readers/viewers thus vicariously expend their pity or fear on the character they are reading about or viewing on a stage. *See* EMPATHY.

CHARACTER: A person in a story; character can also be used to indicate the quality or main characteristic of an individual thing or group of items, such as "the principal character of his novels."

CLIMAX: The point in the story of greatest intensity and usually the time of the strongest emotional involvement by the reader, where the story has a definite turning point in the *action*. Sometimes *crisis* is used in place of climax. *See* ACTION and CRISIS.

COINCIDENCE: Coincidence is present in a story when two or more improbable events occur at the same time with no causal connection or *foreshadowing*. *See* FORESHADOWING.

COMEDY: In literature comedy in its broadest sense is the opposite of *tragedy*. Comedy is associated with smiles, laughter, and humor. *See* TRAGEDY.

COMPLICATION: A *conflict* of opposing forces or the sections in a story in which the characters and events become intermingled and involved. *See* CONFLICT.

CONFIDANT (feminine, CONFIDANTE): A principal *character* in a story who receives the confidence and private thoughts of another *character*, usually the *protagonist*. *See* CHARACTER and PROTAGONIST.

CONFLICT: The situations, difficulties, and problems that arise because of the forces opposing each other in a *plot*. There are several kinds of conflict: man against man, man against nature, man against himself (an inner conflict within a *character*), and man against his fate or destiny. Conflict in a story frequently is a combination of several of the above types. *See* CHARACTER and PLOT.

CONVERSATION TAGS: A term sometimes used for phrases in a story's *dialogue*, such as "he said," "she asked," "they shouted." Conversation tags that excessively rely on adverbial helpers, such as "he said, worriedly," and "she asked, with deep feeling," are very often doing the work that the *dialogue* itself should be doing. *See* DIALOGUE.

CRISIS: The turning point or decisive moment in fiction where the *plot* takes a definite direction. Crisis sometimes coincides in time with *climax*, but not always. *See* CLIMAX and PLOT.

CRITIC: A person who analyzes, interprets, and makes a reasoned opinion or *judgment* on a work of art, such as *fiction*, as to its values and truths. *See* FICTION and JUDGMENT.

CRITIQUE: An interpretive and evaluative opinion, usually in essay form, which critically inspects a work of art, including literature.

DENOUEMENT: The final uncovering of the *plot* where, in some stories, we learn the secret behind the mystery, and in general find out the explanation and the outcome for what has been happening in the story. *See* PLOT.

DEUS EX MACHINA (from Latin—literally god from the machine, an allusion to the practice years ago of the actual bringing an actor playing a god onto the stage by some kind of machinery—ropes, etc.—to solve a problem in the drama): A term used in literary *explication* to refer to an unexpected and often unlikely event, incident or accident that the author seemingly has used to manipulate the *plot*, influence the *action*, or resolve a difficulty. *See* ACTION, EXPLICATION, and PLOT.

DIALOGUE: Conversation of two or more people in a story. *See* CONVERSATION TAGS.

DIDACTIC: Writing intended to instruct or to teach a lesson, particularly when the author's intent is to do so, usually in a moral sense. Often an author's overemphasis on didactic purpose can interfere with the artistic quality of his story. *See* PARABLE.

DIGRESSION: An irrelevant, unrelated event or other material introduced in a story that departs from the central theme or action of the plot.

DRAMATIC IRONY: A term meaning that the readers/viewers have information that the characters/actors involved do not know.

DRAMATIS PERSONAE: The characters in a literary work, particularly a play's listing of the characters in the program. *See* CHARACTER.

DYNAMIC: Often used in reference to a *character* who changes or develops during a story's development, and also used to describe the advancement and *movement* of the *action* in a *plot*. *See* ACTION, CHARACTER, MOVEMENT, PLOT, STATIC, and TEMPO.

DYNAMIC CHARACTER: A *character* in a story who changes in some way as a result of the development of the *plot*. *See* CHARACTER, DYNAMIC, and PLOT.

EFFECT: The totality of the story's emotional impression on the reader. The main effect of the story's *action* usually should not be weakened by any *digression*. *See* ACTION and DIGRESSION.

EMPATHY: The imaginative identification and projection of one's feelings onto a *character* in a story: It also can involve sympathetic understanding by the reader of a person, animal or thing. *See* CATHARSIS and CHARACTER.

EPIPHANY: A manifestation or "showing forth." James Joyce made the term well known by using it to express a sudden insight/revelation of the inner essence of an experience, *character,* or situation in a story. *See* CHARACTER, EXEGESIS, EXPLICATION, and INTERPRETATION.

EPISODE: A portion of the *plot* that is unified by being one continuous *action.* *See* ACTION and PLOT.

EPISODIC STRUCTURE: Used to describe a story that is primarily made up by linking incidents or events that have little if any connection except perhaps a chronological order.

ERZIEHUNGSROMAN (from German—novel of education): A story where the *protagonist* is educated in life, literally an "education novel." *See* APPRENTICESHIP STORY, BILDUNGSROMAN, KUNSTLERROMAN, and PROTAGONIST.

ESCAPE LITERATURE: Stories designed to entertain and/or amuse, such as detective and adventure tales.

EXEGESIS: A close reading, analysis and interpretation of a story or other literary work. *See* EXPLICATION.

EXISTENTIALISM: A broad term when applied to creative literature that involves attitudes that emphasize the meaninglessness of existence in life rather than spiritual essence and involvement, and also the acceptance of the world just as it is without attempting to explain life religiously or philosophically. The existentialist in literature believes he/she alone is responsible for what he/she does and does not do, and that life can have no meaning except that man/woman has to accept his/her "absurd condition" and go on living in spite of one's seemingly purposeless involvement in life.

EXPLICATION (from French *explication de texte*—to unfold from words): A sustained, close analysis of the *meaning* of a story. *See* EXEGESIS, INTERPRETATION, and MEANING.

EXPOSITION: The introductory section in a story that gives needed details and sets the *atmosphere* of the story so that the reader will understand the following *action.* *See* ACTION and ATMOSPHERE.

EXPRESSIONISM: In literature the presentation of scenes, attitudes, and situations so as to reflect the subjective state of the *character* involved. *See* CHARACTER and IMPRESSIONISM.

FABLE: A short, usually brief tale developed to present a moral truth or teach a lesson.

FALLING ACTION: The second half of a *plot* that follows the *climax,* made up of events in the *resolution.* *See* CLIMAX, PLOT, and RESOLUTION.

FARCE: *Comedy* based on broadly humorous and exaggerated situations and not on subtleties of *character* and *plot.* *See* BURLESQUE, CHARACTER, COMEDY, PLOT, and SATIRE.

FICTION: The opposite of historical or factual writing, and thus relying for its source on the author's imagination and creative capacities.

FIRST-PERSON POINT OF VIEW: A story told through the author's use of an "I" *character,* relating his/her experiences and telling in the first person what he/she did. *See* CHARACTER, NARRATOR, and POINT OF VIEW.

FLASHBACK: The presentation in a story of an earlier *episode,* event or incident that is out of chronological order. Some authors use flashbacks to add *suspense* to the story and also to avoid excessive reliance on a basically chronological narrative. *See* EPISODE, RETROSPECT, and SUSPENSE.

FORESHADOWING: An indication, often very slight, in a story of some aspect of *character* or *plot* development that will occur later. Foreshadowing is closely connected with the *organic* development of a narrative. *See* CHARACTER, ORGANIC, PLOT, and SURPRISE ENDING.

GENRE (from French—a kind or type): A term used to classify kinds, types, and categories of literature and art by either technique, form, purpose, or subject matter.

HAMARTIA (from Greek—tragic flaw, weakness, or shortcoming): Hamartia in a *character* is defined by poor judgment, weak character and/or a hereditary flaw in his/her nature. *See* CHARACTER, HUBRIS, and TRAGIC FLAW.

HERO (or HEROINE): A *character* of physical or moral courage admired for his nobility or distinction who is the main focus of interest in fiction/drama. *See* CHARACTER and PROTAGONIST.

HUBRIS (or HYBRIS): The kind of pride—a self-destructive and overweening pride—that causes misfortune and usually the downfall of the *protagonist.* *See* HAMARTIA, PROTAGONIST, and TRAGIC FLAW.

IMAGERY: The use of language to represent actions, objects, or persons in a descriptive, imaginative way.

IMPRESSIONISM: The depiction in literature of scenes, emotions, or characters with broad simplicity and little elaboration of details, and usually meaning today that the author has presented these scenes and characters subjectively just as he/she saw them or felt them at a specific time and/or place, and not as the scenes or characters actually are in real life. *See* CHARACTER and EXPRESSIONISM.

IN MEDIAS RES (from Latin—in the midst of things): Beginning a narrative with an important event at the mid-point of the *action* or *plot* rather than beginning the story chronologically. *See* ACTION and PLOT.

INTERIOR MONOLOGUE: A term often used to describe the internal thinking of a *character*, with these thoughts usually jumbled, without punctuation and grammatical order, just as the mind of the *character* conceived the thoughts. *See* CHARACTER and STREAM OF CONSCIOUSNESS.

INTERPRETATION: In literary criticism, the explanation of what is obscure or ambiguous. *See* AMBIGUITY, EXEGESIS, and EXPLICATION.

JUDGMENT: A critical term used by some along with *taste*, sometimes synonomously, in making critical estimates. Judgment implies discriminating perception or discernment in literary *interpretation*. *See* INTERPRETATION and TASTE.

KUNSTLERROMAN (from German—novel of the artist): A story that traces the development of the artist's own life. *See* APPRENTICESHIP STORY and BILDUNGSROMAN.

LEITMOTIF (from German—leading motif): In music, a marked melodic passage associated with a person, idea or situation, repeated throughout the score. Similarly in literature, a recurrent word, phrase, situation, or idea used in association with the element of the story.

MEANING: A term used sometimes in literary criticism to indicate that which an author has had as his/her intent, purpose or aim in writing a story. In literary criticism there can be, for some critics, four possible levels of meaning: the literal, the allegorical, the spiritual, and the moral. *See* ALLEGORY, THEME, SYMBOLISM, and UNIVERSALITY.

MELODRAMA: Literature and drama overly dramatic or romantic and thus sensational and sentimental in its situations and *action*. *See* ACTION and ROMANTICISM.

MONTAGE: A procedure, often used in movies, to project a series of quick impressions and/or scenes and pictures to establish a certain *atmosphere* or to move the story along quickly in time. *See* ATMOSPHERE and IMPRESSIONISM.

MOOD: A term used to indicate in a literary work the emotional disposition or feeling the author expresses towards his/her theme or story. Note the subtle difference between mood and *tone*. *See* TONE.

MOTIVATION: The inner causes that bring a *character* to take some kind of *action*. Motivated *action* caused by the personality and beliefs of a *character* usually leads to the reader's acceptance of such *action*. *See* ACTION and CHARACTER.

MOTIVE (or MOTIF): In literature and art the guiding and/or controlling idea manifested in all or part of a creative work. *See* LEITMOTIF.

MOVEMENT: A critical term used to indicate whether the *plot* of a story has dramatic *action* that is slow, fast, weak or strong. Also, a progression or development of ideas or *action* toward a specific result. *See* ACTION, DYNAMIC, PLOT, STATIC, and TEMPO.

MULTIPLE MEANINGS: Often used in place of *ambiguity*, indicating a literary work has various levels or kinds of *interpretation*. *See* AMBIGUITY, INTERPRETATION, and SYMBOLISM.

NAIVE NARRATOR: A simple *character* who narrates the story, but whose naivete or innocence causes him/her not to comprehend aspects and implications of the *action* which the reader usually can easily understand. *See* ACTION, CHARACTER, and NARRATOR.

NARRATOR: The person telling the story, who could be an "I" *character* with the author using the *first-person point of view;* or the author can have a third person (he or she) to tell the story by using the *third-person point of view;* or the author can use the *omniscient point of view* and be like a god in seeing all and knowing all. *See* CHARACTER, FIRST-PERSON POINT OF VIEW; THIRD-PERSON POINT OF VIEW, OMNISCIENT POINT OF VIEW and POINT OF VIEW.

NATURALISM: The application of the concepts of scientific determinism to literature, meaning that man has no control over his life, that he has no choices and no options of any kind because his heredity and environment have determined his fate. A *character* in a naturalistic story thus cannot do anything about what is causing him/her to be what he/she is and what he/she is becoming. In naturalism, the story materials are presented with a fidelity to actuality and truth as in *realism*, but the author selectively chooses these materials and forms them into a pattern of his/her own design, often thus making a philosophical attempt through the story to object to what is happening to a *character*. Sometimes this somewhat loose philosophical statement is a protest against the disinterest and lack of concern by society for a *character* or a group of people. *See* CHARACTER and REALISM.

NOVEL: A fictitious prose story of considerable length.

NOVELLA (or NOUVELLA or NOVELLETTE): A short *novel.* *See* NOVEL.

OBJECTIVITY: The lack of subjective involvement of an author in his/her writing, that is, the creative expression reveals little and often nothing about the author and deals with external objects as opposed to thoughts or feelings. *See* SUBJECTIVITY.

OMNISCIENT POINT OF VIEW: A story told by the author where the author knows everything that occurs in the inside and the outside worlds of any *character.* *See* CHARACTER, NARRATOR, and POINT OF VIEW.

ORGANIC (or ORGANIC FORM): A term used in literary criticism to indicate a cause-and-effect relationship of closely related events, thus situations and *plot* development that come about from causes such as *character* traits or personality flaws. As a result, like a living organism, a *character* or story can unfold just as, for example, a plant can grow and bloom as we observe it. *See* CHARACTER and PLOT.

PARABLE: A story that points up a moral or spiritual truth by comparison with another situation or actual event. *See* ALLEGORY and DIDACTIC.

PARODY: A literary work that imitates another and usually more serious literary composition, holding the serious up to laughter and ridicule. *See* SATIRE.

PATHOS (from Greek—suffering or deep feeling): That quality in literature and drama that awakens feelings of pity, sympathy, and sorrow in the reader/viewer. *See* CATHARSIS and EMPATHY.

PLOT: A carefully constructed sequence of interrelated events to achieve a desired effect. *See* SUBPLOT.

POETIC JUSTICE: In a story the operation of justice where there is due punishment for vice and due reward for virtue. Thus bad characters are punished and good characters are rewarded, mainly as the results of actions by characters and the principles, or lack of them, that they have followed in their lives. *See* CHARACTER.

POINT OF ATTACK: The moment in fiction/drama when the main *action* of the *plot* begins. *See* ACTION and PLOT.

POINT OF VIEW: A term used to describe the attitude or position from which an author has told his/her story. *See* FIRST-PERSON POINT OF VIEW, THIRD-PERSON POINT OF VIEW, NARRATOR, and OMNISCIENT POINT OF VIEW.

POT-BOILER: A popular term used to describe a story or other writing that the author wrote primarily to make money and not to create an artistic work.

PROTAGONIST (from Greek—first actor): The main *character* in fiction and drama in which the *action* centers. *See* ACTION, ANTAGONIST, and CHARACTER.

REALISM: Often called the truthful treatment of story material, realism is fidelity to real life in literature. *See* NATURALISM and VERISIMILITUDE.

RESOLUTION: Sometimes called the *rising action*, the resolution is made up of the events in a *plot* that follow the *climax*. *See* CLIMAX, PLOT, and RISING ACTION.

RETROSPECT: A looking back at things past, sometimes used in place of the term *flashback*. *See* EPISODE and FLASHBACK.

RISING ACTION: That part of a story's *plot* where the complication of the *action* begins and then continues to the *climax*. *See* ACTION, CLIMAX, and PLOT.

ROMAN À CLEF (from French—novel with a key): A story, usually a novel, in which actual people and actual events are presented as fiction.

ROMANTICISM: A big term that has a variety of meanings. Romanticism can mean the use of the imagination with great stress on individuality, thus placing the *character* in the center of life's experiences. Romanticism in reference to romantic literature can mean stories that are unrealistic and overidealized, usually by avoiding the harsh actualities of life. *See* CHARACTER and REALISM.

SATIRE: Writing that holds up general or individual vices and follies to ridicule by humor and wit, mainly to bring about improvement in these particular human conditions.

SETTING: The physical *background* or locale in which the *action* of a story takes place. *See* ACTION and BACKGROUND.

SHORT-SHORT STORY: A brief *short story*, with a length of about 500 to 2,000 words. *See* SHORT STORY.

SHORT STORY: A brief prose story usually having a length of about 500 words (*a short-short story*) to about 15,000 words. *See* SHORT-SHORT STORY.

SLICE OF LIFE (translation of the French *tranche de vie*): A complete, highly detailed, and unordered segment (or slice) of life presented without comment or interpretation. *See* NATURALISM and REALISM.

SOLUTION: A term used to mean a set of circumstances that affects the explanation, the outcome, the clearing up, or the *denouement* of a *plot* and its *complication. See* COMPLICATION, DENOUEMENT, and PLOT.

STATIC: Used in reference to a *character, situation* or *plot* that changes or develops little during a specific *action* or the entire story. *See* ACTION, CHARACTER, MOVEMENT, PLOT, SITUATION, and TEMPO.

STREAM OF CONSCIOUSNESS: A term used to describe the flow of mental activity—conscious and/or subconscious—running through the mind of a *character. See* CHARACTER and INTERIOR MONOLOGUE.

STRUCTURE: The organized framework, the arrangement of parts or the interrelationship of the structural elements in a work of literature.

STYLE: The mode, manner, or distinctiveness of an author's arrangement of words by the combination of that which is to be expressed with his own individual creativeness in writing.

SUBJECTIVITY: A term used to designate writing that involves some or much of the author's own individuality—his personal views and/or attitudes toward life. *See* OBJECTIVITY.

SUBPLOT: A secondary or minor sequence of events in a literary work which may complement or contrast with the principal action. *See* PLOT.

SURPRISE ENDING: A sudden or unexpected turn-about in action at the end of a story or drama.

SUSPENSE: That element in a story or drama that brings to the reader/viewer apprehension, anxiety, and/or interested anticipation about the outcome of the *action* and/or *plot. See* ACTION and PLOT.

SYMBOL: A term generally meaning that the *character*, scene, or situation that the author has used to represent something else has a value different, in a connotative way, from its concrete reality. The symbol thus can be used to represent a group of meanings that are highly suggestive in *interpretation* and often *ambiguous. See* ALLEGORY, AMBIGUOUS, INTERPRETATION, PARABLE, and SYMBOLISM.

SYMBOLISM: In interpreting literature, symbolism means the use of a *character*, or scene, situation, or some object to suggest something else or represent something else. *See* ALLEGORY, AMBIGUOUS, MULTIPLE MEANINGS, PARABLE, and SYMBOL.

TALE: A simple story with an uncomplicated *plot. See* PLOT.

TASTE: The discernment, appreciation, and critical *judgment* used in evaluating a work of art or a piece of literature for its beauty, proportion, congruity, symmetry, or whatever is needed to make for excellence in creative expression. Taste may also be evident in the end results of the creator (the artist or writer), the reader/viewer, and the critic. *See* JUDGMENT.

TEMPO: Literally the rate, rhythm, or pattern of movement within the *action* and *plot* of a story. *See* ACTION, DYNAMIC, MOVEMENT, PLOT, and STATIC.

THEME: The principal and dominating idea in a story, and thus the abstract concept represented by the totality, the combination and the involvement of each *character,* the *action,* and the *plot.* *See* ACTION, CHARACTER, MEANING, PLOT, and UNIVERSALITY.

THIRD-PERSON POINT OF VIEW: A story told by the author's using the limited viewpoint of a single *character* such as he/she did this and that. *See* CHARACTER, NARRATOR, and POINT OF VIEW.

TONE: A term used to indicate the attitude of an author towards his/her subject. *See* MOOD.

TRAGEDY: A narrative work—prose, drama, or poetry—which excites pity and/or terror by a succession of sorrowful events, miseries, and/or misfortunes leading to an unhappy *catastrophe,* often the death of the *protagonist.* *See* CATASTROPHE, COMEDY, and PROTAGONIST.

TRAGIC FLAW: The defect, weakness or mortal flaw in the tragic *hero* or *protagonist* which inevitably causes his/her downfall and/or defeat. *See* HAMARTIA, HERO, HUBRIS, and PROTAGONIST.

UNITIES: The unities are made up of *action,* time, place—the three principles of dramatic structure. *See* ACTION and SETTING.

UNITY: The organizing principle and/or *organic* cohesiveness in a literary work. *See* ORGANIC.

UNIVERSALITY: The quality of a story with a *theme* and/or *meaning* that can be understood by and applied to all people at all times—thus, a worldwide comprehensiveness and appeal to everyone, everywhere, no matter what country or nationality. *See* MEANING and THEME.

VERISIMILITUDE: In a story the state or quality of being truthful, or presenting in a creative sense the resemblance to truth and actuality. *See* REALISM.

VILLAIN: The *character* in a story who represents an evil or negative force in the plot in opposition to the *hero.* *See* ANTAGONIST, CHARACTER, HERO, and PROTAGONIST.

A Selected Bibliography

The following selection provides an introduction to the short story in particular and fiction in general, as well as including reference works, interviews of authors, statements on writing by authors and critics, and observations on creative achievement.

Anderson, Sherwood. *Letters of Sherwood Anderson.* ed. Howard Mumford Jones and Walter B. Rideout. Boston: Little, Brown and Company, 1953.

Aristotle. *Poetics.* Translated by S. H. Butcher. New York: Hill & Wang, 1961.

Babel, Isaac. *The Lonely Years: 1925–1939, Unpublished Stories and Private Correspondence.* Edited by Nathalie Babel. Translated by Andrew R. MacAndrew. New York: Noonday Press, 1964.

Breit, Harvey. *The Writer Observed.* New York: Collier Books, 1961.

Burgess, Anthony. *The Novel Now.* New York: Pegasus, 1967.

Camus, Albert. *Lyrical and Critical Essays.* Edited by Philip Thody. Translated by Ellen Conroy Kennedy. New York: Alfred A. Knopf, 1968.

Chekhov, Anton. *Letters on the Short Story, Drama and Other Literary Topics.* Edited by Louis S. Friedland. New York: Dover Publications, 1961.

Conrad, Joseph. *Joseph Conrad on Fiction.* Edited by Walter F. Wright. Lincoln: University of Nebraska Press, 1964.

The Creative Process: A Symposium. Edited by Brewster Ghiselin. New York: Mentor Books, 1955.

Criticism: Twenty Major Statements. Edited by Charles Kaplan. San Francisco: Chandler, n.d.

Critiques and Essays on Modern Fiction 1920–1951. Edited by John W. Aldridge. New York: Ronald Press, 1952.

Dictionary of World Literature. Edited by Joseph T. Shipley. Totowa, N.J.: Littlefield, Adams, 1968.

Forster, E. M. *Aspects of the Novel.* New York: Harcourt, Brace, 1927.

Goodman, Theodore. *The Writing of Fiction: An Analysis of Creative Writing.* New York: Collier Books, 1961.

Highlights of Modern Literature. Edited by Francis Brown. New York: Mentor Books, 1954.

Holman, C. Hugh. *A Handbook to Literature* (based on the original by William Flint Thrall and Addison Hibbard). New York: Odyssey Press, 1972.

Humphrey, Robert. *Stream of Consciousness in the Modern Novel.* Berkeley: University of California Press, 1954.

An Introduction to Literary Criticism. Edited by Marlies K. Danziger and W. Stacy Johnson. Lexington, Mass.: D. C. Heath, 1961.

James, Henry. *The Art of the Novel.* New York: Scribner's, 1934.

James, Henry. *The Future of the Novel: Essays on the Art of Fiction.* New York: Vintage Books, 1956.

Lawrence, D. H. *Selected Literary Criticism.* Edited by Anthony Beal. New York: Viking, 1955.

Lubbock, Percy. *The Craft of Fiction.* New York: Viking, 1957.

Maugham, W. Somerset. *Selected Prefaces and Introductions.* Garden City, New York: Doubleday & Company, Inc., 1963.

Millett, Fred B. *Reading Fiction.* New York: Harper & Brothers, 1950.

Myth and Method: Modern Theories of Fiction. Edited by James E. Miller, Jr. Lincoln: University of Nebraska Press, 1960.

Pattee, Fred Lewis. *The Development of the American Short Story.* New York: Harper & Row, 1923.

Readings in American Criticism. Edited by Thomas Elliott Berry. New York: Odyssey Press, 1970.

Schorer, Mark. *The World We Imagine: Selected Essays.* New York: Farrar, Strauss & Giroux, 1968.

Short Stories: A Study in Pleasure. Edited by Sean O'Faolain. Boston: Little, Brown, 1966. See Introduction by O'Faolain.

The Theory of the Novel. Edited by Philip Stevick. New York: Free Press, 1967.

Writers at Work: The Paris Review Interviews. New York: Viking, 1959.

Writers at Work: The Paris Review Interviews—Second Series. New York: Viking, 1963.

Writers at Work: The Paris Review Interviews—Third Series. New York: Viking, 1967.

Writers on Writing. Edited by Walter Allen. London: Phoenix House, 1948.